T0113648

Halldór Laxness

PARADISE RECLAIMED

Halldór Laxness was born near Reykjavík, Iceland, in 1902. His first novel was published when he was seventeen. The undisputed master of contemporary Icelandic fiction, and one of the outstanding novelists of the century, he has written more than sixty books, including novels, short stories, essays, poems, plays, and memoirs. In 1955 he was awarded the Nobel Prize in Literature. He died in 1998.

INTERNATIONAL

ALSO BY *Halldór Laxness*

Independent People

PARADISE RECLAIMED

PARADISE RECLAIMED

Halldór Laxness

TRANSLATED
FROM THE ICELANDIC BY
MAGNUS MAGNUSSON

Introduction by Jane Smiley

VINTAGE INTERNATIONAL

VINTAGE BOOKS

A DIVISION OF RANDOM HOUSE, INC.

NEW YORK

FIRST VINTAGE INTERNATIONAL EDITION, MARCH 2002

English language translation copyright © 1962,
copyright renewed 1990 by Halldór Laxness
Introduction copyright © 2002 by Jane Smiley

The Cataloging-in-Publication data is on file at the Library of Congress.

Vintage ISBN: 978-0-375-72758-0

www.vintagebooks.com

146086900

Contents

TRANSLATOR'S NOTE:

Pronunciation

This is a revised version of the translation of *Paradise Reclaimed* (*Paradísarheimt*) I made some forty years ago. I gladly accepted the invitation by Vintage Books to revisit it and refresh its style; I have also added notes to give context to the historical setting.

In particular, I have used the original Icelandic orthography of proper names; it is no longer considered either necessary or desirable to anglicise foreign names, as used to be the norm.

The modern Icelandic alphabet has thirty-two letters, compared with twenty-six in modern English. There are two extra consonants (ð and þ), and an additional diphthong (æ). Readers may find a note on the pronunciations of specifically Icelandic letters helpful:

ð (Ð), known as "eth" or "crossed d," is pronounced like the (voiced) *th* in *breathe*.

þ (Þ), known as "thorn," is pronounced like the (unvoiced) *th* in *breaths*.

æ is pronounced like the *i* in *life*.

The pronunciation of the vowels is conditioned by the accents:

     á like the *ow* in *owl*
     é like the *ye* in *yet*
     í like the *ee* in *seen*
     ó like the *o* in *note*
     ö like the *eu* in French *fleur*
     ú like the *oo* in *soon*
     ý like the *ee* in *seen*
     au like the *œi* in French *œil*
     ei, ey, like the *ay* in *tray*

Please note asterisks (*) within the text indicate an explanatory note to be found on pages 301–304.

INTRODUCTION TO HALLDÓR LAXNESS'S

Paradise Reclaimed

by Jane Smiley

When Halldór Kiljan Laxness accepted his Nobel Prize in 1955, he spoke of his amazement that "a poor wanderer, a writer from one of the most remote islands in the world" should be so recognized and honored, should find himself in front of "Majesties, ladies, and gentlemen." Several years later, he came to write *Paradise Reclaimed;* in the novel, Laxness revisited these ideas and explored them through the story of Steinar of Steinahlíðar, who is touched and transformed by the intrusion of the great world into his bare corner of Iceland, and then leaves home upon a strange journey of geographic, philosophical, and spiritual discovery. In one sense, Steinar's story (based on the story of Eirikur Bruni, a nineteenth-century Icelander) parallels that of his author, who was a great traveler, and in another, larger sense, it parallels those of many Icelanders after the first settlement of Iceland in the ninth century, who left the country on

perilous journeys, met kings and famous men, saw great wonders, and then returned to resume the lives they had left behind
in a land that was almost unchanged.

When the Nobel Prize Committee awarded Laxness the prize,
they cited his revival of the thousand-year-old Icelandic literary
tradition and his connection to the ancient saga narratives, but
Laxness was far more than a reproducer of medieval modes
and ideas like Sigrid Undset. Though his work was imbued with
traditional poetry and literature, he was very much a twentieth-
century novelist who was thoroughly skilled in social commentary and alive to the issues and questions of his time. His focus
was always on Iceland, but his angle of perception was skeptical
and ironic; his criticism of his native land was sometimes harsh,
and his work was often the subject of controversy and even vilifi-
cation. In his acceptance speech, he reflected upon his position at
home—"Like a sensitive instrument that records every sound,
they have reacted with pleasure and displeasure to every word I
have written. It is great good fortune for an author to be born
into a nation so steeped in centuries of poetry and literary tradition." Laxness was no less skeptical of the movements and fash-
ions of the larger world—one of the tragic ironies of his great
novel, *Independent People,* is that the protagonist, Bjartur, is
tempted by the rise of wool prices as a result of the First World
War to build himself a real house to replace his traditional Icelandic turf hut.

When the war ends and prices crash, the house is unfinished
and must be abandoned. The independent Bjartur, whom we had
met at the beginning of the novel as a youngish man, fired with
the desire to establish himself as a self-reliant small farmer, loses
everything and must start over, stoic to the end and not quite so
independent of the world as he had tried always to be. Steinar,

too, ends where he had begun, but his story is the counterpoint to Bjartur's. When *Paradise Reclaimed* opens, Steinar is a small farmer already, who is famous for the meticulous care with which he maintains his tiny farm. Though he is not one of the important men of his district, he is a man of dignity and unusual skill. He has a stroke of fortune—whether good or ill is open to interpretation—when one of his mares gives birth to a remarkably fine foal of almost uncanny beauty and abilities. Though his children love the horse, when Steinar hears that the King of Denmark is coming to Iceland, he decides to present the animal to him. The King of Denmark accepts the horse, though not quite with the respect that the reader feels Steinar deserves.

More importantly, when Steinar leaves his farm, he encounters a man who will change his life—an Icelandic Mormon named Bishop Þjóðrekur, whom Steinar saves from being tethered to a stone outside a church. Thereafter, Steinar's life grows stranger and stranger. His willingness to be open to experience, to be led from one thing to another, takes him to Denmark, where he meets the king again and gives him another gift, and then to Utah, where he lives among the Mormons for many years, still remembering and loving his family, but unable to hear from them or get in touch with them. In the interim, his family and his farm fall into the careless power of the local sheriff, who ravishes the daughter and whose horse herd destroys the homefield. The sheep are dispersed and everyone in Steinar's family must go into service until at last Bishop Þjóðrekur appears with a message from Steinar, and takes the family to Utah to join him. The wife dies on the ship, and the daughter is seduced by a stranger, but she is later redeemed by polygamous marriage to Bishop Þjóðrekur.

At the very end, Steinar returns as a Mormon missionary to

Iceland. When he finds his small farm, he can barely recognize it, but once he does, he ends as he began, putting stone upon stone, expressing his nature by making order of chaos.

The novel, which has a strange combination of earthy, ironic incident and mythic power, asks us to accept in Steinar a man of radical innocence, who neither ruminates upon nor questions his own decisions, but acts and then accepts the results of his actions. Neither he nor his family doubts that he loves them passionately, even though he abandons them. The narrative chain of causation that is a novel does not become a chain of judgement and blame, but instead deflects those very ideas by disregarding them. A key incident in *Paradise Reclaimed* is the birth of Steinar's grandchild. Everyone in the parish knows that the sheriff has ravished the daughter and impregnated her—the parish is full of his illegitimate offspring. But the daughter repeatedly states that nothing happened and that she does not know how she came to have a child. She is unashamed and resists persuasion. A virgin birth? Why not? Her ignorance, like Steinar's, becomes innocence, and redeems the careless cruelties of the sheriff and the other powerful exploiters she meets who, no matter what they do, cannot change her perception of the world as a place of wonders, of pleasures and pains that cannot be understood, but may only be endured.

If Laxness's major novels are world-class epics by a great writer writing at the top of his form in a sophisticated literary language, this novel is different from them—it is the smaller, more idiosyncratic work of an acute and interesting mind. According to translator Magnus Magnusson, Laxness first became acquainted with the story of Eirikur Bruni as a young man in his twenties, but didn't know how to use it, or perhaps what to make of it, for some thirty years. When he did come back to it, perhaps it resonated with his own sense of where he had traveled and the wonders he had seen. While it doesn't seem to have the sweep and general applicability of the larger works, it functions like a parable or a folktale, not operating out of basic verisimilitude but out of material that is not understandable by reason, only through belief. Eirikur's story was similar to the raw material of the medieval saga writers in that it was a given story, taken from life and known to many. Laxness's job was to make sense of it and find meaning in it, and the meaning he found was in the exploration of innocence.

Steinar and his family are never redeemed because they never fall. Though they act in ways that the world condemns, they never lose either their innocence or their ability to love not only each other, but those around them. They always seek to do good and to be helpful. To be poor, ignorant Icelanders may seem to be a disadvantage, but in the end, their adventures transform and save them from the narrow-minded lives of their neighbors, who would rather tether a man to a rock than listen to what he had to say, or the frivolity of the European aristocrats whom Steinar meets in Denmark, who haven't got the patience either to make good use of the horse he has given them or to open the intricate puzzle-cabinet he constructs for them.

It is Laxness's ironic tone and sly humor that give Steinar and his adventures much of their interest. He is, as always, a master of understatement and juxtaposition. Bishop Þjóðrekur has great regard for his hat—he always wraps it in paper and hides it so that when he is getting beaten up, his hat will remain in good condition. When Steinar decides to go to America, he sends his wife a packet of needles. The packet takes years to find her, but upon receipt, she understands its meaning at once. A woman Steinar meets in Utah (also Icelandic) brings him coffee from time to time. In return he belatedly takes her a load of bricks. The manner in which Laxness portrays these small incidents is very Icelandic—they are full of unexpressed emotions; what is expressed is courtesy, philosophy, acceptance, not exactly wit but something very dry that lies somewhere between stoicism and humor.

Possibly, *Paradise Reclaimed* is not for everyone, but it is a strange and beautiful book, written by one of the twentieth century's most unusual, skilled, and visionary novelists.

PARADISE RECLAIMED

I

The wonder pony

In the early days of Kristian Wilhelmsson, who was the third last foreign king to wield power here in Iceland,* a farmer named Steinar lived at Hlíðar in the district known as Steinahlíðar. He had been so named by his father after the rubble of stones that cascaded down off the mountain in the spring when he was born. Steinar was a married man by the time this story opens, and had two young children, a daughter and a son; he had inherited the farm of Hlíðar from his father.

At this time, Icelanders were said to be the poorest people in Europe, just as their fathers and grandfathers and great-grandfathers had been, all the way back to the earliest settlers; but they believed that many long centuries ago there had been a Golden Age in Iceland, when Icelanders had not been mere farmers and fishermen as they were now, but royal-born heroes and poets who owned weapons, gold, and ships. Like other boys in Iceland, Steinar's son soon learned to be a viking and king's-man, and whittled axes and swords for himself out of pieces of wood.

Hlíðar was built in the same way as the average farmhouse in Iceland had been from time immemorial—a floored living-room and entrance, and a small timber-lined spare room with a bed for visitors. A row of wooden gables faced on to the yard in the normal order of farm-buildings of that period, with an outhouse, store-shed, byre, stable, sheep-hut and finally a small workshed. Behind the buildings the haystacks reared up every autumn and dwindled down to nothing by the spring.

Farms of this kind, turf-roofed and grass-grown, were to be found huddling under the mountain-slopes in a thousand places in Iceland in those days; what distinguished the farm we are now to visit for a while was the loving and artistic care with which the owner made up for what it lacked in grandeur. So scrupulous was his attention to his property, by day or night, that he would never see damage or deterioration of any kind, indoors or out, without making haste to repair it. Steinar was a master-craftsman, equally skilled with wood and metal. It had long been the custom in the district to point out the dry-stone dykes and walls of Hlíðar in Steinahlíðar as an example for aspiring young farmers to follow in life; there were no other works of art in those parts to compare with these carefully built walls of stone. The farms in Steinahlíðar stand on a plain under cliffs which had been the seaboard twenty thousand years before. Pockets of soil keep forming in crevices up in the rock-face and various plants take root in them, which undermine the fabric of the rock. In the heavy rains of spring and autumn the soil is washed away from the fissures, and pieces of rock bounce down on to the farms below. On some farms these stones would cause great damage every year to the meadows and home-field, sometimes even to the buildings themselves. Steinar of Hlíðar often had his hands full in the spring, clearing the boulders from his home-field and meadows—the more so since he was more meticulous than most. Many were the times he had to bend double and straighten up with a heavy boulder in his arms, for no other reward than the joy of seeing a destructive stone fitted with dedicated care into a wall.

It is said that Steinar of Hlíðar had a white pony which was considered the finest animal in the south. This horse was the sort of phenomenon that every farm needs. It seemed beyond serious doubt that this was a supernatural beast and had been so ever since he was a foal, when he had unexpectedly appeared on the scene at the side of a rather elderly white mare which had been running with the herd for a long time in the mountains. At the time of the birth she was grazing at Lónsbakkar (Creek-Banks), but she had been stabled over midwinter and no one had had any idea that she was in foal. If there were ever a case of immaculate conception in Iceland, then this was it. The birth took place in a snowstorm nine days before summer; not a flower in sight, not even a dock-leaf crouching by a wall, certainly no sign of the golden plover yet—the fulmar had scarcely started to hurl itself high in the air to see if the mountains were still there; and suddenly a new creature had been brought into the world almost before the spring itself was born. The little foal ran so lightly at the old mare's side that he could hardly be said to touch the ground with his toes; and yet these tiny hooves were not turned backwards, and this seemed to indicate that he was not a water-kelpie after all—at least not on both sides. But since the mare was unprepared for him, what was this fairy creature to live on? The old mare was brought back to the farm and given hay; and the young kelpie was given butter, which was the only thing that would do in place of the mare's milk that did not exist. And the little kelpie went on being given butter from the churn until he was put to grass.

As he grew he developed handsome lines, a richly arched neck with a full mane, lean flowing hindquarters, long slender legs and well-formed hooves. There was a fine gleam in his keen eyes, and his sense of direction never failed him; he trotted smoothly and well, and at galloping he was quite without equal. He was named Krapi after all the slush and snow there was that spring; and from then on, time was always reckoned in terms of the year of his birth: the spring Krapi was a year old, two years old, three years old, and so on.

Up on the cliffs some ravines had formed here and there which broadened farther up into grassy watercourses. The ponies from the farms nearby often gathered there in a large herd—"up on the Brows," as people said—or else along the riverbanks or the plains by the sea. But because of all the cosseting and the titbits that Krapi had grown used to accepting from the folk at Hlíðar, he often came trotting alone down the mountain or up from the flats straight into the farmyard, where he would rub himself against the doorpost and whinny into the house. He seldom had to wait very long for a lump of butter if there were any available. It was a pleasure to lay one's face against his nose, which was softer than any maiden's cheek; but Krapi never liked being caressed for long. As soon as he had got what he wanted he trotted away along the path and then broke into a sudden gallop as if something had frightened him, and did not pull up until he had rejoined the herd.

The summers in Iceland were long in those days. In the mornings and evenings the meadows were so green that they were red, and during the day the horizon was so blue that it was green. But throughout this remarkable play of colours (which no one paid any attention to or even noticed, for that matter) Hlíðar in Steinahlíðar went on being one of those south-country farms where nothing very eventful ever happened except that the fulmar went on sweeping along the cliffs just as in great-grandfather's day. On ledges and in crevices in the cliffs grew rose root and fern, angelica, brittle bladderfern and moonwort. The boulders kept on tumbling down as if the heartless cliff-troll were shedding stone tears. A good pony can occur on a farm once in a generation, with luck; but on some farms, never in a thousand years. From the sea, beyond the sands and marshes, for a thousand years, the murmur was always the same. Late in the hay-season, when the eggs were safely hatched, the oyster-catcher would arrive in red stockings and white shirt under a black silk jacket to strut aristocratically through the new-mown meadows, whistle, and depart. For all those centuries, Snati the farm-dog was just as full of his own importance as he trotted at the shepherd's side behind the milch-ewes every morning, newly fed and with his tongue lolling out. On still summer days the sound of a scythe being hammered sharp would drift over from the neighbouring farm. There was rain on the way if the cows lay down in the meadow, particularly if they were all lying on the same side; but if there were a dry spell on the way they would bellow eleven times in a row at sunset. Always the same story.

When Krapi was three years old, Steinar put a halter round his neck to make him easier to catch, and kept him in the herd of work-ponies near the farm. By summer he had grown accustomed to the bridle, and learned to walk beside another pony that was being ridden. Next spring Steinar began to break him in to the saddle, and then to train him to trot. In the long light evenings he would give the colt his lead in gallops over the flats. And if the muffled thunder of hooves reached the farmhouse in the early hours of the morning, one could never be quite sure that everyone inside was sound asleep; it sometimes happened that a little girl would come out in her petticoat with fresh milk in a pail, accompanied by a young bare-legged viking who always went to bed with the axe Battle-Troll* under his pillow.

"Is there a better horse in the whole place?" the boy would ask.

"It would probably take some finding," said his father.

"Isn't he quite certainly descended from kelpies?" asked the little girl.

"I think all horses are more or less fairy creatures," said her father. "Especially the best ones."

"Can he then jump up to heaven, like the horse in the story?" asked the viking.

"No doubt about it," said Steinar of Hlíðar, "if God rides horses at all. Quite so."

"Will another horse like him ever be born in these parts again?" asked the girl.

"I'm not so sure about that," said her father. "One would probably have to wait a while. And it could also be long enough before another little girl is born in these parts who can light up a home as much as my girl does."

2

Great men covet the pony

It now so happened that Iceland, in a great surge of national awakening, was celebrating the thousandth anniversary of the settlement of the country, and for that reason a festival was to be held the following summer at Þingvellir, on the banks of the Öxará (Axe River). Word also came that King Kristian was expected from Denmark to attend these millennial celebrations, in order to grant the Icelanders their formal independence—which, come to that, they had always considered theirs but had always been denied by the Danes; but from the day that King Kristian stepped ashore, Iceland was to become by constitution a self-governing colony under the Danish crown. This news was welcomed in every farmhouse in the country because it was thought to herald something even better.

One day early in summer, shortly before the meadows were put to the scythe, a great frenzy seized the dog at Hlíðar in

Steinahlíðar. His hackles bristled horribly at the sound of hooves coming from the main track, and he jumped up on to the roof of the farmhouse as he always did on occasions of great moment; and now there was barking such as once was heard in the days of old at the entrance to Gnípahellir.* Soon visitors with many ponies came riding up to Hlíðar in Steinahlíðar, for in these parts, like everywhere else in Iceland, the main track led right through the farmyards. It was always considered a significant event out in the country when Snati jumped up on to the roof, and hearts would beat faster; it was a portent that these were no vagrants on the way.

It is the story-teller's privilege to give some account of his heroes before they arrive on the scene. These were two eminent gentlemen who rode into the farmyard with a string of horses and grooms in tow. In charge of this company was Sheriff Benediktsson,* but it is no part of this narrative to examine the reason for his journey; the authorities have many occasions to travel. This sheriff had been little more than two years in office; he was a young man, and had been appointed as soon as he graduated. He was considered a poet by the public, but the more modern-minded in the district who wanted to be in fashion called him an idealist. However, there had never been any idealists in Iceland before now, and older people did not understand the meaning of the word; they reckoned that this sheriff was not cast in the same mould as sheriffs of the past had been, and called him two-faced.

The other visitor was the agent Björn of Leirur,* who had worked his way up from nothing and early in life had made use of what were considered his superior talents and intelligence to ensure that he would not have to chase sheep and haul cod. As a

boy he had gone to the trading-station down at Eyrarbakki for
training, and then as a youth had spent a few years with his
employers in Denmark; on his return to Iceland he was appointed
clerk to the previous sheriff at Hof, and received from him various derelict crofts along the coast with significant names like
Bæli (Den), Hnúta (Knuckle) and Svað (Bog). These he joined up
into one large estate on which he built an imposing house; then
he married for money, and employed many workers. He had long
since ceased to be a sheriff's clerk, of course, but on the other
hand he received many business commissions from various other
sheriffs, and now travelled the country as an agent for the Scots,
buying up ponies and sheep on their behalf for gold, which he
usually carried in stout leather bags attached to the pack-saddles.
He would buy up wrecked ships along the south coast, sometimes at auctions and sometimes by arrangement with the
authorities, and in this way he had amassed a pile of wealth that
made the farmers boggle. He was always on the spot when anyone was being forced to sell up through lack of ready money or
farming losses or other misfortunes, and by now he had collected
a large number of farms up and down the country. Wherever he
went he selected good riding-ponies for himself, and paid in gold
whatever price was asked. He was a tireless traveller, fearless in
the face of hardship or danger, a man who never hesitated to ford
the mightiest rivers wherever he came to them, by night or by
day—chiefly, perhaps, because his horses were more reliable than
most. But although Björn of Leirur was now getting on in years,
he had never managed to create sufficient confidence within the
district for the farmers themselves to make him their agent; somehow his popularity was the greater and his reputation the rosier
the farther he was away from home. Björn of Leirur cultivated

Sheriff Benediktsson's friendship assiduously from the moment he arrived in the district; he gave him horses, cattle and land, and attached himself to him as much as possible. It often came about that Björn happened to be going the same way when the sheriff was travelling the district on official business, and then there was much boisterous talk and uproarious laughter with the farmers and farm-folk; there was seldom much brennivín* on the go on those occasions, but usually the snuff was moistened with cognac.

Steinar of Hlíðar was pottering about with his dykes, keeping himself busy until the grass should be ready for mowing, adjusting a stone here and a stone there as he felt the eye demanded. He walked over to meet the visitors, as a good farmer should, and greeted the sheriff respectfully; Björn of Leirur, on the other hand, he greeted according to country custom with a kiss.

"What a hell of a man you are!" said Björn of Leirur, patting him affectionately. "Always adjusting the stones. Always making improvements. Always having fun."

The sheriff's glance was roving along the egg-smooth edges of the stone-work, and he too could not restrain his admiration: "What wonders you could work with stone if you lived in Rome, man, like old Thorvaldsen!"*

"Oh, it would be an ingratitude to God if I grudged the trouble of finding the right stone for the right niche," said Steinar. "It just takes a little doing, bless your heart; perhaps there is only the one space in the whole wall where this stone rightly fits. But certainly I have never envied those who can perhaps amuse themselves better than I can. The finest parts of these walls are not my work at all, however; they were done by my great-grandfather, God rest his soul, who rebuilt the whole farm in the last century after the big volcanic eruptions that destroyed every wall in the place. We nineteenth-century folk have neither the eye nor the knack to make walls the way they used to in the past; and besides, time has worked to their advantage by letting the stones bed down the more snugly, with God's help—and with maybe an occasional helping hand from later generations. Until the next volcanic eruptions, of course."

"I have heard that you never say Yes or No, Steinar," said the sheriff. "I would like to find out if that is true, some time."

Steinar's laugh was a high-pitched titter. "Bless you, I cannot say I have ever really noticed, my dear fellow," he replied; as was the custom of all good farmers in Steinahlíðar, he always talked to people of importance as he would to a brother or rather, perhaps, to a pauper of whom one is fond not so much for his worth as because one detects in him a divine personality. "It probably does not make all that much difference in this world whether one says Yes or No, heeheehee; and now come this way, boys, step inside and have a cup of something to drink."

"Tell me something about that white colt of yours we were admiring out there," said Björn of Leirur. "A fine beast; what's his pedigree?"

"It would really be better to ask the children," replied Steinar. "They think he came straight from the creek. Sometimes I think that children, bless them, get much more out of life than we adults do. To tell you the truth, the horse is more or less theirs."

The sheriff had not dismounted, but Björn of Leirur was walking at Steinar's side, leading his pony, as they went up to the farmhouse. The children had come out on to the paved doorstep. Björn of Leirur kissed them and gave them each a silver coin, as was the custom of decent people.

"Aha! That's a girl I want for a wife when she grows up," he said, "and that's a lad I want for a foreman. But what I was going to say, my dear Steinar, was—what a hell of a man you are to have such a handsome colt! What on earth are you going to do with a horse like that? Aren't you going to sell him to me?"

"Oh, it's a bit early for that while the children still call him a kelpie. I think we should wait until he is just an ordinary horse, the way most other horses are in the end, and the children no longer small."

"Quite right," said the sheriff. "Never sell your children's fairy-tales. Björn has quite enough toys to play with already; he has had two big shipwrecks since Christmas, to the best of my knowledge—not to mention all the better-class housewives and farmer's daughters over in the west."

"Our new sheriff can sometimes make the quaintest remarks," said Björn of Leirur. "They say he's a poet."

"Steinar," said the sheriff, "if you part with that horse, then sell him to me. He is just the sort of horse I need next summer when I ride west to welcome royalty."

"I have never known of a single official who didn't manage to turn a good horse into an old hack within a year," said Björn of Leirur. "But you know me well, my dear Steinar, and you should know perfectly well that if I ever get hold of a good horse I turn him into an even better one."

The sheriff, still in the saddle, lit his pipe and said between puffs, "Yes, you sell them for gold to England where they are blinded and put to work in the coal mines. Happy the horse that becomes an old hack here in Iceland rather than fall into your clutches."

"Fear the Lord, children," said Steinar of Hlíðar.

"Name your own price," said Björn of Leirur. "If it's timber you need for building, just help yourself. I've got plenty of copper and iron, and silver just like dirt, of course. Come and have a look in here and see what you can see."

He tugged a big leather purse out of his topcoat. Steinar went over and looked inside it.

"What would my children say if I were to sell our fairy horse for gold?" he said.

"That's the spirit!" said the sheriff. "Stand up to him."

"If you don't want gold, I'll give you a good cow," said Björn of Leirur. "Two, if you like."

"I can't waste any more damned time hanging around here like this," said the sheriff.

"The whole point is, my dear fellow, that when the world ceases to be miraculous in the eyes of our children, then there is very little left," said Steinar. "Perhaps we should wait for a little while yet."

"Ride the white horse out to Leirur whenever you're in the mood," said Björn, "and we'll both take another look at him and have another little chat. I have always enjoyed looking at good horses."

"Never ride the white horse out to Leirur," said the sheriff, "not even if he offers you a cow in exchange. You would go home that night with nothing in your pocket but a couple of cobbler's needles."

"Oh, hold your tongue, sheriff!" said Björn of Leirur. "My good friend Steinar of Hlíðar knows me well enough to know that I never try twice to buy the same horse off anyone. And we can still kiss each other whether you sell me a horse or not."

And with that the visitors rode away.

3

Romanticism comes to Iceland

Life in Iceland had not yet grown so romantic that country folk would go for Sunday outings on horseback in summer, on the lines of the forest-trips in Denmark; that came later. In those days it was still considered wicked out in the country to do anything simply because it was enjoyable. More than a century previously the Danish king had abolished by decree all forms of entertainment in Iceland. Dancing was the devil's work, and had not been performed in Iceland for many generations. It was not considered seemly for young unmarried people to tramp on one another's toes except at most, perhaps, in order to have illegitimate children. All life had to serve some useful purpose and the glory of God. But the year had its festivities, all the same.

One of the main festivities was when the lambs were weaned and separated from the ewes; this took place around midsummer, when the sun shone all night long. Man and sheep took part in a night-and-day marathon agreeable to God, and the air vibrated with shrill bleating; for sheep lament in the major. The dogs had their tongues lolling out all day long, and many of them lost their bark. When the lambs had been separated from the ewes for a few days they were finally driven far up into the mountains. It was a wonderful excursion for everyone except the lambs themselves.

The herding went on all night, for the most part up along the river from ridge to ridge until the highlands opened out, unfamiliar mountains with unfamiliar waters in between and unfamiliar skies mirrored in them. This was the world of the wild geese, and with them the lambs were to share the sweets of the wilderness for the rest of the summer. Here one could feel the cold breath from the glaciers, and Snati the farm-dog started to sneeze.

A few of the farms in Steinahlíðar always combined forces for this lamb-drive. Women were sometimes allowed to come too; devoted serving-girls had been looking forward to this glorious occasion ever since the previous year, for the monotony of a man's life was as nothing compared to a woman's. Some young folk were allowed to come too, down to more or less grown-up children. One of those was the fair-haired boy from Drangar who had just spent a spring season at the fishing down at Þorlákshöfn and had visited Hlíðar in Steinahlíðar on his way home. He lived a few farms away to the east, where some solitary cliffs had parted company with the mountainside and stood aloof. Little Steina, Steinar's daughter, had been confirmed that year, and to celebrate the fact that she was now a big girl her father had lifted her up on to Krapi's back without saying a word—and this was something that had never happened before; he assumed that the pony would not bolt with her, since the speed of the company was dictated by the sorrowing lambs.

Love, as we now call it, had not yet been imported to Iceland.

People mated without romance, according to the wordless laws of nature and in conformity with the German pietism of the Danish king. The word *love* survived in the language, certainly, but only as a relic from a distant unknown age when words meant something quite different from now; perhaps it had been used about horses. But nature got its own way nonetheless, as has been said already; for if a boy and a girl were not given the chance to make eyes at one another under the long German sermons about pietism, or at the sheep-pens where the bleating is the loudest in the world, they could hardly fail to touch one another accidentally when they were binding hay together in the summer. And although only the soliloquy of the soul was permissible, and the nation's poets could never reveal more of their inner selves in a poem than to say that they laughed at destiny, people had everything in the right place, one feels, even in those days. By covert sign-language and cryptic talk it was still possible to maintain ordinary natural human life in whole districts. Thus, throughout the lamb-drive, Steinar's daughter never once looked at the fair-haired boy from Drangar; always she looked in exactly the opposite direction. But she sat her white pony as securely as if she had never ridden any other.

When they had gone so far into the highlands that Snati had begun to sneeze they came upon a large sunlit lake from which there breathed an eerie coldness. Suddenly the boy rode right up to her side and said, "Weren't you confirmed this spring?"

"Yes, I was a year behind. I was to have done it last year, but I would have been a little too young then."

"When I called at your place on my way home from the fishing, and saw you, I could scarcely believe my eyes."

"Oh, I've probably become a horribly big and ugly fool now. The only consolation is that I'm small inside."

"I've also got plenty of time left to learn some sense, although I learned a lot from going to the fishing, come to that," he said.

"I still believe a lot of things which perhaps aren't true," she said. "And the rest I don't understand."

"Listen," he said, "why don't you let me have a quick ride on the white horse? Your father can't see us behind this hillock."

"Are you out of your mind? Imagine my letting you have this horse up here on the moors, with lakes all round us! He's a water-horse."

"A kelpie?" he asked.

"Didn't you know that?" she said.

"His hooves aren't turned backwards, as far as I can see."

"I never said he was a kelpie on both sides," said the girl. "Just a minute, I think someone's calling us."

"I'll talk to you later. Soon. I'll come and call on you," he said.

"No, please don't, for heaven's sake. I'd be much too scared. You don't know me at all, anyway. And I don't know you at all, either."

"I didn't mean I was going to come at once," he said. "Not today, and not tomorrow. And not the next day, either. Perhaps when you're seventeen. I'll be nearly of age then. I hope you won't have sold this colt to Björn of Leirur by the time I come."

"I'd be so shy I'd hide in a cupboard," she said, and with that she turned her horse away from the boy so that she would not have to look at him; and besides, their fathers had just about ridden up to them.

"We must not let the outside flank of the drive fall behind, my dears," said her father.

The other farmer said, "I'd be very surprised if those two haven't started thinking some rather pleasant thoughts."

4

The pony and fate

A lamb-drive at midsummer on a pony descended from kelpies, and a breath of air from the glaciers—those who have been on such a journey in their youth dream of it forever afterwards, however long they may live, and finally with the wordless emptiness of regret and resignation to death. She only rode Krapi this once; why not always from that day onwards?

"I mentioned last year, Steinar, that you should let me have the white horse this summer when I ride west to welcome royalty," said the sheriff. "It is of no little importance to arrive at Þingvellir* well-mounted on such an occasion—as much to impress other districts as the Danes themselves."

Steinar of Hlíðar laughed his high-pitched titter. "I have often admired the sheriff's horses," he said. "Wonderfully reliable beasts, and fine at fording rivers, no half-measures about that. I can say nothing about the king, of course, but I would dearly love to see the sheriff in this country who would be better mounted."

"Yes or no?" said the sheriff. He was in a great hurry, like all officials, and had no time to listen to evasions.

"Hmmm," said Steinar of Hlíðar, swallowing carefully. "The point is, my dear friend, that this pony you refer to is completely untried and scarcely even fully broken in. But it so happens that he has become a fairy-tale horse for the children here, and his value, if he has any, is what he is in the eyes of the children while they are young and small."

"It is downright dangerous to let children ride unbroken horses," said the sheriff. "Children should be strapped on to docile old hacks."

"I have not really made much of a habit so far of letting them ride him," said Steinar. "But, if you will allow me to say so, I like to use our Krapi as a model when I tell them stories of grander creatures, like the horse Grani that Sigurd the Dragon-Killer rode when he went to fight the dragon Fafnir, or the late Hrafnkell Freyr-Goði's horse Faxi, the beast that the god Freyr inhabited on the strict understanding that whosoever rode him, apart from Hrafnkell himself, should forfeit nothing but his life;[*] nor am I accustomed to forget Sleipnir,[*] who pounds along the Milky Way so hard with his eight legs that the stars are sent flying; or else I tell them that the colt is perhaps a kelpie that came straight from the creek there."

The sheriff lit his pipe. "It is no use serving up old legends for me, my lad," he said. "I can invent my own fairy-tales, thank you. You peasants always forget that Sigurd the Dragon-Killer went to hell a long time ago with the dragon and all the rest of the paraphernalia. But you allow Björn of Leirur to rob you of anything he likes, even your souls if you had such things and he happened to want them."

"I cannot say I had thought of letting old Björn ride very far on our Krapi," said Steinar. "Not but what Björn has deserved nothing but good as far as I am concerned."

"The day may come, my friend, when you will part with this pony for less than nothing, and you will have cause to regret your refusal to sell him to me," said the sheriff, and mounted.

Steinar of Hlíðar once again laughed his squeaky titter as he stood on the paving. "I am well aware that it has never been thought proper for a poor man to own a fine horse," he said. "And I realise that this is why you important people are now making so much fun of me, bless your hearts. One must just take it as it comes. But the fact of the matter is that it may not be so very long before this horse ceases to be more remarkable than any others; and perhaps that day has already arrived, even though I am reluctant to believe it."

Once again it was borne out that the more insistent the demands on Steinar of Hlíðar became, the more amiable became his falsetto giggles; but the Yes which was anyway the most alien of words to him always withdrew farther and farther until it disappeared entirely into that infinity where the word No belongs.

But Steinar of Hlíðar liked to have his little joke just as much as the eminent did. There were more than a few smiles when word got around that he had refused to sell both to the sheriff and to Björn of Leirur a pony for riding to Þingvellir—but was now letting it be known that he intended to ride there himself after the hay-making in order to pay his respects to the king.

It had long since been decided what gentry from the district were to ride west in the sheriff's party, and it goes without saying that Steinar of Hlíðar was not one of them; but he seemed to have no misgivings about going on his own.

It was undeniable that there was something about this horse which contrasted sharply with other horses and made them look inferior: something about his gait, his bearing, the look in his eyes and the quality of his responses which at the very least suggested that it was not quite right to say that the horse, as a species, had ceased to evolve ever since the unicorn's horn was lost . . . that its development was not entirely finished even though there had evolved on it just about the most perfect form of foot ever known, one toe in a fixed shoe. This particular horse was at least in his own way rather like the Pope: not only above other horses, but above all his surroundings—meadows, waters, mountains, everything.

There was no doubt at all that this was the horse that Steinar of Hlíðar was going to ride to see the king—or rather, as he put it to his neighbours with his usual modesty, "Our Krapi is going to Þingvellir to greet the king, with the fellow from Hlíðar on his back." But there was no lack of wits in the district to turn the phrase round and say that the white horse from Hlíðar was going to ride on his master's back to Þingvellir to see the king.

Although Krapi was as gentle as a babe in the farmyard, and felt quite content when he was haltered in the home-field, he was a very different creature when it came to catching him out in the pastures. Near the farm he behaved like a model prisoner who deserved every privilege, even the privilege of being released at the earliest opportunity. But out in the open spaces he was his own master. If anyone tried to fetch him from the grazing down by the sands when he was with the other ponies, he would glide away from his pursuers like a breath of air; the more they tried to

approach him, the farther he left them behind; and the faster
they came at him the more he resembled the wind itself and
went sweeping away over scree and mud, water and earth-slips,
as if they were level plains; and when he grew bored with the
game he would head straight for the mountains. And that was
how it was on the day that Steinar of Hlíðar went out to the pastures with a bridle behind his back to catch the colt unawares on
the day before he was due to set off. The pony bolted, tossing his
head in all directions as if something had frightened him, then
galloped perilously up the steep mountain-slope and disappeared
over the ridge. It meant that Steinar now had to comb the mountains with the help of his family to drive all the ponies down so
that Krapi could be captured in the corral. When they had
chased the pony up over the Brows they saw him standing alone
high on a knoll, looking towards the glacier and neighing loudly.

"Have a good long neigh at the glacier, my lad," Steinar
shouted at him, "for you may be having a change of scenery
soon."

The dust of the delegation of dignitaries and notables had
long since settled on all the tracks of Steinahlíðar, and the sound
of their hooves had mingled with that of other notables and roy-
alists from farther west. Government officials were to welcome
the king when the royal ship docked at Reykjavík, and sheriffs
and members of Parliament were self-appointed guests at the
forthcoming royal banquets in the capital. On a peaceful late-
summer day, when nothing moved except for an occasional tern
drowsing on the track and an oyster-catcher stepping elegantly
through the meadows, right in the midst of the hush that falls
upon those who remain behind when the great have ridden off to
their revelry, the farmer of Hlíðar in Steinahlíðar saddled his

pony and rode off by himself. Snati the farm-dog was locked indoors. The wife stood on the paving and wiped away a dutiful tear as she watched her husband ride off down the path, and the children stood on either side of her, having put their arms round the pony's neck and kissed him on his fragrant muzzle for the last time. They did not move until their daddy had crossed the screes and disappeared to the west behind the shoulder of the hill.

5

The sacred lava violated

In Brennugjá (Burning Rift), the place in Þingvellir where people used to be burned at the stake, a small gathering of farmers had collected at dusk that late-summer evening on the day before the king's arrival. The scree under the cliff was almost hidden by moss, and on one moss-grown block of lava the height of a man someone had clambered up to make a speech to his fellow-countrymen about a matter of no little importance. A few inquisitive souls had drifted up to hear if anything of interest were going on, and among them was Steinar of Hlíðar; he had his riding-crop in his hand.

As far as he could make out from a distance, it seemed to Steinar that this man was quoting something from the Bible, but he was astonished to note that the pious expressions usually worn by an audience on such occasions were not in evidence now. Indeed, most of the bystanders were looking rather indignant, and there were some who made no secret of their disapproval of

what was being said. The speaker was constantly being interrupted, and some of the catcalls were distinctly discourteous;
there were other people who just shouted and laughed. But the
speaker was never at a loss for an answer and never became confused, although his delivery was by nature a little awkward.

He seemed to be about Steinar's age, big-boned and high-
shouldered but rather thin, with a gaunt face that was pitted
with pockmarks or scored by suffering; his whole appearance
bore witness to some exceptional experience. At that time, most
Icelanders had rounded cheeks under their whiskers, and their
adult tribulations were as natural to them as the sorrows of childhood; even the oldest men had the same expression as children.
Many people in Iceland in those days had a sort of pink, transparent skin; their colour varied between a cold blue-red pallor and a
deep-blue flush, depending on the weather and the nourishment
they were getting. But this man was almost greyish-brown in
the face, not unlike the colour of glacier-rivers or warmed-up
coffee with skimmed milk added. He had a shock of thick, tou-
sled hair, and his clothes were too big for him, but he was no
scarecrow for all that.

And what was this man talking about at Þingvellir near the
Öxará out with the official programme for the great national celebrations, when every honest breast in the land was swelling
with pride and the hope of better times to come?

Steinar of Hlíðar asked who this preacher might be, and
received the reply that he was a heretic.

"Oh really?" said Steinar. "I must say I would not mind having
a look at such a person. We see many strangers in Steinahlíðar,
but most of them seem to have the right ideas about the Almighty.
Excuse me, gentlemen, but what is this man's heresy?"

"He's over from America to preach some revelations from a

new prophet who opposes Luther and the Pope, some fellow
called Joseph Smith, apparently," said the man Steinar had
addressed. "They have several wives. But the authorities have
burned all his pamphlets with the revelations in them, and now
he's come to Þingvellir to see the king and get permission to
print more heresies. They immerse people."

Steinar moved in closer. By this time there was no longer any
question of a formal speech being delivered. The stranger's
preaching had so incensed everyone that he was scarcely given
time to finish a sentence before the audience were shouting cor-
rections or demanding further explanations. Some were now so
impassioned that they could scarcely find words of sufficient
abuse to apply to this heretic.

"What proof does this fellow you mentioned have that people
ought to be immersed?" yelled one heckler.

"Was the Saviour himself not immersed, then?" replied the
speaker. "Do you think the Saviour would have let himself be
immersed if the Lord had acknowledged child-baptism? In the
Bible there was always baptism by immersion. There is no child-
baptism in God's Word, no sirree. It never occurred to anyone to
sprinkle water on infants before the third century, at the beginning of the great Apostasy, when unenlightened and ungodly
people got the idea of cleansing children who were to be sacri-
ficed to a copper god, yes sirree. They called themselves Christians but they worshipped the fiend Satan. Then the Pope
adopted this perversion, of course, like all other heresies; and
Luther followed him, even though he boasted he knew better
than the Pope."

One person asked, "Can Joseph Smith perform miracles?"

The speaker retorted, "Where are Luther's miracles? And

where are the Pope's miracles? I've never heard anything of them. On the other hand, the whole existence of the Mormons is a miracle, from the moment when Joseph Smith spoke to the Lord for the first time. When did Luther speak to the Lord? When did the Pope speak to the Lord?"

"God spoke to the Apostle Paul," said one learned man.

"Oh, that was rather a brief interview," replied the speaker. "And God never bothered to give the fellow more than the one audience. On the other hand, the Lord spoke to Joseph Smith not once and not twice and not thrice but one hundred and thirty-three times, not counting the principal revelations themselves."

"The Bible is God's Word here in Iceland," said the earnest theologian who had spoken previously. But the preacher was quick to reply: "Do you think that God was struck dumb when He had finished dictating the Bible?" he demanded.

A witty heckler shouted, "Not dumb, perhaps, but at least dumbfounded at the thought that Joseph Smith was going to come along and bastardize it."

"Dumb or dumbfounded, I'm not going to argue the point with you, my friend. But I get the impression that you believe that God is utterly silenced? That He has not opened His mouth for nearly two thousand years?"

"At least I don't believe that God talks to fools," said the heckler.

"Quite so," said the heretic. "I suppose He is far more likely to talk to respectable farmers and sheriffs, and perhaps a pastor or two? But allow me to add one word, if I may, since you were asking about miracles: what miracles do you have to set against the fact that God led Joseph Smith to the golden plates on the Hill Cumorah, and then by direct revelation showed the Mormons the way to the Promised Land which is God's home and the kingdom of the Latter-Day Saints in Salt Lake Valley?"

"Hey, wait a minute," said the heckler. "Since when has America with all its hordes of gangsters and beggars become God's Kingdom?"

Now the Mormon had to swallow carefully once or twice.

"I must admit," he said at last, "that one's tongue can sometimes get tied in knots here in Iceland, and it takes an effort for unlettered folk like myself to untie it. There's only one thing I want to say to you, because I know I am speaking the absolute truth: everything the Saviour and the Pope's saints tried to do but couldn't, even though all your Lutheran kings tagged along behind them, Joseph Smith and his disciple Brigham Young achieved when they, at God's express wish and command, led us Mormons to God's own city of Zion descended upon earth; and over that country there shines a glorious light. There you will find God's Valley of Bliss and His millennium on earth. And because this valley lies far behind the mountains, moors, deserts and rivers of America, and secondly because America preserved the Lord's golden plates that Joseph found, the mere name of America is sufficient praise."

"Yes, and of all the swindlers and vagabonds in America, Joseph with his plates was the worst," shouted one of the crowd.

"Where is *your* promised land?" retorted the speaker.

"In heaven!"

"Ah yes, just as I thought. Is that not pretty high up in the stratosphere?"

Another said, "It would be fun to have a look at these golden plates. I don't suppose you have a fragment of them handy? Even just a list of the natural resources in Zion?"

"In Salt Lake Valley it's quite usual for any one farmer to own ten thousand ewes in addition to other livestock," said the Mormon. "How are the prospects in *your* millennium?"

This report about sheep-farming in the Promised Land seemed to take everyone aback for a moment.

"Our Saviour is our Saviour, God be praised!" testified one God-fearing man, as if to brace himself against this enormous holding of sheep.

"Yes, and is Joseph perhaps not Joseph?" said the Mormon. "That's what I would have thought, even though I'm not very learned. Joseph is Joseph. God be praised."

"The New Testament is our witness!" shouted the man with the clergyman's vocabulary. "He who believes in Christ does not believe in Joseph."

"That's a lie!" cried the Mormon. "He who believes in Christ can certainly believe in Joseph. No one but he who believes in the New Testament can believe in the golden plates. But he who calls the New Testament a hoax made up by vagabonds and asks 'Where's the original?'—*he* can't believe in Joseph either. Such a person would tell you he puts the New Testament and the golden plates of Joseph in the same category. Such a person says, 'Just as the Saviour's friends concocted the New Testament, so Joseph's friends invented the golden plates.' Such a person will try to prove to you that the Saviour and Joseph were both dishonest men. Dear brethren, we Mormons do not speak to people who talk in the way I have just described. They are beyond the pale."

"I seem to recall, my friend," said one well-to-do farmer, "that you were just telling us how many ewes you had. Ten thousand, wasn't it, eh? How about now telling us how many wives you have?"

"How many wives did people in the Bible have? People like

Solomon, for instance, who was at least as big a farmer as you?"
said the Mormon. "And didn't Luther allow the Elector of Hesse
to have more than one wife? And why was the papacy abolished
in England? Only to allow old Henry to have several wives."

"We're Icelanders here," said a voice from the crowd.

"Yes, and Icelanders have always been polygamists," said the
Mormon.

There was a gasp from various good folk in the audience.
Some shouted, "You're lying!" Others challenged the Mormon to
prove his statement.

"Well, they certainly were when I knew them," said the Mormon. "It was just that any one man was free to turn any number
of women into harlots instead of giving them honourable status
with the seal of matrimony, as we Mormons do. Mormons don't
let nice young girls waste away before their eyes in shame and
humiliation if they refuse to marry the first lout who proposed to
them. Many fine girls, on the other hand, are happy to share a
good man rather than make do with some boor all their lives. We
in Salt Lake Valley don't want to rear harlots or old maids or dis-
graced mothers and widows for vulgar people to gossip about.
But when I was growing up in Iceland the country was crowded
with such women. Children were given fathers and women married off for the most part according to whose reputation needed
salvaging. I myself was conceived and reared in this form of
polygamy. People said I was a pastor's son. It was the custom of
those in authority who had to travel a lot to sleep with whatever
women happened to take their fancy, married or unmarried. My
mother was forced to seek refuge in the Vestmannaeyjar, and
died there from the contempt with which she was treated; and I
was brought back to the mainland and reared in her parish. An

orphan, usually an illegitimate one at that, was never a person of much standing in Icelandic society. I was invariably given a change of clothes and a haircut on the first day of summer. The sack on which the dog had lain at the door all winter was dusted against the wall, then a hole was made for my head and that's what I was given to wear. Polygamy has always been practised in Iceland, but that's how it actually worked out for the women and children. It wasn't perhaps quite so bad in my time as before, when the unlawful wives of polygamists were put to death by drowning in a pool here at Þingvellir for giving birth to children. With us in Salt Lake Valley, on the other hand . . ."

When he had reached this point in his argument it was obvious that various upstanding farmers in the audience felt he had gone quite far enough. Some said they had not ridden to Þingvellir from distant parts just to see the sacred lava violated and the place defiled with foul talk about eminent folk and decent farmers. From all around came shouts that the heretic had gone too far. Several good people went up to him and tried to topple him off the stone. The Mormon peered at them over his spectacles and stopped short in mid-sentence, dropped his preacher's attitude at once, and said quietly in an ordinary tone of voice, "Are you thinking of laying hands on me?"

"If you insult this holy sanctuary with one more word from your shameless and ungodly mouth, you'll suffer for it," said one topbooted gentleman, walking briskly up to the stone on which the Mormon stood.

"I shall stop now," said the Mormon. "I always stop when people are going to beat me up. God will conquer without Mormons having to brawl. Goodbye, gentlemen, I shall take my leave now."

They cried, "Fie on you!" and "Shame on you for taking the Lord's name in vain!"

The Mormon clambered rather stiffly down off the rock. Two or three respectable farmers seized hold of him, not to help him down but to take him to task. They gripped him tightly and exposed him to the crowd, so that whoever was so minded could come forward and deal with him. One topbooted gentleman stepped up and kicked him. Another good man came and struck him twice on the face.

There was a bystander with a riding-crop in his hand nearby, rather an undistinguished, clumsy-looking fellow.

"Good, there's a riding-crop," said a stout gold-braided man with a goatee beard. "You there, spindle-shanks, lend the lads your riding-crop."

"It so happens, heeheehee, that so long as I am holding it this riding-crop has human intelligence, as one might say, though not very much, it's true," said Steinar of Hlíðar, with a falsetto giggle.

Anyway, whether or not it was because they failed to get a loan of Steinar's riding-crop, they stopped giving the Mormon a beating. They released him and told him to go to hell. He shuffled away down towards the water, straddle-legged and stooping a little from the waist. In characteristic and ingrained Icelandic fashion he was jeered as he departed. Some shouted "America!," others "Salt Lake Puddle!," while others just shouted obscenities; but the Mormon neither turned his head nor quickened his pace. It did not take long for the crowd's vehemence to simmer down, and the people dispersed. Soon there was no one left in Brennugjá except Steinar of Hlíðar sitting on a stone with his riding-crop.

Steinar was one of the uninvited guests at Þingvellir, repre-

senting no one in particular—scarcely even himself, and certainly not his pony; representing, at the very most, perhaps, just
his riding-crop. Accordingly, no arrangements had been made to
receive him; there was no reserved bed for him at this great
national festival except the moss that covered the sacred lava, and
no other refreshment than the breeze that the guardian-spirits of
the country breathed. After entrusting his pony to the ostlers
earlier in the evening, he had found himself alone with only his
riding-crop for company; and since he now happened to be in
Brennugjá with nowhere else to go, he began to look around for a
spot where the moss grew thickly enough to blunt the sharp
edges of the rocks.

And while he was busy with these thoughts, after all the
people who had got so excited about the Mormon had left, he
suddenly noticed that the speaker had returned to Brennugjá.
He had never gone farther than just out of sight round the first
curve of the cliff after all, while tempers in Brennugjá were cool-
ing down. Now he was peering about in the late-summer twilight as if he had lost something, and did not take the trouble to
greet Steinar even when he walked right past him.

"Good evening, friend," said Steinar of Hlíðar.

"Are you going to use that riding-crop on me?" asked the
Mormon.

"I have never made much of a habit of beating people with
riding-crops," said Steinar. "I am looking for a spot where I can
bed down for the night."

"I don't suppose you've seen my hat, have you?" asked the
Mormon.

"I fear not," said Steinar. "As far as I could see, you were hatless when you were making your speech."

"I stuck it in a hole before I started," said the Mormon. "I always hide my hat before I make a speech. You never know what they'll do to your hat."

Steinar of Hlíðar readily offered his help in looking for the hat, and for a long time they searched the moss-grown scree at the foot of the cliff. The light was now failing fast. At last Steinar happened to catch a glimpse of some monstrosity glistening among the rocks. It was the hat; it had been wrapped in transparent paper.

"I don't suppose this is your hat, is it?" said Steinar.

"A thousand thanks," said the Mormon. "You're a man of luck. This hat and a change of underclothing is all I have left since they took my pamphlets away from me. And if I lost it, it would show that I'm not man enough for my hat."

"And you keep it wrapped in grease-proof paper," said Steinar.

"Yes, that's what is always done in America when they are good hats. It's to keep them from getting wet if it rains. Grease-proof paper repels water. The hat is always as good as new."

"Really?" said Steinar. "But what I find most remarkable is all that excellent land you said there was over in your part of the world."

"Yes, you people in Iceland can beat me and kick me just as you please," said the Mormon. "My land is good."

"You must be used to most things by now," said Steinar.

"Oh, this affair tonight was nothing," said the Mormon. "I have seldom escaped so lightly. I have three times had a thorough beating, several times a black eye—and one of my teeth is loose. I have travelled through whole counties where I have nowhere been offered so much as a bite of food or a sip of water, never mind a roof over my head. Orders had gone out from the sheriffs and pastors."

Steinar of Hlíðar was not in the habit of criticizing others, but now he could not restrain himself from repeating an old saying which is normally used when little fellows get uppish with their betters: "Wipe my arse, Mr. Lawman!"

"But that was nothing at all compared with taking my poor little pamphlets off me," said the Mormon. "I travelled 2,000 miles across America, most of them on foot, all the way from Salt Lake Valley to Dakota, until I finally found the one and only printing-press in the Western hemisphere that possessed the letters þ and ð so that I could get my pamphlets set up in type; if you search there long enough you will find some paupers like me from Iceland living on a riverbank behind the forests. When my pamphlets had been printed out there in Dakota I set off with them for Iceland. And now there is none left."

"Excuse me," said Steinar, "but what did these misguided people do with the pamphlets?"

"That's easy," said the Mormon. "They sent them to Denmark—Iceland's brain has always been in Copenhagen. They told me that the Danish ministries would have to decide. So now I have come to Þingvellir to waylay the king. I have heard he is a German peasant, and I have met many of them in Salt Lake Valley: Denmark's brain has always been in Germany. But Germans don't belittle Icelanders, on the other hand, and for that reason I can expect more of a German than a Dane. I am going to ask him why I cannot have books just like anyone else in this kingdom."

"That is sensible of you," said Steinar of Hlíðar. "He is said to be a good king."

6

The millennial celebrations. Icelanders reap justice

This book does not profess to give the history of the festivities which were held at Þingvellir to commemorate the thousandth anniversary of the settlement of Iceland* and to welcome the Danish king. Detailed accounts of these events were compiled at the time, and later some excellent books were written. But there were one or two not entirely irrelevant incidents, in the judgement of some, which never received attention in those worthy publications. This is the story of one such incident, only to be found in some of the less significant books, which are none the less true for all that.

But first, a few words on a topic that people now are apt to overlook: there was a time once when Icelanders, despite the fact that they were the most indigent nation in Europe, all traced their ancestry back to kings. Indeed, in their literature they have given life to many kings whom other nations had made little effort to remember and who would otherwise have been consigned to oblivion in this world and the next. Most people in Iceland traced their lineage back to the kings who were written about in the sagas; some only claimed descent from warrior-kings or sea-kings, others to remote petty kings in the valleys of Norway and elsewhere in Scandinavia, or to the leaders of the Norse warriors who served in the Varangian Guard under the emperor in Constantinople;* but a few claimed descent from kings who, it can be proved, were actually crowned. No farmer was considered worth his salt if he could not trace his genealogy back to Harald hárfagri (Fine-Hair)* or his namesake Harald hilditönn (War-Tooth).* All Icelandic genealogies can be traced back to the Ynglings and the Scyldings*—if there happens to be anyone left in the world who knows who these folk were. It was child's play for most of the Icelanders to prove kinship with Sigurd the Dragon-Killer, King Gautrekur of Gotaland,* and Ganger-Hrolf;* but those of yet more recondite erudition could claim connection with Charlemagne and Frederick Barbarossa, or could work their way right back to Agamemnon, noblest of the Greeks, the conqueror of Troy. Learned foreigners called the Icelanders the greatest genealogists in Europe after royal pedigrees had been denounced as pomp and vanity as a result of the French Revolution.

Many people had ridden to Þingvellir just to see with their own eyes what manner of man it was to whom the saga-writers of old had given life in their books. Many of them claimed kinship with much greater princes than King Kristian Wilhelmsson; and although the farmers gave due respect to the high rank and royal title that the Danes had conferred on this foreigner, it is unlikely King Kristian ever in his whole life found himself in a company

of people who considered him so inferior to themselves in pedigree as did those stunted rickety peasants tramping around in
their crumpled cowhide shoes. It has never been forgotten in Iceland that it was only with the help of Icelandic genealogies that
this offspring of German cottage-nobility, reared as a foster-child
in Denmark, could trace his ancestry back to King Gormur gamli
(the Old)* of Denmark—who, according to some, never existed
at all. But it is a measure of King Kristian Wilhelmsson's qualities that, despite his humble origins, the Icelanders have always
esteemed him more highly than most other Danish kings; and it
goes to show that even in a nation of fanatical genealogists there
are people who at a pinch can value some things more highly
then the ancestral seed which flowed a thousand years ago. Kristian Wilhelmsson had one outstanding attribute which, despite
his lowly antecedents, won him the Icelanders' regard and even
their admiration, and that was his horsemanship. It is an Icelandic dogma that kings should be able to ride well; indeed, a
man on a good mount is respected above all others. White horses
have always been considered one of Iceland's greatest glories, and
farmers competed to supply them when royalty was riding
through their district. Also, in those days most Icelanders took
tobacco through the nose from wooden flasks or horn receptacles;
this tobacco is called *snuss* in Low German, and Icelanders respect
any man who accepts a pinch from them. It is said that King
Kristian Wilhelmsson, too, liked his snuff.

It is not to be denied that the Icelanders were glad to receive
their new constitution from the Danish king—but not exuber-
antly so. In fact, they completely forgot to thank him for it during the festivities. There was only one man there who had the
presence of mind to thank the king for the gift on the Icelanders'

behalf—albeit uninvited and unauthorized; and this was the Danish baron who had drafted the constitution for the king. Perhaps too many Icelanders felt that the gift merely represented something which was already theirs by right and did not go far enough, at that. The king, for his part, quite forgot to thank the Icelanders for what they thought the most significant thing they gave him in return, which was the poetry composed in his honour. Some poets composed as many as eight poems about him. It is not the custom in Germany to compose poetry in honour of county governors, Electors, or even the Kaiser, and Kristian Wilhelmsson was left wide-eyed and open-mouthed as a procession of poets stepped forward one after the other and recited verse at him; he had never heard verse before, and did not know what it was.

It is said that on the morning after the main ceremonies at Þingvellir some of the grooms were trying out the horses which the king was to ride on his way back to the capital. A crowd of farmers had gathered round to see how good the horses were and how they performed. Among them was Steinar of Hlíðar, holding by the bridle his aforementioned white horse, Krapi. When he had watched the royal grooms putting the horses through their paces for a while and seen what they could do, he led his own mount away and headed for the huge marquee where the king was at table with his courtiers and the sheriffs of Iceland. Steinar greeted the sentries and asked to see the king. They were reluctant to pay any heed to this stranger's request, but finally it was brought to the attention of one of the officials in attendance to the king. This man asked Steinar why he wanted to see the king; Steinar replied that he had urgent business with him—he had a gift to present to him. After a while the courtier returned

to say that the king never accepted gifts from individual com-
moners, but that Steinar was to be permitted to come inside and
pay his respects to the king while he was at table.

Inside the marquee sat a crowd of gold-braided men of rank,
some of them drinking beer. There was a rich aroma of cigars,
which the gentry held glowing between their teeth, emitting
thick plumes of smoke. There were Icelandic as well as Danish
notables there, and it was only to be expected that some of them
should look askance when a plain farmer without official recognition came walking in.

Steinar of Hlíðar doffed his battered cap at the entrance to the
marquee, and smoothed down what little was left of his hair. He
made no attempt to straighten his shoulders or stick out his
chest; his walk was a clumsy trundle, like that of all farmers, but
there was no suggestion from his bearing that he thought himself more humble than anyone present. He looked as if nothing
came more naturally to him than meeting kings; nor was he
there on any commonplace mission.

He made straight for the king. Then he bowed to him courteously, but not too low. The famous men who sat nearby forgot to
carry food to their lips. A sudden silence descended on the marquee. And now when Steinar of Hlíðar stood facing royalty, he
once again smoothed his hair down across his brow; then he
began to speak, addressing the king as befitted a good Icelandic
farmer in the sagas:

"My name is Steinar Steinsson, from Hlíðar in Steinahlíðar,"
he said. "I bid the king welcome to Iceland. We are of the same
kin, according to the genealogy which Bjarni Guðmundsson of
Fuglavík prepared for my grandfather. I am of Jutland origin,
descended from King Harald hilditönn, who fought the battle of
Brávellir."*

"I beg your Majesty's indulgence," said one of the notables in Danish, edging his way in front of Steinar and bowing to the king. "I am this man's sheriff," he said, "and it is not with my consent that he comes barging in on you like this, sire."

"We are pleased to hear what this man has to say," said the king, "if you would interpret for us."

Sheriff Benediktsson spoke up at once and said that this man had bidden the king welcome, with the observation that they were distant kinsmen. "I crave your Majesty's pardon that our farmers all speak like this," he said. "They cannot help it. The sagas are their lifeblood."

King Kristian replied, "This has just about convinced me that most kings would find it does not pay to argue genealogies with farmers here in Iceland. Has this gentleman anything else to say to us?"

Steinar Steinsson continued his address:

"Since I have heard, my dear and excellent king, that we have much in common as regards lineage and standing (for you, I understand, are a farmer from down south in Gotaland), I wish to proffer you the thanks of my district for giving us what is already ours, namely, permission to walk upright here in Iceland. No one can receive a better gift from those in power over him than permission to be what he is and not something else. And now for my part I wish to return your generosity in my own modest way. In my family we have always had good horses; and I myself am said to have a not unhandy colt, as my sheriff can confirm better than anyone else, for he is one of the eminent men who have offered to buy him in exchange for gold and gratitude. And now, since you have brought us justice to this country, I am going to hand over the reins of this nag as a token gift in return. The beast is now in the care of their lordships at the door; but I would be grateful if I could have the bridle back at your earliest convenience."

Kristian Wilhelmsson first had this speech translated into Danish; but he was still not fully clear about the meaning of it, and so he called upon his page to translate it into his mother-tongue, German. The more interpretations he was given of it, the more remarkable a speech he thought it.

"Let us go and see this animal," he said at last.

They walked to the entrance to the marquee, where a groom was holding the pony by the reins and a crowd of people had gathered from all sides to have a look at so admirable a mount. The pony was trembling slightly at the withers; he did not like being handled and stared at by so many people. The king saw at once that this was a handsome creature; he went over to the pony and patted him gently but firmly, as all good horsemen should, and the pony calmed down. He turned to some baron who was standing nearby and said to him in German, "Perhaps I am after all the right sort of barbarian chieftain to be king over the Ice-landers. But I shall not accept anything for nothing from these farmers. Let it be paid for in full from my exchequer, through the proper authorities."

Then the king took leave of Steinar of Hlíðar with a hand-clasp, and said that he would never forget such a gift. He also said that Steinar should just mention his name if ever he found himself in any difficulties, for Steinar would always have the king for a friend.

Steinar of Hlíðar thanked him for the kind reception and walked away out of sight of his king and his pony, away from the great millennial festivities.

7

Church-going

Steinar of Hlíðar hoisted his saddle on his back and set off for home. He took the track along the south side of the lake through the wood which has stood there for thousands of years and is unique because it never grows taller than the height of a man, or higher than a man can reach; everything above that is sheared off by the cold. All these stunted trees bent to the will of the wind. Then he followed the paths along the stream that flow out of Þingvallavatn (Lake Þingvellir) towards the lowlands and the main track to his home district. He walked all day and far into the night; it had begun to rain and the ground was wet, giving off a wonderful aroma. Midsummer was past, the two months when night did not exist; but one could scarcely call the nights dark yet. An occasional farm-dog gave tongue as he passed. He came to a meadow full of haycocks, where he put the saddle down for a pillow, spread hay over himself, and munched half a rye-scone that tasted utterly delicious, even though it was

45

as tough as a saddle-flap. It was the last of his provisions. Before
he fell asleep he recited to himself:

> *Wet and weary down I lay,*
> *Far too tired to wander;*
> *Saddle down among the hay*
> *In the meadow yonder.*

Next morning he called at a farm. The farmer was already up,
and he asked the visitor if he were a Mormon. Steinar of Hlíðar
said he was not—"unfortunately not, I almost said," he added. "I
come from Steinahlíðar, farther east."

"Well, if you say you're not a Mormon, you aren't one," said the
farmer. "I've never heard of a Mormon who didn't acknowledge
he was one before being asked, even though he knew it would
cost him a beating."

"We are all inclined to take pride in our heresies," said Steinar.
"I in mine, you in yours. By the way, could I ask you for something to drink?"

"Girls!" the farmer shouted into the house. "Give this man
here a drink of whey. And a bit of cod's head."

Soon the sun shone from a clear sky. By the afternoon one
could see mirages. The sea rose trembling into the sky. The Vestmannaeyjar had floated up to heaven.

Steinar of Hlíðar had almost forgotten that it was Sunday,
until a crowd of churchgoers rode past him. Someone said he had
a fine saddle there.

"Indeed I have," said Steinar. "And a riding-crop, what's more.
But the bridle I have mislaid."

They offered him a pony, but he preferred to walk. The farmers said that this was unlike folk from Steinahlíðar.

"That's quite right, good people," said Steinar. "This is just a little fellow passing through—so little, in fact, that he cannot become any smaller by not being on horseback."

Steinar reached the church on foot much later than the others; when he arrived at this unfamiliar place of worship, everyone had already gone inside for the service. Outside, there was that peculiar sense of human withdrawal that pervades a parish-of-ease every Sunday between noon and three in the afternoon. A few ponies stood drowsing in the corral; but the dogs sprawled around at the lich-gate or the church-porch and howled at the Vestmannaeyjar because they had floated up to heaven. There was not a human being within sight. The glad sound of singing could be heard from inside the church. Steinar was pleased when he realised that he had arrived in time for the second benediction.

But as he followed the path up from the farmhouse to the church he caught sight of three old tethering-blocks standing in a field; they were no longer in use, because either the farm had been shifted or else the church had. When he looked more closely at the boulders, however, he saw that some large and untidy bundle had been tethered to the middle block. He went over to see what it could be, and found that it was a man.

"Well I never," said Steinar.

This man had been gagged and bound and the rope made fast to the iron staple in the boulder. Steinar went up to him and contemplated the state he was in.

"Can I be right? It's surely not the Mormon, is it?" he said.

The prisoner was hatless and his mop of hair stuck out in all directions. In daylight his colour was reddish-brown, like a tanned hide, and the gag made his face look distorted. Steinar of Hlíðar at once set about removing the gag, which turned out to be a round stone picked from the mud. The man spat a few times when he had got rid of it; there was some dirt in his mouth, and his gum was bleeding slightly. The two men greeted one another.

"You have had a bit of a roughing up," said Steinar of Hlíðar, and went on untying the rope.

"Oh, I've known worse," said the Mormon, and reached into his pocket for his spectacle case. "I'm lucky they did not break my glasses."

"What a way to treat a stranger," said Steinar of Hlíðar. "And these are supposed to be Christians!"

"Am I muddy at all?" asked the Mormon.

Steinar coiled the rope up carefully like the tidy man he was, and laid it on the tethering-block. Then he brushed the Mormon down a little.

"There is little I can say," said Steinar. "Criticizing others will not make me any bigger."

"When have Christians behaved in any other way?" said the Mormon. "They began to fall into the Great Apostasy right from the days of the Primitive Church."

"Excuse me, but where is your hat?" said Steinar.

"It's safely hidden away," said the Mormon. "But it's very odd that they should never try to take my topboots away, considering how good they are."

"You must be a fearless sort of man," said Steinar. "It's just as well, if you have to put up with injustice."

"Big dogs are the worst," said the Mormon. "I've always been a bit scared of dogs. I was bitten by a bitch when I was small, actually."

"Where are you going now, if I may ask?"

"I'm on my way to the Vestmannaeyjar. The people there used to be the worst rogues in Iceland, but now they are the best of the lot. The Latter-Day Saints are given sanctuary there."

"Did you get hold of the king?" asked Steinar.

"What business is that of yours? Who are you?"

"My name is Steinar Steinsson, from Steinahlíðar. I am the man who was looking for a spot to bed down at Þingvellir the other night."

"My goodness, hallo there, friend!" said the Mormon, and kissed him. "I had a vague feeling I recognized you. Thanks for the last time. No, I did not meet the king—the Icelanders saw to that, all right. But he sent me his greetings, and said that Joseph Smith was certainly not banned in the Danish kingdom."

"Are you getting your pamphlets back?" asked Steinar.

"Not from the Icelanders," said the Mormon. "But one of those gold-braided Danes put my case to the king, who is a decent German. He came back and said that I could have all my stuff back if I cared to go to Copenhagen for it. That's the Germans all over. And if the Danes have lost them, the king promised that I could have as many pamphlets printed in Copenhagen as I wanted and then take them to Iceland and give them away or sell them just as I wished—it had been unlawful of the Icelanders to take them off me in the first place. I knew that already, for that matter; and also that the Icelanders were a much more insignificant race than the Danes—although the Germans, of course, are much better than both."

"You are perhaps on your way to Copenhagen now to have the new pamphlets printed?" asked Steinar.

"Books don't make themselves, my friend," said the Mormon. "The printing isn't the whole of it, by any means. It's a fearful prospect for an uneducated farmhand from the Landeyjar (Land-Isles) to have to start composing books to convert a nation like the Icelanders. The only consolation is that the Lord is Almighty."

"Indeed He is," said Steinar of Hlíðar. "And perhaps we are still in time for the second benediction even though it is on the late side now."

"I have already tried to go to church once today, and I am not trying again," said the Mormon. "It is unnecessary to get oneself thrown out of chapels like these more than once a day. You go yourself, brother. And give my regards to God. What we humans have to put up with from God is as nothing to what God has to put up with from humans in this country."

"Farewell then, friend, and may God be with you," said Steinar of Hlíðar.

But when the Mormon had gone a little way across the field he turned towards Steinar again; he had forgotten to thank him. Steinar had not yet gone into the church, but was picking his way carefully through the dogs at the lich-gate.

"Thanks for setting me free!" shouted the Mormon.

"Hold on a minute," said Steinar. "I forgot something."

He picked up his saddle and hoisted it on his back, then walked across the field to the Mormon again. "I think it is rather too late to go to church in any case," he said. "Perhaps we can keep each other company for a step or two."

"Hallo again," said the Mormon.

They walked away from the church together. When they reached the edge of the field the Mormon leaned down and pulled his hat out of a niche in the wall; it was carefully wrapped in grease-proof paper as before. There was also a bundle nearby containing the Mormon's change of underclothing. He smoothed his hair into place with his hand and placed the hat neatly on his head in the sunshine.

"I forgot to ask you your name," said Steinar.

"So you did," said the Mormon. "My name is Bishop Þjóðrekur."

"Well I never," said Steinar. "That's quite a thought. As I was going to say: that's a great country you come from."

"Isn't that just what I was telling you? What of it?"

"I have been thinking about it since that evening at Þingvellir," said Steinar. "And I am no more likely to forget it after this. Anyone who goes out of his way to get himself beaten up and tethered outside a church because he refuses to recant—there must be something in what he believes. I cannot understand why people in this country should be put off from going over to your country simply because there is immersion there. I think you are probably right in what you say, that according to the Bible there ought to be immersion. Why do the Icelanders not want to go from a bad country to a good country since it costs so little?"

"Oh, I never said it costs little," said Bishop Þjóðrekur. "You picked me up wrong there. You can't get much for little, my friend, no sirree."

"Of course, I should have known," said Steinar. "I should have guessed that immersion alone does not take you far. What costs you nothing is worth nothing. Excuse me, but what has it cost you, if I may ask?"

"What's that to you?" asked the bishop.

"I was thinking of myself," said Steinar, "and how much I was man enough to afford."

"That's your own affair," said Bishop Þjóðrekur. "But if we come upon a stream of clear water I could immerse you."

"And then what?" asked Steinar.

"You have freed me," said the bishop, "and you are due your own ransom. But I can only say in the Apostle's words: silver and gold have I none, but such as I have I give thee."

"Ah well, bless you, it is a kind offer and a kind thought," said Steinar. "But if you are heading south for Eyrarbakki I think we are at the crossroads now and our paths must part for a while. It has been very pleasant meeting you. So goodbye for now and may God be with you for ever and ever, and think kindly of me."

"And the very same to you, my lad," said the Mormon.

"And if you ever happen to be in Steinahlíðar, no one will set the dogs on you at Hlíðar."

With that they parted, each on his own way, one to the east and the other to the south. But when they were a stone's throw from one another, Bishop Þjóðrekur suddenly came to a halt.

"I say, there!" he shouted. "What's your name?"

"Oh, did I not tell you?" the other shouted back. "My name is Steinar Steinsson."

"Were you asking what it cost me to become a Mormon?" asked Bishop Þjóðrekur.

"Forget it, friend," said Steinar.

"Only the man who sacrifices everything can be a Mormon," said the bishop. "No one will bring the Promised Land to you. You must trek across the wilderness yourself. You must renounce homeland, family and possessions. That is a Mormon. And if you have nothing but the flowers that people in Iceland call weeds, you must take your leave of them. You lead your young and rosy-cheeked sweetheart out into the wilderness. That is a Mormon. She carries your baby in her arms and hugs it close. You walk and walk, day after day, night after night, for weeks and for months, with your belongings on a handcart. Do you want to be a Mormon? One day she sinks to the ground from hunger and thirst, and dies. You take from her arms your baby daughter who has never learned to smile; and she looks at you with questioning eyes in the middle of this wilderness. A Mormon. But a child cannot get warm against a man's ribs. Few can replace a father, none a mother, my friend. Now you trudge alone across the wilderness for miles and miles with your daughter in your arms; until one night you realise that the biting frost has nipped the life from these tiny limbs. That is a Mormon. You dig a grave with your hands and bury her in the sand, and put up a cross of two straws that blow away at once. That is a Mormon. . . ."

8

Secret in mahogany

Now the family at Hlíðar were continually glancing out towards the shoulder of the hill to the west, where travellers from the south were first to be glimpsed. The plan was to have some milk in a pail and a lump of butter ready to thrust into the pony's mouth when he came back from his long and tiring journey as ravenous as a wolf.

The golden plover was curiously subdued that summer, and scarcely a whistle was heard from the oyster-catcher. It was also one of those late-summer times when the cliffs of Steinahlíðar sent back no echoes. One shouted, but received no reply. The fulmar drifted silently under the black cliffs.

When it was two or three days past the expected time, the children thought they could make out yet another vagrant coming round the shoulder of the hill with his knapsack on his back. But as the stranger approached, they seemed to recognize his walk: with every step he would put each foot down twice, as if he were testing ice that might not be quite safe. When he reached the edge of the home-field he stopped and ran his hand over the wall, adjusting a stone here and there and fitting in some small ones which lay loose nearby.

Steinar's little daughter stood outside on the paved doorstep and suddenly burst into tears.

"I knew it, I dreamt it," she sobbed. "I knew this would happen. Everything's finished now."

And with that she rushed into the house and hid.

Steinar came walking into the farmyard with his saddle on his back. He greeted his wife and son affectionately, and asked where little Steina was.

"Where's Krapi?" asked the viking.

"It's a long story," said Steinar. "But here I am with the saddle at least. And the riding-crop."

"He has sold the horse, naturally," said his wife.

"A small man cannot carry a big horse," he said. "So I gave him to the king."

"How silly of me," said his wife. "You gave him away, of course."

"I had the feeling, somehow, that the only proper owner for such a horse was the king," said Steinar.

"I'm so glad you didn't accept money from the king, my dear," said his wife. "I have no desire to be married to a horse-coper."

"And anyway, money for a horse like that! It's absurd, is it not, my dear?" said Steinar.

"Our Krapi cannot be valued in money," she replied. "Good health and peace of mind are the only real blessings in life; whereas all life's evils spring from gold. Oh, you've no idea how glad I am and grateful to God that we never see gold here at Hlíðar!"

"On the other hand, the king promised me his friendship," said Steinar.

"There you are! When has any crofter in these parts ever been given the king's friendship?" said the woman. "God bless the king!"

"What have we left to be fond of now?" said the boy, and started to cry like his sister.

"A man can never discover his real worth until he has renounced his horse," said Steinar.

"Stop making such a fuss, silly," said the boy's mother. "You don't understand what a father you have. How do you know the king won't summon him before long and make him his counsellor?"

This was enough to console the boy, for he was a true viking and king's-man.

"I was only sorry I forgot to get the bridle back," said Steinar. "But we can manage somehow, I expect."

He took the saddle over to the outhouse.

It was late in the autumn when a sheriff's messenger came riding into the farmyard, stepped on to the paving, pulled out a letter with an official seal on it and handed it to Steinar of Hlíðar.

In those days it was unusual for a sheriff to send a special messenger to peasants unless to tell them that their possessions were being confiscated for some valid reason, or to give them notice of the date on which they were to be evicted. A letter of the kind that was now delivered had never been received by an ordinary peasant in Iceland before, as far as is known. This document stated that His Majesty the King of Denmark sent Steinar of Hlíðar his most gracious greetings and favour as before; it was the king's pleasure to invite this farmer to pay him a visit in

Denmark, and the keeper of the royal purse had been instructed to defray the costs of his passage and all the expenses of his sojourn in the royal city of Copenhagen. The king wished to receive Steinar in person at whichever of his palaces he happened to be residing when Steinar arrived. This royal invitation was inspired by gratitude for the pony which the king had been given by this man in Iceland, and which was now called Pussy; Pussy was a great favourite in the palace, particularly with the children in the royal household. He was stabled at the Bernstorff Palace, the king's summer residence outside the city.

It was not considered proper for sheriff's messengers to accept hospitality from ordinary farmers when they were on official business: "We royal officials don't have time to sit down." But curiosity kept this one lingering on the paving while Steinar read the letter.

"This is a good letter, to be sure, and of great importance," said Steinar when he had finished reading it. "You deserve to be given a gold piece for it—not that there is one available here, nor likely to be, either. Indeed, my dear wife says that gold is the source of all ill-fortune in men's lives. Convey my respects to the king. Say that I shall come to visit him at the earliest opportunity. And would you remind the master of the royal household that I forgot to remove the bridle when I handed the horse over in the summer; I would be glad to have it back whenever possible."

It was mentioned earlier in this book that Steinar of Hlíðar had the reputation of being a skilled and ingenious craftsman; his neighbours always brought their broken implements and household utensils to him for repair, and he would make them all as good as new. And now as winter approached he was more and

more to be found away from his family, sitting in his workshed
and tinkering with bits of wood. But it was all rather trifling and
did not appear to be anything special, and he would toss his carv-
ings aside like any other idle pastime. But if he were ever passing
near the shore he would always pick up a few likely-looking bits
of wood from the littoral farmers who collected driftwood. He
pottered about like this all winter. He was always reciting an old
stanza to himself while he was busy with the wood, one from an
old ballad involving the hero Þórður hreda (Menace);[*] he never
recited the whole verse at a time, but always in snatches, a line at
a time. This is how it went:

> *She gave food for hungry hound,*
> *She gave bed for sleeping sound;*
> *She was merry above all,*
> *She was very liberal.*

But however much he carved and whittled, the wood was
never the right size, it was either too long or too short, too thick
or too thin. And so winter passed and the bustle of spring began;
and one day Steinar came into the kitchen with all his winter's
work in his arms and thrust it on the fire under the kettle. Then
he began to clear his hayfield of all the stones which had spilled
down off the mountain during the winter, and to touch up the
wall around it.

During the summer, people asked him if it were true that he
were going to visit the king soon, but he always changed the
subject. When the hay was safely stacked, however, and the
approach of autumn brought ease from toil, he once more had to
make a journey along the coast and then, as he had so often done

before, he asked leave to poke around in the farmers' woodpiles; but he could find nothing to his taste in most places, and almost before he realized it he had gone all the way down to Leirur.

Old Björn of Leirur was his usual genial self; he kissed Steinar affectionately and ushered him into the house, and asked what he could do for him. Steinar said he needed a few good pieces of wood, a spot of mahogany, preferably, even though it were no more than half a puppy-load: "And I beg you now, dearest friend, not to hold against me my boldness a year or two back when you offered me gold and I refused it."

"You've always been a hell of a man," said Björn of Leirur, "and I've never thought more highly of you than when you refused to sell me a pony that time—but you were even more of a true Icelander when you turned the sheriff down too. That's the kind of saga-men we need nowadays! No crawling around on your knees for you! Pay heed to no one lower than the king! Some bits of wood, did you say? Mahogany? I know it's the choicest wood in the world, and the only wood that is worthy of you. Now it so happens that I was having a Russian shipwreck dismantled down on the shore here the other day, and the whole thing was done up in mahogany. Go ahead and help yourself to whatever there is."

"I can hardly manage to buy for more than about 75 or 80 aurar," said Steinar. "I can give you a note for that amount in my account at the store in Eyrarbakki."

"We king's-men and saga-Icelanders are never such small fellows that we grudge one another a horse-load or two of mahogany," said Björn of Leirur.

"I am a poor man," said Steinar, "and I cannot afford to accept gifts. It is only rich men who can afford to accept gifts."

At all events, Björn of Leirur took Steinar out to the field where the mahogany was stacked under cover.

But even though Björn of Leirur refused to listen to any mention of payment, Steinar of Hlíðar was not the man to accept more than a modest amount of mahogany. Björn and two of his men helped Steinar to load it on to a pony; then he saw him off down the path and kissed him: "Goodbye, and may God be with you for ever and ever, you hell of a man, you."

Steinar of Hlíðar mounted and rode off, with the mahogany-laden pony in tow. Björn of Leirur closed the gate of his home-field. He was wearing big topboots, and did not get his feet wet. But just as he was tying up the gate he remembered a little trifle, for Icelanders never remember the main point of their business until after they have said goodbye. He gave Steinar a shout and said:

"Listen, my dear chap, since you happen to live on the main track, would you not let me graze my colts on your pastures for a night or two if I should happen to be driving them down this summer for shipment to the English?"

"You will always be welcome at Hlíðar with your colts, night or day, bless you, my old friend," Steinar called back. "The grass does not care who eats it."

"It may well be that I'll have a few drovers with me," said Björn of Leirur.

"You are all welcome at Hlíðar for as long as you can find houseroom there," said Steinar. "Good friends make the best guests."

9

Steinar leaves, with the secret

She gave food for hungry hound,
She gave bed for sleeping sound.

Who was the woman who performed such prodigies of hospitality, people asked? Was it the Good Fairy of days gone by, or the Norns who decided men's fates? Or was it the good housewife of Hlíðar, who never doubted her husband's superiority in anything and thought it a measure of his integrity that he refused to accept gold? Or was it the blue-clad elf-woman who for a thousand years has been seen wandering alone over the heather moon beside the cliffs on hot summer days? It could hardly be His Royal Majesty of Denmark himself, could it? Or was it just that shallow jade whom some people call Mother Earth? Only one thing was certain: the woman was no more overpraised in this ballad than is the custom in Iceland when the talk is about anything of value.

As the winter wore on, Steinar of Hlíðar would all the more often shut himself away in his workshed with the door locked from the inside; and whenever he came out, he would lock the door again and put the key in his pocket.

"Daddy," said the girl, "when we were small you used to tell us everything. Now you don't tell us anything, and lock yourself in when we are curious."

"We have almost worn out the shoes of our childhood, my little darling," said Steinar. "Our fairy-tale horse has now become a royal pony and is called Pussy."

"Yes, but you could tell us just a tiny little bit sometimes, Daddy, even though it's only a fairy-tale. We are so longing to know what you're making in there."

"Perhaps with God's help I shall manage to concoct some little trifle before spring—and then I shall open up the workshed for you," he said.

And that is just what happened. In spring, when the land was freeing itself from its bonds of ice, Steinar called his children into the workshed one day and showed them his completed handiwork. It was a casket, most beautifully finished. It was quite unvarnished, and therefore retained the natural colour of the wood, but the surface was highly polished as if it had been kneaded between the hands; and this had been done with such artistic skill that the wood seemed to have surrendered and allowed itself to be moulded like wax. It was taller and longer than most other caskets, but did not seem to be larger; all its proportions were somehow unique; there was no other casket quite like it. And it was as agreeable to the eye as it was pleasing to the touch.

It was divided into several compartments of different sizes. Under the largest compartments, which were detachable, was the bottom; but there was more to that than met the eye, because under it there lay three, some say four, secret compartments which no one could open except by an ingenious special device which will be dealt with shortly. But first the locking mechanism of the casket must be described; it is said to have been the most complicated and cunning arrangement that had ever been known in Iceland, and many delicate operations were required to open it. On the lid there was a large group of numbered studs which had to be adjusted according to an intricate formula before the casket could be unlocked; to do this, one had to start with the seventh stud and end with the sixth, and with that the lid would open. Steinar had no alternative but to set the formula to verse in order to commit it to memory. It was a long poem, composed in a verse-form which only Icelandic farmers know, and for anyone who did not know the poem off by heart it was an impertinence even to attempt to get the casket open.

Steinar recited the poem to his children and opened the casket according to its instructions; and the children gaped as if thunderstruck by this miracle.

POEM TO OPEN A CASKET

First you shove the seventh out,
Eleven can soon be moved away;
Flip the fourth one round about,
For the ninth to come in play.

Now you press the second spur,
And see the eighth come swinging round;
Then the third can start to stir,
And thirteen moves up with a bound.

The fifth is now at last set free,
And fourteen slides down with a click,
Give the twelfth a twist with glee,
And turn the sixth one with a flick.

You who seek life's happiness,
Set ten and fifteen on their own;
And you will glimpse just how intense
Is God's glory. But leave it alone.

With fourteen clues I've favoured you,
To find the gold that's hidden well;
But still there's yet another clue,
And that one I shall never tell.

Steinar's daughter asked what was to be put into all these compartments.

"The large compartments are for silver," said Steinar.

"What about the trays that are divided into four?" asked the boy.

"They are for gold and precious stones," said Steinar.

"Then I don't understand what is to go into the secret compartments," said the girl.

"Then I shall tell you, light of my life," said her father, and laughed his falsetto titter. "That is the place for what is costlier than gold and precious stones."

"What could that be, Daddy?" asked the girl. "I never thought that such a thing existed."

"It is the secrets which no one else will ever know until the end of the world," said Steinar, and closed the casket.

"Is all that gold ours, then?" said the little viking. "And all these precious stones?"

"And what secrets do we have, Daddy?" said the girl.

"Why did God create the world with compartments for silver and gold and precious stones, my children?" asked their father. "And with so many secret compartments as well? Was it because He had so much ready money that He did not know where to keep it all? Or was it because He Himself had something on His conscience which He had to hide away in holes?"

"Daddy," said the young girl, staring spellbound at the closed casket, "who's going to open up the casket when we are dead and no one remembers the poem any more?"

The news of this masterpiece of carpentry spread far and wide, and many whose journeys took them near Hlíðar knocked on the door to ask if they could feast their eyes on this phenomenon. Others travelled miles for this specific purpose. And many offered large sums of money for the casket.

Late that summer, Steinar made it known that he was going to travel to Denmark to visit his Krapi, and that he was going as the guest of King Kristian Wilhelmsson of Denmark. He made his preparations to the best of his ability. A renowned seamstress from another district made up a suit for him of blue homespun, and he ordered a pair of topboots from Eyrarbakki. He left home in the middle of the night without saying goodbye to his children; but before he went he looked at them for a moment as they slept. Steinar was 48 years old when he undertook this journey.

His son Víkingur had just been confirmed, and his daughter Steina was almost sixteen. And although the departure of this home-loving farmer gave his family cause for tears, there was consolation in their pride at having a father whom foreign kings wished to have at their side, just as in the sagas. His wife wiped away her tears on the corner of her apron and said to her neighbours: "It is not surprising that kings should send for my Steinar. What a wonderfully peaceful world it would be abroad if there were more like him there. I'm quite sure there will be God's heaven on earth when men like my Steinar can influence kings."

These were Steinar's circumstances when he set off on his journey: as was said before, the land he farmed was his own, inherited from his father. The farm was worth twelve hundreds according to the old system of valuation, whereby one hundred was equivalent to the price of a cow. He owed no man anything, because in those days farmers had no credit, nor was there any money available for lending. If any farmer got into difficulties, he just had to sell up. Steinar owned thirty milch-ewes and a dozen non-milkers, two cows and a year-old heifer, and five work-ponies which for the most part fended for themselves. The cow has always been the people's bread and butter in Iceland, and the sheep their ready cash. In modern terms, the income from one sheep is equivalent to two days' pay for a labourer, but in those days there were no wage-earning labourers. Of thirty sheep on a farm, ten were required for maintaining the stock; thus, Steinar only had the income from twenty sheep for his ready cash, or in other words the equivalent of forty days' pay for his year's expenditure. With this income he bought rye-meal and barley and other necessities from the store at Eyrarbakki, two days' journey away; this was the largest trading concern in the Danish overseas empire, and customers came to it from many hundred of kilometres away. A few old ewes were slaughtered every year for meat, and clothes were home-made from waste wool. Shoes were also made at home, from untanned hide dipped in alum, and it was always impressed on the children that they must not put too much strain on the shoes by treading hard on the ground. Fish and dulse were bought from the littoral crofters in exchange for mutton, and sometimes, when provisions were low, Steinar would himself go and spend a fishing-season at Þorlákshöfn in an open boat. With any luck he could earn himself a few baskets of fish off that surf-tormented coast where relatively more Icelandic fishermen were drowned in storm and tempest almost every winter than soldiers were killed in wars.

10

Concerning horse-copers

Meanwhile, Steinar of Hlíðar had gone west and boarded ship and was now on the high seas bound for foreign lands. He had not set off until late in the hay-season, when most of the hay had already been secured, and he expected to be back late in October on the last autumn sailing. At the farm were only a woman and two children to clear up the autumn work. And the nights were growing dark.

Petroleum was so expensive in those days, compared with farmers' means, that one could hardly say there was much illumination in farmhouses during winter; even fish-oil, which had been the staple source of light in Iceland from the very beginning, was itself now becoming a luxury. The few pints of petroleum which served as the year's supply of light at Hlíðar were reserved for the dark days of midwinter, and people tried to make the fullest use of what daylight there was. One banked up the fire and went to bed when there was no longer light enough to work by, and rose at the first streak of dawn, until at last the nights were equally long at both ends; only then did one begin to light the lamp. How long the children found the first few nights after their father had gone abroad!

After a day of toil there was nothing to do except go to bed. But it sometimes happened that those twin travelling companions, Sleep and Dream, were late in calling at the house. In that case the best way to pass the time was to listen for the sound of distant hooves. The children could recognize the hoofbeats of horses from more than one district. It made a change during the quiet of the night to hear riders clattering through the yard and the dog baying up on the roof. And every morning they counted the days until their father was expected home.

On the night which is now to be described, just at the time of the first autumn round-up, everyone in the house had been asleep for a long time. There had been no sound of hooves from any direction all evening. It was raining. At midnight the mother and daughter woke suddenly from deep slumber at a deafening tumult outside, as if the world were falling in. Then someone came to the window and said "God be with you!," as was the custom in those days. The women threw on some clothes in haste and opened the door. Outside, the rain was lashing down. A burly man, dripping with rain and wearing a voluminous coat and enormous topboots, seized them in an embrace and kissed them. He smelled powerfully of horses, with a mixture of snuff and cognac as well. There was rainwater in his beard, and clammy moisture in the tufts of hair on his nose.

"It's only your old friend Björn of Leirur," the visitor said when he had finished kissing them in the darkness. "We were just coming from east of the rivers, a few lads and myself with one or two horses. The wretched beasts are getting a bit tired.

The boys haven't slept for two days. We haven't a dry stitch up to the armpits. What a God's mercy it is to be able to kiss such warm and dry people! But tell me, by the way, is my good friend Steinar still at the king's coat-tails?"

The housewife said that Steinar was in Copenhagen and not expected home before the end of October: "But if this house is of any use to you, then you are welcome here. As you know, my dear Björn, there's not much in the way of luxury here to offer to the gentry; but still, what's good enough for my Steinar should be good enough for the king, that's what I always say."

"As if drenched people can be gentry, my good woman!" said the visitor. "The main thing is to get a drop of warm soup, even though it's only cow-soup. The other matter I have already discussed with my friend Steinar a long time ago—indeed, he offered me it unasked, as my two lads here remember from when they were helping him load up his horse with mahogany: 'You will be obliging me, my dear chap,' he said, bless him, 'if you would rest up in my pastures next time you are driving horses. The grass does not care who eats it.' As far as the boys are concerned, they can bed down in the lamb-shed, if they could just have a wisp of hay to lie on."

"Well, my dear Björn," said the woman, "it so happens that we have nothing better for soup than some barley. We haven't done any slaughtering at Hlíðar yet. Everything is waiting for Steinar. But there is some dried fish, although that's not much of a feast for the nobility. And you are all welcome to share the three bunks in the living-room here, except that you yourself will have the bed in the spare-room, of course."

"Is that not just like you, my dear?" said old Björn. "And as for the soup, I could well believe that we have a shank or two of mutton tucked away in our saddle-bags, if you have the barley."

The woman told her daughter to fetch some brushwood and sheep-dung to revive the fire.

It was quite an occasion. Half a score of dripping visitors filled the living-room and the family had their hands full pulling off their outer garments. A small lamp was lit, but one could still hardly see one's nose for all the steam from the sodden clothing. Those who had no change of clothes borrowed some. There was some schnapps to keep the strength up while waiting for the soup; and that started the singing. The soup did not arrive until the night was nearly over, and some of them were already asleep by then. They shared the bunks out amongst themselves, but some had to go out and see to it that the ponies did not stray.

At dawn the housewife thought it safer to send her daughter to the spare-room to help the champion off with his things, rather than let such an inexperienced young girl stay longer in the living-room waiting upon a crowd of high-spirited horse-copers who furthermore had been at the bottle.

"Thanks for the offer, dear woman," said Björn of Leirur, and kissed her goodnight. "It doesn't come amiss to have such a lissom young creature to wait upon an old fellow who is numb and stiff from the glacier-rivers."

It was an old Scandinavian custom in all decent farms for a woman to be provided to help a visitor off with his clothes when he retired.

"Well, well, my little lamb," said Björn of Leirur.

He was so big and bulky that he almost filled the little room. He patted the girl on the cheek and the head, the way one pats a dog; then he casually ran his hands over her breasts, stomach, and buttocks, squeezing them briskly the way one does with sheep to see if they are in good flesh. The girl gasped.

"You've come on a bit since I saw you out there in the yard with your father that time, poor little thing," he said. "I'll soon have to be making an offer for you. My old woman is nothing but rheumatics and grumbles nowadays, I'll be needing a house-keeper before long."

It was as if the girl withdrew even farther into her shell at these words. She hung her head a little and was rather at a loss for an answer.

"We never say Yes, Björn," she said, and looked him full in the face for a moment despite her fears. "My brother Víkingur sometimes says No, of course, but Daddy doesn't like that because he says it means the same as Yes."

The man-mountain had now seated himself across the side of the bed; he leaned back against the wall and stretched his legs out to the floor. The girl knelt down in front of him and tried to pull off his vast topboots, which are popularly known as waders and are fastened to the waist with suspenders. Under them he was wearing stockinged trousers. He was neither so wet nor so cold as he made out; and perhaps not so old, either.

He said, "You've now at least reached the age, little one, when sometime or other a young lad must have sneaked up and said something to you in secret which it was no use answering with nothing but hiccups."

"I won't deny it," said the girl. "It was the year before last. I was riding Krapi on the lamb-drive. And at sunrise, when we were up in the mountains, a boy said to me, just like that, 'Would you give me a ride on the white horse?' It's the first time a stranger has ever asked me for anything like that. What could I say? I haven't recovered from it yet."

"Since you could neither say Yes nor No, I can't see that it

would have cost you much to dismount without saying anything, my lamb," said Björn. "He would just have got on the
horse's back, the young rascal, if he had any presence of mind."

"His father and my father arrived just at that point," said the
girl. "Otherwise I don't know what I would have done."

"One hopes he had the nerve to give you a casual hint of some
sort, next time you met," said Björn.

"I didn't go to the lamb-drive the next spring," said the girl.
"Nor this spring. When Daddy gave Krapi away, I knew I would
never be going on a lamb-drive again."

"And you haven't met since?" said Björn.

"We've maybe just had a peep at one another in church," said
the girl. "He doesn't seem to have forgotten that business over
Krapi. Perhaps he never will."

"There's not much stuff in these young lads yet, little one, pay
no attention to them. You young girls are better off helping
us old fellows off with our things, you know where you have
us then."

"I don't think you're so very old, Björn," said the girl. "And I
don't think Daddy is, either. When I was little I used to snuggle
up under his beard to go to sleep. But since then it's as if everything has somehow become so distant."

"Yes, childhood is soon faded into the distance, my little
chicken," said Björn, "and things get worse and worse for you
until you're bedridden with old age, and then things start getting a little better again, thank God. And come on now, dry my
toes for me, my little mouse. What the devil's the point of fording three glacier-rivers a day, anyway!"

The girl said, "Daddy used to sing me a little song once; it
went like this:

Come and lay your cheek on mine,
Though mine is cold and hairy,
But yours is peach and petal-fine,
My pretty little fairy."

"I'll just have to take your daddy's place for you, little lamb, while my old friend Steinar is with the king," said Björn. "And now just pull these English trousers off me, and then there's not much left except my birthday pants. You're a real treasure—not the same at all as the old devil of a woman who was wrestling with me out east in Meðalland the other night. A thousand thanks."

"There are no thanks necessary for a little thing like that," said the girl, getting to her feet and rubbing the numbness from her bare knees where she had been kneeling on the floor; she was scarlet in the face now. As she turned to go, she said he was not to hesitate to call out for anything he wanted; and she added, out of the goodness of her heart and the trusting innocence which is instinctive to young girls: "It is my life and joy to look after visitors who wake people up in the night."

"Now that you've bedded down all us horse-dealers in your own bunks, what are you going to do yourselves, you poor creatures?"

"Mother is staying up to dry all their clothes in the kitchen," said the girl. "Víkingur and I will lie down on the saddle-turves in the outhouse. It makes a nice change. It will only be for a short while, it's nearly dawn."

"The very idea, child!" said Björn of Leirur. "Do you think for a moment that I'm going to allow a little girl with such long fair hair and rosy cheeks and a body like fresh-churned butter to go and lie on a scrap of turf out in a shed on my account? No, we may be quick to buy and sell horses, but we're not so quick at sending our girls away. Here, let me put this pillow at the foot of the bed there, and you can creep into bed with me like the Beauty who freed the Beast from a spell once upon a time."

11

Money on the window-sill

When daylight came, it is not too much to say that the family at Hlíðar were startled, for Steinar's hayfield and meadows were swarming with a greater horde of ponies than had ever been seen in those parts. It was a magnificent herd of beasts. Some accounts say that there were 300 ponies grazing at Hlíðar that morning; others say 400. There had been a lot of rain for the last few days, and the ground was soft. The chafing of the ponies churned it up and turned it into mud wherever they thronged together. Already during that first night the home-field had been trampled beyond repair. All these ponies had travelled miles from their home districts, and so were restless and unruly; the colts were alternately frisky and frightened, and kicked out at every wall in sight. Already during that first night large gaps had appeared in the dry-stone dykes that had been built by the master-craftsmen of Hlíðar, generation after generation.

When the girl woke up that morning she found herself alone in the room. It was broad daylight. She was still wearing the ragged old petticoat she had hurriedly thrown on the night before. Her visitor was away in his long topboots. When she had a look through the window she saw that their home-field and meadows were all dense with ponies; and while she was standing staring at this in amazement, she happened to catch sight of a red coin on the window-sill. She took this strange object through to the kitchen and showed it to her mother, and told her how she had found it on the window-sill of the spare-room on her way out.

"Well I never!" said the woman, taking the coin and studying it. "I suppose it was inevitable that this day would dawn, like all other days; but I always thought that the Saviour would spare me as long as possible from having to touch the metal your father Steinar least desires. This is gold, you see, the stuff that creates all the evil in the world, my child. No one in Hlíðar has ever touched this kind of metal before. How does it come about that you bring this evil object from the room our visitor used?"

"I slept the night there," said the girl. "And when I woke up there was nothing there except that."

The woman stared at her daughter dumbfounded. When she finally found her tongue she spoke in that suppressed tone of res-ignation which was current in Iceland for as long as people believed that everything bided its time: "May the Lord have mercy on all wretched creatures, and most particularly on those who have no wits. Did I not tell you to sleep on the saddle-turves out in the shed, child?"

"Indeed you did," said the girl. "I simply don't understand myself. I had helped him off with his things and had got to my feet. I had said goodnight and was on my way out. I swear it, I was on the point of leaving the room. Then he said, 'Where are you going, little one?' And when I told him that I was going out to the shed to sleep, why, then he started insisting that it was out of the question for me to have to lie on a scrap of turf out in the shed on his account. Anyway, not to make a long story of it, before I knew what I was about I was in the bed beside him and fast asleep."

"You poor little fool," said her mother. "And what then?"

"Nothing," said the girl. "The next thing I knew, it was morning, and that thing was lying on the window-sill."

"Am I really to believe, my child, that you have slept the night with Björn of Leirur himself, no less!" said the woman.

"Mother dear," said the girl, "I don't believe for a minute that old Björn is as bad as he is said to be. He certainly did me no mischief, stupid though I am."

"I suppose you know you're a fully grown girl now and can no longer go to bed beside a man," said her mother.

"What, me?" said the girl, on the verge of tears now at her mother's words. "How can you say such a thing to me, Mummy, you who know better than anyone else, except perhaps the Saviour, that I'm still just a little girl and think about nothing all day long except my daddy and how it can be that he went away. And anyway I didn't undress at all."

"How much are you wearing underneath?" said the woman. "There, isn't that just what I thought! If you've never had any idea before this how things are with you, poor wretch, then it's time you started thinking about yourself, after last night."

"What has happened to me, then, Mummy? Won't you tell me?"

"As if you had no knowledge of him, child!"

"I only just felt there was a person there," said the girl. "He's so big and brawny as everyone knows. And I'm big and brawny now, too. And the bed scarcely has room for one, even."

"He must have pressed up against you just a little bit, child," said the woman. "They used to in my day, at least."

"I was dead tired and fell asleep at once," said the girl. "And Björn had started snoring. If there was any pressing after I was asleep, how was I to know about it? I don't think there was very much. At least I never woke up; I wouldn't even call it a nightmare. And I didn't wake up until this minute, in broad daylight."

"Why have you got that gold coin in your hand, then?" said the woman. "Leave it where you found it. You can't have forgotten that Björn of Leirur and the sheriff and the king himself all offered gold in exchange for our Krapi; and what did your father reply?"

What astonished the family at Hlíðar, although it would not have been proper to mention it, was that the visitors showed not the slightest signs of packing up and leaving. On the contrary. During the morning, provisions and other supplies arrived for them on pack-ponies. They pitched a tent in the stackyard. It is considered small-minded in Iceland to ask visitors what is keeping them; but there was no attempt to disguise the fact that they were waiting for more horses to arrive. It was now clear, too, that the horse-copers were in no need of cow-soup, even though they had made out the previous evening that they would put up with anything, however humble. Some of the visitors lay in the living-room all morning, to the accompaniment of resonant bass snoring; others squatted on the paving at the door and crammed themselves with snuff from wooden flasks and horns as they kept an eye on the herd. One or two were drunk. Some dashed around on their ponies rounding up unruly colts. The neighbouring farmers were out in force to guard their own acres against this swarm of ponies which was like nothing so much as the plagues that befell the world in the Bible. The horse-copers gave the women meat and flour, and got them to cook soup and bake bread. They had boxloads of butter. They certainly showed no lack of liberality towards the housewife. If they handed her some coffee which had been roasted in her utensils, it was never less than a pound. The children could gorge themselves on sugar and Danish whey-cheese. Whole herds of ponies were sent off in one direction and replaced by others from elsewhere. More drovers arrived and bedded down in the tent, using armfuls of hay from the stack, and young Víkingur was hired as an extra drover and sent off on long journeys.

A few days later, Björn of Leirur returned. It was nearly midnight, and everyone was in bed.

"Where's Steina?" he shouted from out on the paving.

The housewife put her head out of the door of the shed, ready to wait upon him. He kissed her and pushed her back inside and said he only wanted young girls. Steinar's daughter had awoken by this time. She warmed up some soup for him in the middle of the night; then she had to make coffee, and then hot toddy; and finally help him off with his clothes, for he had been floundering through glacier-rivers as usual.

"You forgot your gold coin here the other day," said the girl.

"It was yours, little one," said Björn of Leirur. "For helping me off with my things."

"Daddy and mummy say that gold coins are the source of all evil," said the girl.

"Give me a hand again, little one," said Björn of Leirur, and laughed.

Early next morning he was off again to buy more ponies, leaving behind a gleaming silver dollar on the window-sill.

It was a memorable autumn.

Alien ponies reigned over the fields of Hlíðar, and the horse-copers ruled over house and home. The bed in the spare-room was always made up for Björn of Leirur, who sometimes came and sometimes not. If he came, it was in the middle of the night, and always wet from the glacier-rivers.

"Where's Steina?"

Steinar's daughter was never allowed to leave his side, waking or sleeping, as long as he was there. And the girl's mother was becoming more and more resigned.

One autumn day just before the second round-ups, while the farm was still under siege, it so happened for a change that a visitor from within the district came riding into the yard and asked to see the housewife. It was the furrier of Drangar, three farms or so farther to the east, and father of the boy who had not been given a ride on the white pony during that lamb-drive.

The visitor was ushered into the spare-room.

"There has been plenty happening here, dear lady," said Geir of Drangar.

"Six hundred horses, day and night," said the woman. "And just the two of us wretched women, apart from the boy, who has anyway been hired as a drover. May the Lord have mercy on us all."

"I would not exactly call you dumb animals," said the farmer. "But one would have expected a little more spirit from house-wives here in these parts."

"Didn't you hear me telling you that we have neither sense nor speech?" said the woman. "We haven't even got a rattle for the horses. Steinar has never wanted anything to do with such frivolities. Here at Hlíðar the only possession we have ever had is the head on Steinar's shoulders."

"Meddling has never been considered much of a virtue, to be sure," said the farmer, "and everyone has the right to dispose of his own property as he sees fit. Everyone can see that Hlíðar is turning into a morass which will grow no grass for long enough. However, my real reason for coming here today is that I have had wind that my son Jóhann might be thinking of coming here to have a word with your young daughter Steina sometime soon. Hmmmm! It occurred to me that someone or other who wished you well might have a word with the sheriff to see if he can use the powers of the law to put a stop to this wanton destruction."

"To tell you the truth, neighbour," said the woman, "it so happens that the man who drives the horses provided evidence that it had all been arranged by agreement with my dear husband. So I have to content myself with believing that He who created the plants will make the grass grow again sometime here at Hlíðar. But it does no harm to have good neighbours for all that, and you and your son are always welcome here, the sooner the better, by night or by day."

As Geir of Drangar rose to his feet to take his leave, he glanced towards the window and noticed some money lying on the sill. There was one large English golden guinea and many gleaming Danish silver dollars.

"You seem to have hooked a good catch here at Hlíðar," said Geir of Drangar.

"Old Björn of Leirur always leaves something in the mornings before he goes off," said the woman. "But we have never learned to handle money here at Hlíðar; we don't even dare to touch it. I suppose his idea is that little Steina should have it as a reward for helping him off with his things. The thought's the same, even though we leave the money lying there untouched."

"Listen, Björn," said the girl the next night as she knelt on the floor and pulled the clammy, muddy clothes of the traveller who was readier to ford glacier-rivers on horseback than any other man: "There is always one gold coin on the window-sill there."

"What did you expect?" said Björn of Leirur. "Gold is for maidens. A man only gives it once to the same woman."

"But now there's this heap of silver coins as well," said the girl. "Mummy and I are frightened of it. What are we to say to Daddy when he arrives?"

"Silver is for girl-friends," said Björn of Leirur, and laughed.

A few days later the girl woke up in the spare-bed one morning, rose to her feet, looked out of the window, and saw that there was snow everywhere. It was the first snow of the winter, late in October. In the autumn darkness it had spread itself over the country, clean and white. She was amazed that there was not a single pony to be seen. Nor were there any tracks in the snow; the ponies had all been driven away during the night, before it started to snow. The trampled ground lay out of sight beneath the snow. Not a sound was to be heard anywhere. No strangers snored in the living-room. Farm and farmland had been whisked into a cold, white world of silence. Seldom have so few missed so many horses.

"The dear Lord be praised," said the girl.

Then she noticed that a handful of large copper coins had been added to the precious golden guinea and the pile of silver pieces on the window-sill.

12

The sweetheart

As time wore on the folk at Hlíðar often thought they caught a glimpse of a man coming along the main track round the shoulder of the hill, particularly at twilight. He always seemed to have that circumspect, conscientious way of walking, putting each foot down twice with every step as if testing whether the ground were bearing. But it was never he. Usually it was just one of the elves. The children went to sleep tired after the autumn round-ups, only to be afflicted by the same dream night after night: they dreamed that their father was wandering along an endless road through the autumn darkness in some foreign land, and could not find the way home. The first snows had disappeared, to be sure, but the birds did not return, not even the fulmar or the skua; there was just the raven's back glinting blue in the white autumn sunshine. The berries were soft and the heather red. The land was utterly silent. The sky was also silent. There was frost at night now. The trampled turf round the farm and the tormented meadows were frozen hard. It was now November and the last autumn boat had already reached Iceland. The stones came tumbling down the mountainside at night.

The boy who had not been given a ride on the white pony was at the door, offering his hand to the housewife.

"I was just passing," he said.

"You'll be wanting to talk to Steina," she said.

"Not about anything particular," he said.

"I'll call her," said her mother.

"Not if she's busy," said the visitor.

"She's in the pantry, churning," said the woman. "Perhaps she would like to wipe the butter from her face before she talks to a young man."

"It doesn't matter," said the boy. "I can come back around Christmas."

"Around Christmas?" said the woman. "It's nowhere near Christmas yet, thank goodness. It's nice to see youngsters with some modesty; but it can be overdone."

"I just wanted to see a little something I know she has," said the boy. "But if she's busy it doesn't matter, just give her my respects. Some other time, perhaps."

"Go on with you into the pantry and see her, lad," said the woman.

She was standing bare-shouldered in her petticoat with the glistening turf-wall behind her, churning with that special motion, rather slow but rhythmical, which the task demands: as if the person and the implement were inseparably fused in some strange dance. She did not falter when the boy appeared in the doorway, ducking low. The butter had splashed up on to her bare arms and neck and face. She blushed and smiled down at the churn, but one must never stop in the middle of a churning.

"Won't you please turn that tub upside down and have a seat?" she said.

When he had seated himself she looked up from her work and said, "White ravens are rare visitors, I must say. What's new?"

"Just the usual," he said. "How are things with you?"

"Fine," she said, without pausing for a moment in her churning; but she kept peeping up at him, curious and shy at the same time and smiling a little, until she could no longer restrain herself. "What's happened to you?" she said. "Have you shrunk? I thought you were much bigger and broader."

"It must be because you've filled out so much yourself," he said, and could not take his eyes off this big, sturdy girl before him.

"We stare at one another and scarcely recognise one another, it's so long since we met," she said. "But perhaps you're just cold. Why did you never come?"

"Did you expect me?" he asked.

"You said you were going to," she replied. "I relied on that."

"But we've seen one another at church now and again," he said.

"I don't call that seeing one another," she said. "I'm just ashamed of being all smeared with butter like this when you finally do see me. But you'll get some buttermilk soon."

"If only there were no worse smears than butter!" said the boy. "And buttermilk is always buttermilk even though it's really only a form of skimmed milk."

"Was there anything special you wanted?" said the girl.

"I've heard it said that you've got yourself a gold coin," he said.
"Who says so?"

"It's said to have been put on your window-sill—one of those big ones that are valid throughout the world."

"It's no secret as far as I'm concerned, I suppose," said the girl. "I'll show you it when I've finished churning."

At last the churning was finished. She took the unkneaded butter from the churn and put it into the trough dripping with buttermilk, then went to the kitchen to get a scone from her mother, for one always has hot rye-cakes with new-churned butter. Three things, according to the poets, are considered bliss in Iceland: hot rye-cakes, plump girls and cold buttermilk. With a liberal thumb she spread this lovely butter straight from the churn on to his cake, and gave him a jug of buttermilk to drink. She had fetched a knotted kerchief from under her pillow on the way, and now she took from it the gold coin and showed it to him.

"What a whopper!" said the boy. "I could well believe it's worth the price of a cow. How did you get hold of it?"

She clicked her tongue as if there were nothing to it. "What, that?" she said. "Someone left it behind. You can have it if you like. Daddy's expected home from Copenhagen today or tomorrow, and I can't think what he would say if he found gold here."

"From whom did you get it?" asked the boy.

"From Björn of Leirur," she replied.

"What for?"

"Helping him off with his things."

"Was that all there was to it?"

"The man was soaked," she said. "He had been buying up horses all over the place and fording glacier-rivers up to the armpits. There wasn't a dry stitch on him when he arrived here, at night."

"He's a dirty shit," said Jóhann of Drangar.

"That's the first time in my whole life I've heard such a nasty thing said about any living person," said the girl, and now there was no smile in her expression. "Nor is it true, either. Björn of Leirur is one of the nicest people there is."

"And I'll bet it's the first time *that*'s ever been said about Björn of Leirur," said the boy. "Everyone knows that he marries off at least three or four girls a year, not counting those he doesn't need to marry off because they're married already; and then there are those he refuses on oath to acknowledge."

"I don't understand what you're talking about," said the girl. "Is this meant to be some sort of riddle?"

"It is to be hoped you never need to understand it," he said.

"Clever, aren't you?" she said. "You're a good one, I must say."

"You forget I'm nearly three years older than you are and that I'll be doing my fourth season at the fishing at Þorlákshöfn this winter."

"That thing you said, I suppose that's what you call seamen's talk?" said the girl. "But I can tell you this, that it would be hard to find a more pleasant and straightforward person than Björn of Leirur. I was always shy of people until Björn started staying here. I simply can't tell you how horribly shy of you I was. I was ill for two years because I didn't dare to give you a ride on the white horse during the lamb-drive."

"Since you're no longer shy, I think you should tell me why he has you in with him at nights."

"Who says so?" said the girl.

"That's what the horse-copers are all saying," he replied.

"Why he has me in with him! Björn of Leirur? Now I've heard everything! Obviously for no reason whatsoever. You laugh? I never believed you were like that."

"Why don't you answer me?" he said.

"I don't owe you an answer for anything," she said. "It's just that an insignificant little girl happens to like it when a grown man takes the trouble to talk to her like a human being."

"And then what?"

"What do you think, for example?"

"Obviously a fellow like that starts some funny business at once," said the boy.

"Funny business?" she echoed. "If you mean kissing and cuddling, then I can't imagine anyone less liable to that sort of thing than Björn of Leirur."

"But you yourself said that you pulled all his clothes off up to the armpits," said the boy.

"That's not what I said at all," she replied. "It's a different thing entirely, and no secret at all as far as I'm concerned—I even told my mother about it—that often when I had pulled his things off for him he would say: 'Stretch out here on the bed beside me, little one, rather than curl up on a scrap of turf out in the shed.'"

"Although I'm no expert in this sort of thing," said the boy, "I can hardly believe that a fellow like Björn of Leirur would leave a girl alone once she was in bed with him."

"I know nothing about that," said the girl. "He always left me alone, anyway. I just became sleepy and tired when I was near him, and I had no sooner stretched out beside him than I was dead to the world."

"Didn't he touch you at all, then?"

"I can only remember the one time when he pressed up against me a little bit accidentally in his sleep, and I woke up with a start as if I'd been dreaming something; but I was asleep again the next moment. And after that I was never aware of him except of course that he's a big, burly man. And I can tell you that I've never slept so soundly as I did with him. I didn't even stir when he climbed over me in the mornings when he left."

The visitor stated at the girl dubiously.

"How is a man to understand women?" he said. "There aren't more strange creatures. One either has to believe them or not. I prefer to believe you, Steinbjörg. And now I must be getting on. Thanks for the cake and the buttermilk. . . ."

". . . And the coin, Jóhann," she added. "The gold coin. It was about time I made it up to you for not letting you ride our Krapi, who's now with the king anyway and is called Pussy."

"It didn't matter at all," he said. "Goodbye, then. Maybe I'll put your coin in my pocket after all—on account. And thanks."

She looked at him, brimming with gratitude to him for having come, and regret that he should have to go so soon. She could not stop herself blurting out, "I think you've just grown bigger and broader, even in this short time."

"It's the cake and the buttermilk," he said. "And the butter from the churn."

She watched him ducking through the door, and perhaps she felt a shade of disappointment. But just as he was about to vanish into the pitch-dark corridor he remembered something and came back in to see her. He looked at her a little uneasily and seemed about to say something.

"What now?" she said, and laughed a little, scarlet in the face.

"It occurred to me to ask," he said. "Was there only one?"

She had to think a little before she knew what he was getting at, and then her smile vanished.

"Wait a minute," she said.

She untied her kerchief and brought out a collection of gleaming silver dollars.

"There you are," she said. "I'd be glad if you would take them. I'm sure Daddy wouldn't like it if he saw them in my possession."

He took the silver and saw that it was good quality, right enough. "But," he said, "what I meant was—were there no more gold coins?"

She looked at him in some surprise. And then the words of wisdom—or folly, rather—from Björn of Leirur came to her mind.

"A woman only gets the one gold coin," she said. "After that she only gets silver."

"Yes, exactly," he said. "It's just as I thought. You have surrendered something only gold could buy."

13

Of emperors and kings

Steinar of Hlíðar did not return to Iceland with the last boat of the autumn. Finally his wife saw no alternative but to turn to the pastor.

She rode to see him and said, "I have come here because you stand closer to Providence than anyone else, even the sheriff. Do you think my husband is still alive?"

The pastor replied that although the autumn ship had arrived without him, no one had heard any suggestion that he was dead when the ship left Copenhagen.

"Could he possibly be dead, nonetheless?" she asked.

"Ahem, not exactly," he said. "Not entirely."

The woman said, "Well now I ask you, because my ignorance is immense and never more so than now, and your wisdom correspondingly profound: can it be that he is perhaps not entirely alive, either?"

"There could well be something in that," said the pastor.

"So you think there could be something in that?" said the woman, and stared out into the blue, while deep within her the tears froze.

"Perhaps not more than is necessary," said the pastor.

"It's no joke being a simple-minded creature," said the woman. "So I ask you to overlook my folly if I ask: if my husband Steinar is not exactly and perhaps only to a certain extent dead, what entry is to be made in the parish register? On the other hand, if there may be something in the possibility that he is dead, even if it is only just a little bit—how much is that to be reckoned in tears?"

"I know that it is all a question of tears, dear lady," said the pastor. "How many, how large. In this instance I would say: ahem—should we not leave the matter open until spring?"

Then he leant across to the woman and whispered, "I have heard it hinted that your husband Steinar is one of those who have met a Mormon. I understand it happened over in the west in the summer the king came over. Some say that he released a Mormon who was tied to a boulder."

About a month before Christmas, when the tears at Hlíðar had ceased to be merely a film of hoar-frost and had become solid ice, a letter arrived from father. It had been written in Copenhagen late in October and posted with the last autumn sailing, but there had been no one to speed its delivery once it arrived in Iceland; it was now crumpled and soiled from having often been passed from hand to hand.

"There are many rivers on the way out east to Steinahlíðar," said the woman. "Good news travels slowly but arrives in the end, thank goodness. Bad news always arrives a day too soon."

Steinar wrote that unforeseen delays prevented him from travelling on the autumn boat as planned. It was also too late to pen much news, except perhaps about the casket, just for fun; and also a brief description of his meeting with Krapi. In addition, thanks be to the Lord for keeping the writer of these lines safe in His keeping from the time he rode from home until the writing of these words.

There followed an account of how they came to Scotland, to a place called Leith. Gold-braided officials of the British queen were there to pry into their luggage in order to prevent unlawful goods being smuggled in. They caught sight of Steinar's bedding-roll and asked what it was; he replied, "That is mainly my eider-down." They felt it all over and asked what was inside it, and wanted to see. It was the aforementioned casket. "What infernal contraption is this?" they asked, and tried to open it, which was sooner said than done. Then Steinar brought out the Poem for Opening a Casket and showed them the way to do it, and the casket opened. They asked him how much he wanted for it, but he made no reply and closed the lid. More Customs men of higher rank arrived, and the bids for the casket rose in proportion. Finally the highest-ranking official and head of the whole Customs service in Scotland arrived, and offered English gold to the value of two cows for the casket, and tried for a long time to open it by fiddling with the studs, because he realised that there was no key to it. But the more he fiddled, the more securely locked the casket was. Then Steinar told the interpreters to say that it could only be opened with a poem. A cow's-price for the poem, said the captain; but when he looked at the poem his face grew doubtful. Steinar laughed and patted this nobleman on the shoulder and said through the interpreter that the British queen was a real treasure, but that the whole British Empire could not afford the price of this casket; this was one occasion when gold was impotent. Then he wrapped the casket in his eiderdown again, and the British cursed him roundly and soundly.

There was nothing further to relate of Steinar's journey until he arrived with his casket in Copenhagen. A messenger from the king was at the quayside with a letter which said that Steinar should lodge in the Seamen's Home, at Vestergade 5, in Kristianshavn, where an Icelandic student would meet him and show him the city. Inside the letter was a sum of money for meals in restaurants, for in Copenhagen one could not eat without paying.

"There is no time to say much about Copenhagen, which one could nevertheless write a book about," said Steinar in his letter. "There is one bridge in particular which opens of its own accord, I do not understand how, and big ships sail through it; a remarkable phenomenon. Then there is Thorvaldsen's beautiful workshop with smooth-limbed goddesses and slim-waisted youths; and also some extremely shapely horses ridden by warlike knights. One must also mention the gasworks, one of the finest masterpieces in the country; it provides light and heat for the people. It contains a huge furnace, from which run pipes that go under the ground into the city and up through the walls into the houses. If one now wants to have light or a fire, one unscrews a tap in a brass pipe in one's room and applies a match, and it begins to burn. Many people find this unbelievable, which it is; but it is quite true, and very remarkable. I have not yet mentioned Tivoli, which the Danes have created to resemble heaven and the joys of paradise, although I did not particularly care for it myself," said Steinar. "In my youth I would hardly have been allowed to perform such frolics in public as are practised there, nor would I like to see my children taking part in such games. Several people swarmed like cats up perpendicular poles and then performed all kinds of pointless acrobatics and posturings on bars and ropes; mercifully there were no accidents. There was also a playhouse where some rather pitiable people appropriately tricked out in the weirdest garb entered and frolicked about with somersaults and whacks and various other foolish antics. Some were very scantily clad, particularly the women. I asked what people these might be and was told that the husband was called Harlequin and the wife Columbine; there was also a fellow called Pantaloon making up to the wife. They seemed to me to be altogether rather undependable people. It was all meant to be fun, to be sure, but it is only for those who are not too particular.

"The king's hunting-lodge," said Steinar, "lies in the heart of a fine forest. There are many fallow-deer to be seen running among the trees; they stretch their necks and nibble the branches with neat, dainty mouths rather like lambs' mouths, and their jaws work remarkably fast; tiny muscles in their jaws ripple prettily when they chew. They bound so lightly and gracefully that one can scarcely see their feet touch the ground. How strange that noblemen should go out and destroy such delightful creatures for amusement. But in the olden days," wrote Steinar, "slaughtering was held to be a sacred task and those who performed it were considered to have a special covenant with God; it thus becomes part of a king's high office to go out and slaughter animals. I could not bring myself to go into the palace before I had tried to count these animals."

Steinar then described in his letter how he and his companions went through the gates of the palace. "Here we found dragoons sitting on their horses in full armour," he wrote, "looking very fierce; but, said one of my companions, if one does not try to bid them good morning or anything like that, they leave one in peace." On the lawns round the palace there were some courtly gentlemen and fine ladies playing games with bat and ball, and some lieutenants who were strutting about on the paving in gold-trimmed attire asked who these visitors might be. Steinar replied that it was a man from Iceland who had been invited by the king to meet a horse.

"Is that an infernal contraption you have there?" they asked.

"It can hardly be called that," said Steinar. "This is just a little casket, and there is a poem to go with it."

Then they let them in.

The king was in his salon. He came over to meet his guests and greeted them graciously, although he seemed a little preoc-cupied and slightly weary underneath it all. He first asked how Steinar and his family were keeping. Then he thanked Steinar for the pony Pussy, which he said was a very good pony, and a great favourite with the royal grandchildren when they came there on holiday; he was used for drawing a little pony-trap in the royal flower-gardens, and could easily pull three children, or even four. Steinar asked whether there were no riders at court who enjoyed giving a mettlesome horse a good gallop over the Zealand plains. One dignified gentleman replied that some of the younger lads might mount Pussy on occasion but that it was safer to lead him by the bridle because he had a tendency to kick out and bolt. But in Denmark, said the king, referring to that country as if it were some peculiar foreign place he was not very familiar with—in Denmark it is considered cruelty to animals if adults ride ponies. Quite recently someone was convicted in court because he had been seen riding an Icelandic pony through Copenhagen. "But," said the king, "we who have ridden these little creatures our-selves in Iceland laugh at that sort of thing."

When the king and his visitor had exchanged a few words about the pony, Steinar spoke up and said that he had a gift he wished to present to the king, a box that he himself had put together for holding gold, precious stones and secrets. Then he laid the casket before the king and opened its intricate lock in a trice. The king gave thanks for the gift and praised Steinar's ingenuity profusely. "But the poor fellow rather found himself in difficulties when he tried to open it himself," wrote Steinar.

"This is something I must show Valdemar," said the king.

He called his son, Prince Valdemar, over and made him greet this farmer from Iceland, which the prince did most graciously, and then began to talk about the pony Pussy, saying that he was very fat but rather restive, like all Icelanders if they were not handled correctly. Prince Valdemar then tried his hand at the casket, but could not get the knack of it. After a while he said that it was the devil's own job to open it, and it was best to let the Tsar of Russia deal with this sort of apparatus. He went out on to the veranda and summoned the king's guests, the people who had been playing out on the lawns, and said that a man from Iceland had arrived with a fiendish puzzle which demanded even more intelligence than playing croquet. The mention of Iceland roused great mirth outside. Soon a host of people came streaming into the salon, and these were certainly no flea-bags or parish paupers or work-house orphans, according to Steinar; he wrote in his letter that he would have thought that his leg was being pulled a bit too hard if anyone other than Kristian Wilhelmsson, who was an honest and upright man, had told him the names of the new arrivals.

It so happened that just at this time King Kristian's children and their families had all come to visit him for a holiday. "These children," wrote Steinar, "have become kings and queens in their own right throughout the world, or have a crown on the way. I shall mention first the one who rules the Greeks, for he came

over to me and offered me his hand—an exceedingly courteous
and kindly man," said Steinar, "bald and with a long beard. Next
came the Prince of Cymru or Wales, who is married to Kristian's
daughter Alexandra and is the man destined to rule the British
Empire and also become emperor of India; he often rules the
country when his mother, Madame Victoria, is away enjoying
herself. He did not trouble to greet me, which one could hardly
expect anyway. He was the first of the crowd to go over to the
casket and now he started examining it, but rather petulantly.
This Edward is a venerable-looking young man with extremely
well-groomed shiny hair and full cheeks; but I can well understand why anyone who will have to rule the British Empire does
not look too cheerful. Then came a brisk-looking man with a
bald head and rather kindly eyes, and a beard not unlike Björn of
Leirur's: he was dressed like someone who had never been associated with warfare, but most people would be inclined to think
that he had more gold braid than anyone else and wore sword
and topboots night and day, for this was no other than Alexander
the Third, Tsar of Russia. He was the only one of the company
who said a few words to me," wrote Steinar, "and my companion
translated for me afterwards what he had said. The tsar said he
had met all kinds of barbarians in the Russian empire and
beyond, including a Tibetan, but never an Icelander until now.
In his opinion no barbarians looked alike, except perhaps Icelanders and Tibetans; this, he thought, was due to the fact that
they were the two most isolated races on earth, the Tibetans surrounded by too much land and the Icelanders by too much water.
Icelanders, however, were much more of a rarity than Tibetans,
yes, so exceptional, in fact, that he, the tsar, was going to put a
cross in his diary for that day. And when the tsar saw the future
king of Great Britain stooping over the casket, he said to me that

he would have to build himself a palace round his tsardom out in Moscow that would be just as hard to get into, so that the British king could not prise it open. I must say that I found the Russian Tsar a most affable person. And now in swept a group of famous ladies, queens and empresses who all wanted to have a look at the strange barbarian from Iceland. One would certainly have thought some of them generously-built, back home in Steinahlíðar, but there was one, I felt, who outweighed all the others—the lady from Greece, the Grand Duchess Olga Konstantinovna, if I have the name right. She gave me a souvenir medallion. The Tsarina of Russia, Kristian's daughter Dagmar, was also there. Behind them came an army of earls and lords and marquises and their ladies, who are always in the train of emperors and kings and are rated by them no higher than farm-servants and are kept, so I'm told, to help them off with their clothes and even hold them on their pisspots, if you'll pardon the expression. But these all seemed to be pleasant and good-natured people, thank goodness. They all spoke in German, which is the principal language in Europe; Danish they call Low German, and hold in contempt."

Suddenly the whole crowd had moved into the middle of the salon to tussle with the casket, but without any success, and at this some became irritated; the king of Britain was the first one to take a kick at this wretched rubbish from Iceland and said that it was nothing but an infernal contraption. Others said that it was no more than to be expected that Icelanders should embarrass decent folk.

And when Steinar produced the Poem for Opening a Casket they looked at it and said that it only made matters worse; one distinguished gentleman from Britain crumpled it in his fist and threw it to the floor, where it was swept away by a servant. "At that moment some ladies came to tell my interpreter that we were to go into the sitting-room for coffee and cakes; so we took leave of the kings and emperors of the world while they were still straining to get the aforementioned casket open," said Steinar in his letter.

When Steinar had refreshed himself, Kristian Wilhelmsson himself came in and said condescendingly that the master of the royal household had ordered Pussy to be brought to the door of the palace. Steinar and the king went out on to the steps together; and there stood the pony. A red-uniformed coachman was holding the reins tight under his muzzle. The pony was sleek and fat, with a paunch like a lapdog and flanks like saddle-bags, his coat closely curried and shampooed. Steinar could not but think it a change for the worse to see the mane clipped so short and the tail docked right up to the bone. The bridle was mounted in silver, and the headstall was of embroidered leather lined with gaily-coloured felt. Never has an Icelandic pony received such favours before. "I walked over to Krapi," wrote Steinar, "our white horse who issued from the water and can jump up to heaven besides, and I stroked his muzzle. I felt as if he were the horse of my soul. I recognized again the gleam in his eye. The king himself said he could tell from the pony's glance that he recognized his old master, but I felt that he looked at me with an alien expression, like a dead kinsman who comes to one in a dream; and at that moment, indeed, I wished that he did not recognize me at all.

"I asked the master of the royal household if there were no good riding-courses nearby, but he replied, 'Not outside these orchards and flower-gardens.' He then repeated what the king had already told me, that Pussy was used for drawing a children's trap amid the flower-beds; he added that such a kitten of a pony was just a plaything for children, but not entirely safe, because he kicked out or reared if he were not led by the bridle."

After that, Steinar wrote: "Then the king took leave of me and said that I could ask him for whatsoever I wished that lay in his power to grant. I replied with an Icelandic adage, that it is good to have credit with the king. It now so happens, I said, that I have no need of anything that kings can grant; but I left a bridle on the animal by mistake when I handed him over that time, and I would very much like to have the bridle back. The king called the groom over and told him to give this farmer from Iceland as many good bridles as he would accept." And in conclusion Steinar wrote: "And there I left the horse of my soul and the casket of my soul in the king's keeping, but got the bridle and also some pictures of the kings and the queens in all their finery."

At this point in the letter Steinar said that it was now late at night in Copenhagen and he would have to be brief in closing, for the ship would be sailing shortly.

Postscript. "I must not omit to inform you, my dear family, that on the day I took leave of the emperors and kings and their ladies and the Madame Grand Duchess Konstantinovna, it so happened that I went to buy myself, for two aurar, a drink of the water that springs from a rock in the forest, the clearest water in all Denmark: it is called the Kirsten Piil Spring. And there, by the will of Providence and divine ordinance, I met a man whom I had twice come across accidentally in Iceland. Indeed I had begun to think that it had all been a dream. This man is called Þjóðrekur, and he is a bishop. He was standing beside this spring and drinking good water for two aurar. This man is my destiny. Can therefore not come to Iceland for the time being. I commit you to God's keeping in my tearful prayers, and now no more of this scribble."

14

Business matters

Now the snow lay deep over the land; and a great darkness; and no entertainments for the last hundred and fifty years, as was said before; scarcely a light indoors, let alone love or money. But most people understood God, and many could understand sheep (more or less); none the heart. People mumbled old verses to themselves or muttered proverbs, and youth drank life from the sagas. It should be recorded, however, that a certain young lad had become a little smaller than Egill Skalla-grímsson since the previous year; but farming sense had not ousted his viking temperament to the extent of making him put the ewes to the ram. At the end of the rutting season some good neighbours bestirred themselves and made arrangements to provide for the sheep that were still in season at Hlíðar in Steinahlí-ðar. But unfortunately the cows were completely overlooked. There was no one with enough intelligence left on the farm, said the woman.

Late in January, while most of the darkness still lay over the land and the world was lost beneath the snow, it so happened that a magnificent outburst of barking roused echoes in the hearts of the family at Hlíðar. It was a long time since Snati had taken the trouble to go up on the roof, they said; and this was certainly not a matter of baying at the moon—there was a kind of silver edge to his bark.

Soon a topcoated man appeared at the door. The whole house shook when he stamped the snow off himself. He engulfed the mother and daughter in the embrace of his many-layered coat and smothered them with kisses in that vast beard of his reeking of snuff and cognac: "There's no need to feed my ponies, they're fat enough as it is," he said, "and my boys are quite used to waiting out of doors while I'm putting maidens to sleep inside. So they say that our good friend has become a Mormon?" he went on.

"Mercy on us," said the woman.

"Mormons!" said Björn of Leirur. "They're men after my own heart, yes, real men. Twenty-one wives at least, my dear, and each with their own front door and hall and separate room so that there's never any clash within the house. Quite a change from all this hole-and-corner business here in Iceland. Haven't I always said that my old friend Steinar of Hlíðar was a phenomenal fellow? And you're getting along famously, ladies? Fat, eh? Thanks for last autumn. I only came along to run my hands over you. It's essential to be fat, especially inside. I know that my old friend Steinar would not easily forgive me if I let you lose any weight while he's away with the Mormons."

"May I ask," said the woman, "why is everyone always harping on about those wretched Mormons? What sort of fairy-tale is this? I was under the impression that I knew my Steinar just as well as some of the housewives hereabouts, the ones who do all the talking about Mormons. I don't know what opinions they've had about my Steinar up until now, but I can say, stupid as I am, that my husband must have changed a lot in half a year if he's now started having twenty-one wives."

"Dear lady," said Björn of Leirur, "both the sheriff and the king know what kind of person Steinar is. He's not just far above Yes and No, my dear; in the end you get nothing more out of him than a little squeak. He is even above gold. There has never been another man like him in Iceland. A nice thing if I let such a man's womenfolk waste away! Someone said you were short of milk."

"That's not the worst of it," said the woman. "My old Daisy lost her calf in the autumn and is as dry as a bone; and then we forgot to serve the summer-bearing cow—that's how clever we are now on this farm. My daughter has never been near cattle until this winter, and knows nothing about animal breeding; and I've become weak in the head. So it goes without saying we haven't had very much dairy-food to waste. But though young Víkingur is a little pinched-looking and rather listless in his work, no one can say that your handmaiden Steinbjörg doesn't seem to be thriving."

Björn of Leirur went over to the girl and felt her all over until she blushed scarlet and saw spots before her eyes and could hardly stand on her feet.

"Oh, so that's the way it is," said Björn of Leirur. "Well, I'll be damned!"

"I'm always running to the tub of fish-oil that Daddy was going to use for light if the worst came to the worst," said the girl. "I should think I'm almost down to the bottom of it by now."

"I'll bear you in mind when it clears up enough to drive a cow over to you," said Björn of Leirur and stopped fondling the girl. "I have a cow that calved at Christmas—not a champion milker, but she gives a steady yield. But it takes more than a calving cow to sort everything out. It's not enough to serve the cows if no one looks after the girls. I only wish I had a son who would do for this little girl here. No such luck. But something will have to be done, my child."

All the strength drained out of the girl.

"I've been thinking of a young lad not so far from here," said Björn of Leirur, "and if I remember right, you yourselves had begun to have some pleasant thoughts about one another."

The girl was now sitting slumped on the edge of her bunk.

"I'll set you up in a nice little croft and scrape some livestock together for you," said Björn of Leirur.

The girl hid her face in the crook of her arm.

Björn of Leirur sat down beside her and took her in his arms, and on his lap this big girl became small again.

"Eh, what do you say, then, my little lamb?"

"I don't know," the girl mumbled in his ear. "I wish I were fast asleep."

For a long time he lulled her in his arms, saying, "There, there, my lamb, there, my lamb, there, my little creature"; and sometimes he even said, "There, my little scamp."

Her mother sat nearby as still as a statue.

"In my time, Björn," she said at last, "young men used to come along themselves and propose. The risk is all theirs, after all."

"They're much too bashful, poor things, while they haven't

got anything behind them," said Björn of Leirur. "I never ran a yard after a girl of my own free will until I was nearly forty. Now I sometimes marry off three or four a year. And now I'm off. It's blowing up again, anyway."

The visitor thrust his beard into the women's faces and gave them another whiff of snuff and cognac, squeezed himself through the door in his bulky overcoat, and was gone.

When it thawed, two men came up from the littoral farms bringing a full-uddered cow for the folk at Hlíðar, and went back with one of the barren cows. In the eyes of the district, this looked like a straight exchange.

But Björn did not leave it at that. A few weeks passed, and then the stripling from Drangar was at the door one fine day. He was not so much of a stripling any longer, for that matter. He was rather more confident than when he had called in the autumn. This time he did not hesitate to ask for the daughter of the house without any preliminaries. They saw one another in private. First they looked sidelong at one another for a little while, then he began, "You didn't tell the truth."

It is not too much to say that the girl was shocked by such an address. From time immemorial an untrue word had never been heard uttered at Hlíðar in Steinahlíðar.

"I don't know what you're getting at," she said, and looked at him in amazement.

"You said last autumn that nothing had happened," he said.

"What *has* happened?" she said. "I don't know of anything that has happened. Is there something the matter?"

"Not with me," he replied.

"Thank God for that. Nor me, either. I only wish I knew how to talk."

"You have been to bed with a man," he said.

"I just don't know what to do with you," she sighed. "Fancy going on about that still!"

"You have kissed him," said the boy.

"Björn of Leirur," said the girl. "Only when he thrusts his beard into our faces sometimes when he comes here."

It is not too much to say that he was nonplussed by the straightforward way she answered him, but also more especially by the sight of her sitting there on the floor bursting out all over and looking her interrogator straight in the eye. His question stuck in his throat at this candour of heart and soul that faced him.

"Some say that you're getting stout," he said at last. "I think so too."

She said, "I'm certainly not a very good-looking person, that's quite true. But can I help it if I'm growing? I can see you haven't forgotten what I blurted out last autumn, that you were a little slender. I don't know why I said it; but please, you mustn't bear me a grudge over it."

"There aren't many who are as stout as Björn of Leirur," said the boy. "And he's been giving you a cow, too."

"Who says so?" she asked.

"That's what they say," he replied.

"Am I now considered the housewife here?" she said.

"Somehow or other you've landed up in Björn's collection," said the boy.

"Landed up in what?" said the girl. "The things you can think up sometimes! And there was I thinking you were such nice people out at Drangar. Was there anything you came for?"

"One could hardly call it that," said the boy. "As far as I could gather, he's had it all out with you already."

"Out?" said the girl. "How out? And out about what? I'm stumped."

"Didn't he want to have you married off? Wasn't he going to fix you up with a husband?"

"I think you're a little queer in the head," she said.

"Yes, I'm probably a bit simple—at least compared with you," he said.

"Björn of Leirur is always joking with people just to amuse them," she said. "But though I enjoy listening to his blether, I've never heard that anyone is obliged to take it seriously."

"Yes, that's these philanderers all over," said the boy. "They joke and joke and no one takes anything seriously, least of all the women—until all of a sudden they find themselves in bed with them."

"Just to have somewhere to sleep, maybe, when all the other beds are occupied," said the girl.

"They add to their collection wherever they stay the night, these fellows. I understand he's had another one out east since the autumn, and a third one west over in Ölfus. And several more, no doubt."

"You've had your nose in plenty of places, I must say," said the girl.

"These were only the three he allowed me to choose from," said the boy. "But I gathered that you were the one he wanted to subsidize best."

"Do you think I don't know what a tease old Björn is?" said the girl. "I wouldn't half be called a fool if I started to take his nonsense seriously."

"He offered to bestow ten hundreds of land on you," said the boy. "And livestock by arrangement."

"And that's the sort of thing you pay attention to?" she said. "No wonder you think you're quite a man."

"It's up to you," he said.

"To me?" said the girl. "It's nothing to do with me. Just leave me out of your seamen's talk."

"What are you thinking of doing then?" he asked.

"Nothing," said the girl. "We're just waiting for Daddy to come back."

"Once I thought you quite liked me," he said.

"Please don't tease me any more today," she said. "We have a grain or two of coffee. Can we make you a cup?"

He looked at her for a long time and was no longer sure about what he should do.

Finally he rose to his feet, picked up his cap, stared down into it and then turned it over.

"Would you consider marrying me?" he asked.

Now the girl dropped her eyes right down and said, "I don't know. Hmmm. What about you?"

"If I only knew rather better what I was getting," he said. "As I said to Björn of Leirur. . . ."

"What has this to do with Björn of Leirur?" said the girl.

"Land and livestock aren't enough when a man like that's involved," he said.

"Why should we expect anything from Björn of Leirur, a stranger?" said the girl. "Daddy will be home soon and then I'll say to him, 'Will you let Jóhann of Drangar and myself have a part of Hlíðar?' 'But of course,' he'll say."

"Your father is a poor man," said the boy. "My father is also a poor man. What I earned at Þorlákshöfn all went into the farm at home, and besides I've only just come of age this year. It seems to me a matter of course to make use of our hold on Björn of Leirur and insist on straight gold for this. He rides the whole country with the stuff in his saddle-bags."

"For what?" asked the girl.

"To put it bluntly, for the fact that you went to bed with him, as you told me yourself, and let him put you to sleep," said the boy.

"How glad I am I never let you have a ride on Daddy's Krapi," said the girl.

"He threw you an English guinea, but he owes you at least a hundred. I want you to go to him yourself and tell him so."

"If I go anywhere it will be to my father, for he has both gold and precious stones as well as magic charms in secret compartments that no one will ever be allowed to see," said the girl.

15

A baby in spring

In spring no letter arrived, no message, no news at all. The mailboat *Diana* had come and gone, they heard. The folk at Hlíðar waited and hoped right until summer that perhaps there would come at last a crumpled piece of paper that had been soiled by many a grubby pair of hands, just like last autumn, but nothing came. Not even a single lamb came out of the ewes, as they did on other farms; and not much food either. The cow that Björn of Leirur sent could only just keep them in milk, and things would have gone worse for them if a barrel of rye-meal and a box of sugar had not arrived from an unknown source to eke out their larder.

Their land had been completely stripped of turf by the visit of the ponies the previous autumn, but the hayfield was worst of all; no one thought for a moment that it would take a scythe that summer. It was also terrible to see how much rubble had crashed down into the field that winter. How this trim little farm which had always shone so sprucely by the main track with its immortal dry-stone dykes had deteriorated since the previous summer!

The people on the farm felt jaded, but that was nothing very unusual out in the country in spring. Steina in particular complained of distension of the belly, with shooting pains above and below the waist.

"It surely can't be a blood clot?" said her mother.

And when the discomfort had passed, she said, "I think it must just have been growing pains."

One day the girl took to her bed, screaming with pain.

"What if I put a cold compress on it?" said her mother.

When the cold compress had no effect on the girl's illness, her mother said, "Should we not try a hot compress?"

That night the girl could not bear the agony any longer, and her mother sent the boy off on borrowed ponies west over the river to fetch the doctor. It was a journey of many hours.

Next morning, when the sun was already high, the boy arrived back with the doctor. By then the girl had been delivered of a baby boy; her mother had cut the cord. The doctor was furious and asked what he had done to deserve humiliation and mockery in these parts.

"How on earth were we to imagine anything like this?" said the mother.

"Well, what does the girl say?" asked the doctor.

"How am I to know?" she said. "It was my death I was expecting, not that thing."

"You probably know where you've been, little girl," said the doctor.

"I haven't been anywhere except here," said the girl.

"Praise be to God, He has once again proved His omnipotence just when everyone was losing faith, and no lambs came," said the woman.

"You don't need to make any excuses for my sake over this," said the doctor. "You can have all the babies you like. But I'm just not a bloody midwife."

"Truly a miracle has happened here," said the woman. "May I not offer the gentleman a cup of coffee?"

After the doctor came the pastor, but not until Steina was up and about again. He had his big book with him. He too was offered coffee.

He replied, "The poor pastor has never been offered so much as a bite since coffee was discovered. This is my thirty-seventh cup today. I shall soon have to give everything up because of my stomach, just like all other pastors. But perhaps I can scribble down what has happened here before I die."

"There's nothing more than what the pastor sees," said the woman: "the farmer's disappeared, and no one knows whether he is alive or dead."

The pastor put on his spectacles, fished an ink-horn out of his coat pocket, and opened his book.

"Brevity is all that matters here," he said. "Steinar Steinsson, unchanged, except that he went abroad late last summer to see the king. Rumour has it that he has met the polygamist and immerser Þjóðrekur, from the Vestmannaeyjar. Ahem, dear lady; he will show up again if he is not dead. What else?"

"Then there are the children, and me," said the woman.

"Yes, I have a note of everyone I have baptized and confirmed," said the pastor. "Anything else?"

"Nothing except what happened," said the woman. "A baby was born here."

"Ahem," said the pastor. "Eh? Did everything not go as it should, or what?"

"We haven't been able to find any explanation for it yet," said the woman.

The girl was now fetched, and the pastor talked to her in private in the spare-room.

"How long is it since we were tussling over Christianity, little one?" he asked. He was referring to her confirmation; and when she had answered this, the pastor said that many a girl had been made a woman at an earlier age than that. "And I hear the baby is doing well?"

"Indeed he is," said the girl. "And thank you for asking."

"And the father?" asked the pastor.

"I don't know," said the girl. "It just arrived."

"Ahem," said the pastor. "Eh?"

"My mother is always saying that there has to be a father," said the girl. "I just don't understand that. What for?"

"It looks better in the parish register," said the pastor. "What did you get landed in, little one?"

"I didn't get landed in anything," said the girl. "I've no idea what I should have got landed in."

"Oh, one doesn't need to take much off for that," said the pastor.

"I've never taken anything off," said the girl.

"By the way, were there not a few horses here last autumn?" asked the pastor.

"There certainly were."

"They are often jolly fellows, these drovers," said the pastor. "Eh?"

"They didn't amuse me," said the girl.

"It has happened before in these parts that a girl has been helping a visitor off with his things late at night, well now, and what happens? She pulls one way and he pulls the other, if you please. He pulls so hard that before she knows it, she is in bed with him."

"I've never heard that before," said the girl. "What happened then?"

"A baby arrived next spring," said the pastor. "I have it in my book here somewhere."

"I didn't get into bed with anyone," said the girl. "My brother and I were told to go out to sleep on saddle-turves in the shed."

"The blessed child must have come into existence somehow," said the pastor.

"That may well be," said the girl. "But not by any human agency."

"Well I'll be damned!" said the pastor. "Did no one help the poor wretches off with their things when they arrived dripping wet with water?"

"I sometimes helped old Björn here in the spare-room at night," said the girl.

"Björn of Leirur?" said the pastor. "It could have been less, I suppose."

He pulled the stopper from the ink-horn and made ready to dip his pen.

"Well, shall we not just write the old fellow down and be done with it?" he said.

"The pastor decides what he writes, I'm not writing it," said the girl.

"You must know how babies are made, my little chicken?" said the pastor.

"Oh, I was never confirmed for knowing that," said the girl. "The first thing I knew, something had started to grow inside me. We all thought I was growing so fat from drinking fish-oil from the tub. And then suddenly a baby arrived."

The pastor had laid down his pen.

"Someone said there were gold coins sometimes," he said. "Eh?"

"Good Heavens above!" said the girl. "I would never have thought that story had spread so far. It's quite true, I was given a gold coin last autumn. I then gave it away to the boy I thought so good-looking when I was little. I gave him the silver coins too. I gave him everything except the copper."

"So there was copper too?" said the pastor. "That was not so good."

"I never asked Björn of Leirur for anything," she said.

"Those who give copper are not good people," said the pastor. "Not to girls. Some say Björn of Leirur is a brute."

"That's not what I said," the girl replied. "I wouldn't dream of starting to speak ill of people."

"A nice chap?" asked the pastor.

"He smells absolutely wonderful," said the girl. "And clean hands. Very soft hands, too, come to that, for a man."

"Quite so," said the pastor. "Eh? Were you laughing, little one?"

"A fool often laughs at his own thoughts," said the girl. "He just had to touch me and no more with his fingertips at night, and I fell fast asleep—that's what I was laughing about. I was as safe with him as with my daddy."

"Asleep, yes. Exactly," said the pastor. "Eh?"

"I sometimes threw myself down at the foot of his bed when it was so late that there was no point in going out to the shed to sleep," said the girl. "I know that one shouldn't talk about such things. But I just wanted to say that old Björn isn't a brute or unpleasant, far from it."

"Did you notice at all where he touched you?" asked the pastor.

"No, I certainly didn't," said the girl. "Did I not tell you I had fallen asleep?"

"Would it have been above or below the diaphragm?"

"Diaphragm?" said the girl, quite baffled. "I haven't the slightest idea where the diaphragm is, even. I never bother my head about people's insides."

"Yes, one has to watch out for these fellows even though they may not be Mormons," said the pastor. "Take care not to become a Mormon woman, my child."

"If Daddy is a Mormon," said the girl, "then I want to be a Mormon woman."

16

The authorities,
the clergy, and the soul

A few days after the aforementioned visitation, a letter arrived from the sheriff: in view of rumours concerning the paternity of the child born to Steinbjörg Steinarsdóttir of Hlíðar, and her own unclear answers to the parish pastor's questions, an inquiry into the whole case was requested. The girl was therefore required to present herself at Hof on such and such a day.

It has always been considered rather beggarly to travel on foot in Iceland; but the folk at Hlíðar had no choice now, for the ponies were in mediocre condition, if that, and had scarcely recovered from the winter. The birds circled the girl's head as she walked. She took off her socks and hitched up her skirt and waded across the cold mountain-streams. It was an enjoyable journey at the height of spring. She could feel the smell of the sea and the land at one and the same time. But when she reached the Jökulfljót (Glacier River) she had to go by ferry.

Because she had been walking since early that morning and it was now nearly noon, there was so much milk in her breasts by this time that she saw no alternative but to ask the housewife at Ferjukot to have a word with her in private. The woman asked where she came from and who her people were, and then led her into the pantry.

"Is there any news out your way in Steinahlíðar?" asked the woman.

"Nothing particular that I know of," said the girl. "Everyone hale and healthy. But there have been a lot of stones down off the mountain this winter."

"What a shame," said the woman. "But have the livestock done all right?"

"My goodness, yes," said the girl. "No question about that. Although there aren't very many lambs at Hlíðar this spring. And the horses didn't come through the winter all that well—I'd have been riding today otherwise. There was a time, once, when we had a good horse. But excuse me, is there anything new in your part of the world?"

"Nothing to speak of," said the woman. "Except for a fellow who forded the river today with seventeen horses."

"That can only have been Björn of Leirur," said the girl, and laughed.

"So you're on your way across too?" said the woman.

"Oh, they were writing me some letter or other," said the girl. "I think they're all going round the bend."

"Men are always the same," said the woman. "And now I'll just put this cloth on you again. I think that's all there is for the time being." And she showed the girl how much there was in the bowl.

"A thousand thanks for your help," said the girl, and was grateful that the woman had not started asking why such a little girl had so much milk in her breasts.

Then the woman said, "Aren't you hungry and thirsty? Can I not offer you a little refreshment?"

"Thanks all the same," said the girl, "but I haven't time to sit down. And now I feel so much lighter. Goodbye and thank you again, and think kindly of me."

"The same to you, my dear," said the woman, and kissed the girl out on the paving. "Just go straight on. My husband's down on the bank with the ferry."

"Your field's becoming really lovely," said the girl. "I only hope I don't tread on the buttercups."

"Thank you," said the woman. "May God be with you."

The girl walked straight across the field, taking care not to tread on the buttercups.

Then the woman called out after her. She was standing in the doorway and her voice was now dry and harsh as if she were a different person altogether; she even knew the girl's name although she had not asked for it, and now she used it.

"Little Steinbjörg," she said sternly.

The girl stopped in her tracks and looked round. "Were you calling me?"

Then the woman said, "Make the old devil pay. It would serve him right. You girls shouldn't put up with these good-for-nothings he buys you for husbands."

On the far bank of the river stood a young man with two ponies. He was waiting. The girl walked towards him when she stepped off the ferry. He had dismounted and was standing leaning against the neck of his pony, which was a little restless.

He watched her gait as she approached him. It was Jóhann of Drangar. He greeted her while she was still some distance away.

"Hullo," she said. "What a very polite good morning you give nowadays. From miles away, even. How did you learn to say good morning so nicely?"

"It's all coming on, gradually," he said.

"Are you waiting for something?" she asked.

"For you," he said.

"How did you know I was coming?" she said.

"I know that you're to be questioned," he said. "I've been interrogated already."

"You should have lent me one of your horses since we were going the same way."

"I'm clearing off now," he said. "And anyway I haven't got another saddle."

"I'm pretty used to riding bareback," she said.

"You never let me have a ride on the white horse the other year," he said.

She looked at him wordlessly, her face flushing, and then lowered her eyes. Then she went off on her way again.

"I was talking to you," he called out after her.

"I thought we had done all the talking there was to do, this winter," she said.

"I was going to tell you that Björn of Leirur has fixed everything up with me," he said. "The minute the sheriff starts asking, then hurry up and say it was me."

"What do you mean?"

"It was me who gave you the baby," he said. "Then there will be no more questions. We'll get married."

"I think you must be out of your mind," said the girl. "I've never heard anything like it in my whole life."

"You just say that I met you once in the pantry when you were churning," he said, "and I put you down on the butter-tub. I suppose you realise that it needs a man to start a baby."

"I don't understand men," said the girl. "If you are a man, that's to say."

"You ought to be far enough advanced to know how animals breed."

"Do you think I'm some sort of animal?" said the girl. "Do you think I'm a cow?"

"The pastor insists on a father for the child; and when the sheriff asks, you only need to say that I pushed your skirt up over your knees a little," said the boy.

"If the sheriff asks," said the girl, "then I'll tell him what I think is true. Anything else I cannot do, will not do, and don't know how to do."

"Don't you understand that we have been offered money?" he shouted after her. "And land?"

"I certainly haven't," said the girl.

"Don't you understand that both of our futures for the rest of our lives depend on this?"

"I have no desire for a bought good-for-nothing," said the girl.

He mounted his pony brusquely and shouted after her, "You'd rather sleep with old Björn for a Króna!"

At that she halted, turned round, and asked: "Who got that Króna?"

He dug his heels into his pony and rode away.

The sheriff was lying on a sofa in his shirt-sleeves, reading a thriller and smoking a pipe. The girl was taken up to his room

by the back stairs, but on the way she was given a plate of porridge in the kitchen. The sheriff puffed away at his pipe. It was
like a haystack on fire. He began to laugh aloud at what he was
reading. Finally he caught sight of the girl.

"What do you want?" he said, getting to his feet

"I got a message to come," she said. "About a baby."

"Oh, so it's you, you poor little soul," said the sheriff and
began to inspect her and feel her. "It's awful to see how young
you are. What a bloody old scoundrel he is, that fellow. People
like him should be fleeced and put on the parish. But the way
things are, my lamb, it's the lesser of two evils to let yourself get
hitched with that boy I was examining here this morning; even
though he isn't up to much. It's no fun for any woman to get
landed with one of Björn's illegitimate children. But tell me,
what the devil draws you all into that old rascal's bed? I never
manage to get myself a wench, and I certainly don't consider
myself less of a man than old Björn. I just have to be content
with sleeping with the sheriff's wife, thank you."

The girl was quite nonplussed; and besides, she was frightened of the sheriff.

"Do you hear what I'm saying?" said the sheriff. "I'm saying
that if the clergy start insisting on a formal court hearing over
this, which would be just like Pastor Jón, for he's a cussed sort of
fellow, then remember that I'm trying to help you. Whatever I
ask, you don't utter a cheep except for the one thing, that it was
that young devil—what was his name again?—it was he who
came to you in the outhouse, or was it in the byre. . . ."

"It wasn't in the pantry either," said the girl.

The sheriff was taken aback at this, and echoed the girl's reply
in surprise: "Not in the pantry either? Well, where then? Anyway—he spread you on a box."

"Am I some sort of animal?" said the girl, and looked up at the sheriff with innocent eyes. "Or perhaps some dead thing that can be spread on a box?"

But now the sheriff had had enough. His patience was at an end. He stamped on the floor.

"What's all this damned impertinence?" he said. "What's the point of having authorities for such people? Do you take me for some sort of freak who pronounces virgin births here before God and the king? People who behave like this should be flogged. I'm not listening to any more nonsense; you'll do as I tell you, my girl."

Later that day the girl was brought into the court-room. The sheriff was sitting there dressed now in his official blue uniform with gold buttons and gold-braided cap. The recorder with the book was also there. Pastor Jón sat by himself at a window gazing out at the home-field where his horses were grazing. No one looked at the girl as she sidled in through the door with palpitations in her eyes. The sheriff told the man to bring the records book over; he preferred to have it lying in front of him. Some papers fell out when he opened it. He whistled tonelessly. Absently, and without looking up, he began to mumble something to the effect that according to a written deposition from the undersigned parish pastor, of such and such a date, etc., hmmm, there had been unclear answers about the paternity of the child born to Steinbjörg Steinarsdóttir, of Hlíðar in Steinahlíðar, on the part of the said girl to the aforementioned parish pastor. "Oh, I'm not going to read out all this rigmarole; as far as I can see the whole case is settled. Here lies a signed declaration by Jóhann Geirason, of Drangar, in which he confirms that he is the father of the child and offers to swear it on oath. . . ."

"Hmm?" asked the pastor.

"What's that?" said the sheriff sharply.

"I am only an ignorant clergyman, of course," said the pastor. "And that is probably why I have never heard that a male person can swear paternity on oath."

"What, then?" asked the sheriff.

"That he can, in certain circumstances, deny paternity on oath," said the pastor.

"Swear what you like, my good man," said the sheriff. "I'll have your horses saddled for you at once. I don't give a damn what you think or what side you are on."

He glanced formally down at the records book again: "I submit this document to you officially as a basis for lawful registration in the paternity case under discussion. And now I see no reason why anyone should ever again be bothered with any more twaddle about this affair within my jurisdiction."

Now there was silence in the court-room. It was one of those rare silences that are most reminiscent of the silences in *Njall's Saga.* The flies on the window-panes had fallen to the sill. Finally a sort of interrogatory *hmmm?* escaped from the pastor; and this *hmmm?* was directed at the girl.

"I don't know," said the girl.

"What don't you know?" asked the sheriff.

Eventually the girl replied, with a gasp, "I don't know how babies happen."

The others looked at one another dumbfounded. Finally the pastor popped a quid of tobacco into his mouth.

"This matter is not on the agenda," said the sheriff. "We are not here to investigate natural history. This particular baby has demonstrably been born, and its paternity established. That is all there is to it."

"Ahem," said the pastor. "Eh? Am I not right in thinking that I heard you mention someone else's name the other day, little one?"

"The case is closed as far as I am concerned," said the sheriff. "I shall have your horses saddled."

The pastor went on doggedly:

"Might I just ask one small question before we set off?" he said. "Tell me, my dear: the boy who signed his name to that document there—when did he lie with you?"

"Never," said the girl.

"Just so," said the pastor. "Exactly. Then perhaps I might ask the sheriff to let the horses graze for a minute or two yet. May I draw the sheriff's attention to the fact that the girl does not acknowledge the undersigned person as the father of her child?"

"No wonder," said the sheriff. "She doesn't understand you. Your speech is too archaic. I don't understand you either, mercifully. It is pointless trying to stir up trouble here by asking questions in saga-language."

Then the pastor asked, "When did you sleep with the boy from Drangar, my dear?"

"Never," said the girl.

"But a little with Björn of Leirur, I believe?"

"I told Pastor Jón the whole story the other day," said the girl.

"Excuse me," said the pastor, "but does the sheriff think it important that children be given the proper father?"

"I don't give a damn," said the sheriff. "No one has complained."

"Does the sheriff deny the necessity for the cure of souls in Iceland?" asked the pastor.

"I don't see how the way people mate concerns religion at all," said the sheriff. "What does it matter to Jesus how mammals breed? But the clergy have their own taste, of course. Theology is welcome to site the soul in people's genitals for all I care."

"And I suppose it is no concern of the sheriff's if a child is made a changeling, nothing more nor less, right from its birth, so that this individual will never be able to prove who he or she is? Not to mention the fact that such a thing should be done before the very eyes of the pastor, who is nevertheless appointed to act according to his conscience and the laws of the land!"

The sheriff's expression was now poker-faced.

"What do you request of me?" he said.

"I ask that this wretched little parishioner of mine be granted justice and truth for herself and her child," said the pastor. "I ask leave to make a statement in court."

"Fetch the court-witnesses from the turbary," the sheriff told the recorder, and then added: "They don't need to wash."

Two of the sheriff's tenants, authorized for this task, entered the court-room. They were upstanding, self-composed and intelligent to look at, but no one needed to be in any doubt about what they had been working at. They laid their turf-cutters aside at the door.

The court was now convened at the request of the parish pastor of Steinahlíðar. He stated his complaint, which he said he had hoped could have been dealt with out of court; but since his statements and arguments out of court had been doubted and ridiculed by highly-placed personages, he could see no alternative to a formal hearing in order that the truth be brought to light.

The sheriff rapped the table with his mallet and ordered the pastor to stick to the point.

When the pastor had finally presented his case, the girl was interrogated. She said that she had never tried to conceal the fact that she had lain on a bed beside Björn of Leirur. But when she was questioned more closely, she could not understand at all what they were getting at. The court-room euphemisms about intercourse between men and women were as incomprehensible to her as the everyday expressions about the same topic. She was familiar only with the vocabulary and activities of saints and angels. She had never been told how babies were conceived in the womb, except in the case of the Virgin Mary. Nor had she ever been present when ewes were put to the ram. And when she was asked how she thought such things came about, she replied simply with these holy words: "God is almighty."

"I call upon the pastor to explain to this ignorant creature what she is being questioned about in this court," said the sheriff.

Pastor Jón took another quid of tobacco and began to expound this remarkable wisdom to the girl in open court with high-flown words and phrases, until the girl buried her face in her hands and said, "I want to go."

"Does the clergy wish to ask the witness any further questions?" asked the sheriff.

The pastor replied that since the girl had now been given this essential instruction in natural history, the time had come for her to answer the question of how much she had taken off, that time last autumn.

"I didn't take anything off," said the girl.

"I asked you the other day if it were not possible that you had half-taken off your drawers," said the pastor. "Eh?"

"I hadn't any drawers on," said the girl.

"Oh! That changes everything," said the pastor. "If I had only known that! Ahem. In that case I am sure you must have been aware at once of anything unusual. Will you not tell us about it?"

"I fell asleep," said the girl.

"And the man?" asked the pastor.

"He slept," said the girl.

"Wasn't it a squeeze?" said the pastor.

"I won't say it wasn't a bit of a squeeze," said the girl.

"But not excessively so?" asked the pastor. "I mean, not so much that it hurt?"

"Perhaps just a little bit, once, after I was asleep," said the girl. "But I knew it was accidental. And I fell asleep again at once."

"Ahem," said the pastor.

"Anything else?" said the sheriff, and looked at the pastor.

"No, thank you," said the pastor. "I would just like to sum up what has come to light, as I see it from my point of view. She was in a room with a man at night-time. She was sleepy. She accepts his invitation to lie down beside him. She becomes drowsy at once, and in no time at all she falls into the sort of deep slumber which overtakes a weary young creature. Both for this reason, and on account of her exceptional inexperience and ignorance, she is not clear about what happened thereafter. It is now for this court to consider what did in fact take place and assess the results."

The girl was staring straight ahead, stupefied, and had slumped into a huddle as if all her bones had been removed. Her face began to twitch, and now she said, catching her breath, "I want to go home."

The tears that began to spill from her eyes were opaque and thick, as if they were excessively salty. They poured down in swift streams and she made no attempt to wipe them away, nor did the sheriff or the clergyman. She went on looking straight ahead of her, the way desperate people do when there is no longer any point in looking around for help.

The sheriff ordered the document signed by Jóhann Geirason, of Drangar, to be read to the girl. In this document, the undersigned confirmed that he was the father of the child born to Steinbjörg Steinarsdóttir, of Hlíðar. They had plighted their troth in childhood and kept full faith with one another until it happened one day last autumn that they had met in the pantry at Hlíðar, when she was scantily clad; and there and then a child had been conceived, which was the child that had now been born and which, under offer of oath, was the child of Jóhann Geirason and no other man. The sheriff now called upon the girl to state her testimony concerning this document. The girl made no reply.

"What else happened in the pantry?"

"I was churning butter," said the girl.

"What then?" asked the sheriff.

"I took the butter from the churn and put it in the trough," said the girl.

"One could scarcely have a baby from that," said the sheriff. "And what then?"

"A little buttermilk dripped from it," said the girl, with her hands to her face.

"And then he spread you out on the butter-box and began to talk affectionately to you, wasn't that it?"

"We don't have a butter-box," said the girl.

"But he pushed your skirt a little up above your knees?" said the sheriff.

The girl went on crying.

"Don't you understand I'm trying to help you, girl?" said the sheriff. "And now I'm going to make one last attempt: were you wearing anything underneath? If you weren't, I adjudge the boy to be the father. Otherwise the whole business is futile."

The girl slumped over the little table she was sitting at and mumbled into her elbow these words, shredded by the sobs that racked her:

"I want to go to my daddy."

17

Water in Denmark

The pristine spring which has its source right here
By Kirsten Piil was first created clear;
And later, for the benefit of all,
Was channelled by the Count von Reventlau.

This poem has been incised for many generations on a stone slab beside the Kirsten Piil Spring in Denmark, where the good water wells up. If there has been any other spot, since Moses struck the rock with his staff, where such an excellent mineral spring is to be found, it is not recorded in any books I know. This water has a gentle refreshing quality that spreads from the tongue to every part of the body. World-famous poets who have written about it call it not only the healthiest water there is but also the noblest drink to be found in Denmark. Whosoever sips this water and looks sunwards at the same time is granted at that moment a glimpse of celestial life, more particularly a blissful foretaste of the nirvana which is described in the books of the East. It is beyond the scope of earthly science to analyse the elements of this water or to define whence its healing properties arise; one can only praise Nature and bless her creator for the taste of the refreshing drink that gushes from the rock. Have I mentioned that the sick and the sore gain marvellous relief from this water? Even the prisoner in his dungeon finds release in it, for this pure drink gives a man strength, greater than any medicine can provide, to bear his fate; and for that reason a cupful of this water that wells up gently from its rock is offered at night to the person who is to be executed at dawn. Whoever drinks of it dies happy and at peace in Denmark. This water costs two aurar a cup.

Now we return to Steinar of Hlíðar at the point where he had taken leave of the king after visiting his pony, which had achieved greater worldly success than any other animal born of a mare in Iceland. He had made the greatest emperors and kings on earth bow down over a little casket, and all their power and wisdom put together had not sufficed to open it; there was no help to be gained from God's grace, which all such folk include in their titles; and besides, they had lost the poem.

Outside the palace gates, Steinar said to the student, "I am thirsty. I have heard that not far away from here is the finest watering hole in Denmark; its name is the Kirsten Piil Spring. I have resolved to go there for a drink."

The student replied that it was rather a novel experience to hear farmers from Steinahlíðar giving lessons about drink to students in Copenhagen. He confessed that he himself had never heard of this drink that Steinar mentioned, despite the fact that Icelandic students had been hanging around the place for nearly three centuries. According to him they had never bothered to get to know any other entertainment or pastime there in Denmark than drinking; and students thought it a bit hard for peasants to arrive from Iceland and start to teach them about drinking in

Denmark. Here in the forest, said this student, there were many good taverns which were great fun to visit and which served the most excellent drinks. He thought it opportune to celebrate this new era in Iceland's history, when a clodhopper could make fools of emperors and kings, just as in the old Legendary Sagas, and have his hack fattened up and set above the king's counsellors in Denmark. He said that Icelandic students would drink for a long time in Denmark before another such day arrived.

Steinar said he would be glad to celebrate the day by tasting the best and most famous drink in Denmark. They now asked the way to the grove where the Kirsten Piil Spring flowed from its rock, as was said before. But when the student saw the water he lost interest in the celebration. He hastily bade Steinar farewell and disappeared.

Steinar walked over to a group of people who sat pensively in a glade in the wood; there did not seem to be many estate-owners among them. They had tired themselves with roaming through the woods and had decided to buy some of the water that was eulogized in the old inscription. There was a light breeze blowing from the Sound. Some were sitting on metal chairs at little tables, and were drinking the excellent water with every sign of satisfaction in the sunshine. Many others were standing in a queue at the counter waiting their turn to be served. Steinar spent a long time spelling out the poem inscribed on the stone in Danish, and the words underneath: "Two aurar per glass, six aurar per jug." When he had read enough he joined the queue to await his turn to buy some water.

When he had bought himself some water he lifted it carefully to his lips where he stood. He was very thirsty by now, and was refreshed in body and soul with every sip. And while he was smacking his lips and thinking to himself what a great and good woman she must have been who discovered this water in days gone by, and how her name would forever be remembered with gratitude by the Danes, he happened to notice a man sitting alone at a small round table under a tall tree, with his back turned towards him. There was something potent about the back of his head; it was no longer young and vigorous—indeed, there were hollows between the sinews, and the wrinkles on the back of his neck made an intricate pattern; but it was still remarkably erect, and sat well on the shoulders. He had taken off his hat, and indeed his bristling tufts of hair made his head rather unsuitable for wearing one. His whole head was deeply sun-tanned. This man was having a drink of water from the Kirsten Piil Spring. Now he pulled from his pocket a small package wrapped in newspaper, which turned out to contain tough rye-bread. He started to chew it, using this good water to wash it down. On a chair beside him lay a fine hat as good as new, wrapped in grease-proof paper. Steinar walked over to him and greeted him:

"It is a small world, I must say. It is good to see you again, my old friend."

"Same to you, my fellow-countryman," said Bishop Þjó-ðrekur; he always broadened his vowels, like most people who have modelled their speech on English. "Have a pew, friend. Yes indeed, it's a small world, especially at this particular end of it. May I not buy you some water?"

"Thanks for the offer, but there is really no need," said Steinar. "I was just finishing a cup."

But Bishop Þjóðrekur insisted on going over and buying a full jug of Kirsten Piil water in Denmark for himself and his compatriot. When they had started sipping it, Bishop Þjóðrekur said, "Who are you again, friend?"

"My name is Steinar Steinsson of Hlíðar in Steinahlíðar. Quite so. We first met by the Öxará, at Þingvellir, when the king came; and then we met outside a church in the south."

"Well, hallo again, friend," said Bishop Þjóðrekur, standing up and kissing him. "Thanks for the last time. How are things?"

"Oh, not so bad on the whole," said Steinar of Hlíðar. "After we parted the year before last it was remarkably fine up until Christmas, but after Christmas it was pretty cold, with a lot of snow, and stormy weather right through the spring, with snow-showers at midsummer. The summer was a bit wet . . ."

The Mormon interrupted him: "It's because Icelanders don't have any overcoats," he said. "I never owned an overcoat until I went to Utah. But in Utah, of course, there is no need for over-coats. I don't care in the slightest what the weather was like in Iceland the year before last. How are you yourself, my friend?"

"Oh, this old fellow from Hlíðar just happens to be in Copenhagen and is drinking Kirsten Piil water," said Steinar.

"Yeah, you've said it, every person is a vessel," said the Mormon, "and it matters a lot that good water should be put in this vessel. Mrs. Peel was a remarkable woman. I come out here by steam-tram twice a week to have a drink. It is like Utah water."

"That reminds me, when you mention water—are you still immersing?" asked Steinar.

"What do you think, man?" said Bishop Þjóðrekur. "Do you think the Saviour let himself be sprinkled while he was an infant in Bethlehem? What happens when a child is sprinkled with water? It's only the pastor's hand that gets baptised, and the poor child is still as unbaptised as ever. There can be no doubt about that. Didn't I tell you that long ago? It's not much good telling people things just the once. I've been sitting here in Copenhagen all summer preparing a pamphlet on it in Icelandic which I shall print and take over with me to replace the ones they stole off me. Yes sirree."

"Was that not just the authorities?" said Steinar.

"There have never been any thieves in Iceland except the authorities," said the Mormon. "They stole everything from my mother, including her good name, even though she was a saintly woman. They had already stolen everything from me before I was born—except the sack on which the dog slept; I was finally allowed to put that on as my Sunday best. No sirree. It was Joseph Smith who raised me up and gave me a country. And now tell me something about yourself, my boy. What are you doing here?"

Steinar replied, "I don't remember whether I told you, when I untied you that time with God's help, that I had just been giving the Danish king a horse. I'm a little like the fellow who rode off to market one morning to buy something for his children. He was a white horse, slightly dappled. In actual fact, he belonged to my children. Anyway, the king invited me home to visit this horse. I have just been there. The biggest emperors in the world and their ladies were all gathered there, and I brought them a little casket. Here are their pictures I was given in return. Quite so. But the poor bridle the king owed me is probably lost."

Steinar dipped into an inside pocket for these pictures which the emperors and kings, empresses and queens had given him of themselves, and put them on the table. The Mormon wordlessly unwrapped his hat from the grease-proof paper and put it on; and it was undeniable that this smooth, split-new hat blended ill with the wrinkled, dust-grimed, weather-beaten face of the Mormon, rather as if a foreign visitor had forgotten this contraption somewhere and left it on top of a lava-outcrop.

"We Mormons only put on a hat for protection against the sun," said Bishop Þjóðrekur. "Did I hear you correctly?"

He put on his spectacles with great ceremony, tilted them on the tip of his nose, and drew down the corners of his mouth as far as possible; but he still had to hold the pictures at arm's length in order to see them. For a long time they both studied these snaps of gold-braided gentlemen and queens with enormous frills and flounces. There was no human virtue, no exploit and no heroic deed which had not left its mark in some decoration on these people's breasts. Steinar gave a ghost of a titter.

When the Mormon had studied them enough he wrapped up his hat again in grease-proof paper, glanced sidelong at Steinar, and took off his spectacles with as much ceremony as he had put them on.

"What are you doing with all this useless trash?" he asked.

"Forgive me if I stand up for my kings, friend," said Steinar of Hlíðar. "And no less for the poor emperors. Even if it were only King George of Greece, who is the least important of all the people in these pictures and is said to be on the dole in Greece (what the Danes call not having two pennies to rub together)— he is at least by rank and title high above every Icelander there is, even if one includes the Mormons too, I should think. Heehee-hee. And he has a well-built wife, besides. These men are much closer to God than we are, insofar as they play a greater part in ruling the world."

"Yes, if they are not just damned robbers," said the bishop. "And now I'm saying more than my prayers. But let me ask you one question before I shut up for good. You say you gave them your casket. Before that you said you had given them your horse. What are you expecting from these people?"

But Steinar was now totally absorbed in contemplation of some beautiful flowers which were growing there in Denmark in a small bed just across from them.

"How lovely the blessed flowers are in this country. And to think that it is autumn," said Steinar.

"Yes, it's all one vast vegetable-garden," said Bishop Þjó-ðrekur.

Then Steinar of Hlíðar said, "When I looked at my little Steina sleeping so peacefully in the midst of this appalling world—she was about three years old then, I think—I suddenly realised that the craftsman who fashioned this world, if such a person exists, what a matchless person he must be! My God, my God, I was saying to myself: to think that such beauty and delight must soon pass away. Later I had a son, who was like Egill Skallagrímsson and Gunnarr of Hlíðarendi and the Norse kings all rolled into one. He slept with a wooden home-made axe under his cheek at nights, because he was going to conquer the world. Hmmm. Incidentally, what is it again that lies on the far side of the wilderness you were mentioning that other time?"

"I should think it is a casket," said the Mormon.

"Quite so," said Steinar. "And what sort of a casket would it be?"

"A tabernacle," said the Mormon.

"Exactly," said Steinar. "Well I never. You don't say so? Excuse me, what sort of a container is that?"

"Do have a little more cold water," said the Mormon.

"You ought to describe this container you mentioned to me a little," said Steinar, "so that I have something to think about on the way home to Iceland instead of my own little casket; but especially to be able to tell the children about it."

"My friend Brigham Young, Joseph Smith's heir, staked out the ground for it the year after I crossed the wilderness. Then we started building. It is two hundred and fifty feet long, a hundred and fifty feet wide, and eighty feet high. The lid rests on forty-four pillars of sandstone. When we built it, there was a thousand-mile trackless trek to the nearest settlement to the east to buy nails, and eight hundred miles to the west down to the sea where one could also have bought some perhaps. So we decided not to buy any nails."

"It would be interesting to know what holds this huge container together," said Steinar. "Is it jointed?"

"Joseph Smith was never at a loss how to hold together even bigger things, my friend," said the Mormon.

"And what do you keep in such a large vessel, if I may ask?" said Steinar.

"The Holy Spirit," said the Mormon.

"Exactly," said Steinar. "Just as I thought. I am beginning to see just how much my own little casket was worth! But how did you go about getting the Godhead in?"

"We built an organ for it," said the Mormon. "We sought out the choicest wood and brought it three hundred miles by oxen. It is the finest wood for music in the whole of America. The Holy Spirit does not live in words, although it sometimes has to resort to them when dealing with unmusical people; the Holy Spirit lives in music. When they were both ready, the organ and the Tabernacle, the Spirit was so pleased that it came to stay there of its own accord. Yes sirree. The greatest maestros in the world have travelled to Utah specially to play on this instrument, which they say gives forth more moving sounds than any other mortal instrument."

"This is all most remarkable," said Steinar. "For a man who usually comes home from market with nothing but a few cobbler's needles, that's something at last to tell his children."

"There are few people in Iceland who have been accused of

lying as often as Bishop Þjóðrekur," said the Mormon. "And you should not believe me, either. Seeing is better than hearing, my friend. Go and see for yourself."

"I think I would give quite a lot to be able to go and see your casket," said Steinar. "Happy the man who has a share in such a casket. It could well be the treasure worthy of my little daughter who slept so well, and the little boy I mentioned. If I were not setting off for Iceland on the steam-ship the day after tomorrow, I would readily take the trouble of trekking across the wilderness for the sake of the children."

"God's charges are certainly high," said the Mormon, "but He never gives short measure."

18

Visiting the Bishop's House

We have now heard how Steinar of Hlíðar in Steinahlíðar left Iceland to visit his horse at the Danish king's residence; how he delivered the gift he brought and received for it few thanks and fewer titles, and then started to drink water in Denmark. But as was previously explained, this water brought him a drinking-companion who was to mould his destiny for a time—the man who was once tethered to a boulder outside a church in Iceland.

After a while, Steinar revealed his curiosity to see this country that the Lord of Hosts had indicated as part of true doctrine. If all the needs of soul and body were provided in that country, then Steinar thought it obvious that Joseph Smith propounded a truer doctrine than the Danish kings, and he wanted his children to benefit therefrom. Hence it followed that he, old Steinar of Hlíðar, on behalf of himself and his family, should become a disciple of this revelation; but he added that he was sadly short of the funds required to betake himself across land and sea to the other side of the earth. But the hardest thing of all would be to explain such a journey to his family.

"What God inspires you to, you need neither explain nor justify to men," said Bishop Þjóðrekur. "It has never been reported that the Saviour made any long speeches to His mother when He left her to go forth and redeem the world, or the prophet Joseph when he said goodbye to the cattle-bums in Palmyra and went off to restore Christendom. And since you deserve nothing but good of me, my friend, I shall see just how much I can scrape together for your sake."

In short, Steinar was now so overwhelmed by the news that Zion was to be found on earth, with vacancies available, that he did not catch the last autumn ship to Iceland. His funds were now exhausted, and he went into town to do some trading. On one and the same day he visited a butcher, a baker, and a rope-maker and offered to sell them some excellent pictures which royalty had given him. They told him to go to hell; such pictures, they said, were no ornament to a home, and anyway they were printed in the newspapers every day; the butcher said that pictures of royalty made everyone in Denmark sick. The rope-maker said that pictures of kings were not worth the string people needed to hang themselves with. But the baker said that Steinar could have one pastry gratis for each king. Then Steinar went into a shop to see a girl he knew sold haberdashery, for he had once bought from her a button for his overcoat. He gave this girl the medallion from Olga Konstantinovna, whom he described as nearly a perfect example to other women, both in beauty and modesty. The shop-girl thanked the Icelander courteously for the gift, and gave him a packet of needles in return.

Not long after the ship for Iceland had sailed, Bishop Þjóðrekur of Utah came to visit Steinar in the Seamen's Home.
Steinar was sitting in his cubicle, eating pastries and thinking
rather melancholy thoughts. The bishop, without any philosophical preliminaries, pulled out of his pocket his purse, which
was wrapped in a handkerchief fastened with three safety pins. In
this purse were some American dollars which he gave Steinar to
pay for his fare to God's City of Zion. He told Steinar to join a
company of Scandinavian Mormons who were on the point of
leaving after they had been properly immersed in clean water as a
token of baptism and spiritual salvation. There were also some
others, their dependants, who had shown inclinations towards
being converted. Þjóðrekur asked Steinar whether he wished to
embrace the Gospel, which is what Mormons call it when someone is converted to the true Golden Book from Heaven which
Joseph Smith found on Hill Cumorah. Steinar replied that he
was a poor man with no resources other than his little bit of commonsense, which he on no account wanted to ignore, however
small it might be; he said that persuasions which people adopted
in defiance of their commonsense would not be much of an asset
to them, least of all when the need was greatest. A country which
prophets, apostles, and church-fathers preached from a Golden
Book could not be justly praised until one had actually lived
there; because the human heart is not discriminating, although
some people have excellent hearts, of course, and there is no limit
to the absurdities of which the head can convince one; but the
mouth and the stomach are the most dependable organs, unpalat-
able as the fact may seem. Þjóðrekur replied icily that he had no
wish to trick anyone into believing the doctrines which Joseph
and Brigham had propounded; every single person was free to
make his own body the touchstone of truth, particularly those who

think that the soul is an imbecile. If Steinar, at the end of his explorations in the Territory of Utah, thought that God had told lies to the Mormons, he could go right back to where he came from. They agreed on these terms that Steinar should go to America without immersion.

Þjóðrekur said that this group was first to sail to England and there await a ship to take them across the Atlantic before Christmas. He said that they were not to expect to receive any great privileges in England; and this, indeed, turned out to be correct, for they were given labels around their necks like cattle bound for the slaughterhouse, and were herded into emigration camps for three weeks with few comforts and only soup and dry bread to eat. But when they reached the Mormon office in New York, said Bishop Þjóðrekur, no one would need to chew dulse nor drink water; they would get steak and milk more than once a day, and heaps of vegetables; there was no question of gruel there, he said, which turned out to be true; there were many who would have liked never to leave the place.

"After that you will be put on board a steam-train," said the bishop. "It runs for a long time through low-lying and fertile countryside, and then over extensive deserts which were utterly trackless in my time, so that we had to pioneer our own paths over the rugged, rocky ground. Now there are no hindrances on the way, except for the bison which wander across the rails in long lines and obstruct the train. The wilderness is overgrown with a type of fibrous-rooted brushwood that the natives call sagebrush, which needs no water and is fatal to all animals. Red-skinned men sometimes come creeping out of this brushwood; in attitude of mind and accomplishments they are not unlike the Icelandic saga-men of old—they use bows and arrows like Gunnarr of Hlíðarendi and never miss their mark. It is not so unusual for the passengers to have to get down from the train and do battle with them."

Steinar said, "The last thing I expected, when I left Iceland, was that I would have to fight Gunnarr of Hlíðarendi."

"When you eventually reach journey's end in Salt Lake Valley," said Bishop Þjóðrekur, "do nothing except ask for the main road to Spanish Fork, and say you are from Iceland. Everyone will kiss you in welcome. Ask to be directed to the mail-coach for Provo. From there you go on foot, following the main road all the way. On your left and a little ahead of you lies a higher mountain than Icelanders have ever seen, named Mount Timpanogus after a Red Indian queen. The ravines in it are ten times deeper than Almannagjá (Everyman Chasm). Here Icelanders can indulge themselves herding sheep in leafy woods, with no storms to care about and therefore no need for schnapps, either. Right at the top of this high mountain, at about twice the height of the glacier Öræfajökull there grows an innocent and kindly tree known as the poplar aspen. I keep two flocks of sheep on this mountain. But that's just by the way. Where had we got to? Just be careful not to stray from the road, my friend. All of a sudden you will find Mount Timpanogus behind you, and a new mountain appears; it looks as if it had been cut with scissors from a folded piece of paper. This is called Sierra Benida, where the sun rises over Spanish Fork; some old woman went up there once with a bucket and spade to prospect for silver and gold. You carry on along the main road and ignore all other houses until you come to one that stands at the crossroads. This is No. 214, the Bishop's House. Inside the gate, the sagebrush grows all the way up to the veranda, for I want to have the desert all around

me and in it I want to die. There is a veranda along the whole
front of the house on the ground floor, and that is where the door
is, with two windows on either side. The house is built partly of
bricks, which I baked myself, and partly of logs. The upper
storey stands on pillars. On the upper floor there is a balcony
with a carved balustrade. Many a good man has slept up there,
for in the Territory of Utah it is healthy to sleep outside except in
midwinter, which barely lasts until February; and there is none
of these appalling late-winter months as in Iceland, when people
starve and the livestock perish.

"Don't trouble to knock on the door, for we disapprove of
knocking. Three sisters will come out to meet you with my middle sister's children; but you are not to give any of them my
regards. Tell them I send them nothing, but will be back myself
in three years; I am with the king, composing a pamphlet for
the Icelanders. The sisters have plenty of pigs and fifteen sheep
and as many vegetables as they wish, as well as Pastor Runólfur
to hold services for the sheep in his frock-coat. We call him
Ronki. Say that you are to sleep upstairs on a bench on the balcony. If you want a job, have a word with the old one with the
spectacles. On the other side of the road, just a stone's throw
away, is my bricklayer's yard; tell the woman that you have permission to go there to make bricks if you like. Tell her to have
some clay fetched for you, and get some straw from Ronki. Tell
the middle sister to make sure that the children come to no
harm, because I am not in a position to look after them. I cannot
help being always a little anxious about children. Tell her that
truth must always take precedence, and this is something
women must learn to accept. And tell my poor old María that if
the King of Angels has ever sent a truly saintly person to the

Vestmannaeyjar, then it is she. And remember, if you are ever immersed, to have yourself immersed as well for all your dead kinsmen whom you don't want to consign head-first to Hell. You can sell the bricks or give them away as you think fit. For my own part, I have given away more bricks than I have sold. Bricks are a good gift, which is more than you can say for gems; and a Christian gift at that."

Steinar Steinsson of Hlíðar thanked Bishop Þjóðrekur with all his heart and kissed him in farewell. But when they had said goodbye, Steinar remembered that he had forgotten a small trifle:

"Since it looks as if you will be in Iceland before me," he said, "and it could well be that you happen to meet a little woman under a big mountain, I want to ask you to give her this packet of needles."

And with that they parted.

Steinar knocked three times on Bishop Þjóðrekur's door after travelling halfway round the world. It was in a broad desert valley which turned green in winter, in contrast to valleys in Iceland; and lo! to the north stood a high mountain which made Iceland's mountains look like hillocks, the way a troll makes men look like dwarfs; and to the east stood a barren hill, no doubt full of silver and gold, as neatly and symmetrically shaped as if it had been cut with scissors.

The woman who came to the door—it was the one with the spectacles—was shrivelled with age and deeply wrinkled. She said imperiously, like an elf-woman, "Who is rapping at this house?"

"It is only proper to give a knock for each one of the Trinity when one knocks at a bishop's door, and good day to you, good woman," said the visitor.

"The Holy Spirit is not praised by knocking," said the woman. "But we allow Lutherans to give two knocks, in the name of the Father and the Son."

After this reprimand she changed her tone, offered the visitor her hand, and asked what she could do for him.

Steinar explained how it came about that he was standing there, and that he had been sent by the bishop himself. He delivered his message that the bishop did not actually send his regards in the mundane sense, and did not send his sisters any of those gifts which could be considered a vanity in this world, but his blessings instead, with assurances of everlasting exaltation and glory.

"You spoilt it there," said the woman. "Rikki would never say any such thing. How is he, poor fellow?"

"He asked me to say that he was in Denmark, where the king lives, composing a pamphlet for the Icelanders, and would not be back for three years."

"Do you hear that, sisters?" said the woman with the spectacles, and in a twinkling two other women appeared on the scene. "Our Rikki is with that terrible man who drank the lifeblood of Icelanders for many centuries until we had nothing but the shirts on our backs, and some not even that."

"I would rather not hear people speak ill of Denmark," said Steinar, "least of all now that I have just arrived safe and sound in Heaven. For I can testify that Denmark has water called Kirsten Piil water, the best in the world. Bishop Þjóðrekur and I partook of that water together."

"Now we've heard everything, María dear," said the middle sister, who was comparatively young and brisk. She was leading by the arm an ancient purblind woman who was shaped like a flour-sack. The old woman's fingers were twisted out of shape like frost-tormented twigs; and the backs of her hands were swollen. She was practically bald. And when she smiled there were no teeth to be seen, just a maternal warmth that would, however, scarcely have appealed to anyone but infants; and perhaps men under sentence of death. At her skirts there clung some wide-eyed children.

"I can see that you must be the woman I was to ask to take care that the children came to no harm," said the visitor, shaking by the hand this middle sister who was so plump and buxom.

"Hark at him, María, how formal he is," said the middle sister, and slapped her thigh.

"It is only proper in a bishop's house, at least to begin with," said the visitor.

"How can Rikki imagine that the children could come to any harm before María's eyes!" said the middle sister.

"For goodness sake ask the visitor in and cook him some dinner," said the old woman María, and it turned out that she could neither say *r* nor *s* on account of her toothlessness.

Steinar Steinsson doffed his hat involuntarily. He took hold of the old woman's warped hands and kissed her reverently to show her his respect, but did not manage on this occasion to repeat the message that Bishop Þjóðrekur had asked him to deliver to her.

"The poor man, to come all this long way on his own," said the old woman, feeling Steinar Steinsson with her twisted fingers both on the face and the body. "It's quite sure that God has something in mind for us all. I am pretty certain I still have some grains of coffee in the tin since our Lutheran was here the weekend before last."

"Only if Pastor Runólfur has not appropriated it as usual," said the middle sister.

This was the sort of house which used to be found in Iceland

in occasional places, but was rare in other countries: its doors
stood open to visitors and passers-by night and day, with refreshment always on hand however long they might wish to stay. Such
houses never seemed over-crowded. No one ever objected to dis-
agreeable visitors, although there were many who were not particularly congenial. The host never expected any payment of any
kind for the hospitality; it was taken for granted that all travellers were destitute, and that rich people did not move from
their homes. At Bishop Þjóðrekur's house in God's City of Zion
the only demand made on visitors was that they should walk
straight in without knocking. Lutherans would be forgiven for
two knocks; a third knock was an affront to the Holy Spirit.

Most of those who were put up in Bishop Þjóðrekur's house
were homeless Icelanders, some of them newly arrived, while
others had managed to find the truth in the Promised Land with
their unreliable heads and even more undiscriminating hearts,
but rather less with the more dependable organs. Many of Þjóðrekur's guests made their own homes eventually. Among those
who had been there a long time was the Reverend Runólfur, former pastor for Hvalsnes. On account of a divine vocation he had
abandoned his living in Iceland to serve the smallest and sorriest
Lutheran church in the world, which three eccentric families had
founded right in the heart of God's city of Zion. After he came to
America he gradually became a Mormon, and was baptised by
immersion. Shortly thereafter the windows of the Lutheran church
were boarded up. No one really knew what it was that impeded
Pastor Runólfur's advancement in Zion, for there were few who
pursued correct thinking with greater zeal than he after his con-
version, and even fewer who had a better knowledge of what they
believed; for he, as a man of learning, had closely studied the
Golden Book as well as the Prophet's revelations and books of

the original saints. Other men, some of them ignorant and indo-
lent, swarmed up the ladder of ecclesiastical preferment straight
from the floor of the byre, as it were, and became counsellors in
their Wards, as they called their parishes, or even Ward Bishops,
if they were not hoisted straight up into the Stake (which super-
vises the bishoprics) and made Elders, Seventies, Melchizedek
High Priests or even Apostles before the cow had time to low
thrice. But Pastor Runólfur willy-nilly had to stick to these fifteen ewes that Bishop Þjóðrekur had put in his charge six years
ago, on the day he was immersed. He had still advanced no farther than the post of Ward Assistant. Yet no one was better
suited to rally the waverers, and especially to wrangle with
Lutherans; he wrangled some of them out of the house and others
off their land and some even out of the country. It could well be
that this talent for disputation was considered a two-edged
weapon, and give the Mormons cause for alarm. But the fifteen
ewes in his care, whose numbers he had to keep steady however
many of them were slaughtered, even if they were all put to the
knife at the same time—they took to the pastor and throve, particularly their tails, which were not at all like the tails one sees in
Iceland, but long and full. Bishop Þjóðrekur was so tolerant in
religious matters that he instructed the three sisters always to
run up a new Lutheran frock-coat for Pastor Runólfur when the
old one was worn out, in accordance with the custom that an
army general who has been taken prisoner by the enemy is
allowed to wear his uniform as long as he so desires, and his
sword too if it is not lost or broken. This short, nimble-footed
slender man with the watery eyes and the face pulled crosswise,
always frock-coated in the desert—this was the man who undertook to train Steinar Steinsson in correct thinking.

And since Pastor Runólfur was a most knowledgeable man,

and somewhat free of tongue, he was quick to give strangers an insight into people's affairs in the district, including the family relationships in the bishop's residence. Runólfur said that Bishop Þjóðrekur owned three wives, but that people believed that he had only ever loved the woman he had brought from Iceland into the wilderness, where she had perished of thirst. He had buried her in the sand. After her death he carried their baby in his arms farther into the wilderness for a while, but the child's life ebbed away until all movement was stilled. Bishop Þjóðrekur buried it in a sand-dune and planted over it a cross made of two straws. This child was said to have been a little girl. Bishop Þjóðrekur was one of the pioneers from Iceland who had bought the Promised Land for the price it was worth.

Crossing the wilderness in the same party in which Bishop Þjóðrekur had brought his beloved and lost her was a middle-aged woman, travelling alone; she was called Anna, and wore iron spectacles. She was fifteen years older than Bishop Þjóðrekur. She had shared her water-supply with the mother and daughter to the very last drop. She relieved him by lulling the baby to sleep at night after Þjóðrekur's beloved had died; and for this, Þjóðrekur was grateful to her. When the survivors reached the Kingdom of Saints, he proposed to her and married her at the same time as he sealed a union to all eternity with the one who now lay in the sand. Anna had since then been in charge of his household, and was known as Járnanna (Iron-Anna). They gave the church one half of everything they earned, and fasted four times as often as the laws prescribed; they baked bricks and built houses for people and raised Welshmen and Danes, as well as Icelanders, out of the holes in the ground in which the pioneers lived, and which were called dugouts. For this and many other social deeds Þjóðrekur was made Ward-leader, Elder, High Priest, Bishop, Stake-president, and one of the Twelve Apostles of the Lamb, according to the Saviour's choosing in the Prophecy of Nephi in the Time of Grace and the Dispensation of the Fullness of Times. This was the man whom the Icelanders had bound to a tethering-block, gagged, and beaten during divine service.

Wandering about in Salt Lake Valley and its environs at that time was a destitute woman who said she had been born into this world in Colornay. Some learned Englishman in the Stake thought that this was a town in France; but later it turned out to be a place in Iceland called Kjalarnes. She was a tall and stately woman; she had been held up by a troop of soldiers (when people in America say that someone is held up, they mean that he or she was threatened at gun-point). At this time the Federal Government of the United States had begun to send to God's City of Zion armed troops to persuade the saints to abandon the Moral Law which had been manifested to them by God and proclaimed by the Church, including holy polygamy. These troops had put the girl in the family way. Next year she was held up by Redskins; these men use bows and arrows and kill people with great artistry, like Gunnarr of Hlíðarendi, as was written before. On account of these hold-ups the innocent girl was ostracised by various nationalities, particularly by the Welsh and Danish, who at that time vied with one another in living the pure life in Spanish Fork. There were not many people who wanted to have such an outcast in their homes, and she often had to spend the night in the tamarisk thickets on the banks of the salt-springs where frogs croaked and grasshoppers and crickets chirred. Her young children also slept with her there. One Christmas, Bishop Þjóðrekur rescued this wretched woman and her two children from the hollow in the ground where they were living, and said that it was contrary to Joseph's Book and the doctrines preached by Brigham Young, the Prophet's dedicated disciple, that women should be bedded out in the open by soldiers and Redskins to no good purpose. The Lord had purposely instituted polygamy by direct revelation in order that no woman should have to lie outside in ditches with her family at Christmas. It was the express duty and law of the Church of Latter-Day Saints that Mormons should protect as many women as possible with the seal of eternal matrimony instead of making them outcasts and jeering at them. On the basis of this conviction, Bishop Þjóðrekur invited Madame Colornay into his house and took her to wife along with Járnanna, whose spectacles were then becoming badly rusted. He also sealed to himself the children she had conceived during the hold-ups, and begat a couple more with her himself. With this, Bishop Þjóðrekur earned himself still more respect in Spanish Fork; it showed how much he excelled other men, in that his benevolence and wisdom matched his fearlessness towards the prejudices of the Welsh and the Danes. And no one supported him so steadfastly in this act of piety as his first wife, Járnanna.

Nor did Bishop Þjóðrekur's standing in the district lessen, particularly in the eyes of the wives he had already, when he decided to marry for a third time and seal to himself in heavenly matrimony poor old María from Ampahjallur, who was fully seventy years old, crippled with arthritis and blind. She too had trekked across the wilderness.

This María hailed from the Vestmannaeyjar and had never been associated with a man in her life. She had come to America as a servant to a family from the islands. It was her task to carry the children across the wilderness and support their sick mother.

Then the mother perished, as was the custom in the wilderness at that time. María did not abandon the children when the journey was over; she reared them herself and sewed every stitch of clothing they wore, taught them Hallgrímur Péturrson's Passion Hymns, and told them parables about saintly people in the Vestmannaeyjar. She never let an angry word to man nor beast pass her lips; she was also one of those Icelanders who never speak ill of the weather. When her orphan brood had flown away and scattered to the four corners of the earth (some had gone to the war), she took upon herself another family of children who had lost their bread-winners. This brood too she reared to adulthood with wisdom from the Vestmannaeyjar and long night-vigils of knitting and washing even though she was now nearly blind; but most particularly with the kind of affection that fears nothing and grudges nothing. Time passed, and soon these children too were gone into the wide world to acquire all the things that María Jónsdóttir had never enjoyed. But word got around that there was an Icelandic woman who could bring herself to love other people's children, and so María was asked to look after some orphaned Danish children in the holy city that the wicked called Salt Lake Puddle. She set off towards this good city, bent with age, half-blind, and destitute. The Danish children did not understand the Passion Hymns and so she had to make do with telling them parables about good folk in the Vestmannaeyjar and about young birds called puffins which were pulled out of their burrows in the cliffs there and made into puffin soup, until these children too were ready to say goodbye. The old bent woman was left behind on the broad streets of the holy city, alone, friendless, and homeless. And when she went out for a stroll she was knocked down on the road and injured. The police took her to a hospital there in Salt Lake Puddle. She said her name was María Jónsdóttir from Ampahjallur in the Vestmannaeyjar. It was then advertised in Spanish Fork that a lone and blind old woman from the Vestmannaeyjar, Iceland, had been found lying injured on the road. No sooner did Bishop Þjóðrekur hear this than he harnessed his horses and drove his carriage to Salt Lake Puddle. He went to see the woman in hospital and greeted her respectfully and asked her to marry him with due seals of eternal matrimony in the temple before God. Then he gave her a dollar to buy herself coffee. He told the hospital superintendent to send him word when her broken bones had healed, and he would return to fetch her in his carriage. When the time came, he married her with all proper ceremony and took her home to the Bishop's House, 214 Main Street, Spanish Fork. María took it upon herself to rear the children that Madame Colornay had brought into the world, and taught them Pastor Hallgrímur's beautiful prayers as well as pious tales from the Vestmannaeyjar. María said she hoped that the Lord of Hosts would be pleased to send her other people's children to have around her for as long as she was granted grace to be able to knit a sock.

19

God's City of Zion

The hoofbeats of cantering horses, large and small, sounded on the road, and the creak of axles and wheels. The foals that trotted behind looked confident but a little pensive. Men and women went riding past on important business, the women on saddles but the young boys riding bareback in pairs on old hacks, as they do in Iceland when they are herding cows. The neighbours stepped up on to the veranda to greet the visitor from Iceland. They asked for news of home. But no sooner had he started to talk than a distant look came into the eyes of the questioners. Iceland vanished as soon as its name was spoken. Their speech was as perfect, certainly, as the chirping of birds, and so polished on the outside and scrubbed on the inside that it took particular dexterity to introduce a foreign phrase; but if one used an old proverb or some well-known quotation from the sagas, people smiled amiably and absently, and had already forgotten it.

The weather in Iceland last year and the year before last concerned them no more than the hydrocarbon halo around Sirius. News of men and affairs in Iceland only prompted them to expatiate on the great events of the present Kingdom of Saints and cite Joseph Smith's Golden Book, or praise his successor Brigham Young, that chosen leader who towered over not only the mountains of the Territory of Utah but the whole of the western hemisphere as well. Iceland, with its little parish officials and low mountains, its ever-hungry soil-grubbers who composed ballads, and its one (at most) well-to-do person per district—was it any wonder that such a country, in the minds of these Zion-dwellers, had faded away to the far side of the moon? Seldom had a country been so utterly lost to a people as Iceland was to those Mormons.

Pastor Runólfur always took newcomers from Iceland into the enclosure to show them the sheep he looked after for Bishop Þjóðrekur, to let them admire how beautiful and thick their tails were compared with the stumps on Icelandic sheep.

This is the place, Brigham Young had said when the Mormons finally came down off the plateau on to the shoulders of the mountain and looked out over the great basin with its unbroken soil, spring streams and cool groves. The Mormons never tired of recalling how only half an hour after their arrival in the Promised Land they unloaded an apology of a plough from a ramshackle cart which some emaciated oxen had dragged step by step in the name of Jesus across the endless wastes of America; now these bullocks stood there with the placidly sullen expression of beasts in the Bible, with blood on their hooves, shaking their heads so that their slaver glistened in the blazing sun and drinking from a stream; and the men had started to plough.

After the stories about the trek across the wilderness came the episodes from the life of the early settlers, when everyone lived in dugouts—trenches which they raftered with ropes or roofed over with hides. Very few of the people had any clothes other than the hides of game-animals; some managed to get skins of mountain-goats or antelopes, others of deer or bison from which they made skin-hose or moccasins. Gradually the age of wool began, the days of the spindle and distaff. Brigham Young himself testified in all sincerity about the saints who were in his company, that some had blankets but many had none: "Some had shirts, but I think there were also some who had none, neither for themselves nor their families," said the pioneer who led people to a greater bliss in this world and the next than most other leaders have ever done.

When they had sown their grain that first year, a host of grass-hoppers swooped on the crops like a cloud-burst. The people tried every means to beat them off, but the grasshoppers showed no signs of moving once they had settled. People could see their precious grain, which they had gone to such pains to transport, being utterly destroyed before their very eyes, and starvation and death looming. But God, who never failed his prophet Joseph, sent the bird which the Mormons have ever since held dear; it was the seagull, and Mormons call it their bird. The gulls flew a thousand miles from the sea to their help, and ate up all the grass-hoppers. And the saints of the wilderness had their first bread.

Spanish Fork was now full of homely farmhouses built of sun-baked bricks; the log-cabins were disappearing fast, and in the dugouts lived only the occasional Lutheran. Practically everyone had a best-room with a picture of the Prophet and his brother Hyrum and also of Brigham Young. On the table lay the Book of Mormon and The Pearl of Great Price. Those cultural institu-

tions that transform a village into a town were already in existence: a community centre, Post Office and a shop. God (in the
person of Zion's Co-operative Mercantile Institution) owned the
shop. His eye was painted over the shop-doors, surrounded by
rays like the spines of a sea-urchin, and the slogan "Holy is the
Lord." The Church owned the community centre, and the Territory owned the Post Office. The Church owned the right to allot
land; in addition to the wilderness, it owned mountains and hill-
pastures where sheep could fend for themselves. The Church had
also started to compete with the pagans at mining ore; and it
owned the water which was led from the hidden arteries of the
mountains to irrigate the fields. All the arrangements prescribed
by the Church authorities, even if alterations were made in the
original arrangements, bore witness, altered or unaltered, to
God's personal guidance and what was called correct thinking.
Everything people earned or acquired proved that the doctrine
had its origin in cosmic law. New shoes and a new hat were matter for eulogising the Church of the Latter-day Saints and the
prophecies of the great leaders. Mules, these rather solemn beasts
which combine the best qualities of the horse and the ass except
the ability to breed—were they not remarkable proof of the
Golden Book's special guidance in all things, large or small?
Who, more than the saints, had made of this unique and model
creature such a useful servant? Steinar Steinsson was shown a pri-
mary school where a specially-trained English-speaking teacher
was employed to instruct the common children in the learning
that would enhance a man's status in the world. These men and
their wives who had lived there in dugouts two decades earlier
and wrapped themselves in skins for their faith in the Prophet—
could there be more tangible proof of the truth of these prophe-

cies than such a fount of wisdom for the populace? Even the most progressive nations in the world, which had for long enough lived in the shelter of one special grace—where were their schools for the common people? Only the children of the wealthy and the unrighteous received any schooling in the Old World. Come and see for yourself one day how happy the children are to be able to listen to a man of learning! Was it not as if the children who once had been laid to rest in the sand were here being re-born into a life of happiness? Or take this pram, for example! A pram, just fancy that! Yes, all hand-made by a skilled Mormon, copied from a pram in a catalogue from New England. On four wheels, upon my life and soul. See how the superstructure is made from artistically twisted metal rods: they first go in a circle and then into another circle, sometimes like the figure 8, sometimes like the letter *S.* Who but counts and barons could have dreamed up such a treasure in that part of the world where correct thinking does not prevail?

"But there is one thing perhaps which proves better than any-thing else how far this nation has advanced, and that is the sewing machine. I could only just pronounce the word," said Pastor Runólfur, "because I had heard it in the capital. Was there any sewing machine where you lived, in Steinahlíðar?"

"I must admit there was not," said Steinar Steinsson.

"There you are!" said the Reverend Runólfur. "Only counts and barons abroad have sewing machines; yet here in Spanish Fork there is a sewing machine. You run a piece of cloth through it and in a trice it has become a garment that fits you like a glove. The cosmic wisdom that lives in the words of the Prophet and the deeds of Brigham Young does not manifest itself exclusively in enormous truths which can only be encompassed in the brains of fearfully large-headed University professors; no, it lives also in the sewing machines of people who yesterday had correct thoughts, certainly, but no shirt. It is the bliss of mortal man to have been led to this land."

"It cannot be denied," said Steinar Steinsson, "that it needs a lot of philosophy to match a sewing machine."

Unfortunately they never got round to showing Steinar this sewing machine at the time, and whenever he asked about it later some hitch always cropped up. But nevertheless the little fellow from Hlíðar was convinced that everything there testified to the cosmic wisdom, even the cross on the Lutheran Church, because it had been broken off.

Small things and large things alike contributed to convince him. The time now came when Pastor Runólfur felt that Steinar was sufficiently convinced and began to think in terms of having him immersed, but said that he could not bring himself to have him baptized in the customary village pond which was full of poisonous trout, serpents, and insects that bit people in the leg. He said that he wanted to round off Steinar's instruction by taking him to the capital city of the faith, which was called Salt Lake City, whatever some wits were pleased to call this holy shrine amongst cities. He wanted to show Steinar the glory of the city and then take him to one of the Elders and have him consecrated in a temple service.

"When you yourself have been immersed according to ritual," said Pastor Runólfur, "you have the right to have any of your departed kinsmen baptized whom you think worthy of it; you have yourself immersed once for each of them, so that they have the opportunity to build a holy sanctuary in that world of light they now inhabit. Perhaps I could scribble down their names now so that we can apply for a recommendation for them from the Elder."

Steinar tittered, as was his custom when faced with a problem, and replied after a little thought that neither his father nor his mother was among those he thought needed baptizing in the world of light they inhabited now, because he knew of no couple more patient than they in adversity nor more constant in giving to everyone his or her due; he reckoned they had been a particularly unpretentious couple. He said he had a long way to go before he would be competent to improve such excellent people's circumstances with God.

"But," he added, "there are others of my kinsmen I am more concerned about than mother and father and for whose sake I would gladly let myself be immersed again once or twice. First of all there is my progenitor Egill Skallagrímsson and my ancestors the Norse kings, and last but not least King Harald hilditönn of Denmark, who was the first of my line."

Salt Lake City is a place, of course, where the highest truth is a little complicated in parts, as is only to be expected; but the more simple facts are more obvious than in other cities. It is quite impossible to get lost in it. One can see the whole city lying in its basin under the Wasatch Mountains. It is laid out according to the fundamental principles of logic and the first diagrams in the geometry book. One always knows where one is in that city; and one also knows at once in what direction and how far away other places in the city are. It is a city where the cardinal points have been revealed to people through God's inscrutable power and grace. For a man newly-arrived from a country where the nation had grown bent at the knees from riding too much along narrow bridle-paths—was it any wonder that he was impressed by the fact that God had prescribed in public writ that the streets there should be as wide as the home-fields in Steinahlíðar?

Was it likely that the streets of Zion in Heaven were any wider than these streets in Zion on earth? Steinar thought it better to pace the streets out for himself rather than have to rely on guesswork or hearsay about it. When he and Pastor Runólfur had measured the streets at a few points and found that they were nowhere less than two hundred Icelandic feet in width, they sat down on a kerb-stone, wiped the sweat from their brows, and brought out paper and pencil and began to multiply the width of the streets by their length.

Pastor Runólfur asked whether Steinar did not want to see the house where Brigham Young kept his twenty-seven wives, this man who had laid out the city according to God's wishes. Steinar agreed willingly and said that, all things considered, he thought it no less a feat to have so many wives than to stake out God's City of Zion upon earth. They came to a long wooden house, in which there were certainly plenty of doors; these doors were in a row along the whole length of the house. To match them, jutting from the roof directly above each door was a little garret where each wife had a boudoir with a window. The whole house was exceptionally well-built; the outer planking was fitted together with painstaking care and painted grey with a tinge of blue. All the doors had the same fittings and the same doorstep, twenty-seven copper door-handles and as many locks. From every door there breathed coolness without any whiff of human habitation; there were no finger-marks visible on the doors or bolts. The house was imbued with some incorporeal cleanliness akin to frost-work or even mirages. At the garret-windows were the same white clean curtains, twenty-seven times over. And as Pastor

Runólfur and Steinar stood out in the street holding their breaths and gazing at this smooth and silent shrine of cleanliness, they had the feeling that twenty-seven women were laughing at them behind the curtains; they even felt a little self-conscious.

Pastor Runólfur whispered, "I am ashamed to say so, but every time I look at that house I am reminded of the monster which came ashore at the Vestmannaeyjar when my late grandfather was the pastor there. It was an enormous, slimy, lump-sucker of a thing. People went for it and stabbed it with twenty-seven big knives, but all that the stabbing did was to open twenty-seven greedy maws. Sometimes I can't help thinking about Buddha's belly, which is inhabited by ten thousand women."

"Although it is as peaceful here as a graveyard," said Steinar, "and no one seems to want to bite us, it was never considered good manners in Steinahlíðar to stare up at people's windows without making oneself known."

"Ought we to knock and ask for a sip of water? No one could find fault with that," said Pastor Runólfur, and began with clerical elegance to finger his cravat, which in fact had not existed since he ceased to be the pastor for Hvalsnes.

"Although I am thirsty, I think I shall refrain from having a drink in this house," said Steinar of Hlíðar. I suggest we go on our way."

When they had set off he continued, "I always pitied blessed Abraham, whom God forced to have two wives, to say nothing about old Solomon, whom God castigated with three."

"Three hundred," interposed Pastor Runólfur.

"It makes no difference to me whether it was three or three hundred," said Steinar. "I always name the lesser number. Many a man with only the one wife is inclined to think that when God instituted the sacraments he forgot one, the sacrament of divorce.

I have been married for nearly twenty years, come to that. And yet, when I stood for the first time on Bishop Þjóðrekur's threshold and was greeted by three sisters, I realised that God is always right—just as much when he ordained monogamy as when he ordained polygamy; twenty-seven wives, one door; one wife, twenty-seven doors."

When Steinar Steinsson first heard the Tabernacle mentioned, and was told that it was a casket, he had confused the word with "tobacco" and thought it was a snuff-mull. On this particular day he stood at last before the doors of this marvel of architecture, the greatest in the Western hemisphere. It was built to measurements that God intimated to Brigham at a time when nails had not yet been seen in God's city of Zion, or any other devices for holding a building together. This building is lower in relation to its length than any other structure of comparable size. Icelanders call it God's Word-Hall, meaning God's mouth, because its proportions are the same as the inside of the human mouth. The faithful say that with such a mouth did God speak to the Church Fathers. The acoustics are so remarkable that if the name of the Lord is whispered at the altar it can be heard as a shout at the door. Steinar and Pastor Runólfur borrowed a pin from a distinguished-looking lady who was studying God's miracle with a very patronizing air; and when they dropped the pin at the innermost part of the chancel everyone jumped and thought an iron bar had fallen on the altar. Pastor Runólfur went over to the lady and returned the pin to her with thanks and asked rather smugly whether she were not now convinced that Holy Wisdom, as it was called in Greek, was more present here than in other kingdoms. Steinar had now obtained permission to climb up into the roof of the building and clamber along the cross-beams and rafters to investigate for himself exactly how the All-Wisdom had built it without having to make a seventy-day trek across the wilderness to buy nails; and he was rather impressed to find that the learned architects had been inspired with the idea of using thongs of ox-hide. There was also an organ there with wooden pipes whose timber had been gathered in some far-off magic forest. While the two Icelanders were in the Tabernacle the organist came in and played on it so beautifully that they said afterwards that while the music played they had stood there as if rooted to the floor, unable to move a muscle. Although they had never heard music before, they were so impressed by the extent to which God had finally managed to lead mankind on the road to perfection that tears were still streaming down their cheeks after they were out in the open again.

In a yard a stone's throw to the east they caught sight of a string of oxen that had just arrived with some sledges loaded with gigantic granite blocks. Pastor Runólfur said that the main temple of mankind was being built on the other side of the street there. Already, its steep walls were soaring heavenwards. This granite, which was unique in the world, was brought from a quarry in a mountain far away in the wilderness. It took a month to haul each block to the site, and teams of oxen had toiled at this task night and day for many years. The oxen stood there slavering in their harness, and still wearing their Biblical expressions as before. It was not the first time that this cloven-footed species had hauled the materials required for praising God in the way He deserves; Pastor Runólfur mentioned in this connection the Pyramids, Borobudur in Indonesia, the Ziggurat, St. Peter's Cathedral and many other structures.

These two Icelanders stood for a long time looking at the oxen standing there with eyes half-closed in divinely exalted rest while they waited for the cud to pop up through their gullets. The builders were arranging pulleys and tackle and getting ready to unload the granite blocks.

Steinar Steinsson could not resist saying, "It's amazing how far man's wisdom has led him. It would be difficult to do anything but follow such chosen leaders who have shown themselves as practical as the late Joseph Smith and his successor Brigham Young."

Pastor Runólfur did not take his eyes off the oxen. Just like the time earlier that day when they had been staring at the house with many garrets, and the pastor had alluded to the Vestman-naeyjar monster, he now made a comment which came rather like a bolt from the blue (and this perhaps was the clue to the enigma that few could explain, why such an excellent clergyman in this community of saints should be allotted no other task than that of looking after fifteen sheep which had no other merit than the fatness of their tails):

"I am not at all impressed," said Pastor Runólfur, "at how far man's wisdom has managed to lead him; besides, it is not very great. What does surprise me, on the other hand, is how high their folly, their downright stupidity even, not to say their complete and utter blindness, has managed to raise them. Other things being equal, I prefer to follow the folly of man, for that has brought him farther than his wisdom."

The oxen had started to chew the cud.

20

Learning to understand bricks

In the baptismal register of the temple he is entered as Stone P. Stanford. No one is very sure where that curious P came from; some think it was one of Pastor Runólfur's notions. In the brick-layer's yard, as it is called, clay is mixed with straw; the straw binds the clay together. When the bricks have been moulded they are baked in the sun, that sun which the Lord of Hosts has given to people of correct opinions. Under this sun the porous lumps of clay are transformed into bricks. The stones that tumble down off the mountains of Steinahlíðar on to the home-fields are as froth compared to the hand-made Utah stones sun-baked by the grace of God. This particular brickyard lies east and a little to the south of the present monument to sixteen Icelanders who were among the first to trek across the wilderness. With Bishop Þjóðrekur's permission, Ronki took Stanford to the yard and summoned the necessary people who could teach him the fundamentals of brick-making and provide him with the materials. Steinar walked around the place and studied the bricks and fingered the alien walls like a blind man. He introduced himself to the various kinds of clay. A brick-maker must be up early in the morning and have a supply of moulded bricks ready before dawn so that the sun has enough work to do when it rises.

"The Passion Hymns say it is only the ungodly who get up early," said a dawn passer-by, only a moderately saintly person, who said he was on his way home to bed. "In fact, only those who cannot sleep for wickedness, like Pastor Runólfur," he added.

"I find it distressing," said the bricklayer, "to have nothing for the sun to shine on immediately it rises. And so I am kneading a little clay."

"The sun shines on lots of things," said the passer-by, "and not all equally beautiful."

"In my opinion nothing the sun shines on is evil," said Stone P. Stanford. "If the cosmic law were not tolerant by nature, it would have created nothing but sun, and no clay. Excuse me, but where are you coming from at this time of day?"

"Since you are so tolerant," said the passer-by, "I suppose I might as well tell you. I am coming from my mistresses. I am a Lutheran."

"You should become a Mormon, my dear chap," said Stone P. Stanford. "Then you would be at liberty to have a long lie with your womenfolk."

"That's a liberty I least desire," said the Lutheran. "No one understood that better than Joseph the Prophet. He looked enviously at every coffin on its way to the grave that winter when God had commanded him to marry his sixth wife. Could I ask you to do me a little favour?"

"What is that?" asked the bricklayer.

"Would you let me hide this bottle of schnapps in one of your brick-piles?" said the Lutheran.

People who wanted to build houses for themselves or for others came by on the road where the bricklayer was standing in his yard. They weighed his bricks in their hands with an expert air and said that they were poor adobes. And crooked, too, what's more. A house built with them would soon collapse. Stanford explained that he was only making them for fun, in order to get to know bricks; he said he had for a long time wanted to understand this form of stone. "And anyway I am a light sleeper once the winter passes; and there are no women to keep me back in the mornings."

"There is never any winter here to pass," they said. "It's not like in Iceland, where winters pass. I would sleep until midday if I made such bad bricks and had no wife either. These bricks are only worth half as much as Bishop Þjóðrekur's bricks."

"I never imagined for a moment that I would be reckoned half as good at bricks as Bishop Þjóðrekur," said Stanford. "That's good enough for me. Help yourself to these bricks and do what you like with them, friend."

They drove off with Stanford's bricks and gave little in exchange. But soon afterwards some other people arrived, saying that they had heard about these bricks and would like to have a look at them. Stanford had more bricks by now. They said they were really handsome bricks and offered high prices for them and, what is more, paid for them cash down. This former farmer from Steinahlíðar, who had scarcely ever seen minted silver before, now stood there in the middle of the Promised Land clutching a handful of large silver dollars. The sun shone on the money.

After that people kept dropping in, some with mules, and drove away with the bricks he had created; and he was left standing there with money in his hands.

Stanford felt that his understanding of bricks was not complete because he had never been present when walls and other structures were being built of this kind of stone. He now got permission to accompany his products to the sites where they were being used. As was previously written, the settlers in Spanish Fork, some of them Icelandic, some Welsh and a few of them Danish, were so well off by this time that they were tearing down as fast as they could the log-cabins which their sainted fathers, the desert-trekkers, had built for themselves when they crawled out of their dugouts.

It is obvious that a man descended from many generations of expert wall-builders in Steinahlíðar who had only had mountain-rubble to work with would not take long to learn to lay stones whose shape he himself had determined. People were soon beginning to admire the house-walls he built, and said that nowhere could one see such symmetry in brick-laying, always excepting the bricks that Bishop Þjóðrekur himself had laid; in Spanish Fork people went by the old German adage, that no one is better at anything than the boss. People asked how it came about that an unknown incomer could build walls of such artistic texture. Stone P. Stanford replied, "Brick, by the grace of God, is mankind's most precious stone. That is because the brick is rectangular. That is what Bishop Þjóðrekur taught me when we drank water together in Denmark."

"Are you a Mormon or a brick-worshipper?" people asked. "In Brigham Young's mansion there are many doors," said Stone P. Stanford, and tittered.

Since manual skill was promptly appreciated in Spanish Fork

at its true worth, the bricklayer found it hard to avoid working night and day for other saints. Although his palms were often sore to begin with, particularly when he willy-nilly had to grasp handfuls of silver, he never disguised the fact that he thought that Providence had, contrary to expectation, proved a surprisingly nimble guide during these latter days.

On one occasion during an evening meeting in the church, when he had been called upon to step forward, he spoke as follows:

" 'This is the place' is what the divinely-inspired leader is reported to have said when Salt Lake Valley opened out before the slavering oxen with blood on their hooves and the men who had managed to cross the wilderness even though their children and sweethearts still tarried in the sand. Sometimes I have the feeling that I am dead and have come to the land of eternity. Of such a land it says in a hymn I once knew, that there stood a wondrous palace on pillars, inlaid with gold and brighter than the sun. I certainly never had many dreams of inheriting this palace for myself, for I am someone whom the Lord has scarcely intended to enjoy complete and utter happiness, but rather for my little children whom I left sleeping so beautifully and for the wife who was so compliant to her husband. When I now look back across the ocean to the land whence I came, I glimpse behind me a sparse and barren coast, as the hymn puts it. There stands my family, and looks sorrowing out to sea."

The generations march by, obedient to their destiny, but in Spanish Fork there still stand houses built with such reverence by this man Stanford. His walls attract the eye more than other walls, and make one want to touch them with one's fingers. Nor was this man who had made a casket for emperors and kings thought less of a craftsman in wood than in stone.

One day Stone P. Stanford was in his brickyard when a woman came by. She was good-looking and well-dressed, but a little past her prime; she was pale of complexion but dark of brow, with a veiled but penetrating gaze. She halted, leaned up against the fence that enclosed the brickyard, and stared at Sierra Benida in a trance. The sun was low in the west. Stanford greeted the woman; and when she bade good evening in return, her thin and brittle voice betrayed more self-pity and despair than circumstances seemed to warrant.

"Who are you, my good woman?" asked Stanford.

"Well, I don't rightly know," she replied. "I am probably your elf-woman here. Certainly, you've never seen me even though I walk past here every day at about this time when I go to the store."

"Many people walk past here," said Stanford. "This is a broad and handsome road."

"It's little wonder you don't notice an eyesore like me," said the woman.

"To tell you the truth, it is the mules that catch my eye most of all, I am so unaccustomed to them," said Stanford. "They are remarkably distinguished beasts."

"Sorry," said the woman. "Unfortunately I'm not a mule."

She burst into peals of laughter at the fence, and it was as if some inner tension had snapped.

"Ronki says you are called Stonpi," said the woman. "Is that true?"

"I'm ashamed to say that I, like you, no longer know myself," said Stanford, "let alone what my name is. Heeheehee."

"No wonder you don't know yourself," said the woman, and now she was no longer laughing. "Anyone who doesn't know others doesn't know himself."

The bricklayer stopped thinking of his bricks for a moment and went over to the woman at the fence and almost stealthily allowed himself to announce his old name: "Old Steinar Steinsson of Hlíðar. But perhaps not." When he had gone back to tend to his bricks, he added this philosophical epilogue: "Quite so."

"And I was once called Þorbjörg," said the woman. "Now I am called, at best, Borgi, and my daughter is called nothing at all."

"How extraordinary," said the bricklayer. "Hmmm. It has been wonderfully seasonable here this summer so far."

"Seasonable?" said the woman. "What's that?"

"I just meant that God can never be overpraised for the weather, like everything else," said the bricklayer.

"Is He not being praised here incessantly?" said the woman. "I haven't noticed any stinting of the prayer sessions. Even if you're only offered a cup of mineral water from the spring, you get a rigmarole along with it. I say for myself that I would rather have a good cup of coffee without the prayers."

"That's perfectly true, pious sir, as the woman said to the ghost; or was it to the devil?" replied the bricklayer. "And now I shall tell you what happened to me. After drinking water in Denmark nearly a year ago, I lost all desire for coffee."

The woman sighed wearily. "That's the way it always goes when you want to give someone a treat: he doesn't need it. When everyone has become sainted and is in Heaven, it's impossible to do anyone any good. Or any harm either, come to that. It's the same as in prison: everyone has everything. I had thought it would be a real act of charity to bring a lonely stranger coffee, even though it were only once a week."

"I am ashamed to say that I am not so sainted that I would turn up my nose at a cup of coffee I was offered out of kindness," said the bricklayer with a titter. "There is more to Heaven than mineral water alone. But once a week, my dear—is that not too much? Should we not say once a year? I could perhaps give you a hand some day with a brick or two if any of your walls needed repairing here and there. Hmmm. Incidentally, did I hear you aright, my dear, is the Gospel beginning to stick in your throat a little?"

"I believe what I like," said the woman in that petulant tone of voice which never left her except when she burst out laughing. She kept on staring out over the brickyard and right through her interlocutor to the mountain on the other side. "Once, when I was a girl, someone tried to explain the Gospel to me. I laughed so much that I had to be carried out on a stretcher. I married a man who was a Josephite."

"My word!" said the bricklayer. "Excuse my ignorance. What does your good husband believe in?"

"He believed that the Saviour would be coming soon," said the woman. "And he believed that when the Saviour came, He would first go to meet a man whose name I forget, who lived in Independence, Missouri. Is that wrong?"

"It is at least a most remarkable idea," said the bricklayer. "And since you have a husband, I would be just as pleased to have a talk with him and be allowed to call on you at home and drink some coffee with you both and discuss these phenomena."

"Yes, you're welcome to drink coffee with him," said the woman. "You see, he left for Independence, Missouri, eighteen years ago, to wait for Jesus Christ to descend from Heaven."

"Independence, Missouri. How extraordinary," said the bricklayer. "A remarkable place, indeed. We were always taught, back home in Iceland, that when the Saviour returned He would arrive in Jehashaphat Valley."

"If the Saviour returns at all," said the woman, "why should He not come to Independence, Missouri? But as far as I'm concerned, it doesn't matter whether He goes there or to some other place. I only know that my husband turned up missing."

"Oh, really?" said the bricklayer. "Turned up missing? You have my sympathies."

"Oh, it's not really the first time they've turned up missing hereabouts," said the woman. "They turn up missing in droves. But I think it pretty hard that the saints who can still be accounted for here in the Valley should not offer a respectable widow a helping hand, instead of exposing my daughter and myself to Lutherans. Excuse me, but has anyone left a bottle of schnapps anywhere here in a brick-pile, if I may ask? If so, I want to ask you to show me where it is, so that I can smash it against a stone."

21

Good coffee

From then on the woman brought this bricklayer coffee in a bottle once a week. She put the bottle in a sock and tucked it away under her coat. He thanked her each time most profusely for her generosity and produced the mug which he normally used for a drink of water. But he never drank more than half the bottle, and always made the woman take the rest back home with her.

"My husband always drank a whole bottle," she said.

"But then he was a Josephite," said Stone P. Stanford, but apart from that he took care not to remind the woman of how things had gone with this man.

Then the woman laughed.

She was not particularly talkative, and when he made some remark she was often so preoccupied that she did not hear what he was saying and was only roused by her own laughter.

"A thousand thanks for the coffee," he said.

"You're welcome," she said.

But when she had given him coffee for a few weeks, she suddenly said, right out of the blue, "How is it that you have been a Mormon all this while and haven't got yourself any wives yet?"

"I have one, and that is sufficient for me," he replied, and tittered.

"One wife, what's that?" she said. "It certainly wasn't considered much in the Bible, at least. Perhaps you're not a genuine Mormon?"

"I know some Mormons who are certainly no more imperfect than I and don't have any wives at all," said Stanford, naming as an example his comrade, Pastor Runólfur.

"Oh, Ronki?" said the woman and laughed. "You surely don't think that Ronki is good for anything, do you? No, it's a poor Lutheran who isn't better than old Ronki."

"You are talking about the one subject in which no male can pass judgement on another," said Stanford, "and so I say nothing."

"I wouldn't be surprised if you're still a bit of a Lutheran at heart," said the woman.

Once again, it was just before sunrise when the Lutheran returned. He went over to the brick-pile and could not find his bottle of schnapps.

"I never really liked the look of you much, and now you've proved me right," he said. "Where's my schnapps?"

"A woman came along," said the bricklayer, "and took the bottle out of the pile and broke it against a stone."

"Oh, the bitches!" said the Lutheran. "They're always themselves, day and night: they even go to the length of ransacking a pile of bricks and stealing one's last drop of consolation."

"She is a generous and capable woman," said the bricklayer.

"Since you allowed them to treat my schnapps like that, it is my dearest wish that you get to know them better. And with that I'm off, insulted and without a drink. Good night."

"It is really time to get up, so I can hardly bring myself to bid you good night; but may God be with you nonetheless, even though you wish me ill," said the bricklayer.

He accompanied his visitor out of the yard as a host should.

"To tell you the truth, I think you ought to marry this woman," said the bricklayer, putting his hand on his visitor's shoulder when they reached the gate.

"I would perhaps have done so if her daughter had not threatened to palm a child off on to me," said the Lutheran tearfully.

"All the more reason," said the bricklayer. "Embrace the Gospel and marry them both, my friend."

"Women are my ruin," said the man, wiping his face with his sleeve. "These dragons use me as a plaything and torment me. I try to betray them, but they hound me down and say they love me. If I had no schnapps to take refuge in, I would be dead."

The bricklayer replied, "That is the difference between the Latter-Day Saints and the Lutherans. The Prophet and Brigham want to give women a share in the honour and dignity which men have achieved in the eyes of God. Women are neither tobacco nor schnapps. They want to be wives, in a house. That is why Bishop Þjóðrekur married not only Anna with the iron-rimmed glasses, but also Madame Colornay and finally old María from Ampahjallur from as well."

The following week, when the woman arrived with coffee in a sock, Stone P. Stanford had vanished. He had gone off to do some bricklaying and perhaps even some joinery in various places. He was only in his brickyard for an hour at the very most to prepare the sun for its day's task at a time of day when neither Mormons nor Josephites were awake. But one day towards autumn, when the chirring of the cicadas was at its loudest and the frogs were roaring at the salt-pools, he was back in his brickyard.

"So that's how unfaithful you are," said the woman, popping her head over the fence. "You simply run away from me. I would never have believed it of a man like you, to make me wait all summer with the coffee. I was beginning to think you had turned up missing."

"That is the way we bricklayers are," he said. "All of a sudden we just turn up missing. Quite so."

"Before I lose you again I'm going to try to persuade you out to visit me at home at the far end of the street," said the woman in a high-pitched, distant voice. "I have been wanting you to have a look at something for me. Everything's falling down about my ears."

Next evening he borrowed the bishop's pram and put in it twenty-four bricks to take as a present for this stately seamstress and dream-woman.

She had a little corner house, No. 307. The brickwork was badly in need of repair in places; these were obviously poor adobes. He also thought the garden rather neglected. But to make up for it there were plenty of gaily-coloured drawers hanging on the line. He took the bricks out of the pram and stacked them neatly at the door.

She came out wearing an apron and flushed in the face from baking him a berry pie.

"Where are you going with that pram?" she asked.

"I brought some bricks with me," said Stone P. Stanford.

Prams were one of those quite unpredictable things that roused this woman to laughter; perhaps also bricks. She stopped dreaming her sorrowful day-dreams; instead she shut her eyes and threw herself headlong into the surf-topped ocean of laughter, where she was tossed from wave-top to wave-top until sorrow washed her ashore again and she opened her eyes.

Stanford was favourably impressed by her home; indeed, she had tidied up the room and closed all the doors. The pictures on the wall of the Prophet and Brigham Young were veritable masterpieces. But the bricklayer was really astounded to find that in this very place, right in the middle of the floor, should stand the proof that Pastor Runólfur had adduced for his thesis that in Utah man had achieved prosperity through having correct thoughts: a sewing machine. The machine stood on a special table in the middle of the room, as if the house had been built round it.

"I would never have believed that this machine would be found at a Josephite's," said Stanford.

"But I always thought it was Josephites who invented the sewing machine," said the woman.

"Is that so?" murmured Stanford, running his hands over this prince of machines cautiously and reverently, as if he had come across a bird or a flower in the middle of the wilderness. "What is the extension of the Golden Book itself if it is not a sewing machine? And that reminds me that when I took leave of Bishop Þjóðrekur in the city of Copenhagen where we had been drinking Kirsten Piil water, my prospects were so gloomy, and the poverty of my soul likewise, that I could only afford a packet of needles to send home to my wife."

"All I know is that the very best Elders in the Church come to me with their wives and daughters, sometimes on horseback, sometimes in sprung carriages. In that cupboard there I could show you a row of half-finished dresses for people in Provo, all made from pure silk in the latest New England fashion and so low-necked that you haven't seen the like since you were being suckled."

Her coffee warmed the cockles as always, as one says in Iceland about a really hospitable pot of coffee. He drank two half-cups with a long interval in between, and on each occasion he ran his palms over his hair (which in fact was all gone by now), either because he felt it standing on end or because his scalp broke out into a sweat owing to the unspeakable power that lay latent in the coffee. The woman contemplated him deeply out of her long, dark subterranean dream. She was one of those women who had been graced in her youth by some muscular restriction at the corners of the mouth; this not only tempered the smile, but quite literally restricted it. And though it had often been stretched by involuntary spasms of laughter, it quickly reasserted itself, but had still not turned altogether into a wrinkle or a grimace, the way in which all the world's beauty does. The woman stared sleepily straight ahead and right through the man, occasionally drawling some low-voiced, worried remark and sighing.

"How are the women looking after you at the Bishop's House?" she asked.

"Turkey and cranberries, dear lady," said the bricklayer. "When I look at the tables of plenty in this land of the All-Wisdom, where parts of more animals than I can name lie side by side on the board, as if in a millennium, and the milk so rich that it would truly be called cream among people who had not yet found the truth—is it any wonder that I am impressed by what

people can manage to conjure up out of these salt-flats if they
have the right book? If it were not wicked to say so, the only
thing this little fellow from Iceland misses is some sour blood-
pudding. Heeheehee."

"Excuse me, but have you anywhere to sleep?" she asked, sunk
in thought.

"What's that?" said the bricklayer. "Where do I sleep? I really
cannot remember, dear lady. I don't believe I have ever noticed.
It makes no difference where one sleeps in God's City of Zion,
the air is everywhere just as all-embracingly pleasing. Sometimes
one stretches out on a bench out in the garden, with a jacket
round one's head for the flies; sometimes up on the balcony if it
rains. This summer I often spent the night in the brickyard on
top of my bricks. Now that it is getting cooler at nights, I
stretch out on Pastor Runólfur's floor. But I cannot deny that I
am just beginning to wonder whether I should not build myself
a little shed; but not for my own sake."

"I understand," said the woman.

"I have no doubt told you already that I have a wife," he said.

"Was that not on the other side of the moon?" asked the woman.

"Does that not rather depend on which side of the moon one
happens to be oneself?" said the bricklayer with a smile.

"Whichever side she is on, does she not live in a house where
she is?" said the woman.

"Heavens above, one can put a name to anything," said the
bricklayer. "But that is not the whole story: this good woman
bore me two children."

"Aren't they doing all right?" said the woman.

"Thank you for asking," said the bricklayer courteously. "When
I looked at them sleeping when they were small, their happiness

was so beautiful that I almost felt sad to think that they would have to wake up. Once I thought that I could buy them a kingdom for a horse. But little came of that. And yet. Who knows? The night is not over yet, as the ghost said."

"I shall give you this house," said the woman. "The house we are in now. If your wife comes, I shall not take from her anything she has a claim to. The only thing I ask in exchange, for my daughter and myself, is a share in a good man's status."

He had not recited a verse to himself since the year in which he made the casket; but now he had started to rock back and forward and chant the way he used to:

> *She gave food for hungry hound,*
> *She gave bed for sleeping sound.*

"This one wife was for me the same as Bishop Þjóðrekur's three wives, Brigham Young's twenty-seven wives, and the ten thousand wives that the god Buddha is said to have in his stomach."

All at once the corners of her mouth started straining, until she burst. She laughed long and heartily.

He stopped his chanting and looked at her. She said, "I only hope that this wife of yours wasn't like the monster that came ashore at the Vestmannaeyjar when Ronki's grandfather was pastor there."

She heaved a sigh, and was no longer laughing.

He did not let himself become confused, but said in a rather more deliberate tone of voice, "This woman's indulgence towards me was not based on how much I could enhance her status in the eyes of man and God, for I have not yet been man enough to give her anything apart from that packet of needles. You will see from that, my good woman how likely I am to make other women more estimable in God's eyes, when that was all I could do for the one who was all women to me."

A little later the bricklayer sat down and embarked on a letter to his benefactor, Bishop Þjóðrekur, who was now travelling some distant road. He said in his letter that it was unnecessary to try to express his thanks for the doctrine that the bishop had brought him and which had this advantage over other doctrines, that those who believed in it, prospered. He said that the more he contemplated the book that Joseph found on the hill and which Brigham upheld to the people thereafter, the less value he found in other books. "It is difficult to doubt that a book which can make roses bloom on a barren branch must be right. And in that case, the truth is something different from what we once thought," said the bricklayer, "if it is as a result of a lie that the wilderness has become green pastures or golden acres of maize and corn."

Then he described freely how he himself had made good in God's City of Zion, which he referred to as the Territory of Utah, as it was now called. He had become both a bricklayer and a housebuilder in Spanish Fork and its environs. He had been put in charge of other bricklayers and been paid foreman's wages, and double pay had also been forced on him for toying with carpentry. He said the only reason he had accepted the money was his certain conviction that he was now in the land of divine revelation. He had been elected Ward Assistant and instructed to prepare himself for ordination which would authorise him to conduct ceremonies within the Ward. Although he was not an eloquent speaker, he had also been requested by the Stake to sit on the committee of the Young Women's Mutual Improvement

Association, where one discussed such things as the proper attitude towards proposals and how the behaviour of young people
during courting should best be harmonised with eternal matrimony sealed with the authority of High Priesthood. An Elder in
Salt Lake City had said that he, Stanford, should be prepared to
be elevated to the Stake. "The only thing," wrote the bricklayer,
"that grieves me in all this is that my mentor, Pastor Runólfur,
the most learned and wisest of men, should not have been nomi-
nated to this position first. I cannot bring myself to accept
preferment as long as my worthy spiritual father is given no pro-
motion."

Finally he reached what was meant to be the main point of
this letter. He said he had to admit that he sometimes noticed a
certain coldness towards him from others; indeed, he himself felt
misgivings about his own failure to fulfil the divine Moral Law,
and most particularly to live up to the divine revelation concerning holy polygamy. Certainly he never for a day forgot God's
command that righteous men and true Latter-Day Saints should
take unto themselves several wives under the seal of everlasting
matrimony, and thus deliver them from physical loneliness, spiritual distress and lack of glory in the eyes of God. He was
appalled at the tragedy, he wrote, of strikingly capable women,
in every way deserving of heavenly matrimony, running around
with Josephites, while their daughters fell into the misfortune in
their youth of taking up with Lutherans, so that the names of the
poor creatures became almost unmentionable in human society.
He could also well appreciate the golden example that Brigham
Young set the world when he had a house built with twenty-
seven doors. But his, Stanford's, weakness was no less great; in
particular, he felt himself to lack the courage to undertake the

responsibility of managing several wives while he had still not fulfilled his obligations towards a certain house and home with which he was not entirely unacquainted at a certain place in the world.

His children, who had slept more beautifully than any others—what had they not deserved? Everything except what he himself was man enough to provide for them. "When they were reaching the stage of waking up into a world that was no longer a fairy-tale book I found their presence becoming more and more unbearable because of my utter failure to be worthy of them," he wrote. And the woman who was so loving and compliant to her husband—her he left, and went on his way. He took with him a horse and a casket, which he called the horse of his soul and the casket of his soul; no doubt he hoped to buy happiness with them in the marketplace; or at least an earldom. But got a packet of needles.

Thus ended the letter from Stone P. Stanford, bricklayer, of Spanish Fork, God's City of Zion, Territory of Utah, to Bishop Þjóðrekur, Mormon, presumably touring somewhere in the Danish Kingdom *P.S.* "I enclose in bank-notes fares for my family and ask you to bring them over with you when you come; I shall try to have finished building them a brick house. *St. P. Stanford.*"

22

Good and bad doctrines

Mine is a bad doctrine," said the Lutheran. "And, what's more, I cannot substantiate my doctrine. The man who has the best doctrine is the one who can prove that he has the most to eat; and good shoes. I have neither, and live in a dugout."

"I've heard that one before many a time," said Pastor Runólfur. "Those who never have anything to eat or to wear are never tired of declaring their aversion to people who have plenty of food. And yet one of the Prophets said that a man needs to have food and clothes in order to perform virtuous deeds. You forget that every single thing contains a higher concept—good broth no less than a pair of topboots; the Greeks called this the Idea. It is this spiritual and eternal quality in all existence and in every thing by which we Mormons live. If anyone is so incompetent that he has neither broth nor topboots, nor the manliness to raise himself from a dugout, he is not likely to have a spirit, or eternity, either."

"I don't care," said the Lutheran. "No one will ever make me believe anything other than that Adam was a dirty shit. And Eve was no improvement."

At that time there was a great furor over the published dogma that Adam was of divine nature no less than the Saviour, on the grounds that God Himself had gone to the trouble of specially creating them both. With this, the Lutheran had touched upon a topic that really roused the defender-of-the-faith in Pastor Runólfur.

"I might have known you would bring that up," said Pastor Runólfur. "It has always been the sure sign of a drunkard and philanderer when he starts to abuse poor old Adam. Anyone who has anything on his conscience immediately slaps the blame on him. But I can assure you that Adam was a perfectly sound chap. Those who run down Adam are children of the Great Apostasy and the Great Heresy. Do you think that the Lord of Hosts would have debased Himself by creating a rotten shit? Or even a Lutheran? Do you think that when God made Adam He used material inferior to what He used when He made the Saviour? I deny absolutely that there is any fundamental difference between Adam and the Saviour."

"May I ask, what did this Adam ever accomplish?" said the Lutheran. "Did he ever make any money? I've never heard it said that he got himself a house, far less a carriage; not even a pair of shoes. He probably just lived in a dugout like me. And what did he have to eat? Do you think he had broth every weekday and turkey with cranberries on Sundays? I wouldn't be surprised if he never had a square meal except for that apple his old hag offered him."

Thus they went at it hammer and tongs in the brickyard night and day, but never more fiercely than just before daybreak. Pastor Runólfur made a habit of waylaying the Lutheran at dawn on his way home from his mistresses to his Welsh wife in the dugout. It has never been worked out just how much of a theologian this intemperate dugout-dweller really was, and perhaps he was no more of a drunkard and philanderer than the unpleasantness of his homelife warranted. But for all that, Pastor Runólfur held him directly answerable for Luther's heresy in particular and the Great Apostasy in general. And no matter how worn out the Lutheran might be, he was always just as eager as ever to stand up for Luther there in the middle of the road. He only asked his antagonist, Pastor Runólfur, leave to pop into the brickyard where he always had a drop or two left in the bottle carefully hidden in the pile of bricks for bracing himself before his wife woke up to read him the morning's lecture. Stone P. Stanford never revealed where the Lutheran kept this mercy-font except for that one occasion which has already been related. But just as soon as the Lutheran had got hold of his bottle in the brickyard, no power in the world could hold him back any longer from his endless disputation with Pastor Runólfur—which seemed, indeed, to have an independent life of its own. Stanford, busy preparing the sun for its useful daily task, often heard the din of their disputation blended with the dawn chorus of the birds; on the one side schnapps, on the other side the Holy Spirit.

But one day the page was turned, as it were: at dawn there was nothing to be heard but the song of the birds and the chirring of insects instead of theological disputation, and Stanford heard it rumoured that the destitute Lutheran had moved from the district.

Time passed. And then it so happened late one evening, when

Stanford was in the bishop's brickyard stacking new-baked
bricks, that all of a sudden an unknown visitor appeared before
him as abruptly as when one sees a vision. It was an extremely
young woman. She was one of those youngsters who suffer so
overwhelmingly sudden a growing-up that physical maturity is
upon them the moment they wear out their childhood shoes. She
had a rather hard-boiled look on account of some gratuitous
experience of the world, and did not know how to return a civil
greeting.

"Mother sent me," said the girl, and bit her lip instead of
smiling. "I was to bring you coffee."

"It is not the first time in the history of Mormonism that
people have been sent something good," said the bricklayer.

She handed him a bottle inside a sock. Stone P. Stanford
recognised both the sock and the bottle.

"This is the next best thing to meeting your mother herself,"
said the bricklayer. "A very good day to you, my dear, and my
warmest thanks to you both. To get coffee this year, too, from
Madame Þorbjörg, the seamstress—I can hardly believe my luck.
It would have been quite enough to give me coffee while I was a
complete stranger here, without overwhelming me with kindness after I have become an everyday sight and when all reasonable folk have long ago discovered what an ordinary sort of
fellow I am. And now, little girl, be so good as to have a seat on
these new-baked bricks over here while you tell me the news."

The girl sat down on the bricks, bit her lip and was silent.

"It is a long time since there has been coffee in my mug, if
only I have not lost it," said the bricklayer, searching around for
it. When he had found his tin mug he reached forward with it
and asked the girl to pour. He went on chatting with her so that
the coffee session should not be an entirely silent one.

"Somehow I had an idea that my friend, Madame Þorbjörg Jónsdóttir, had a daughter, even though I saw little sign of it that time I paid a visit to your house. You will have been born by then, I fancy, and not all that recently, either."

"I should jolly well think so," said the girl, and snorted contemptuously. "I was practically in labour already!"

"All the doors were shut, if I remember," he said.

"Of course they were all shut," she snapped back at him.

"It is a good custom and a fine rule to close the door, I was taught back in Iceland, even though there was no great surfeit of doors in people's houses there," said the bricklayer.

At that the girl sat up straight and said accusingly, "Just so long as nobody is locked in."

"Oh, perhaps not every pleasure is to be found out of doors, my dear," said the bricklayer.

"They call us Josephites," said the girl. "Every time I went out, the children jeered at me that we drank coffee."

"People are sometimes pretty empty-headed," said the bricklayer. "And the greatest empty-headedness of all, I think, is to jeer at people who are different from oneself. It was endemic in Eyrarbakki, once upon a time. From there it must have spread all the way east to the Rangárvellir (Rangriver Plains) and then to America. Some people say it is wicked and ungodly and sinful to drink coffee. These people are undoubtedly right as far as they themselves are concerned, and accordingly they should never drink coffee. Then there are other people who can quote medical books to prove that coffee damages the heart, not to mention the liver, stomach and kidneys in this temple of God which is the human body. These people should not drink coffee either. But speaking for myself, I always drink coffee when I feel that it is offered in all sincerity, but never more than half a cup."

"It wasn't only that we drank coffee, come to that," said the girl.

"I can understand that," said the bricklayer. "You lived by yourselves. But all the same it will have been a consolation to know that one had a father who was a thinking person. No one but a thinking person would go away from such a splendid woman as your mother, and such a promising daughter, in order to receive the Saviour in Independence, Missouri."

"My father may well have been doing some deep thinking when he left mother," said the girl. "But he didn't have to think very deeply to run away from me, because I wasn't born until the year after he turned up missing."

"How very ashamed I am of myself for being so bad-mannered towards you and your mother, never getting round to doing a few repairs to your house as I had more or less promised. But one has little enough time for doing friends a favour when one is pottering about for oneself. Bricks are difficult things to understand, no less so than the Golden Book itself. And then there is all the church work to be done for the Ward late into the night every evening; and in addition we sometimes have tasks given to us by the Stake, which unlettered people like myself find difficult and slow work. What leisure have we left? Somehow I have never been able to get the knack of not sleeping at night, at least until the birds start chirping. And it is not much better now that I am beginning to build myself a house. But I know of one good man who is a real friend of yours."

"Old Ronki?" said the girl. "He could well be a fine fellow for all I know; he can at least chase away other people who are perhaps not worth so much in his eyes. But what do you get from him instead? Whatever is left of the soup at the Bishop's House at night after bedtime! I don't call that being a man. And I don't care even if there are occasionally some dry shreds of turkey on Sunday evenings."

"You have a lot to say, my dear girl," said the bricklayer. "Perhaps I might venture to ask you a question or two more?"

"I didn't think you were such a fool as to need to ask what happened," said the girl.

"My word! Has something happened?" said the bricklayer. "Here? In God's City of Zion?"

"Everyone knows perfectly well that I had a baby," said the girl.

"Well now, since you tell me you have a baby, my dear, then I wish you still more luck and blessings than before," said the bricklayer. "I should think so, indeed. Anyway, to change the subject, what great pleasure I take in these dear little quails which visit me here sometimes in the brickyard; see how agile they are at running obliquely, just like knights on a chess-board, heeheehee. It is a solemn moment first thing in the morning when the birds wake up. Sometimes at dawn a man would call here who said he was a Lutheran, and was always quoting the verse about the evil-doers in the Passion Hymns: 'early their sleep is shattered.' In the end one is no longer sure which is the greatest evil-doer, the man who gets up early or the man who goes to bed late. I have a vague recollection that he used to have a bottle in the brick-pile there."

"That's him," said the girl. "That was mother's paramour. But it was a straight lie to say he gave me schnapps, just like all the other things of which she accused us. Even if I'd been tied hand and foot, and someone had held my nose, I would never have allowed a drop past my lips. But it's another matter altogether when you've been locked in a room with a man who's been drinking schnapps, as mother sometimes did to me when she was angry with him; it's like being locked in with a baby: one tries to make sure it doesn't come to any harm; and one tries to keep it amused. So one gives it the first toy that comes to hand to make it stop whimpering. Whether he was a Lutheran or something else, as if I should be asking him that! I haven't even asked what it is to be a Josephite."

"Where do you and your mother hail from, if I may ask?"

"What a question to be asking!" said the girl. "It would be better to ask my mother! Or else Ronki—he was grandmother's pastor in Iceland when the old woman was converted and ran off with the Mormons. Get mother to tell you how she came here in her youth, long before the trains started going. All of a sudden one fine day Ronki arrived in his frock-coat, all the way over here to God's kingdom to try to convert them. He held services up on the hill here in an ugly little church which can only hold one mule at a time, and put a cross up on it. But he was too late: mother was engaged to a Josephite. Then he himself embraced the Gospel and started looking after the bishop's ewes. He could well be a fine fellow for all I know, and he certainly helped us to get hold of a sewing machine so that we could earn a living. And now that we've sold it because no one wanted us to do any sewing after I had a child by a Gentile and we don't dare to be seen out of doors, scarcely even to go to the store, and anyway we've no money to buy anything, he collects the day's scraps from the Bishop's House and brings them to us at night. But he's no man. And it's no lie when mother says we would rather drown ourselves in a salt-pool than have to take Ronki in."

23

Delivering
a packet of needles

Meanwhile, Bishop Þjóðrekur had been travelling around
Iceland for two years preaching the faith to people and
immersing them, after spending a winter in Denmark composing a pamphlet for the Icelanders and having it printed. In Iceland he spent most of his time in areas where no Mormons had
been before; his preaching provoked very little interest and even
fewer beatings. As regards his pamphlet, this Apostle has
declared that it is the only religious book which has been
hawked around Iceland by special permission of the Danish king
directly against the will of the populace, particularly the sheriffs,
and the first book composed by an Icelander in Icelandic in
which the religious ideas were not all on loan from the Danish
king. He said he never grudged the Danish king's destitute
slaves in Iceland the beatings they gave him; their blows affected
him about as much as when a pauper beats dried fish up in Lan-
ganes. Of King Kristian Wilhelmsson, Bishop Þjóðrekur has said

in print that the king was the only person in the kingdom who considered the Prophet Joseph's authorized missionary his equal in matters of faith, and for that reason he had Bishop Þjóðrekur's undivided respect; indeed, this king was a countryman of the spiritual father of the Danes, Luther himself. Þjóðrekur the Mormon had now been beaten up so often and in so many places in Iceland without any result that most people, one might say, could no longer be bothered with it. Wherever Bishop Þjóðrekur took jobs during his missionary tour he earned everyone's respect, according to the weekly *Þjóðólfur.* The Mormons have a law, instituted by God through the mouth of the Prophet, that the Apostles of the Gospel should not set forth with a purse, but should earn their own keep on missionary journeys. Bishop Þjóðrekur had been a labourer for two summers up north, and worked on a fishing-boat for a season in the east and one in the west.

Towards the end of the second summer that Bishop Þjóðrekur spent in Iceland on this occasion, he remembered that he had an important errand to perform south in Steinahlíðar before he left the country—to deliver to a woman there a packet of needles, etc. This he had promised to some man or other in Copenhagen nearly three years previously. It so happened that he had to pass through this district on his way west at the time of the autumn round-ups. He had nothing with him except his hat wrapped in grease-proof paper according to American custom; in his knapsack there was nothing but a shirt, a rye-loaf and a little candy for children. His pamphlets were all used up. His topboots were still in as good condition as they had ever been. It is said that on rugged mountain-tracks with razor-sharp stones, and also on the trackless lava wastes, over sands and through swamps, even when he waded across rivers, he always took off his topboots, tied them together by their laces, slung them over his shoulder and walked barefoot. This earned him respect in Iceland.

It was the time of year when the hay from the home-field had long been safely gathered and the grassier meadows mown; the sparsest patches were now being scraped. When Bishop Þjóðrekur reached Steinahlíðar he asked the way to Hlíðar. People looked at him in amazement. Some did not know of any farm of that name. Others said, "You must mean the gravel patch where Björn of Leirur grazes his wild ponies."

Finally he reached a spot where the main track led past a ruined croft. Here there were high walls of stone, most of them in a sorry state. The famous dykes that once had enclosed the home-field were also dilapidated, and in some places it was obvious that gaps had been deliberately torn in them to make access easier. The grass had been so cropped to the quick that nothing remained except a clump of marsh marigolds, and where the earth had been stripped clean of turf there was chickweed growing. But there were still plenty of stray animals, both sheep and ponies, regaling themselves on the roots. The rock-falls from the mountain had been sufficient by themselves to make the home-field uncultivable. The farm itself was derelict. The roof had been torn off and all the timber carted away. The tumbledown walls had been engulfed by dock-plants. Two redpolls flew startled out of the herbage and vanished. The bishop had not had any dinner, but yet he seated himself on the door-paving and picked his teeth with a straw for a long time. An air of desolation breathed over the ruins.

"There have been rare goings-on here," the Mormon said at last to some passers-by who roused him from his trance.

"What makes you think that?" they asked.

"Two redpolls flew out of here," said the Mormon. "Where are all the people, bless them?"

He got little information out of these wayfarers except that the people had long since been scattered to the winds: the husband was believed to have run off and taken to that Mormonism heresy, and the agent at Leirur had appropriated the farm; according to some he had given the daughter a baby, but he had certainly never acknowledged it. None of the passers-by was so well-informed that they knew exactly where the rest of the family had ended up. "The parish council placed them," they said; one thought in the uplands somewhere, but another thought that some of them at least were down by the coast.

"It's heavy hay in this damp!" said the bishop when he eventually found the girl busy raking. The ground was level here, and the pasture ran in a pointed tongue to the sands. Here one could hear the ceaseless muttered thunder of the south-coast breakers. It was on the banks of one of the rivers from Steinahlíðar; at this point it had become calm and broad and no longer entirely clean.

The girl pushed back the damp hood from her forehead and looked up. He walked over to her and offered his hand and greeted her. She stared at him without a movement in her body or soul.

"I was told that you would be the girl," he said.

"Yes," she whispered. "I am the girl."

"I cannot remember exactly whether I was to bring you greetings, but I'll do it anyway, even though I have been chewing on them for long enough," said the bishop.

"From mother?" said the girl, and a spark of life stirred in her.

"No, from old Steinar—I don't remember his patronymic—of Hlíðar in Steinahlíðar, if you know of him," said the visitor.

At these words the girl became even more speechless than before; until her face suddenly disintegrated. The days of her childhood suddenly came rushing back to her without any warning, all in the same flash, when she heard the name. She let the tears course freely down her cheeks, like a child, without lowering her head or trying in any other way to hide her face; and without making a sound.

"I would have come to see you earlier," he said, "if I had suspected how things were."

The girl turned away, sniffed loudly, and started to rake again.

"I had no idea how it was until two birds flew up out of the ruins of your old home," he said behind the girl's back. "It is the story of us all. How often have birds flown up out of my own ruins! Sit down on that tussock, my dear, while I see if I haven't got anything left in the bottom of my bag."

He brought a piece of candy out of his knapsack and offered it to the girl; she stopped raking again, accepted the candy, and put it in her mouth. Then she dried her eyes and thanked him. "But I cannot sit down," she said. "I'm in service here."

"You are an honest girl," he said. "But while a visitor is talking to you, no one can order you about. Courtesy comes first."

She paused with her rake in mid-swing and began to stare at him again.

"What's your name?" she asked.

"My name is Þjóðrekur, I am called The Mormon."

"Is it true then that they exist?" she asked.

"Unless they have all dropped dead," said the bishop.

"Is there no one who tells the truth?" said the girl.

"I don't expect your father would have voyaged far across land and sea if he had thought me a liar," said the bishop.

"It's no good telling me fairy-tales any longer," said the girl.

"Do you think I don't know now that Heaven and earth are two different things?"

"Thy Kingdom come, on earth as in Heaven," said the Mormon. "Is that just a bit of sarcasm by the Redeemer?"

"I don't understand Bible talk," said the girl. "Not any more."

"God's Kingdom is in Utah, which is adjacent to Heaven with no gap in between," said the bishop. "In that Kingdom lives your father."

"Either he exists or he doesn't exist," said the girl.

"In the eyes of Mormons, no one is dead. With us there is only one Kingdom which is and ever shall be," said the bishop.

"Yes, it's just as I thought," said the girl. "And now I must carry on with the raking."

Now the bishop became a little irritated.

"And I say not!" he said. "You shall not carry on with any raking whatsoever. I have come to fetch you all and take you to your father. Where is your poor mother? And there is also a brother of sorts, I believe—yes, and that's not all, according to the stories I have heard. Direct me to them all."

"If I had not stopped believing in fairy-tales, I would think you were Death," said the girl. "Or at least the old ogress Grýla.* Excuse me, but are you a pastor?"

"I come from your father," he said.

"Are you quite sure you haven't got the wrong person? Was it not some other girl you were looking for?" she asked. "Don't you think you've got the names mixed up?"

"Was it perhaps not he who had the horse?"

"Yes, we had a horse," she said.

"And a casket?"

"A casket?" she said. "How do you know that? Is it then

absolutely true that my father is still alive, not according to any Bible, but as if he were sitting here on this tussock? Am I not dreaming, as always?"

The bishop met the boy at the other end of the district, where he was working for his keep. He was busy bringing in dried peat on pack-ponies. He also had peat in his nose and mouth. The boy wore a hat much too large for him, and under it was a shock of matted hair, discoloured by sun and rain.

"You look as if you haven't had a haircut since the first day of summer, lad, just like me in my young days," said the bishop. "What are your plans?"

"I'm going to drive these peat-ponies home," said the boy.

"Leave them be," said Bishop Þjóðrekur.

"My master is at home waiting for them," said the boy. "He's stacking peat. I don't suppose I could ask you for a pinch of snuff? I've run out."

"Let me see your nose," said the bishop. He went up to the boy and scrutinized his face closely. "My goodness, if it isn't tobacco. I thought it was peat! That's something you won't have learned from your father."

"My father is dead, somewhere abroad," said the boy.

"I wouldn't be too sure of that, my lad," said the bishop. "I don't suppose he is any more dead than I am."

"I don't believe he would have let us all go on the parish if he had been alive, for he was descended from both Egill Skalla-grímsson and the Norwegian kings, and Harald as well," said the boy.

"Go over to that stream, my lad, and wash your nose, both inside and out, while I lead these pack-ponies home and hand them over to the farmer," said Bishop Þjóðrekur. "I am going to release you from your contract. Then I am taking you with me to show you how dead your father is."

"Has he got some terrible illness?" asked the boy.

"Oh, just the usual things, my lad," said the bishop. "A cold when there are colds about. And perhaps a little flatulence from eating too many pancakes at Christmas and such-like."

"Did you see him yesterday?" asked the boy.

"Yes, yesterday about three years ago."

"Was it after he disappeared?"

"You might say I saw him off," said the bishop.

"Was he buried?" asked the boy.

"Not that time, lad—however often they may have buried him since."

The boy gaped at him inanely, took off his hat and scratched his head, and pondered how he should react to this news.

"I still think there must be something in the story that father's dead," he said at last, but perhaps more from obstinacy than conviction, and stared after the bishop as he led the string of ponies back to the croft. After hesitating for a while, however, the boy walked down to the stream and started washing his face.

Steinar's wife was traced to a croft far in the uplands, where she toiled to support herself and her two-year-old grandson.

She was now broken in health and unfit for outdoor work, so she was left to look after the house while the crofter and his wife were out in the fields. She came to the door with Steinar junior. Bishop Þjóðrekur greeted her with a handshake and delved in his pockets for a lump of sugar for the boy.

"The people are out in the fields, bless them, late as it is," she said. "They said they would be on the far side of the six o'clock cairn, cutting hay for the pastor's lamb. I'll direct you to them."

"Who are you, missus?" he asked.

"I am a widow," she replied. "We used to live at Hlíðar in Steinahlíðar. Give the man a kiss for the sugar, Steinar dear. I don't recognise you, although I lived for many years on the main track. You must be from the east."

"You can certainly say that again," said the bishop. "So far east that it has become west again."

"Oh, the poor man," said the woman. "I'm just a parish pauper, and I'm afraid I can't act the housewife. But I need hardly say that my dear departed husband would have invited you in to rest your weary limbs on the bunk while you were giving us your news, if he had still been with us and in my shoes."

"The thought is as good as an offer," said the visitor. "And thank you all the same. But it so happens that here in Iceland I feel more at home at a tethering-block than on a bunk. It was at a tethering-block that we first met, this man you mentioned and I. You were asking for news, missus. I'm not particularly well-informed, but there's one small item I can tell you. You called yourself a widow, but I can inform you that you were wrong there, missus. You're no more a widow than I am. Your husband sent me to you and asked me to give you this packet of needles."

The woman brushed the mists of the world from her eyes with one hand while she accepted the packet of needles with the other. For a long while she peered at that little black paper folder; her eyesight was failing her now.

"These needles will come in handy," she said. "What was often a need is now a necessity—if only my eyesight were better. Yes, I've heard many an unbelievable story in my days, and yet true. And it's many years now since I began to get this feebleness in the head and this weakness in the heart, so that I'm ashamed to say I scarcely know whether I'm in Heaven or on earth. But one thing I've always known: the All-Wisdom is just as close to my Steinar whether he's alive or dead. Fancy him sending me a packet of needles! The Lord be praised. And now it wouldn't come amiss to have a scrap of thread!"

"The All-Wisdom can never be over-praised, missus," said the bishop.

Somehow, the woman was so entranced with this packet of needles that she forgot to ask any more questions. Or else she felt that the man who had sent her a packet of needles must be living in such a state of grace in Heaven and on earth that there was no need to ask anything further. Faced with a weather-beaten traveller from afar, she could only think of the rivers which constitute such a severe obstacle to travel in that part of the country.

"Have the rivers not been terribly high after all this rain?" she asked.

"Are you much for rivers, missus?" he asked.

"No, thank the Lord," said the woman. "I've never had to cross a river in my life, except for our farm-brook. My Steinar forded big rivers."

"That may all have to change, missus," said the visitor. "I have come to fetch you and take you to him. I have his letter here to prove it. I'll show you it. He is building you a brick house."

"Excuse me, but to whom am I speaking?" she asked.

"My name is Þjóðrekur, a Mormon," he replied. "Are you hard of hearing, missus? I was sent to you by your husband, Stone P. Stanford, in the Territory of Utah, in America. He wants you to join him there."

"You look such a calm person, and you certainly sound reliable," she said. "But since I am now keeping an eye on my grand-

son here, I don't think I'll be doing very much travelling. My
Steina is still only a little girl, and the parish council decided
that she was too young to have maternal instincts, so they handed
him over to me. Now I have become nearly as fond of him as of
his grandfather. I hope I shall always have a Steinar by me as long
as I live. A thousand thanks for bringing me this packet of needles. He was a very gifted man; and he was a very skilled man;
and he was a light. Yes, and how attached he was to his children.
Who knows, perhaps he will come down to us out of the clouds
one day! And now I mustn't stand here enjoying myself any
longer, there's all the work still to be done in the house."

24

The girl

Everything on the other side of the river now belonged to Leirur. Björn the agent bought up the crofts that had stood on the coastal plains listening to the thunder of the surf beyond the sands for a thousand years. He broke up the farms and added the land to his own estate.

One late-summer evening, on the way home from the hay-making in darkness and drizzle, she waited for an opportunity to lag behind the others: Yes, I am the girl. While the others went to have their supper and rest their weary limbs, she turned back and headed down towards the river. She knew the ancient ford that the old crofters, now long since gone, had once used; she had made a little cairn of three stones at the point where the ponies could cross. Despite the darkness, she managed to find her stone marker. Then she waded into the river. The water seldom reached above her knees, but in places the river-bed was treacherous underfoot. In daylight she knew where it was safe to cross, all right, but in the darkness she could not pick out the landmarks; twice she blundered into quicksands and had to turn back. At the third attempt she thought she could just make out the far bank about twelve feet away, when suddenly without any warning the water was up to her armpits and she was gasping and calling to God for help. As on so many other occasions, God was not slow to react, and created a sandbar for her that had never been there before and now rose up in the middle of the river. And just as she was losing her footing in the icy water she managed to scramble on to this newly-created sandbar. Luckily the river was shallow on the other side of it, and soon the girl was standing on the grassy bank and was wringing out her clothes.

Björn of Leirur was the only one of the peasantry in those parts who used lamplight, even though it was now nearly autumn— but seldom more than for one evening at a time, for this great traveller was seldom at home for many days in succession. When he was at home he used to sit downstairs in the room facing east. If he were not chatting to visitors from here, there and everywhere, he would be going over his accounts. His was the only light that shone inland, and on late-summer evenings it could be seen all the way from the main track that skirted the mountains. Sometimes it glowed all through the night. It was not only a sign that the agent was at home; it was the light of the world for the whole district.

She was worn out after a summer of drudgery, long days of toiling in the rain with her rake far into the night. But now all at once it was as if an exhausted traveller had been wafted on to well-rested horses, or as if the wings of fairy-tale had sprouted from her shoes. Her feet bore her lightly over clogging mires, moors and bogs as if they were level fields. So sure-footed and keen-eyed were these magic steeds that they never once stumbled even in this unfamiliar country in the rain-driven darkness.

The light that cast its wan rays over the plain drew nearer, until she was at the house itself. The big downstairs windows of the east gable-wall belonged to his study where his lamp now burned, that intermittent light. The curtains were not drawn. She pressed her face to the window-pane and peered in. The lamp stood on his desk. He was sitting hunched over his letters and ledgers with his nose right down to the paper, holding a magnifying glass to his eye with one hand, and with the other restraining his beard from flowing over the pages. She rapped on the pane with her knuckles, and he gave a start and looked up. He did not call out the customary response to the person who greeted him in God's name, but laid a finger to his lips towards the window as a warning not to make a sound. Then he left the room. He opened the outer door, groped his way along the side of the house and round the corner, and caught hold of this stranger. He quickly realised that it was a girl, and led, pulled and carried her in, all at the same time. When he had brought her into his room he drew the curtains.

"What a terrible mess!" he said, and kissed the drenched girl. "Did you fall into the river? Welcome, anyway. It's a long time since anything flew into my arms."

"Do you recognize me?" she asked.

"I hope you haven't mistaken your man," he said. "And even if you have, I've never yet mistaken a girl."

"I knew I wouldn't need to make any apologies to you, Björn," she said. "It may well be late, but we've met one another at night before now. We girls are no doubt all the same. I am probably not the first who was afraid of not reaching you before your light went out."

"Old philanderers never get to bed until all hours," he said. "They want to put off waking the wife as long as possible. We are mourning the fact that we no longer ford glacier-rivers on horseback, which is the next best thing to sleeping in a maiden's arms; we are becoming unduly storm-bound by our firesides, we old fellows."

"I have stared across the river towards you all the time since the nights started drawing in," she said. "I sometimes see your lamp burning. Twice I have waded across the river to you, but each time I waded back over to myself and went home and took off my wet clothes. But now I have come all the way. I want a word with you, Björn."

"Are you going to start discussing important matters with an old fellow like me at this time of night?" said Björn of Leirur. "Well, say your piece, my lamb, but keep your voice down, for sound carries far in this house. I must build myself a stone house some time. Now I'll light a pipe. It is anyway just about the only wisdom you'll get out of me, if I can puff out a little smoke."

"Because we are all the same, and it's impossible to be mistaken about girls, I know exactly what you imagine I am going to speak to you about, Björn," said the girl. "But you are wrong. I have come to ask you what you think about my father."

"Your father? What might the matter with him be?"

"Do you think he will ever come back again?"

"Why do you ask me that?"

"I must sound funny, talking like this," said the girl. "Other people don't understand how attached we were to him. I used to pray to God every night to be allowed to die before father ever

released my hand from his. One day he rode away on our white
horse and came back on foot."

"He would have been better to sell me the nag," said Björn of
Leirur.

"Another time he set off with his wonderful casket."

"He got the mahogany from me," said Björn of Leirur, realiz-
ing at long last who the girl was and whom they were discussing.
"Incidentally, what was in the casket, again?"

"There was a big compartment for silver," said the girl. "And
a drawer divided into many small compartments for gold and
precious stones."

"What the devil for?" said Björn of Leirur.

"And finally there was a secret compartment for what is more
valuable than gold," said the girl. "But he never came back, not
even on foot."

"He was a queer fish, right enough," said Björn of Leirur. "I
think he is best left where he is, my lamb. You wouldn't be any
the happier for seeing him again. People say I don't do much for
my children; but what did he do for his?"

"He did a lot for me," said the girl.

"Such as what?" asked the agent, who was now puffing at his
pipe with furious energy.

The girl said, "I remember once outside a church. There was a
fearful crowd of strange dogs there, as always outside a church.
They were crawling round people's legs everywhere. I was only
about five years old, I think. Somehow or other I got separated
from my parents. I couldn't see anyone nearby who could rescue
me if the dogs were to bite me. And I started to whimper. Then
suddenly a big warm hand enclosed my own. It was Daddy. He
had such a big warm hand. And now I have come to you, Björn,

because I have no one else to go to, and I know you would never dream of telling me anything but the truth: is he dead?"

"What an absurd thing to ask! What, Steinar of Hlíðar dead? Him? Dead my foot! Don't you know he's with the Mormons, child?"

"Is there some truth in the story, then, that these Mormons exist? I have always had the suspicion that when someone had gone to the Mormons, it was the same as saying he had passed away or been gathered to his fathers. I have always thought that Mormons were in Heaven."

"You surely don't think that everyone is dead and gone to Hell except those you can actually see with your own eyes up to the crutch in the marshes, do you?" said Björn. "If you want to hear about someone who is dead, I'll tell you who it is—it's me. It's me who is sunk deep into this quagmire. What good have I got out of fording glacier-rivers night and day to bring people gold? Not a single damned thing, except my rheumatism. And almost blind, at that. No, my child, our Steinar is not dead. I am sure he has at least seven wives over there with the Mormons."

"Though he had only one wife at the other end of the earth, or even none at all, he is dead just the same," said the girl. "We would not recognize him again. It used to be quite enough just to be able to see father's face, and then everything was right with the world; he did not need to say anything. It did not matter in the least if one of those snowstorms blew up in Steinahlíðar, a blind blizzard driving in from the east; inside our house it was sunshine. Even though we had nothing to breakfast on, it didn't matter. One morning we woke up and he was gone. Anyone to whom we have said goodbye in our thoughts is dead. Night after night during that winter he did not come back, when I had gnawed the blankets all night and could feel the dawn in the air and my mouth was dry and swollen—I would suddenly find myself whispering, God, God, God, yes, yes, yes, You may keep him beside You because You created the world. And with that I would fall asleep."

Björn of Leirur gave a perfunctory laugh, bent over the girl and kissed her. "You can be quite sure, my lamb," he said, "that the day will come when I no longer have a bite to eat and can only crawl around the house here, blind and crippled; and then you will catch a glimpse of someone coming from the west, and it will be old Steinar of Hlíðar on his white horse, with his saddle-bags bulging with gold and schnapps."

"I don't think I would even dare to stroke his horse's muzzle," said the girl. "The person who comes back is never the same as the one who went away. And daddy's little girl no longer exists either. No one knows that better than you."

"Listen to her!" said Björn, and yawned.

"A man has arrived in the district," said the girl. "He came to me out in the meadow today and told me to sit down on a tussock because he had something to tell me. He is from the land of the Mormons, and has come to fetch me. He said he was sent by my father. He gave me two days to get ready."

"Are you crazy, girl?" said the agent, waking up. "Do you know where the damned place is? It's on the other side of the moon. You must just have fallen asleep on the tussock there and dreamed it all."

"Then I was also dreaming of my death," she said.

"If in fact it was a man, and even a Mormon, probably that devil from the Landeyjar who has been slinking around the country recently according to the papers, well then, what are you going to say to him when the two days are up? What are you going to do?"

"Oh, nothing much, I don't suppose," said the girl. "I shall just wait out there in the fields until he arrives with mother and my brother Víkingur and takes me along too."

"What about the boy?"

"What boy?"

"Our boy."

"Is he yours, then?"

"Whose do you think he is?"

"I gave him to mother."

"No one is taking the boy a single step out of this district, least of all to that arsehole of a place on the other side of the moon," said Björn of Leirur.

"You have always said the boy wasn't yours," said the girl. "And so he wasn't mine either, of course. He just started growing there inside me of his own accord, just as when God created the world out of nothing and then Himself at the same time."

"There's no need to pretend to be any more stupid than you are, my girl, when you're talking to me," said the agent.

"Do you think I didn't know you did something funny to me when I pretended to be asleep?" asked the girl.

"There is no bridge between a man and a woman," he said. "No man knows what any woman knows, and it will never be known until a pair of conjugated twins are born, a male and a female child in one body."

"Whose business was it what I knew?" said the girl. "Mother's? Or my sweetheart's? Certainly not. Perhaps I should have started preaching about it to Pastor Jón? Jesus doesn't care at all how mammals breed, as the sheriff said. And besides, they could never prove that I had been awake. But those days are past now, like other days. Whether I was dreaming or not, there's one thing certain: in two days' time I shall not be here."

He put his arms round the damp, warm girl and clasped her to his beard and his corpulent body, and stroked her.

"Call me your little scamp once more before I go, and then I'm away," said the girl.

"My poor little scamp," said Björn of Leirur, kissing the girl with that huge beard of his that reeked of snuff and cognac. "I'm going straight to the sheriff tomorrow to adopt the boy. I rode past the croft this summer and saw him playing among the tussocks. He has the looks of my late grandfather, who was a great man and a poet. I promise you that I shall make this little boy a sheriff. I shall make him a national poet. We'll go and fetch him. You shall not spend another day in these marshes. Don't think for a moment that I'll ever let you fall into the clutches of the parish council again, let alone the Mormons. I'm going upstairs to wake the men and tell them to fetch horses. We'll ride away."

"Where to?" asked the girl.

"Who the hell cares? I've had quite enough. I'm packing it all in—marshlands, shipwrecks, cognac, mahogany, horses; and these highflown plans for a steamship with these rich fellows in Reykjavík; and the rheumatism; and the great Vestmannaeyjar monster. We shall ride west tonight and board ship, you and I and the boy, and arrive in fairyland before bedtime, ahead of the Mormons. Now I'll pop upstairs and put on my topboots."

He released her from his embrace where she had snuggled half-suffocated under his beard. She stood there in the middle of the room. There were pools on the floor from her sodden shoes. She had seen everything through a haze until now, when for the first time she noticed the leather-upholstered mahogany chairs he had accumulated from many shipwrecks. Although one did no more than breathe in this room, one could not escape the smell of cognac and tobacco. A cat lay motionless on a cushion in an armchair, asleep.

The east wind kept hurling the rain against the windows in squalls. The girl stood rooted to the floor, and the pool at her feet kept on growing. And the cat kept on sleeping. But the man who had been embracing the girl did not return. Were his top-boots lost? Were the men, not long in bed, difficult to rouse from their slumbers? That could surely not be a dead cat? thought the girl. Or was it all a dream, even her tracks on the floor? She went over to the sleeping cat and stroked it. The cat did no more than half-open its eyes, lift its head slightly, stretch itself, and yawn; and then fall asleep again. Perhaps it had thought that this strange girl was its dream; and so perhaps she was.

At long last she heard stealthy nocturnal footsteps on the stairs and out in the corridor. Then the door was opened with the kind of cautious care that makes the hinges squeak. In came an old woman with a bent, almost hunched, back, her face still numb with sleep and her wispy grey hair tied in tight plaits no thicker than ordinary twine. She was wearing a night-gown that was so loosely buttoned that one could see down the front how her breasts sagged as limply as empty purses; but she had put on her black pleated skirt before coming down to meet the visitor. Blinking, she looked at the soaked girl, offered her hand, and asked, "What brings you here, my girl?"

"Nothing," said the girl. "I was having a word with Björn. I wanted to see him about something."

"Are you not from Steinahlíðar?" asked the woman.

"Yes, I am from Hlíðar in Steinahlíðar," said the girl.

"Poor thing," said the old woman. "Was it not you who lost your father?"

"Yes," said the girl, "he is with the Mormons."

"Good heavens!" said the old woman. "Compared with that, it's a blessing to be able to see your loved ones in the graveyard."

"At least they don't come back," said the girl.

"It's a little late to be visiting, little one," said the woman. "We mustn't keep my poor Björn up too late unnecessarily. Can't you see that he's an old man now, and nearly blind, and needs his sleep at nights?"

"I have never thought of Björn as old at all," said the girl. "Some people say he gave me a son."

"Yes, the things people can say about my Björn!" said the woman. "Are you dripping, my dear?"

"I'm in service on the other side of the river," said the girl. "I waded across."

"It's nice when young people want to go into service," said the woman. "But it's terrible the loose living that goes on nowadays at night. Hadn't you better be hurrying off home now, poor thing, so that you can get up in the morning? I'll lend you my riding-cloak to put on. Would you like a lump of sugar? Unfortunately the fire under the kettle is out."

25

Travel episode

When Björn of Leirur went to see the sheriff and complained about the fact that a foreign agent was moving round the country like a moor fire and buying up decent people on behalf of the Mormons, so that Iceland was in danger of depopulation, the sheriff said, "Decent people? What sort of people are they? Do you mean parish paupers or saga-heroes?"

"You remember the girl from Steinahlíðar who had a virgin birth?" said Björn. "The Mormons have managed to get their noses into that, of course. I am thinking of adopting the boy legally."

"You will adopt precisely damn-all boys whom you have denied on oath, making a laughing stock of my office," said the sheriff.

"That's a lie, I never denied the boy on oath," said Björn of Leirur. "On the other hand, there was nothing I could do if his mother insisted that it was a virgin birth."

"Yes, I'm branded as an idiot," said the sheriff, "for not sending you all to jail where you belong."

"Just re-open the case as if nothing had happened," said
Björn. "I demand that the Hlíðar folk be restrained from leaving
while the case is being investigated."

"Have you considered what sort of a favour you are doing the
taxpayers by interdicting parish paupers from emigrating?" said
the sheriff. "I know of parish councils that thank God for the
chance of being allowed to pay them their fares to America."

"Well, I'll take matters into my own hands, then," said Björn
of Leirur.

"That's up to you, but don't involve me in anything, and try
to keep out of jail. And now let's talk about something more
congenial. Do you want some cognac?"

"What have you got?" asked Björn of Leirur.

"Napoleonic," said the sheriff. "And getting down to something that is worth spending words on—we have had an offer of
a trawler in England, a big ship, my lad. It goes on steam. In one
single season it can catch as much as all the seamen in fifty fishing stations in Iceland put together. On a ship like that there's
no question of the men lying on their bunks all day long, reading
about saga-heroes while they wait for better weather. In a few
years' time, fishing smacks and schooners will have become
objects of public ridicule, and no one will know what a rowing-
boat is. It just needs a final bit of drive for our company to be
formed in Reykjavík. If a few sound fellows like you put up five
hundred hundreds of land or so, in addition to cash, a certain foreigner is prepared to guarantee a bank-loan for us. After a year
we would be ladling the gold from the sea."

Björn of Leirur protested that all the stuffing had gone out of
him now, and that he suffered from nightmares: "It's all up with

me. And anyway I don't understand big business. All I understand is how to accept nice shiny guineas from the Scots for horses and sheep on the hoof. As you know," he went on, "it has always been my ideal to restore gold in Iceland. Some of my happiest moments in life have been spent in counting out genuine money into the hands of farmers and seeing their eyebrows shoot up. Very few of those with whom I had dealings knew the stuff. Some of them said to me that they thought gold only existed in ballads. One man said to me that modern gold was all counterfeit; all the genuine gold in the world had been sunk to the bottom of the Rhine in the days of the *Edda,* he said. Those are the kind of people with whom I can do business, not the big boys in Reykjavík, and least of all with foreign bankers."

The sheriff offered to lend him English statistics about trawler profits, but Björn of Leirur said he was too weak in the eyes now to read statistics and too weak in the head to do sums. The sheriff brought out the statistics nonetheless and read out some figures to the agent and explained them to him.

"Yes, that may well apply to the English," said Björn of Leirur. "But there's a difference between Peter and Paul. I don't know how to look after my money once it's put into a trawler."

"Trawlers are trawlers," said the sheriff. "And fish have still got little enough sense to go into the net without pausing to ask whether it belongs to Björn of Leirur or to the English. I don't see why foreigners should scoop up all the fish around Iceland's shores while we ourselves sit on dry land and read thrillers and wait for good weather; or how a progressive chap like yourself can carry on fleecing these peasants who are stuck here hemmed in between river and seashore. For my own part I confess that I shudder at being called sheriff over these people. It is as ludicrous to administer justice to destitute people as it is to fleece them. Now's the chance for us two, you and me, to give the English a roasting."

In the end they both started doing sums. They did all sorts of sums for the rest of the day, and restored Iceland's national economy on paper and consigned decent parish paupers and saga-heroes to America to ease the burden on the taxpayers. It was not surprising that the Mormons were forgotten during this game.

"Since you cannot be induced to grant interdicts against slave-traders from Mormony, I'll have a word myself with my lowland tenants down here. I'm not used to letting any shrimp of a sheriff trip me up," said Björn of Leirur eventually, when he had mounted his pony that evening.

"Keep out of jail, and come and see me again," said the sheriff in parting.

And now to tell of the encounter at the Jökulsá.

Early next morning a small and rather unwarlike company could be seen plodding along the main track westwards from Steinahlíðar. In the van was Þjóðrekur the Mormon, barefooted and leading an old pack-pony laden with the sort of bits and pieces that do not deserve any elaborate description in a book. Behind him trailed the family which the Mormons had confiscated: the wife, her daughter and the boy Víkingur who, in the bishop's opinion, had not had a haircut since the first day of summer. Nor should it be entirely overlooked that Bishop Þjóðrekur, in addition to carrying his boots and hat slung over his shoulder and walking barefoot, as was said previously, also carried in his arms the little boy who had created such a mystery in the district; and now over the bishop's shoulder the child opened his hand towards the mountains which were taking leave of these people.

"It's as if he wants to take these mountains with him," said his mother, and laughed.

"He will get better mountains instead, like Sierra Benida where the sun rises over those who think correctly," said Bishop Þjóðrekur. "Not to mention Mount Timpanogus, which is named after a red lady and has poplar aspens."

"Where is the company bound for, if one may ask?" said passers-by, stopping in the middle of the main track and eyeing these people who from their lack of ponies did not seem destined for fame, even though one of them was a fresh-complexioned young woman in the full bloom of youth.

"If you were sent to ask, my lad," replied Bishop Þjóðrekur, "then we are on the way to paradise on earth, which wicked men lost but good men found again."

The ferryman and his wife gave the travellers curds and then coffee and cream on top of that, which they said was wholesome; and they gave them this piece of news: "There were some men around this morning, some of them people of no little account and with horses to match. People like that never deign to ask for a ferry when they come to glacier-rivers. And there was certainly nothing very threadbare about their leader."

"Is that any of my business?" said Bishop Þjóðrekur.

"Not unless they were wanting to have a word with you."

"Were they perhaps thinking of beating me up?" said the bishop.

"I don't know," said the ferryman. "But you are welcome to shelter here until the sheriff has been fetched."

"I never laugh as loudly as when I hear sheriffs mentioned," said Bishop Þjóðrekur, but he did not laugh, for it was an art he had never learned.

When they came down to the ferry they caught sight of mounted men on the sands on the far side of the river. They seemed to be waiting for something, and kept a close watch on

Þjóðrekur and his companions. One of them put a telescope to his eye.

The ferryman's wife drew the girl aside as she bade her farewell at the edge of the home-field.

"You can see him standing there with the telescope, ready to snatch the child when you step ashore on the other side. Remember what I said to you the year before last: make the old devil pay. Don't let him have the boy except for a really large sum, cash down."

"Just take it nice and steady, lad," said Bishop Þjóðrekur to the ferryman. He seated himself carefully on the grass and put on his topboots. Then he put on his hat just as it was, wrapped in its transparent covering. Then they carried their baggage and the pack-saddle on to the boat, and let the pony swim across unencumbered.

No sooner had they pushed out the boat than those who lay in wait on the other side rode down to the landing-point opposite. Some of them dismounted, others remained on their horses. They exchanged sardonic witticisms and laughed uproariously. There was no sign of any weapons, but on the other hand Björn of Leirur had put on his topboots and was standing in them on the other bank. He was trying to focus the telescope but his pony would not let him; it kept on tugging at the reins Björn was holding, pawed the ground and chewed the bit, snorted and tried to rub its bridle off against its legs or against its master's shoulder.

When it was obvious that Bishop Þjóðrekur was determined to put out into the river, the ferryman disposed his passengers in the skiff, with the women in the stern and the boy Víkingur on the thwart by his side; in the bows sat the bishop, with the child wrapped in a blanket asleep in his arms. The river was shallow on the near side but deepened gradually into a fast-running channel the closer one went to the other side. The ferryman's technique was to row upstream first of all where the water was shallow and sluggish, and then let the current carry the boat downstream while he steered for the landing-place with an oar. Bishop Þjó-ðrekur, however, now asked the ferryman to head straight towards the men, "For I need to have a word with them," he said, "before we enter the channel."

The ferryman replied, "If we head straight across river we shall enter the current just where it swings out into the middle of the river, and then we could either be swept back to this bank or else be driven on to a sandbar."

"Be that as it may," said the bishop. "I want to have a word with these men from out on the river rather than be driven help-lessly ashore at their feet."

"I cannot vouch for this old hulk, she only hangs together from sheer habit, and she could come apart if we deviate from the course I have steered her for a generation. She can't stand the strain of the current from any other direction than the one she is used to."

"Have no fear, lad. I am the bishop," said Þjóðrekur.

The ferryman steered the boat in the direction the bishop had indicated. When they reached the point where the current began to grow stronger, Þjóðrekur told the ferryman to hold the boat on the oars. Then he called over to the men on the far bank: "Are you waiting for anything, good people, or were you wanting to have a word with us?"

"This is a public ferry," said Björn of Leirur.

"It does not seem to me proper for men with such fine horses to crowd into this little tub," said the bishop. "Why don't you ford the river on horseback? Who are you, anyway?"

"The agent at Leirur," came the reply.

"Oh, that doesn't cut so very much ice," said Bishop Þjó-ðrekur.

"I know who you are," Björn of Leirur went on. "And let me tell you that we don't need to ask a crazy Mormon how to conduct our journeys here in the south."

Bishop Þjóðrekur replied, "Since you call me a crazy Mormon, then my opinions challenge your opinions to a duel. Which of us has the more correct opinions will be proved by seeing which of us is better off when the ultimate reckoning comes."

Now Björn of Leirur was getting really roused.

"I have no opinions at all, luckily—before seven o'clock at night," he said. "Then I know whether I want beefsteak or salted meat," he shouted, and all the champions on the riverbank laughed. "And now stop hanging about in the middle of the river, the child will catch cold."

"What's this child to you?" said the Mormon.

"I've come here to fetch it. I'm going to adopt it."

"Who gave you the documents for that?" asked the Mormon.

"The Government authorities are on my side," said Björn.

"If you mean sheriffs, my friend, they can eat their own dirt," said the Mormon. "My documents are from King Kristian Wilhelmsson himself."

Þjóðrekur now asked the ferryman to let the boat drift downstream, but to be careful to keep the channel between themselves and the champions standing on the bank.

Björn and his men mounted and moved off to keep abreast of the boat. The river deepened and broadened, with a steady current, and both banks fell away. The boat was no longer familiar with the river when she left her customary course, and now began to creak rather ominously. The women began to feel dizzy.

Steinar's wife pushed her hood back, raised her eyes to Heaven and began to sing the hymn, "Praise the Lord, the merciful King of Heaven." The agent shouted from the bank, and could only just be heard above the noise of wind and water. He said that although the Mormon was evil and damned, he trusted the ferry-man, his friend and compatriot, not to take part in murdering the child.

"I can't hear what you're saying," said the ferryman.

"Come closer," said Björn.

"If you frighten me away from the bank by threatening my passengers, I cannot vouch for their lives. There is a strong current here, the boat is leaking, and the oars are rotted."

"Try to come back into earshot again," said Björn of Leirur. "My eyesight is failing, but isn't there a fair-haired young girl in the boat with you, red-cheeked and well-built? I want to speak to her if she agrees."

"Have you anything still to discuss with this man?" asked the bishop.

The girl asked to be rowed closer to the bank, in case this man should have anything important to say to her. "What he says is up to him," she said.

"I have come here with many horses and followers and plenty of money," shouted Björn of Leirur. "Everything except good eyesight. Will you ride away with me? I am going somewhere I can get my sight back. I shall bring the boy up and provide for him. He will have all the education he can cope with. I shall make as much of a man of him as can be done for anyone in this country. When I saw him this summer in the uplands I said to myself: this boy and his mother as well shall be mine before the summer is out."

The housewife of Hlíðar kept on singing without listening, staring up to the heavens: "Praise the Lord and join with his angels in song." But the girl's dizziness out in midstream overpowered all emotions.

Bishop Þjóðrekur shouted, "You shall never take this boy alive, my friend."

"Why are you sticking your nose into the boy's affairs, foreigner?" asked the agent.

Bishop Þjóðrekur raised the boy aloft and said, "I, Þjóðrekur, bishop and elder of the Church of the Latter-Day Saints which stands in heaven and on earth, by immersion do here and now consecrate this child in water and spirit, and seal him to myself before God and men in this world and the next for all eternity. And after that I shall drown the child in this baptismal water here in the river, rather than let him fall, alive or dead, into the hands of the man who has addressed us from the bank."

Þjóðrekur now removed the blanket in which the boy was wrapped, and the child started to cry at being woken in such strange surroundings. The Mormon paid no attention, but began to loosen the boy's ragged clothing with hands whose clumsiness only made him all the more resolute, until finally he held the child naked in his arms in that ramshackle boat out in the middle of the river. The child cried with all its might. The men on the bank huddled in a group and told Björn that the Mormon had now taken all the child's clothes off. Björn asked them if they thought it possible to reach the boat on horseback and try to rescue the child, but this suggestion got short shrift; they said it was quite impossible to ford the river there because of quicksands. And now, they said, he is holding the child aloft, naked, and is loudly declaiming some rigmarole; and now he has lifted the child out over the gunwale, and plunged him into the water.

They said there was no doubt that the Mormon was determined to drown the child.

Now Björn of Leirur interrupted the speaker and told all his men to mount up at once and ride away before infanticide was done. The whole company responded at once and rode off out of sight as hard as they could.

While this was going on, and the bishop was immersing the weeping and terrified child naked in the glacier-river, the boy's mother reacted as she always did in times of trial: she simply let things happen to her, and when the point was reached where words ceased to have validity she became oblivious to everything around her. She leaned back against her mother's hymn-singing breast and fell into a faint, and the whites of her eyes glinted between her half-closed lids as she swooned.

When she came to her senses again she was lying on the river-bank with her head on her mother's lap: the hymn was over. The Mormon was sitting on the sand cuddling her son against his skin under his shirt, to warm him. Gradually the child's racking sobs died down as his terror abated, until he fell asleep against the warm hairy chest of this bishop who a short while ago had been planning to murder him, or rather had been ensuring for him the eternal life of the saints of Zion.

It was a pleasant autumn day; the soft breeze wafted the soul high above time and place, and here and there the occasional blue sheen of a raven glinted in the white sunshine over the sand. Bishop Þjóðrekur took off his topboots and removed his hat with its covering, as a sign that the ceremony was over for the time being; and the sun made up for it by breaking resolutely through the clouds. He tied the shoelaces to a specially-made loop on the hat, and then slung the lot over his shoulder, the boots behind and the hat in front. They headed in a straight line west across

the sands; at the far end of the sands they encountered another
river, with an unknown ferryman on the one side and no troop of
champions on the other; and indeed there was little immersing
or baptising or infanticide for the rest of the day. They were now
in another district. Steinar's wife could now no longer walk, and
had to be carried on top of the baggage.

In this new district the blue raven cawed with bell-like tones
in the sunshine, for this wise song-bird had modelled himself on
the bells of the small churches of the littoral, like foreign toys
washed ashore from shipwrecks. The little boy eyed the ravens in
silence from the bishop's shoulder; he did not have the confi-
dence to reach out towards them until he was in his grandmother's arms on top of the baggage. This area was called the
Landeyjar from the grass-patches that retained moisture and
were left there when the turf was stripped by erosion and turned
into sand. These grass-patches could provide the sparse popula-
tion with a reasonable livelihood; the farmhouses stood on humble hillocks which were often no more than turf ramparts against
erosion. On the other hand, the mountains had all taken to their
heels as the travellers approached, as if they feared that these
people were going to drag them off to the Mormons, and had not
halted before they were far inland—in direct contrast to the
mountains of Steinahlíðar which had come rushing headlong
down from the hinterland right up to the people's faces, as it
were, in their eagerness to be taken along by the little boy.

"If it isn't, it isn't," said Bishop Þjóðrekur, looking all around
him at this low-lying district which somehow glided unnotice-
ably into the sea and then merged into the sky. "It's nothing,
really," he went on, "but yet the place has a faintly familiar look
about it. Over there, where you can see a smudge of cliffs in the
sea, that's the Vestmannaeyjar, where my mother was sent to give

birth to me; I always thought the biggest rogues in Iceland lived there, until sister María Jónsdóttir from Ampahjallur told me they were all saints. Now the ground starts rising a little, and then I am sure I shall get my bearings properly."

It was late afternoon, and the sun was shining full in their faces as the ground gradually began to rise from the flats.

"I don't suppose you can see a little green hillock at the foot of a rocky outcrop over there?" said the bishop. "Let's go over and see if we can't wring some supper out of them, and perhaps some milk from a cow of three colours for the boy. It's called Bóla in the Landeyjar, that farm. It's where my people came from originally; the parish council sent me to work for my living there when I was four years old. My mother was too broken in health to be able to support me; she was in service in the Vestmannaeyjar."

When they reached Bóla in the Landeyjar, where they had been going to get milk from a cow of three colours for the boy, and perhaps other delicacies as well, there was unfortunately no one at home except for two marsh marigolds which had started sprouting that autumn among the reeds beside the farm-brook because they were expecting a little boy who was going away; but the farm itself had been derelict for more than forty years. The tumbled turf walls had long since fused and were overgrown. And just to keep the picture accurate, there were also two phalaropes nodding and bowing in the two-foot-deep pool in the farm-brook. No sooner had the boy been lifted down off the pony than he ran down to the brook to pull the marigolds that had been waiting for him, and to try to catch these well-mannered birds. His mother sat down on a tussock and stared entranced with questioning, wondering eyes at this remarkable frock-clad young gentleman, as if she had never seen anything like it in her life; and perhaps she had not. The bishop lifted the old woman

and the baggage off the pony and did not seem appreciably disappointed that the farm was now derelict.

"We shall just have a bite of our own, then, others have had to
do it before," he said, and began to unwrap their provisions. In
no time at all the black pate of a handsome rye-loaf was glinting
at the mouth of the knapsack. "This one hails all the way east
from Skaftártunga, no less!" said the bishop. "Kneaded and baked
by a saintly person. I have been keeping it in the hope that I
would be given the chance of eating it in good company. I wonder if I can find that famous doorstep somewhere around here,
and offer you a seat on it; it is a slab which has haunted my
dreams for long enough."

The farmhouse paving, in fact, was now almost smothered by
the grass, but Bishop Þjóðrekur knew where it lurked and did
not take long to recognize a corner of it which was still visible
above ground.

"Do have a seat," said the bishop. "It was on this slab that the
dog of blessed memory used to lie on my frock until the first day
of summer."

They sat down on the paving of Bóla in the Landeyjar. The
bishop said grace and thanked the Lord on high for having saved
the wanderers from the clutches of the unrighteous earlier that
morning and admitted this young boy into the communion of
souls and led them all to a green site beside a little brook where
two marigolds grow and the smallest birds in Iceland bob their
curtseys. Then they ate the appetising jet-black bread from out
east in Skaftártunga, and had the setting sun for butter.

Then the bishop began to give them instruction there on the
hillock.

"These ruins," he said, "bear witness that every dwelling shall be laid waste if the people do not have correct opinions. Even though this was excellent farmland, the young were kept alive on bone-jelly and whey from midwinter until the cows were out at grass and beginning to yield some milk. When my master went to buy meal down at Eyrarbakki the week before Easter and came back with one pastry a head as a treat for the family, he always took care that there should be no pastry for the foster-child. I was invariably thrashed every morning for uncommitted crimes. I never managed to go through this door, in or out, without treading on the tail of the dog and being snapped at. Mercifully, the water here was good. Indulge my laziness, Víkingur lad, and go and fill that mug from the brook for us. And what do you have to say about all this, missus? In your shoes, most people would be yearning for the country where the truth lives."

"Oh, yes indeed," said the worn-out woman. "It was not to be that I should never leave my home and hearth. Indeed I feel as if I have already left this world and have come to a new one. But to be quite candid, let me tell you that in my time here on earth there were two kinds of farm. There were farms where people had food and clothing, and there were farms where people had neither. But I don't think that it went by whether people had correct opinions; and luckily not the opposite either. I knew of people who never had a ghost of an opinion in their heads, and not that much kindness in their hearts, either; they lived on a barren moorland croft, but there was never any suggestion that they ever had to go hungry—indeed, they were rolling in fat. People who never have any opinions about anything attract profusion and plenty. It would be nice to be able to say that good and gifted people who adhere steadfastly to correct doctrine are provided with food and clothing in proportion; but that is not the case. In our household at Hlíðar there was always a shortage of the good things of life for which one gives thanks to God; and yet it would take some looking to find a man who had a better understanding of most things than my Steinar."

Bishop Þjóðrekur did not at the moment care to enter into dispute with this homeless woman; instead he sipped the water that her son Víkingur had fetched for them from the brook, and changed the subject.

"It is good to come across one's own stream again," he said, "and be able to drink it with people whose feet are on the very threshold of the sacred city. Yes, these were glorious days, missus, when one wore the sack from under the dog and was thrashed every morning for the sins of the unlived day. No one here, with the exception of that little boy who is messing about in the mud beside the birds, has the glorious days yet to come. Praise be to the Lord for this water."

"I have been wanting to ask the bishop something for a long time," said Víkingur Steinarsson. "How much would a pair of shoes like the ones you are carrying cost? And where can they be obtained?"

Bishop Þjóðrekur replied, "No Lutheran could ever obtain a pair of boots like these, my lad. Boots like these are only made by saints. These shoes are a proof, my boy, that the Church of the Latter-Day Saints is founded on the All-Wisdom. If Lutherans ever obtain shoes, it is merely by chance. They manage to lose them in a year and never get another pair again. Yes sirree. No sirree. Not even one in a hundred in Iceland can obtain a pair of boots. These shoes have been a much stronger argument for me in arguments with Lutherans than any quotation from the prophets. On these boots one could climb most of the way up to the moon."

26

Clementine

In a cavern, in a canyon,
Excavating for a mine,
Dwelt a miner, forty-niner,
And his daughter Clementine.

All day long one could hear this dance-tune on the emigrants' deck of the liner *Gideon* which was transporting people from the Old World to the New. Each and every one had his own goldmine on the other side of the ocean, and the song adjusted itself to the hope, as always. Young girls in far too heavy coats, some of them from the Carpathian Mountains, strolled hand-in-hand along the decks with the words of the song dancing in their eyes, alight with hope, and the wind in their hair on this morning of eternity. This song was the only one with any meaning for the young country lads, who were probably Gascons, in their black pea-jackets and embroidered shirts; or an apprentice from Bavaria with the broad-brimmed hat of his craft and wearing trousers so wide that they looked like a skirt on each leg. This was the tune that was danced to on the deck far into the night, and again on an empty stomach first thing next morning;

it was played on harmonicas and mouth-organs, strummed on lutes and mandolins, and ground out on barrel-organs. It carried from the bar, blended with the bitter-sweet aroma of beer and, from the kitchens, mingled with the reek of vegetables and singed fat: Clementine, the romanticism of the age that went to America, with the characteristically melancholy note of the refrain:

Oh my darling, Oh my darling,
Oh my darling Clementine,
Thou art lost and gone forever,
Dreadful sorry, Clementine.

For the first few days after leaving harbour in Scotland the sea was calm. They all wanted to escape from the overcrowding and stuffiness below decks in steerage, and treat themselves to some inexpensive luxury such as the breath off the sea or the rays of some poorer star like the ones which shone on Steinahlíðar. Families gathered together in groups and sat or squatted on the deck. They removed the newspaper wrappings from their salted ham, home-baked rye-loaves and mandolins. The boys were sent for beer, and now there was feasting of a kind that made the entertainment provided by the emigration agents look pale by comparison. These people sang and talked in languages that no one understood except themselves; and so did the salted hams, pumpernickels and mandolins. Soon they all joined hands and started dancing in a circle. There were also plenty of young people who were going on their own or with a few companions to dig for gold in America. They and their friends gathered together on deck in the evenings under an oil-lamp and displayed whatever accomplishments they might have; some did sword-dances, others made prodigious leaps, clapped their hands and uttered shrieks and yells that outmatched anything to be heard in Iceland. This was all part of the dance. The brother and sister from Steinahlíðar gaped at the men fearfully. Here was the entertainment which had been banned in Iceland two centuries previously by royal decree, under pain of Hell. Here was no question of sparing the shoe-leather by treading lightly on the ground, as children were taught in Iceland; and all the musical instruments which the Danish king found sinful were here on show. The brother and sister from Steinahlíðar were the only young people in the world who knew no other entertainment than going to church, not even going round in a circle. They stood apart from the crowd and held hands and for a long time they did not understand what was going on. What was the meaning of it? Was this the correct way to behave? Look at that one doing a somersault in the air and landing on his feet! Was this perhaps a new way of going to Communion?

"It pierces the marrow of my bones," said the boy, when the din of the bagpipes and drums was at its most frantic.

"I am almost glad that mother is ill, so that she does not have to see and hear all this," said the girl. "I am sure she would never recover from it. Goodness me, I'm going to run away and hide!"

But despite all the goings-on they did not run away and hide, but stayed where they were, like two mooncalves.

> *In a cavern, in a canyon,*
> *Excavating for a mine. . . .*

They forgot time and place. They were spellbound by the kind of enchanted vision which opens the secret pores of the soul to the winds of regeneration. And suddenly, before she was aware of it, someone had grasped her round the waist; she was snatched from her brother's side; a man was holding her in his arms and had begun to whirl her around; he was from a nation that dances the mazurka to Clementine. And now this young girl in her fetters of homespun found that inside this woollen guise there lived another girl who understood rhythm and followed it without making too many mistakes, and who knew instinctively this art that the Danish kings had forbidden to Icelanders. What was it that suddenly started stirring in all her limbs with such unnatural ease that one met oneself and did not know who it could be?

They were unused to seeing many strangers at a time, and inexperienced at distinguishing between foreigners (particularly in a herd), just as it is practically impossible to distinguish between the oyster-catchers that step aristocratically in flocks through the new-mown hayfields; and the faces of the people somehow blurred into a sea of porridge whenever the Hlíðar children tried to differentiate one from the other, and melted away like the bubbles in a simmering porridge-pot. This mob of foreigners, their shipboard companions, was one huge whale, a monstrous beast which stuck together of its own accord like the Vestmannaeyjar creature, with such and such a number of maws. It did not occur to them to single out any one individual in their minds, or to try to get some idea of which ones came from Norway and which from Montenegro. They had become like the English officials who interviewed them at the emigration office: these Englishmen thought they spoke Finnish because they came from Iceland. When Bishop Þjóðrekur said that they spoke Icelandic, the Englishmen retorted curtly, "Yes, and isn't that just another kind of Finnish?" To the Hlíðar children, just as to the Englishmen, foreign tongues were either Finnish or yet more Finnish; with the best will in the world it seemed to them that this multi-mouthed monster always talked the same language, as far as they could hear. They had the impression that no one in this mob was a foreigner except themselves. But now the girl suddenly discovered that a particular individual had started to dance with her. She could not see him yet, admittedly, but she could feel him. And most particularly she could feel how the movements of his soul aroused due responses in her own; or rather—life had begun to flow. But she did not even dare to glance at him during the dance, neither when he pulled her close (for then she did not want him to suspect that she was conscious of herself) nor when he moved away from her again—for that would have been nearly as inconsiderate as asking one's husband for his name on the morning after the wedding-night. Still, she got an impression of a tall and broad-shouldered young man, slim-waisted and supple to match. Quite accidentally she caught a suggestion in the lamplight of a sun-tanned manly chin and a lock of blond hair which he flicked back behind his ear. He said something to her which was quite definitely Finnish, and she was careful not to try to guess what he meant. If he were asking what she was called, she thought it a blasphemy not to conceal her name and her identity, language, family, people and country. What did such things matter? Life has no name.

When she had danced for so long that she had not only forgotten that she did not know how to dance, but had forgotten everything except the dance, he suddenly stopped. "One minute," she thought she heard him say. He put his arm round her waist and led her out of the dance circle. She felt as if she were floating on unfamiliar planes of air, borne aloft on a soft breeze. They drifted through the open door of a room where some men were sitting crowded round little tables and having a drink. There were two men sitting drinking on their own at one table, and she realised

that they must be his comrades, for they applauded him boister-
ously for having got hold of a girl. They rose to their feet and
bowed to her and said, as far as she could make out, that she was
a fine piece. Then they made her sit down between them. They
made another attempt to converse with her, but their language
was Finnish and yet more Finnish. Even so she could not help
laughing at their eagerness and this seemed to delight them, for
she had excellent teeth, like all people who do not eat bread. She
contemplated them while they were struggling to converse with
her, and saw at once that her dance-partner, with his blue eyes
and blond wavy hair, was much the most handsome of them.
One of his companions was long and dark-haired, which made
her think of a raven; his hair was as coarse as a horse's mane, his
cheeks hollow, and his hands were large and numb-looking, ice-
blue hands ruined by chilblains, for the knuckles were badly
swollen; or else they had been wrecked by poor implements. His
cold glittering eyes began at once to probe into her half-angrily,
as if he thought she were concealing under her clothing something out of which she had cheated him. She was not fully recon-
ciled to him until he produced a mouth-organ and began to play
with great skill on this instrument, which was swallowed up in
his blue hands like a pea in a barrel. While he was playing the
mouth-organ she had a chance of observing the third man in the
party. This one effaced himself as much as he could and preferred
to stay in the shadow of his companions; and this was because
he had a gaping hare-lip and a cleft palate. His complexion was
pasty from drudgery, and there was nothing but down left on the
crown of his head; his teeth betrayed him as a bread-eater. But in
Iceland the girl had been brought up to pay no heed to people's
external appearance, for human virtues do not all reside in the

face; she gave no hint that she preferred her dance-partner to his comrades. And when Blue-Hands stopped playing and started knocking the saliva out of the mouth-organ into his palm, she gratefully enveloped him with the candid warmth of her eyes. No sooner had the music stopped before the man with the hare-lip began to display his own accomplishments, which consisted of cackling and crowing as if there were a whole hen-run next door. This amused the girl from Steinahlíðar intensely because she had never heard this fowl before. He could also mimic the unimpassioned and simple everyday clucking of these birds when pecking for grain in the midday quiet. Then Blue-Hands went into action again and produced a deck of cards and launched into a series of card-tricks, some of them so outrageous that his comrades pretended to thump him. Then the man with the hare-lip set about imitating the yowling of lovesick cats behind a house at night. The girl cheered up at all this ingenuity and laughed heartily, for she had never attended an entertainment in her life before. In gratitude she danced with both of the others the next time Clementine was played, for she was now an expert at that dance. They ordered one last round of drinks before the bar was closed and the lights put out, but the girl did not like the taste; it reminded her of stale urine, and she handed her beer-mug to the three men to share between them. After that they sat in a darkened corner of the deck and they sang Clementine to her over and over again and other songs, each one livelier than the last. One of them was holding her ankle. She was not very sure who it was and was not particularly pleased, but did nothing about it until the hand began to steal suspiciously high up her calf; at that she suddenly remembered that her mother was lying ill in the sick-bay and that she was to sleep with her

that night and nurse her. She stood up. They could not understand why the girl wanted to leave so early. "Mamma, mamma,"
she said. They imitated her and laughed. "One minute," she said,
pulling away from them. They laughed even more. In the end
her dance-partner accompanied her on her way and his comrades
generously raised no objections, for he quite indisputably had
first claim on the girl.

But when they were round the corner he stopped her and
started to talk to her nineteen to the dozen. But words were of no
use here. Then he pointed to her and then to himself, question-
ingly. No understanding, no reply. He pointed in the direction
the ship was steaming and pretended to dig and shovel, but she
did not understand properly, for the only shovelling she knew
was dung from the byre. He led her over to a spot where the light
was a little better, and pulled from his pocket a small object
which a fist could easily hide. It was a lump of unrefined ore
studded with gilt particles. Strangely enough, it so happened that
the girl had once before seen the colour that glittered in this dross.

"Gold," she whispered, and got palpitations.

He wanted to give her the piece but at that she became even
more fearful, for she remembered all at once that a girl is worthy
of gold only once in her life. She could not bear to think of the
shame there would be if he gave her gold and it later came to
light that she had been given gold already. "One minute," she
said, thrusting the lump of gold into his hand again, and hurried
away. But when she had left him she began to have doubts
whether there had been pure gold in the lump; the boy was still
only on his way to America, after all. Perhaps he had only
brought out this gold in earnest of the future. By the time she
reached the room where her mother lay she had begun to regret

not having accepted the lump, whether it was pure gold or not. She hoped and prayed that she had not offended the young man by refusing his gold.

And what of the housewife from Steinahlíðar? This woman had set out from Iceland with a feebleness in the head and a weakness in the heart and so wobbly in the legs that she could not even walk across green fields, let alone sands. One might say that she had the desert itself in her legs. On the voyage from Iceland to Scotland the last of her strength ebbed away and she took to her bed, and was scarcely able to rise from it again. At this setback her speech and her memory became blurred. She became so overcome by exhaustion that she could do nothing but lie back in bed. It is not the custom to make much fuss of destitute women from unknown parts who fall ill in emigration camps. Most people in Glasgow thought she was Finnish. Bishop Þjóðrekur gave instructions that her daughter Steinbjörg was not to leave her mother's side night or day while they waited in Scotland, and he himself took charge of the little frock-coated gentleman whom he had immersed in the Jökulsá. And although she and the child were at last getting to know one another, she, too, handed him into the bishop's care when they embarked on the emigrant ship; indeed, they were already father and son, as far as she could understand from the complicated formulas the bishop had declaimed out in the river. The bishop managed to arrange permission for the girl to sleep near her mother at night aft in the sick-bay. There were several other peasant women from Europe in it; one, who could not move a muscle because of some internal ailment and was green in the face, was hurrying to join her son in New York; another had broken a hip during all the rough and tumble that attends lower-class flittings, and the general opinion was that she could certainly not survive another such fracture. Here was a collection of people who, in the English idiom, were past all needs except for a last white shirt. Forbidding-looking iron bedsteads jutted out from the walls, and in a corner behind the door a bed was made up on a bench for Steina. Her task was to get up during the night and tend her mother whenever she groaned, and preferably more often than that, and give her medicine. The doctor and the nurse were always in a hurry on the few occasions they drifted in. Early in the morning Bishop Þjóðrekur would arrive with her grandson, and the exhausted woman from Hlíðar was happy when she felt the little fellow clamber over her as if she were the last tussock in Iceland and burble at his granny with the few words she had taught him while they were paupers together.

And now we move on to the point where the girl had said "One minute" and gone below decks after refusing gold. It was around midnight. Her mother was now so weak that she could hardly take her medicine. A light burned faintly in one of those little red lamps which are used at night to comfort the dying. The girl was still keyed up by the warmth she had been given by the goldminer both in the dancing and the music. She forgave him for not having any particular accomplishment such as playing the mouth-organ or mimicking hens. She did not care in the least whether anyone knew how he had obtained the gold, or whether it was pure. And she was most grateful of all to him because it was not he who had been holding her leg above the ankle. She could not bear men like that. And then, before she was aware of it, she had put out the red light which was to have amused the women while they were dying. She tiptoed out again and hurried to the spot where she had said goodbye to him a long time ago. She had somehow got the idea that he was waiting there. But he was gone. Everyone was away except for a man who was embracing a girl against the mast; she almost bumped into them. Of course they were all gone! She could not understand how she could have thought otherwise in the middle of the night. She hurried down below decks and relit the lamp for the women and tried to make her mother drink a cupful of cold water, but most of it just spilled out of the corners of her mouth and ran down her neck. Then the girl went to bed on her bench.

27

One minute

Next day the sea got rougher and the girl asked herself whether she liked the motion or whether she was beginning to feel cold at the temples. But anyway, if one thing were certain, it was that she had completely recovered from that foolishness with complete strangers the night before. Or was emotion just as incomprehensible to her in the morning as it was natural at night?

And then without any warning she saw them come bearing down on her from a distance along the deck. Many a girl has asked herself whether it would not be just an act of courtesy and becoming modesty to look away and show no recognition. Finally they were all three at her side, fully refreshed by their sleep. They greeted her with the words that constituted the spiritual connection between them—"One minute"—and surrounded her. Before she knew it, she was once again standing beside the

bright-haired goldminer. The other two at once started to perform for the girl to make up for the language deficiency, such as
turning somersaults and playing leapfrog, and Blue-Hands tried
to trip up the one with the hare-lip, who thereupon dropped
down on all fours and bounded about the deck roaring like a wild
animal. But the goldminer did not have to do anything, because
he had the lump of gold in his pocket. When his rivals had
started to stand on their heads and walk on their hands for the
girl, he just stood there beside her without a word and put his
arm around her waist.

It had become the custom for her to go to see old Þjóðrekur in
the morning, after breakfast, and take charge of her son for the
rest of the day while she looked after her mother. It had truly
been a happy day that dawned in her life, now that she was a
fully-grown woman, when she had got to know this little boy
whom she had not understood when he was born. And when she
got to know him, she felt sorry that she had missed all his first
attempts to talk; and she also regretted the tears that she had not
been allowed to dry for him. But on this Atlantic morning with
storm in the offing and a long slow swell, her new-found friend,
the one who wore a frock-coat, had all at once slipped her mind
completely. She did not come to until Bishop Þjóðrekur was
standing beside her in his topboots and hat, with the boy in his
arms. He asked who these nincompoops were who were standing
on their heads nearby, but she could give him no answer.

"Who are you, gentlemen," he asked in English, but they did
not understand the language.

"I don't understand them either," she said, disengaging herself from the man who was steadying her as the ship rolled, and
went over to her son. "The fair-haired one is the Goldminer,"

she added, just to give the bishop some satisfaction. "The dark one with the chilblains I call Blue-Hands. But the one with the hare-lip I think of as the Hen-Keeper, because he can make the cockerels crow and the hens lay eggs. But now it's time to see to my son."

It is not too much to say that the three artistes were shocked when they saw this girl of little more than confirmation age take a child in her arms and betake herself off with an ancient old American with grease-proof paper around his hat; they felt that this madam had played them a really dirty trick. But later that day they had found out all about these people from the ship's officers: the passenger list said that the one with the grease-proof paper around his hat was a bishop, and the girl a widow. With that their spirits rose again; they forgive the widow and set off to find her again.

And now the little boy found companions who did not stint the fun; they became his playmates, just as they had been for his mother: Blue-Hands with somersaults and music, the Hen-Keeper with a flock of hens, to which ducks had now been added, and even pigs, and finally a howling dog. People gathered round from all sides to listen, and the entertainment was received by the audience with great enthusiasm. But happiest of all was the girl from Steinahlíðar at being able to sit close to a young man who was not associated with any earthly phrase or image but could yet have been the father of this little boy, and feel how he enveloped her with a warmth that was above any games or tricks.

A topic that sometimes succeeds in being fully resolved with the help of long explanations in speech or writing, with arguments and letter, but more often fails the harder it is pursued, can be resolved by dumbness in a single hour. That is why sages believe that language is one of mankind's blunders, and consider that the chirping of birds, with appropriate gestures of the wings, says far more than any poem, however carefully worded; they even go so far as to think that one fish is wiser than twelve tomes of philosophy. The happy assurance that two young people can read in one another's eyes becomes incomprehensible in verbal explanation; silent confession can turn into a denial if the magic spell is broken by words.

> *Oh my darling, oh my darling,*
> *Oh my darling Clementine. . . .*

When Clementine had begun to reverberate again and everyone had found one another on the dance-floor which often reared up like a cliff as the ship rolled, the girl from Steinahlíðar and her Goldminer had also found one another in that all-expressive wordlessness which books can never articulate. In one day they had poured over one another in the language of fish that light of truth which a whole year of daily letters with constantly reiterated vows of eternal fidelity cannot create, not even when accompanied by philosophy and poetry recitations or even songs. They had not been able to tear themselves away from one another all day, when most people had crawled into their bunks and begun to vomit. But the girl somehow felt that the Goldminer shrank from disappearing for a single moment from the sight of his comrades; and she noticed also that they were just as careful not to leave his side, but went on confirming their togetherness with skill and ingenuity, as if each and all of them, by prior arrangement, had a share in any gold lump that any one of them dug up. "How wonderful it can be," she said to herself, "and what nobil-

ity it proves in young men, when they pledge one another a
friendship that can never be shadowed by selfishness, envy or
jealousy." It was also a proof of the Goldminer's high-mindedness
that he treated his comrades in every way as his equals, the Hen-
Keeper no less than Blue-Hands. The humility which displays
itself in valuing the lowest on a par with the highest, and being a
true brother to the one whom nature has inflicted with a cruel
handicap—this was something that Icelanders had been taught
in theory on the principle that the Saviour had bought all men's
souls equally dearly. She was quite prepared to acknowledge this
ideal in practice, although she was ashamed to have to admit to
herself that she could not hit the right rhythm with his comrades
when dancing but trampled on their toes and they on hers until
she landed in the arms of her Pan again.

Some authorities think that the attachment between a boy
and a girl is in some way less valid if the time factor is not given
sufficient attention. Others think that implicit in the theory
about the necessity of a period of courtship are subconscious
associations with the fermentation of certain drinks, such as
mare's milk, or the peculiar fluid which in the *Edda* is called the
mead of poetic inspiration; or even the need to bury certain delicacies in a midden for three years. But one thing is quite certain:
that whereas the patriarchs and greybeards required lengthy
negotiations to conclude the betrothal of a man and a maiden,
Nature often requires only one minute, if she has her way.

In the evening Bishop Þjóðrekur came over to the group of
young people who were struggling to dance in the heavy seas to
snatches of mouth-organ music played by a drunk. Seasickness
was so foreign to them that they delighted in the towering waves
which tumbled them all over the place according to the laws of

physics. The bishop put his hand on the shoulder of the girl from Hlíðar, who had just been pitched into a man's arms in a corner. She rose to her feet in confusion and brushed a stray lock of hair from her hot cheeks; the pupils of her eyes were dilated, glowing.

"I have just come from your mother," he said. "She has taken a turn for the worse, I fear. Your brother and the boy are both in bed in my place, and I am now going back to see to the child. If I were a young girl I would not hang around so much with vagrants from Galicia tonight."

The girl flinched at this admonition from the bishop, and the terrified look of a sleepwalker invaded her face. She disengaged herself from the Goldminer's arms with the formula they had established: "One minute," she said, and ran.

It was now quite late and there were no other people about apart from those whose incontrollable glandular activity compelled them to dance in a howling gale at night on a floor that tilted fifteen degrees. From cabins and salons all over the ship came the sound of people retching or vomiting and groaning with seasickness. But the girl walked the heaving decks cheerfully and felt no discomfort. She tried to tend her mother, and gave her water and drugs as the doctor had prescribed. She tried to tell the exhausted woman about the weather. She said that young people who could not understand one another welcomed all the pitching and rolling, and she cheered this listless woman with the news that she had met some foreign gentlemen who were very nice to her. Although the woman did not react with any exuberance, she was not dead; she even half-opened one eye and smiled with one corner of her mouth towards her daughter in this aforementioned small red glow, as if to say that the happiness of youth is a beautiful thing and that people should enjoy it

while they could: "I understand you, my daughter," she seemed
to be saying with that half-smile, "and I will not reproach you
for as long as I can see you with one eye, by the grace of God."
And with that she fell into a coma.

The girl began to struggle out of her clothes in the tossing of
the waves. The ship creaked as it plunged into a trough, or clambered up a mountain of water so steep that the propellers rose
threshing above the surface. There was no pause in the groans
and screeches of the engines.

One minute. The words still rang in her ears as she stood there
half-naked and numb as the ship pitched under her, holding on
tight to avoid a fall. The sound of the door being opened was
drowned in the din. It was her Goldminer, intent on compensat-
ing her for the brevity of their leave-taking a short while ago, to
say goodnight and take her in his arms. And now she recalled
Björn of Leirur, who always used to put out the light at this
point. As if nothing were more natural she turned down the
lamp without moving from his embrace, and caught a gleam of
his blond wavy locks at the same moment as the light went out.
While the women carried on breathing their last she inhaled this
youngster who by his mere presence held sway over all her
veins. The moment had arrived that some authorities consider
all-important—so important, even, that nothing further awaits
when it is past. But nevertheless here were no proposals made nor
promises, no confession, compliment nor poetry, let alone any
argument about morals and philosophy. At this moment which
could just as well contain the true essence of a whole life, no
other words were uttered than the magic formula: One minute.

Time dissolved in the heat of this night of oblivion on the
heaving ocean rollers that hurled the ship from wave to wave, to

the sparse breathing of the suffering women and the strains of the lost and gone forever Clementine. The sensations and dreams of the blood's dark night merged into a strange picture-book or ebbed away into oblivion to the accompaniment of the protesting propellers that reared into the empty air on the crests of the waves; and of the mouth-organ outside. She had fallen asleep, and was aware of nothing until she awoke at the man's presence again. The hands which clasped her like an urn were now cold, and refreshed her. And the fire of this wordless night burned on from sleep to sleep, from distant memories of Björn of Leirur's aromatic beard all the way up to the cackling of hens.

As was mentioned earlier, Bishop Þjóðrekur had thought the woman from Hlíðar in rather worse shape when he had visited her the previous evening. The bishop had found her daughter mixed up with some crowd of rascals and admonished the girl until she went below. Then he went to the dormitory where her brother and small son were lying in bed paralysed with seasickness. The bishop could not sleep for worrying about the distaff side of this family he had been sent to fetch home for God safe and sound to a holy land. Again and again during that night he was on the point of going to visit the woman once more to see how she was doing in this tempest, but hesitated to leave the ailing little boy. There was a sage old Mormon from England in there, however, who always woke up at the crack of dawn and started chanting to himself a beautiful Mormon hymn about a poor sorry wayfarer. And now early in the morning, when Bishop Þjóðrekur heard the old Mormon starting to chant, he left the small boy in his care and went off to visit the sick and the wretched, according to the Gospel.

The sea was still high and the sky leaden, but the storm was abating and day was dawning. He groped his way aft along corridors and companion-ways. There was not a soul afoot. Dim lights glimmered here and there. He opened the door of the sick-bay, and found that the light inside had gone out and the patients were lying in complete darkness. He brought out some matches and struck a light. He glanced towards the bench where the girl had her bed, and was astounded to see lying beside her an oldish-looking man, far from handsome, bald, and with a hare-lip, his mouth wide open, and snoring. Beside him this young girl lay sleeping peacefully in all the bloom of her beauty. This sight astonished the bishop so much that he forgot for a moment his mission and went over to the bench and shushed at the sleepers with the sort of noise one makes when driving sheep to their night-pastures. The girl was the first to stir and she opened her eyes. She saw the bishop standing at her bedside, and lying beside her a creature which in her semi-waking state seemed to her to be a monster. With a scream she cringed away against the wall, covering her naked breasts with her hands. At this point her bedfellow awoke too. He rubbed the sleep from his eyes and giggled, so that the deep cleft in his lip gaped wider, but into his eyes came the bestial look so typical of those whom nature has disfigured in this way. He also mumbled a few unintelligible words in a nasal voice as he grabbed for the first clothes he could find to cover up his nakedness, a lean, sinewy, bony, hollow-chested man. He slipped into his shabby shoes, tucked the rest of his clothes under his arm, and went off without a word of farewell. The girl still sat there crouched in a huddle as if she were turned to stone, with her hands fastened in a cross on her breast and fingers splayed, staring after the man in a craze of anguish.

"Pull the blanket over yourself so that you don't catch cold, little girl," said the bishop. "I'm going to see to your mother, who looks as if she is lying in some discomfort. She surely wasn't left unattended all night?"

The woman from Hlíðar had been thrown this way and that by the motion of the ship, no longer strong enough to brace herself against it in the way that people do instinctively in heavy seas, even when asleep, to protect themselves. She was now lying on her stomach with her face jammed up against the bars at the head of the bed. Bishop Þjóðrekur eased her down and laid her on her back. She was cold and heavy, and showed not the slightest reaction to anything that was done to her. One eye was open and the other was half shut. The bishop put on his glasses and laid his ear to her heart. But when he had listened intently for a while he took his glasses off solemnly and put them neatly away in his spectacle-case.

"Your mother has gone on ahead of us to the land, little girl," said the bishop. "Your father and I will baptize her in due course and give her the opportunity to enter the Holy City for all eternity."

At this unexpected new blow the girl ceased all unnecessary sighing over her own manifest fall in the swell, and her face sagged into an expression of vacant relaxation, as if the clockwork of her consciousness had come to an abrupt stop. Then she hunched herself into a ball and turned towards the wall with her knees up to her chin, her plump young body all at once became as soulless and sexless as that of an overgrown child, and the bishop covered her up with the blanket for the sake of modesty before he went away to see the ship's officers.

All that day, and the next, the girl never raised her head from the pillow, took no food and spoke to no one, but merely cowered against the wall. At midnight on the following night the girl's brother arrived with the message that their mother was now about to be buried. She made no reply except to draw the blanket up over her head, and grovelled even further down into the bed.

The storm had blown itself out, and the sea was now comparatively calm. The stars looked down.

On the stroke of midnight the ship hove to for three minutes, and into the sea was consigned the body of this woman who had left home to travel to heaven to meet there the best man she had ever known, who had been dead to her for a long while now. Present at this funeral were the captain and first officer and six able seamen in their Sunday best. There was also the dead woman's son looking a little embarrassed in the too short trousers and mountaineering boots Bishop Þjóðrekur had bought for him in Scotland. The doctor was standing a little apart smoking a cigarette, as was then becoming fashionable. Bishop Þjóðrekur was there with the woman's grandson in his arms in the night cold. Also in the company was the old Mormon who knew how to sing one of the finest hymns that has ever been composed about a lonely wayfarer; this hymn, however, he was not allowed to chant except in silence on this occasion, for it is by law the task of the captain to read the burial service at sea if there is no clergyman present of the sects that Mormons call Gentiles. But Bishop Þjóðrekur nevertheless managed to say a few prayers over the woman's mortal remains in a language that no one understood except God, but not for more than about thirty or forty seconds, for this was no time for dawdling.

The body had not been placed in a coffin, but lay on its bier wrapped in thick sailcloth and wearing a white nightshirt from

The Company; and finally the red and white flag of the Danish king had been wrapped around it as a token of respect; for in the ship's register of the world's nationalities, Icelanders were not reckoned as Finnish, unbelievable as it may seem, but Danish.

"Inside that colourful cloth sleeps your grandmother, my lad," said Bishop Þjóðrekur.

The captain, a short powerful man, grey-haired and ruddy in the face, turned the leaves of his book, stepped forward into the lamplight at the head of the bier, and recited in English the pre-scribed words for burial at sea. Then he beckoned to the Mor-mon. Bishop Þjóðrekur stepped forward and handed the boy over to the old man, crossed his hands on his breast over his carefully wrapped hat, and said:

"This sister of whom we are now taking leave shrouded in red and white attire which is not however her attire, but the Danish king's, is now being welcomed home by God in other attire, the only attire she had left when she left Iceland. And this attire bears an emblem which is above Icelanders and Danish kings; it has on it the image of the Bee-hive, the Sego-lily, and the Sea-gull; it is the emblem of the land that the Prophet gave us with the Golden Book and which will rise in heaven on the day the earth is laid waste."

After that Þjóðrekur took the child in his arms again. The sailors now unwound the Danish king's flag and attached ropes to the bier. Then they lifted the bier over the rail and lowered it carefully down the side of the ship. Bishop Þjóðrekur carried the boy over to the rail and showed him his grandmother going down. The boy stared with big intelligent eyes in the night cold, and was silent; but when the bier slid into the sea and the bonds began to loosen, all he said, with tears in his voice, for they had been the happiest people in the world when they lived together as paupers on the croft, was: "Little Steinar wants to go with Granny."

At dawn next morning Bishop Þjóðrekur opened the door of the sick-bay and went over to the girl on the bench and greeted her. She looked up at him like an animal from inside its lair, without acknowledging his greeting.

"Were you awake, my lamb?" he said.

The girl was silent for a long time, until she replied, "I don't recognize myself. I don't know what I am. Am I a person?"

"I should think it very likely," said the bishop.

"To wake up and have lost everything, and know that one has nothing any more, is that being a person?" said the girl. "Oh, where is our beautiful horse which we once all owned together?"

"There is no gainsaying it: the spirits around you are not at all attractive. I have been standing guard here all night. I had my hands full driving these devils off. First came one, then came another, and then came the third. In their eyes you are the basest of all harlots."

"Was it this then that my father promised me?" said the girl, now overcome by grief. "I beseech you in the name of I don't know whom, save me from it, never again let me be blinded by it. Shut me in. Turn the key."

"I have another idea, my lamb," he said. "And it is in actual fact the same expedient I resorted to on the river last autumn, when Satan stood on the other bank waiting to seize the child: I covenanted him to myself before God. I can think of no alternative than to do the same with you."

"You can do with me what you like, Þjóðrekur," said the girl, "if only you will keep me safe and never let me loose."

"I shall just have to seal you to me by covenant, my lamb, and make you my heavenly wife. Otherwise the shadow of your degradation would rightly fall upon me, not only in the eyes of the Lord, but also in the eyes of your father who deserves better of me than that I should deliver to him a wretch from the rubbish-dump instead of the little girl whom he set out into the world to redeem."

"Dear Þjóðrekur," said the girl and raised herself up with tears in her eyes and reached out her arms towards him. "If you want to make any use of this miserable life of mine, then redeem me, so that I may once again feel the breath of the days when I was little at home."

28

Good broth

The federal government had for a long time shown a disposition to incorporate into its jurisdiction the Territory, as the Utah settlement was called by its inhabitants when they were not speaking Golden Book language. The Latter-Day Saints were not very enthusiastic about any such association. The Government found itself time and time again being forced to send police troops, which were called Feds, to intervene when conflict arose between divine revelation and the U.S. President's views. The biggest stumbling-block of all for outsiders was the doctrine that a woman should be esteemed in heaven and on earth according to who her husband was, and that therefore it was the duty of honest and upright men to give as many women as possible a share in their reputation and thereby to enhance their status. It is always a heavy step for a church to renounce a doctrine which has been confided to it by the Godhead; and this holds good not least for moral tenets which are founded upon self-denial by the individual and social enthusiasm by the congregation, such as had been the case with holy polygamy among the Mormons.

At about this time the main road to Utah had been improved and immigrants began to pour in from the eastern States. This wave of emigration was justified by the phrase "Good Times" which was then coming into existence in America and had never been heard in the world before; such "times" were said to be had in Utah. The majority of these incomers, however, were certainly no Latter-Day Saints, but Gentiles, as the Mormons, copying the Jews, called people who do not recognize the true God. They say that such people belong to the Great Heresy, otherwise known as the Great Apostasy, in which Christians had been ensnared from the third century until the Prophet found The Book on Hill Cumorah. The Gentiles had no sooner installed themselves than they rose up against the Prophet's pioneers, called his revelation balderdash and preached holy monogamy against holy polygamy.

The Government had spies out everywhere in Utah to see if there were not some wretch somewhere sleeping with two or three wives. If any such were found they were dragged into court and ordered to pay compensation to the Government, or despatched farther east and put behind lock and key. Particular efforts were made to punish the most prominent men in every community in order to intimidate the minnows. And now the time came to examine more closely the situation in Spanish Fork, to see who had obeyed God's command in this instance rather than the Federal laws and, if so, was important enough to justify the expense of punishing him.

It was now the turn of Bishop Þjóðrekur, who had committed the crime of raising Madame Colornay, the former ditch-dwelling

child-bearer, as high in the eyes of God as the sainted but barren
Járnanna, and then made things even worse by sealing a marriage before God for all eternity with poor old María Jónsdóttir
from Ampahjallur. The Spanish Forkers told the Feds that the
chap they were looking for was either at the North Pole or in
Finland, teaching people to embrace the Gospel.

It is unavoidable that the narrative should digress for a while
from Stone P. Stanford, master-bricklayer in Spanish Fork, and
the house he built, while events were taking place in other parts
of the world. To ensure that such an excellent bricklayer is not
entirely forgotten in this book or other books, we shall now take
up the thread again at the description of his house. Stanford built
almost the whole house in one summer, baking the necessary
bricks himself in Þjóðrekur's yard. First he built a main house,
but then he began to get big ideas and added an extra building
which he placed at right angles to the other one, as if they
wanted to break apart and go their separate ways.

Such houses were not infrequently built in Spanish Fork in
the search for a more varied and wealthier-looking style than a
pioneer's circumstances had allowed. Several worthy compatriots
said it was a bad move from Iceland to the Land of All-Wisdom
if they and their families had to make do with smaller houses
than the average sheriff's residence in Iceland. No one knew
where the little house that came marching out of the big house
was making for. But in the instructive little anecdotes about England which appear at the foot of the page in newspapers on both
sides of the Atlantic it was always said that people in fine houses
came "down to breakfast," and this was not the least of the rea-
sons why good people in Spanish Fork had their bedrooms
upstairs. Stone P. Stanford did not want to aim lower than other

inhabitants of God's Kingdom on earth. He constructed three rooms downstairs, and in the kitchen he made a recess for himself, the old fellow from Hlíðar, where he hoped to be allowed to sit in peace and quiet when he grew older, picking meat off a leg of salted mutton with his clasp-knife while the young people, visitors and residents, were singing in the sitting-room.

He made the bedroom for himself and his wife as large as the main bedroom in the home of a Welsh sheep-farmer who was living in Spanish Fork at the time and owned twenty-four thousand sheep on the mountain—about as many sheep as all the farmers put together in any ten parishes in Iceland. But he himself never slept there. In the loft of the extra-house, whose gable-wall faced east towards Sierra Benida, there suddenly took shape a room which he had some difficulty explaining when he was asked what it was for.

"When my daughter wakes up on her first morning in God's City of Zion," he said, "the sun will rise over Sierra Benida and shine upon saints: the sun of the All-Wisdom; the sun of the Bee-hive, the Sego-lily, and Sea-gull; and then she will understand her father even though she did not understand him when he was making a casket once. My son, who will be staying at the other end, will also understand on that morning that Egill Skallagrímsson and the Norse kings live here in Spanish Fork, but that they now have the gleam of righteousness in their eyes and have become leaders in the Stake, Seventies and High Priests."

But there was one problem he had not managed to solve, and that was what kind of curtains her windows were to have. Over and over again Stanford had inquired after suitable curtains in the Lord Thy God's Store, which was uncontaminated by merchants, and where an awful eye stared out with rays like a sea-urchin. He had made them unwind bolt after bolt but never found anything approaching the colour and floral design which were to adorn the cloth that was to be between his daughter and this holy mountain. He laid the problem (white or coloured?) before an aged and honourable Elder in the capital city when he had to go in to the Stake on Ward business. People in Salt Lake City were only too willing to provide him with household goods, but curtains for the girl's window were quite beyond them. This slow-spoken Elder, who embodied all the ordeals of the wilder-ness, reminded the bricklayer that there were two things of greater urgency for him now than curtains for his daughter if he wanted to continue along the path he was following: the first was to consider the worthy women who were drifting around help-lessly like flotsam on the salt lake of the wilderness without being able to sink, and to consider whether the time had not come to covenant a marriage of a divine nature with a sister or two and thereby do his stint to strengthen this saintly commu-nity against the Gentiles.

"When Brigham Young was lying at home on his deathbed the Federal flag was flying over his house with the twenty-seven gables, and the Feds were all standing outside, fully armed," said the sage Elder, as if to render any further argument unnecessary. "And the other thing, dear brother, is this: is it not soon becom-ing time to submit yourself to the duty of all good Mormons, and journey to the lands of the Gentiles to teach people to embrace the Gospel?"

Stone P. Stanford came home doubly fortified by the confi-dence in him that had been shown by these necessary admoni-tions. The circumspection and solicitude in these admonitions had been on such a high plane that the more he thought about the matter, the more clearly he understood that he had in actual fact been taken to task: the only correction that is true and precise is the one a man is not aware of when it is administered, but realises tomorrow that he had been flogged yesterday. Towards evening he stood at the window which looked out on the prospect of Sierra Benida, the Blessed Mountain, the mountain whose nakedness is like that of a man who has not merely had his clothes removed, but also his skin and flesh, nerves and blood. Perhaps it was the will of God and the Prophet that between this little girl, when she came, and this mountain, the Blessed Mountain, the Naked Mountain, this Skeleton of a Mountain, there should not be any curtain.

Never had it been so far from the bricklayer's mind as now, when he had pondered the words of the Elder, to think for a moment of living in the house he had built. He put the newly-bought dining-table in the middle of the room with its chairs round it, as if he were going to hold a banquet—and then hung the guests up on the wall: pictures of Joseph the Prophet, his brother Hyram and Brigham Young. He went on pottering about in the dusk, polishing up the woodwork in the house by the light of a lamp he lit. But when he became sleepy he did not stretch out on the big marital bed, but went out to the workshed behind the house as usual. The floor in this shed was the sand of the wilderness. His bed was a frame that he himself had put together, with two props, or rather stools, one for the head and one for the feet. This was where he usually slept, with a blanket to cover him. The death-watch beetle woke up and started to rub its neck when he lit a candle, and there was a rustling from a spider the size of a meadow pipit, which had taken up winter quarters in one of the corners. A wholesome breeze blew in through the open window, and from heaven there shone a star. He emptied the sand carefully from his shoes before turning in.

One evening—it was one of those evenings which are almost exactly the same as other evenings, without even a meeting at the Young Women's Mutual Improvement Association, and the bricklayer was getting ready to eat his bread and go to sleep—one evening he was sent a message asking if he would not like to drop over to the Bishop's House and have some broth. He washed his face carefully as was the custom in Steinahlíðar when people go visiting, and brushed his hands over his bald scalp because he felt that his hair was standing on end as it used to do when it was in full growth.

When he reached the Bishop's House all the windows were lit up. Bishop Þjóðrekur had come home. From the house came an enticing cooking-smell of cabbage and all kinds of other vegetables, all the hospitable pleasures which are contained in American broth. Þjóðrekur had taken off his jacket and was sitting in his chair under the lamp. A seven-year-old boy and an eight-year-old girl were kneeling on the ground in front of him, eyeing their father with awe and admiration; the boy had put on his father's hat, that marvellous hat wrapped in grease-proof paper which had never suffered a stain or a wrinkle. The bishop's little daughter fingered the buttons on his shirt and said, "Oh, what lovely buttons you have on your shirt, Daddy." But Madame Colornay's youngest son, who had not seen the light of day until six months after Þjóðrekur went away, had clambered all over his father until he had pulled off his spectacles.

Stanford had barely had time to greet the bishop before Madame Colornay came sweeping out of the kitchen towards him, a beaming sunshine smile all over, hugging a fresh-coloured young girl from another world who stared straight ahead with huge questioning eyes.

"Praise be to the Lord of Hosts for giving you such a jewel for a daughter, our Þjóðrekur's fourth wife! And now kiss both me and her and all of us and congratulate us," said Madame Colornay. "Don't you think it a blessing to get a fragrant rose into this bone-jelly and old-women's smell, so bright and clean and undefiled in heart and, what's more, just at the time when I can't have any more children? Now life is starting again with sunshine days here in the Bishop's House, like the year after our Þjóðrekur raised me out of a ditch with my small sons who are now grown up and gone to the war. Nothing could ever again cast a shadow on this house if it weren't for the damned Feds (God save the children) skulking around the house here till all hours; one of them very nearly had me trapped in a corner against the water-butt yesterday evening, a fat old thing like me with varicose veins up to the thighs and now gone sexless, thank God."

He kissed his daughter, as was the custom in Steinahlíðar, but rather hesitantly. Then he kissed his son who sprang out of a shadowy corner, but neither the boy nor the girl could utter a word when they met him here in eternity, until he asked his daughter how their mother was.

"Mother is dead—too," said the girl.

Then they told their father how his wife had died at sea, and been buried.

"May the Lord be praised for her," said Stone P. Stanford.

He tittered slightly and added, "My word! It would not matter so much not knowing what to say, if I only knew where I should look."

"Look over here, Steinar dear, and greet your own image," said María Jónsdóttir from Ampahjallur.

She was sitting with the little frock-clad gentleman from Steinahlíðar on her lap. In the single hour that had elapsed since he came into the house, she had practically become his grandmother, the same grandmother for whom he had been pining since she vanished and whom he had half-expected to see again when he came "home," for somehow or other the boy had got the idea that when she was lowered into the Atlantic she had just been taking a short cut to the place for which they were all heading.

"Bend down, Stanford dear, and give him a kiss here on my lap," the old woman went on. "This is the son of your darling daughter, our and Þjóðrekur's fourth sister. I always knew that so long as I lived, God would grant me the joy of having a little boy to hold in these buckled hands, as a saintly woman once prophesied for me in the Vestmannaeyjar when I was young."

Stone P. Stanford now went round and kissed everyone again, and wished each and all of them happiness as sincerely and fittingly as he knew how. Then he asked his daughter for news of Steinahlíðar.

"Oh, everything's all right, I suppose," said the girl, sniffing. "Except that it was a terribly cold spring this year, nothing but rain, rain, rain right until pasturage, and lambs always being drowned in the pools. . . ."

Her brother interrupted, "Steina and I were saying that there probably hasn't been another spring like it in Steinahlíðar since the year the mare threw Krapi. . . ."

"And more stones down off the mountain than ever before, I think one could say," added the girl.

"I assume you mean that the last few winters have been hard on the hay?" said the bricklayer. "It could also sometimes snow in Steinahlíðar in spring; the sheep then blundered through the thin ice-crusts over the hazards, that is perfectly true. What I was going to say: stones coming down off the mountain on to the hayfields, one knows all about that, all right! But there was some consolation in those days in the fact that we had a good horse at Hlíðar in Steinahlíðar, the one you mentioned. Quite so."

They listened in amazement to themselves talking to one another again: three people who all were originally one and the same heart. So this is how reunions were in Heaven! They hastened to fall silent.

"I trust that everything went well on your travels, old friend?" said Stone P. Stanford.

"They didn't beat me very much in Iceland during my last year and a half there. But is that a step forward or a step back?" said the bishop. "It can drive you mad, to wrestle with wool when it isn't even in sacks."

"Oh, it can surely be called a good sign that some people, somewhere, have stopped beating those who think differently from themselves," said Stanford. "You remember where and when we became acquaintances, Þjóðrekur? If I say to you that I live on the other side of the moon, which I have sometimes half suspected anyway, this does not seem to me an entirely valid reason to start beating me up, before you have considered on which side you yourself live. Anyway, we all live a hundred thousand million miles out in the cosmos."

Then the bricklayer lowered his voice, and almost in a whisper asked the great bishop and traveller: "Could I just ask you to tell me one small thing: were the stars present when she was buried?"

"The storm had abated and it was beginning to clear up, and there was bright starlight," said the bishop.

"That was good," said Stone P. Stanford. "That is all I wanted to ask you."

Járnanna brought in the broth in a large pot and laid it on the middle of the table. She asked them all to come and eat, and this remarkably expanded family sat down at table. Járnanna herself did not take her seat immediately, but started to serve the soup into the bowls. It is not the custom among Mormons that it should always be the head of the house who says grace; sometimes it is one of the sisters; and this is due to the fact that the head of the family is often away for long periods doing useful work in distant parts. Járnanna did not sit down this time until she had said grace. She was rather sparing of words, as lean people always are:

"We thank thee, God," she said, "for that our brother has once again performed a prodigy of faith which will long be remembered among saints, and planted a new flower in lovely bloom which will live and multiply for generations here in the wilderness. Amen."

29

Polygamy or death

It is related that two hundred Gentile women got together at about this time and called a meeting in Salt Lake City, calling themselves The Union of Christian Women. The saints considered these women to be offspring of the Great Apostasy. The women, who in fact had never had any revelations themselves, now sent energetic demands to the Congress of the United States of America to take decisive action against the church which claimed to be God's proxy; and they called upon the Federal Government to brook no delay in disfranchising the polygamists and annulling the law and order which the saints had established among themselves. They further declared in this document that the doctrine that many women should share the same man was ungodly, as God had created for Adam only one Eve and not several. At this meeting, which was held in one of the churches of the Great Apostasy, many fanatical and tearful speeches were

made by women with one husband apiece demanding liberation
for women who had to share theirs. In a flood of eloquence they
demanded that their husbands and other monogamists should
put the polygamists behind lock and key. Some suggested making use of a peculiar Anglo-Saxon form of torture, called tarring
and feathering, for those husbands who loved more than one
woman, and also for their wives.

This is not the place for a full account of all the measures and
devices to which the Government authorities resorted in order to
constrain the Mormons in Utah. But to demonstrate that the
gloves were now off in the battle with the saints it has to be told
that, when Stone P. Stanford went to see Bishop Þjóðrekur the
day after his return in order to seek more information about the
important events that a higher Providence had imposed on both
their lives, the bishop was not available. The Feds had arrived at
the crack of dawn and arrested the bishop and driven him away
in a large military wagon. The blossoming household which last
night had gathered round a pot of good wholesome broth to celebrate reunion and soul-salving tidings, and where happiness
was guest of honour, had been crushed by injustice in the name
of justice and by ungodliness under the pretext of godliness.

Although Mormons are always described as inoffensive people,
they were not accustomed to lying down under a beating for very
long. It was not long after the two hundred daughters of the
Great Apostasy had delivered their manifesto that the saints
sounded the trumpets of war. They first summoned local
women's meetings in every single district in Utah to make vows
and pass resolutions publicly. Then the local meetings were to be
summoned to a general meeting in Salt Lake City to promote
unity and solidarity there, and to explain the place and validity

of polygamy in the business of salvation. The womenfolk of Spanish Fork also met in conference and made preparations to go to Salt Lake City and make their voices heard in the national chorus. First they sang some beautiful Latter-Day Saints hymns and then attempted to describe their bliss, each in her own way. They thanked the Lord of Hosts for the revelation of being able to see and understand that woman's salvation consists in having a righteous husband, whose virtuous deeds spoke for themselves; and there can never be too many women sharing in such a man. They said that harmony of spirit, coupled with a tangible share in the divine presence, gave Mormon households a grace which was rarely to be found elsewhere in married life. For every day that God gives us, they said, we thank the Lord of Hosts and His friend the Prophet, the latter of whom instituted here on earth a life of loveliness without envy or jealousy. Who has ever heard that decent women here are thrown on the rubbish-dump, as is the custom among Josephites and Lutherans, whose men go to any lengths to avoid honourable matrimony, or else are unfaithful to their wives when they do eventually marry, and then run away from them? We shall not give up this our life of loveliness as long as we live, however much we are oppressed by the Government and its troops and policemen, its Congress and Senate, orators, newspaper scribes and authors, professors and paltry bishops and even the anti-Christ himself, the Pope. No power on earth will succeed in preventing us from accomplishing God's sacred ordinances, as regards polygamy no less than all the other aspects that God has revealed to us. Polygamy as long as we live, say we women Latter-Day Saints; polygamy or death!

After the district meeting was over the women all took their seats in wagons that were waiting in the road ready to take them to the general meeting in Salt Lake City. Large farm-wagons, normally used for hay and corn, some with teams of four horses, had been furnished with seats and canvas to transport this cargo of blooms. These worthy women glowed with idealism and correct opinions, and wore the cheerfully innocent expressions that are seen at their best on nuns. Some laughed and giggled from the childlike excess of good conscience that borders on being consciencelessness, others went on singing hymns of praise with quavering voices in order to give this great innocence an outlet; a band of young men played a horn accompaniment. Husbands stood on the road with the children to say bye-bye. There was a great deal of indiscriminate kissing. An elderly man came up to one of the wagons, brushed his hair down on his forehead, and addressed himself to a young girl who had taken her place on a seat between two elderly women and was staring wide-eyed into the blue, not even singing, to be sure, because she did not know the words; but one could tell from her bright expression that she was happier than words could say.

"I hope, my dear," he said with a titter, "that you are not disappointed in the country and kingdom I bought for you children. I want to tell you that if I had known of a truer City of God elsewhere I would have bought that for you and your brother."

The bishop's fourth wife looked at her father from the distance which one day must come between two hearts. She answered from the wagon, "What more could I have wished for myself than to be allowed to join these women? I hope the day will never come when I let Þjóðrekur down, for he saved me from that terrible beast whose name I shall never utter."

"Don't say any more about that creature; happy the one who is free of it," said Madame Colornay, who was sitting on the other side of the fourth wife.

"In the Vestmannaeyjar there was only one terrible beast, the beast that has as many greedy maws as it was slashed with knives," said old María from Ampahjallur, who was sitting on this side of the fourth wife with Steinar junior on her knees. And the blind woman added, "But the people with whom I grew up in the Vestmannaeyjar, on the other hand, carried heaven within themselves; even if it was sixty fathoms at the end of a rope down a cliff, fowling, they were at home in God's City of Zion."

Giddup! and the first crack of the whip. The leading wagon had set off, and soon the whole caravan was on the move with its load of women and music. The menfolk took the children by the hand and ran alongside for a good while, waving their hats in farewell, some with jokes and others with prayers of intercession, but they soon had to fall behind; the women waved their kerchiefs from the wagons, laughing and singing to the music of the brass band, and the dust swirled on the road. Gradually the men gave up running behind and waving, and when the outskirts of the town were reached they had all turned for home except one. He suddenly found himself standing alone in the dust, with his hat held aloft; the wagonloads of women had vanished into the distance, halfway to Springville, and the sounds of singing and brass had almost died. He wiped the dust from his eyes after his vain pursuit. But it was not until he had put on his hat again that he noticed he was standing in front of the farthest house at that end of the street, the dilapidated house where the sewing-machine had once lived.

The house had deteriorated badly since he had first gone there a long time ago; and it had not been in very good condition even then. Now there were such large cracks in the walls that lizards had made their homes in them, and elsewhere pockets of soil had formed in the fissures and couch-grass was growing in them. There was not much life left on the clothes-line either, compared with what it used to be—just a few torn and tattered children's rags.

He discovered that he was not the only one who was staring foolishly after the musical wagons: outside the door stood a young dark-haired girl who had inherited everything from her mother except the laughter, and was endowed with most of the feminine virtues except knowing how to say good morning. She was looking towards the road, weeping, with her year-old child in her arms. The little scamp was trying to comfort his mother by twisting her tear-filled nose upwards and poking at her eyes with his soft little fingers. Stone P. Stanford had luckily put his hat on, so that he was able to take it off again to the girl.

"What a rumbling of wagons today, did you not think?" he said, walking over towards her. "May God give you and your son a good day."

There had been no tidying-up done around the house that year, and probably not for twenty years at that. It was amazing how zealously the sagebrush and tamarisk flourished in this patch round the house, and on the whole all the weeds that can flourish in a wilderness. In some places the crumbled adobe had fallen from the house-walls like a landslip. The windows that faced the road had been boarded up. A long time ago the brick-layer had half-promised the woman to see to her house for her; seldom had a half-promise been more thoroughly broken. The bricks he had brought her in a pram when he paid her his visit (blessed memory) still lay on the paving as he had stacked them, except that they were now almost engulfed by weeds and brush. He proffered his hand to the girl, and the girl first wiped her face with her palm and then offered the visitor a hand wet with grief. Then he patted the little boy on the forehead and tittered.

"There is someone, at least, who is not jubilating in God's City of Zion today, despite what one might have thought," he said. "What is there to be done about that?"

"We are Josephites and aren't allowed to go," said the girl, and went on crying.

"Oh dear, if you had only come to me I would quickly have got you a seat beside my daughter, in gratitude for all the blessed coffee," he said. "And even though I am perhaps undependable and promise more than I fulfil, it would have been simple for you to mention it to the man who is an older and truer friend to you than this old fellow from Steinahlíðar."

"You mean old Ronki," said this rather raw-looking girl. "You surely don't think he can command as much room as would do for a woman's bottom? The only thing he can do is to nail boards over our windows when the boys have thrown stones through them. You see, he got used to this sort of carpentry in the Lutheran Church."

"There is no denying that," said the bricklayer. "Too many panes are gone. When I look at this wanton destruction it makes me suffer as much as if I had done it myself."

As has been alluded to already, the sewing-machine no longer stood in the middle of the room; instead Borgi the seamstress, her face swollen with tears, sat at a window at the back of the house doing some darning with needle and thread. The doors that had once been kept so carefully closed in this house were now not only off their hinges but had vanished altogether. And what had become of the cupboards full of the gay ultra-fashionable New England gowns, which were so low-necked that one thought one was being suckled again?

The woman looked at the visitor with her expressive eyes from out of that deep darkness, swollen with tears.

"It has been a long time," he said.

He brushed his invisible hair down over his forehead as always and found a place for his hat on the floor, in a corner, before he offered the woman his hand.

"A very good day to you, my dear Madame Þorbjörg. It is little wonder you cannot remember this old chap, who himself does not even know his own name any more, much less where he comes from. But there was a time when you used to bring me excellent coffee, and lots of it. A thousand thanks for that."

"Coffee!" she repeated in astonishment, as if she had never heard of anything so absurd.

"But He who did not let a refreshing drink go unrewarded remembers it even better," he said.

"Yes, that's true," said the woman. "And I, too, thank you for the bricks you brought here in a pram."

Although she had just been weeping and her tear-glands had scarcely stopped functioning, her sense of humour was so great that the memory of this gift threw her into a frenzy of laughter. She laughed so hard that one could see right down her throat.

"It is truly a Godsend to be able to smile, dear lady," he said.

She stopped laughing and dried what was left of the tears.

"Do please have a seat on my chair," said the woman and stood up. "I'll sit on this stool. No, there is truly no laughter in my heart. But the bloodiest part of it all was seeing women sitting there so superciliously who, to the best of my knowledge, have never once even heard the Prophet's name mentioned, any more than I have. That was the last straw."

"It has always been so," he said, "that the first shall be last and the last shall be first. It is not very long since my daughter heard the Prophet's name mentioned, if she had heard it mentioned at all. Perhaps there is a reason for everything, even for the fact that you and your daughter were not specially invited to a seat in the wagons. If I remember correctly, you once told me that when someone tried to teach you to embrace the Gospel you laughed until you fainted."

"As if one isn't just as dependent on the Prophet whether one believes in him or not," said the woman. "Why do we sit here abandoned like this? The Prophet has pulled everyone away from me. The house is falling to pieces, and why? The Prophet has stoned it. The only thing the Prophet has left me is old Ronki, and therefore I got the leavings of your ox-soup in the Bishop's House the other day."

"It was a great pity about the sewing-machine," he said. "It gave me a shock to hear of it."

"Obviously, it had to go towards my debts," said the woman. "And anyway I hadn't much use left for it because, since my daughter had a child by a Lutheran, not a single saint has wanted me to sew underwear for his wives (not that it can get around very far who sews people's underwear), much less any visible garments that could possibly be talked about in the Mutual Improvement Association, with someone saying: 'That surely isn't from Borgi?'"

"I shall truly do my best to get Pastor Runólfur to take off his clerical coat so that he can begin to earn a living and become at least a Ward chairman, if nothing else," said Stone P. Stanford. "I can see from the way he looks after Bishop Þjóðrekur's sheep that he could be an outstanding head of a family if he would covenant himself just one or two wives in marriage."

"And what about yourself?" said the woman.

"By the way, don't you think I should remove my jacket and take a look at the worst cracks in your walls? To tell you the truth, I freely acknowledge, even though I am sorely ashamed of it, that

I broke my promise to you over a trivial thing I offered to do for you a long time ago. But the night's not over yet, as the ghosts say, heeheehee," said the bricklayer. "Excuse me, but are my eyes deceiving me, if I may ask? Or are the doors in the house gone?"

"We used them for the fire in the cold weather the winter before last, just after my daughter had her baby," said the woman. "We didn't need to shut the doors on one another any more, anyway. Our Lutheran was gone."

The bricklayer now went on a brief tour of inspection of the house, outside and in, and was more and more appalled the more he saw of it. One could scarcely set foot in some of the rooms for ants and beetles, and the brambles and weeds around the house were swarming with wild animals of the lesser orders, most of them harmless, although at one spot there was a glint of the eyes of a viper.

"Well, I shall not detain you ladies any longer on this occasion, and thank you for showing me the house, which could certainly be improved, come to that, like most other human handiworks," he said. "But it is not always so obvious where one should make a start when one is faced with a fallen wall."

"It's a great shame not to have any coffee left nowadays to offer a visitor," said the woman.

"Oh, don't give it a thought, dear lady, I am still living on the coffee I got from you in the past, not to mention the coffee you sent me once by your daughter," said the bricklayer, and kissed her. "Think kindly of me, both of you. And if I should not run into your daughter out in the orchard, give her my warmest greetings; she is a very fine girl, even if she is not simpering all the time, no more than her mother, heeheehee; and that's a grand little boy she has—to tell you the truth he reminds me most of my daughter's son, with whom I was presented right out of the blue here the other day, as it were—or to be more accurate, with God's help, I had never been given; indeed I dare not look in his direction in case I entice him away from a better father than I am. And now, where did I leave my hat, for I hope I did not come hatless into someone else's house? And as far as I can remember I was taking it off to someone out in the road there not so long ago."

The woman made no reply but looked at him from the remoteness of the soul in that huge, deep and tear-filled silence of human life that nothing could break except laughter.

He found his hat at last in the corner where he had put it.

It was not until he had stepped out of the room into the little hallway and had opened the outer door, with due creaking and grating, that he remembered a small matter he had nearly forgotten. He pushed the door to, turned back into the room, and said casually to the woman who had once more seated herself at the back-facing window with her darning: "It is not so easy as all that to get rid of this old fellow from Steinahlíðar once you have hooked him, and that is how it is now. But when I see of what poor adobe the house is built, and your windows all broken by these rascals, and your doors long since converted into kindling, and the sewing-machine that Pastor Runólfur proved to me over and over again was a token of the victory of the All-Wisdom here in Spanish Fork . . ."

"Would it be impertinent to ask what you are talking about?" said the woman.

"Hmmm," he said. "I was just wondering whether I could invite you both to come over to my new house and live there? There is a remarkably attractive view from the attic window looking towards Sierra Benida, which I consider to be the ideal mountain. I will be getting old soon and am making ready to leave here. And then it is not such a bad thing to have around some reliable people, particularly women, who are loyal to one. And I offer you both in exchange the seal of marriage that women need to have in heaven."

Next morning Stone P. Stanford made up his mind to make one more attempt to find suitable curtains for his upstairs window, from which one could see the truth in mountain form, the view which no fabric seemed to be worthy to curtain. Now we shall hear what happened when he set off on his search.

When he had gone a little way along the main road he saw that the householders on both sides of the road were driving sheep from their gardens in great wrath. Finally the ewes clustered together in the middle of the road, bleating irresolutely, and some of them started butting one another as if they could not agree what they should do now that they had no other refuge than the gravelled road where freedom grew, but not grass. The bricklayer counted them from ingrained habit; there were fifteen, all of them with fat tails which far surpassed the stumpy tails on Icelandic sheep.

"What sheep are these?" he asked.

Someone from the neighbourhood, exhausted from driving the sheep out of his garden, answered by asking him whether he did not see that these were Bishop Þjóðrekur's soup-pot sheep: "Would you believe it? Pastor Runólfur just upped and let them free this morning."

Another man joined them and said, "Ronki has quite obviously gone off his head. He was seen at dawn this morning staggering along with his trunk on his back, moving house. He seems to have moved into the dugout where the Lutheran lived."

A third man came along and said, "Have you heard that the

Josephite women threw him out with the porridge scrapings from the Bishop's House last night?"

It was mentioned in this book previously that in Spanish Fork there stood the sorriest Lutheran church in the world; the young Josephite girl had said of it once that there was only room for about one mule to stand upright in it. On top of this box, which stood there up on a hillock, a tower had been stuck, which was little bigger than a good-sized coffee-grinder. And on top of the tower the Lutherans had put a cross, a symbol which the Latter-Day Saints call a heretical token derived from the Pope, an inheritance from the Great Apostasy. There had originally been four windows in this church. But when Pastor Runólfur lost his Lutheran faith and the congregation broke up and scattered to the four winds, the windows were all stoned and broken as is the custom of boys all over the world wherever they see a spiritually dilapidated house. For years now there had been boards nailed over the paneless windows, and there was nothing left of the cross except for a broken stump.

Stone P. Stanford was going past this deserted church which was like the famous church in the poem, the one on the barren mountain, "as deserted as on Judgement Day." But now something new was afoot; someone had put a ladder up against the wall of the church and had managed to climb all the way up to the little tower. He was trying to mend the cross. He was in his shirt-sleeves. His clerical coat, the most distinguished garment in Spanish Fork before or since, had been folded lengthwise, with the lining outside, and laid over one rung of the ladder. Stone P. Stanford stopped on the road, took of his hat and shouted to him, "May God give you a good morning, my dear Pastor Runólfur." But Pastor Runólfur made no reply and carried on mending the cross.

30

Ending

At this stage the management of the Mormon mission to Iceland had been transferred from Denmark to Scotland; that is where the headquarters were, as one puts it nowadays, but in the past it would have been called the archiepiscopal seat. At this seat there was a school at which Mormon priests were trained in the technique of preaching the Gospel in the new fashion to Gentiles of other lands. Stone P. Stanford was sent over there from Utah to study for a winter before he went to Iceland to succeed Bishop Þjóðrekur and other saints who had gone there. The bricklayer is reported to have said later that there he had learned theology with the part of the head that begins above the nose; whereas until then he had drunk it through the nose, like snuff from a wooden horn.

No further matters of theology or holy doctrine will be recounted here at present; the bricklayer himself, indeed, has said that nothing in the instruction at the archiepiscopal school there in Scotland surpassed the propositions that Pastor Runól-fur had preached, and which have already been rendered in this little book. The story now moves on to a day when the birds were tuning up their songs in the trees there in the newly-green slope under Edinburgh Castle. Nearby lies Princes Street, which is broad and sunny and moistened with wholesome showers, more so than most city streets in the world, with the exception of the streets in the aforementioned God's City of Zion, which were measured and laid out according to the principles of the All-Wisdom.

On this day the bricklayer from Utah was strolling along Princes Street to buy himself shoes with thick soles for his trip to Iceland, and perhaps even a good hat. Then all of a sudden some-one came up to him and clapped him on the shoulder among the throng in Edinburgh's main street where all the gentlemen of quality wear skirts. This man was wearing an expensive fur coat and a tall tile hat of the same kind of fur; his moustache had been waxed and the ends turned upwards so that they stood erect like knitting needles. This was clearly no Scottish street-sweeper or shoe-cleaner who had stopped him. But what surprised the bricklayer from Spanish Fork even more was that such a man should shake him by the hand and greet him in his native tongue with all sorts of homely oaths as friends are apt to do: Well, if it isn't the old so-and-so himself; what the flaming hell are you doing here? And so on and so forth.

The bricklayer first blinked hard several times to get the dust out of his eyes and then swallowed carefully once or twice to loosen his tongue; and when he finally spoke it was not without a hint of a sob in his voice, but also with a touch of the laughter which always assailed him when he explained something he considered indisputable.

"My name," he said, "is Stone P. Stanford, bricklayer and Mormon from Spanish Fork in the Territory of Utah. Quite so."

"Bricklayer and Mormon from Spanish Fork, yes, what bloody lunatics you are! But to hell with that, and welcome to you anyway, and now open up and tell me how it is that I can't get hold of as many women as Björn of Leirur and you."

The bricklayer said, "Oh, there's no more to say about an old fellow like this than there ever was, except that my ears tell me that the birds have started to sing rather more than is proper in Scotland on such a day; they are probably doing rather more than saying their prayers, heeheehee."

"Don't pay too much attention to what we are twittering," said the man in the fur coat. "All the same, I'm taking you straight to my hotel over the road here and buying you a glass of beer."

"I cannot exactly say that beer is my drink, my dear sheriff," said the bricklayer. "But I usually accept coffee when it is sincerely offered. It revives the spirit, rather than deadens it, if there is such a thing; and I might then find the courage to ask how it comes about that I should run into the sheriff, bless him, in this great world-street."

"There is nothing lower in Hell than being sheriff over lice-ridden people," said the sheriff. "Never mind. To put it briefly, I have become tired of men who lie on their backs reading sagas while they wait for good fishing-weather. And finally, when it comes, a wave arrives which drowns them. In the hotel I sign myself Governor of Iceland, just for fun, and the doorman gets a penny for believing it every time I go in or out. To be Governor for a penny in the eyes of servants is at least better than being sheriff and judge in reality over people who cannot even achieve the minimum of human virtue because of their poverty. I have three missions in Great Britain: to form a British-Icelandic limited company to run trawlers; to raise capital to electrify life in Iceland; and finally to put the finishing touches to my book of poems."

Not even in God's City of Zion had the bricklayer set foot in such accommodation as the hotel to which his sheriff now brought him. There were carpets on the floor as green and soft as lush meadows. From the ceiling hung chandeliers so spectacular that if Egill Skallagrímsson had set eyes on them he would certainly have fallen into a berserk fit no less frenzied than when Einarr Skálaglamm* fastened the shield, inlaid with gold and jewels, over his bedhead. There were also pictures of queens wearing clerical ruffs, and other distinguished folk who were beheaded in Scotland. The chairs were high, with tall straight backs and carved woodwork, so that anyone who sat in them was bound to feel as if he were mounted on a good riding-horse. Governor of Iceland Benediktsson carried on talking.

It was quite evident that the sheriff had raised himself out of the peatbogs, where justice resides in Iceland, up into a no lesser splendour than the coal-biters of old who raised themselves from the ash-pit; but he had in fact always been well above the general run of sheriffs.

The bricklayer could find no break in the conversation where he could sneak in a few words about the truth which the Latter-Day Saints were given along with Paradise. When he had sat there silently for a long time, either smiling or nodding his head absently, or giggling slightly to himself whenever the sheriff swore, he began to look for an excuse to take his leave. The mail-

boat for Reykjavík was expected that evening, and he had still
various matters to attend to, including buying himself shoes to
go evangelising in.

"I know one who won't take long to go over to Mormonism,
and that's Björn of Leirur," said the sheriff. "I never tired of
scolding him and saying to him, 'You damned old devil, you get
hold of all the wenches I should have had. I'll settle your account
some day,' I said to him but the blame certainly wasn't always
his. For instance, I did everything I could to save your daughter,
but it was hopeless. After God and men had joined forces to save
her reputation and provide her with an acceptable father for the
child, and old Björn had as near as dammit gone on oath, what
was the end of it all? The girl made me a fool and a laughing-
stock in the eyes of the Government. I even had it said to my face
by the Governor that I was the sort of sheriff who pronounces
virgin births. In the end I cleaned the old devil out of everything
he had, in order to buy a trawler. But I never dared to mention
electricity to him, because he doesn't know what it is; he would
have thought it was some remainders of damaged ship's biscuits
I was trying to palm off on him. But give him my regards all
the same, and tell him that the British-Icelandic Company is
under way."

The poet-Governor accompanied his visitor out through the
hotel foyer and kissed him in front of the entrance. The doorman
bowed so low that his coat-tails stood on end, and looked on
with lofty condescension at how graciously the Governor took
leave of the lowest of his subjects. But when the bricklayer had
reached the pavement, the Governor remembered a little something he had left unfinished in his business with him. He hurried
out after him, bareheaded, and shouted in Icelandic: "Steinar of

Hlíðar, am I not right in thinking you are on your way home? Wouldn't you like me to give you a farm?"

"Oh, it is really quite unnecessary, bless your heart," said the man who had suddenly become Steinar of Hlíðar, and turned round there in Edinburgh. "What farm would that be, if I may ask?"

"It is the farm at Hlíðar in Steinahlíðar, which I put up for auction under execution to pay off taxes and outstanding debts, and knocked down to myself to prevent it from landing in Björn of Leirur's collection. If you come with me to the doorman's desk I shall scribble you a note you can stick in your pocket; and the farm is yours again."

The poet-Governor, Iceland's new outpost in the British Empire, unfortunately did not turn out to be the only Icelander who showed no desire to hear about the Golden Book's truth and the land beyond the wilderness which is thrown in with the truth for good measure. For three whole centuries, some say four, Icelanders had made it a rule to believe in dogmas that came from Denmark; indeed Bishop Þjóðrekur had declared that just as the Danes got all their wits from the Germans, so had Iceland's brain—by mistake, it is to be hoped—landed inside the Danish king's head: they too left the Mormons in peace when they heard that Kristian Wilhelmsson did likewise in his own country. But that brings us back to the question that Bishop Þjóðrekur failed to answer when he returned to Utah from his later, and greater, missionary journey: was it a step forward for the Icelanders or a step backwards for them to stop beating up Mormons? In former times, the moment a Mormon stepped ashore in Reykjavík the riffraff and drunkards, who in those days characterised the town, would come flocking round and pursue him with catcalls and obscenities, while the youngsters threw stones or snowballs of slush and mud. If nothing better occurred to them they would shout that the Mormon's head was too big for him, or that he had one leg shorter than the other. Whenever a Mormon tried to hold a meeting in order to publicize such vital matters as immersion and the need to abstain from cursing and swearing, along with information about the breadth of the streets in the resplendent City of Zion, these rioters would immediately surge on to the platform where the speaker was preaching and start giving the saint a beating. Lutheran bishops and divinity teachers busied themselves writing pamphlets eulogising the excellence of Luther and other Germans against the Mormons, because they knew that the Danes believed in Germans; similarly, various Icelanders with a tendency towards mental disorder wrote malicious articles in Þjóðólfur, or plucked verses from the Bible against the Mormons in the hope that this would hustle these terrible people straight to hell.

But now times had changed. When Stanford the Mormon arrived in Reykjavík there was not a single guttersnipe or drunkard in the town who made any distinction between a Mormon and any old peasant from up-country. Most of the mentally disordered had forgotten about Mormons and had started thinking about electricity. In the newspapers of that period there is no mention at all of the arrival of this Mormon, with the exception of an advertisement that he himself inserted in Þjóðólfur; this stated that Stone P. Stanford, bricklayer and Mormon from Spanish Fork in the Territory of Utah, was holding a meeting in the Good Templar Hall on such and such an evening at the end of the fishing-season to expound the revelations of Joseph Smith. This Stanford is the only Mormon who came to Iceland without once being beaten up, and about whom there was published no pamphlet, neither by Doctors nor lunatics, apart from this worthless little booklet compiled by the humble scholar who wields the pen at present.

Stanford the Mormon tried to engage people in conversation down by the harbour where they congregated sometimes in large numbers, especially late in the evening, and looked out over the bay with their wooden snuff-flasks rammed hard up their noses. He also accosted a water-carrier with four pairs of shoes and three battered hats, and a drunken old fishwife with a sack of salt on her back. He asked whether immersion would not do such people some good, and whether he could not lend them a pamphlet by John Pritt. People looked at him and never even shook their heads. Or would they rather, he asked, have that splendid masterpiece on the truth by Þjóðrekur Jónsson from Bóla in the Landeyjar? No one even told him to go and eat his own dirt.

And when the spring evening arrived on which Stone P. Stanford was to hold his lecture in the Good Templar Hall on the revelation, the terns flew past the door and started to hunt for minnows in the Tjörn.* Not a living soul in the town went out of the way to hear about the good country where peace reigned and truth lived. And yet. Two elderly women in ankle-length pleated skirts and everyday blouses, with jet-black woollen shawls wrapped around their heads so that only the tips of their noses showed, came sidling in through the door and seated themselves at the back; perhaps they wanted to hear about polygamy. At long last another person appeared. A dignified-looking and somewhat corpulent grey-beard, obviously practically blind, came fumbling down the centre aisle with his stick and did not stop until he was right below the platform. He laid his hat beside him on the bench; but the stick had become the most important of this man's senses, and he did not let go of it even when he had sat down.

"Fine weather, then, eh?" he said when he was seated, looking straight ahead down the hall; he listened and waited for an answer for a while, and then added, "I presume that a large number of good people have gathered here this evening?"

But when there was no reply from the hall the lecturer himself rose from his seat in a shadowy corner where he had been waiting for a public, and made himself known to this seeker after truth who had conquered his blindness and infirmity in order to gain knowledge about the land of lands.

"Goodness gracious me, it can't surely be Björn of Leirur? Hallo and welcome, my dear old friend," said the man from Utah. "Am I right in thinking you don't see so well? But you must not let yourself be downcast, the only sight that matters is . . ."

"You can quite safely skip that chapter, lad, for I am already saved," interrupted the blind man, feeling with his stick until he found the Mormon, then pulled him towards him and kissed him. "Hallo yourself and welcome, my dearest Steinar of Hlíðar. Your little scamp of a daughter converted me to Mormonism with much more convincing arguments than a fellow like you is capable of."

"Someone else was hinting something of the sort," said the Mormon. "I could not bring myself to ask, for whatever the All-Wisdom has allowed to take place, that and that alone is right. Perhaps I have yet to covenant you to the eternal abode of the saints if we happen to come across a clear stream."

The blind man replied, "Oh, it doesn't make the slightest difference whether you immerse this old corpse or let it stay dry: from now on we both have the same homeland. And if Sheriff Benediktsson had not made me a pauper with his persuasive powers, I would perhaps be in Utah by now to die, instead of sitting in Reykjavík plaiting hobbles for horse-copers to keep myself alive in my old age. They have started hobbling horses now, you see. New masters, new customs."

The Mormon replied, "Perhaps, in that case, I should not delay any more in passing on the regards I was asked to give you from the British-Icelandic Company in Edinburgh. I met our good sheriff in his new fur coat in Princes Street. He took me to a vast salon and bought me coffee and gave me a farm, heeheehee. It was rather like old Kristian Wilhelmsson's little joke when he came over from Denmark some years back and gave Icelanders permission to stand upright in their own homes. But when will Icelanders progress so far that their society will be governed by the All-Wisdom according to the Golden Book?"

"Yes, my friend, you can speak piously, for the Almighty gave you a riding-horse that was better than all my horses, even though I was the best-mounted man in Iceland," said Björn of Leirur. "I shall never forget the time when Sheriff Benediktsson, the most brilliant persuader in the country, was putting out his feelers to get hold of the horse—not to mention the stupid coper from Leirur. Well, at last you've sold the beast for what he was worth. But of Björn of Leirur? A Króna per hobble, that's all this old horse-tamer gets; and even so, his sprig is rooted just as firmly in Paradise as you. The All-Wisdom knows what it is up to."

It had all been very different in the days when sheriffs and arch-deacons made it known throughout their districts that whoever gave shelter to a Mormon for the night, or offered him so much as a drink of water, ought to be broken on the wheel. In those days fugitive saints crept along the sheep-paths late at night like outlaws, or curled up to sleep in outlying sheep-cots, where cud-chewing animals kept them company in winter and toadstools in summer.

But now when this Mormon was nudging his way east through the southern lowlands, and knocking on people's doors, he always introduced himself as a bricklayer and Mormon from the Territory of Utah, quite so, and then waited to see if anyone was going to beat him up. But instead of wrangling with him about correct thinking and then beating him up because of the Prophet's Golden Book, every farmer all the way east to the Rangárvellir said, "Oh, are you a Mormon? Well, good day to you. I've always wanted to meet a Mormon. Won't you come in?"

Or: "Did you say Utah? Yes, it's a fine place, they say, and grand people, too. I once had a kinsman who went there with his sweetheart and a hand-cart. And the women are said to be not so bad, if they're not turned into housewives before they've grown up properly."

Others said: "Hey, come on in quick, lad, I've got plenty of *brennivín*. Tell me how many wives you have."

The bricklayer answered all these questions courteously, but when he came to the last one he used to give a titter and reply with this riddle: "I am covenanted to three wives, my good man: one dead, two living. The first one I sealed to myself while she lay at the bottom of the Atlantic. . . . Of the other two, the one is my mother-in-law, the other is my step-daughter. The day after I sealed them all to me formally and to all eternity I set off for Iceland to teach you to embrace the Gospel. Work it out for yourself now, good brother: how many wives has a bricklayer who is and will always be the most wretched bricklayer of all until the end of time?"

People racked their brains over this riddle, but no one could solve the problem of who could be the real wife of a man who, at one and the same time, married his mother-in-law and step-daughter, as well as the woman who lay at the bottom of the Atlantic. For that reason he was a welcome visitor everywhere.

One Sunday in summer he began to find his surroundings familiar, as if he had been there before. He went up a path to a church which stood close to a grassy hillock. Ponies stood there, drowsing in the paddock, with their tails tied together; there were dogs brawling at the lich-gate or howling at the Vestmannaeyjar where saints are said to live; indeed, the islands had floated more than half-way up to heaven in the mirage. There were no people in sight. From all this he deduced that divine service was at its height, and the glad sound of singing could be heard from inside the church. In the home-field there were three tethering-blocks, half-sunk in the turf; they had been used in former times when the farm and church lay differently in relation to one another, but at this stage they had long been abandoned by God and men as well as by ponies. Stanford the Mormon waited until the service was over, and when the congregation came straggling out he stepped up on to the middle block and began to read from a work by John Pritt. He was half-expecting that some well-to-do farmers and other notables would come over and give a good thrashing to this uncouth fellow who claimed to be preaching correct social principles according to a document that the All-Wisdom dispensed on Cumorah Hill. But as he stood there on the block, reading aloud with John Pritt's voice of truth, and some people had started to listen, who should come out into the field but the pastor himself in cassock and gown. He raised his hat to the speaker, went up to him, reached out his hand, and said, "Would the Mormon gentleman not prefer to come into the church and deliver his intimation from the pulpit, rather than perch on this unworthy stone? The congregation's organist is prepared to play for you whatever hymns you wish to have, and which we can join in and hum."

But when the Mormon began to preach it was received with the kind of amiable indifference that was in fashion among our compatriots in the sagas when they accepted an unknown faith in the year 1000,* and yet did not accept, because they could not be bothered to argue; or when they sat down and tied their shoelaces because they could not be bothered to flee when they were overcome in battle. Icelanders had now completely lost that spark of religious conviction which had shown itself a few years previously when they tied Mormons to boulders. Progress or retrogression? That was the question asked by the finest bishop to travel round Iceland in recent centuries: it is no fun at all to wrestle with a lot of wool when it is not even in sacks.

And before the Mormon realised it he had reached Steinahlíðar. When he came to Hlíðar late one afternoon during the hay-making, he was staggered to find that there was no farm there. And yet he felt that it was only yesterday that he had got up early one morning and taken leave of his children in their sleep, while his wife stood tearfully on the paving and stared after the wisest man in the world as he disappeared round the shoulder of the mountain. Nothing would have seemed more natural to him than to find everything there the same as he had left it, and to be able to go in to his sleeping children and wake them with a kiss. What surprised him most now was that the home-field had become pasturage for alien sheep. That the farm-house should have disappeared would have been bearable had not the paving on which the woman had stood also sunk into the ground. Who were these two silent little birds that flew out of the banks of dock and angelica where the farm had once stood, and vanished into the blue? Had he not put his hand into his pocket and found the letter from a man in Edinburgh that this was his farm, he would scarcely have believed it.

But it was not until he had a look at the boundary-walls that the enormity of it all really struck him. Was it any wonder that it should hurt him so much to see how these masterpieces by his great-grandfather, the model and example for many a district, had gone in a flash while he slipped away for a moment? And the rubble off the mountain scattered all over the hayfield! Then he happened to look up at the steep mountain above the farm, at the fulmar, that faithful bird, sweeping with smooth and powerful and deathless wingbeats high up along the cliff-ledges over-grown with ferns and moonwort, where it had had his nest for twenty thousand years.

He laid down his knapsack with the pamphlets by John Pritt, slipped off his jacket and took off his hat; then he began to gather stones to make a few repairs to the wall. There was a lot of work waiting for one man here; walls like these, in fact, take the man with them if they are to stand.

A passer-by saw that a stranger had started to potter with the dykes of this derelict croft.

"Who are you?" asked the traveller.

The other replied, "I am the man who reclaimed Paradise after it had been lost, and gave it to his children."

"What is such a man doing here?" asked the passer-by.

"I have found the truth, and the land in which it lives," said the wall-builder, correcting himself. "And that is assuredly very important. But now the most important thing is to build up this wall again."

And with that, Steinar of Hlíðar went on just as if nothing had happened, laying stone against stone in these ancient walls, until the sun went down on Hlíðar in Steinahlíðar.

Notes

3   the third last foreign king to wield power here in Iceland: Kristian IX, King of Denmark 1863–1906; he was the son of Wilhelm, Duke of Schleswig-Holstein-Sonderburg-Glücksburg.

8   viking who always went to bed with the axe Battle-Troll under his pillow: Battle-Troll (*rymmaugýgr*): the mighty battle-axe owned by Skarpheðinn Njálsson in *Njáll's Saga.*

10   entrance to Gnípahellir: Gnípahellir, in Norse mythology, is the place where the great Wolf Fenrir would break free from his fetters before Raganarök (Destruction of the Gods).

10   In charge of this company was Sheriff Benediktsson: Einar Benediktsson (1864–1940) became one of Iceland's major poets. He was also a cosmopolite and entrepreneur (see chapter 30). In his younger days, he was appointed a country magistrate (Sheriff).

10   The other visitor was the agent Björn of Leirur: Björn of Leirur is loosely based on a historical character named Þorvaldur Björnsson (1833–1922), a farming magnate who lived at Þorvald-

seyvi at the roots of Eyiafjallajökull. He, too, became an entrepreneur, investing all his money in trawlers, but went bankrupt. He
had no children by his wife, but had two children by Ingvald, the
daughter of Eiríkur of Brúnar (the original of "Steinar of Hlíðar").

12   **there was seldom much brennivín . . . :** brennivín (literally "burnt wine") is a strong spirit, like schnapps, flavored with
caraway seeds or angelica roots and familiarly know as "Black Death."

12   **like old Thorvaldsen:** "Old Thorvaldsen": The Danish
sculptor Bertel Thorvaldsen (1770–1844), the son of an Icelandic
woodcarver. He was Denmark's most celebrated sculptor of his
time, and a leader of the neoclassical movement.

20   **It is of no little importance to arrive at Þingvellir:** Þingvellir (Parliament Plains) is the great natural open-air arena where Iceland's Parliament (the Alþingi) was established in 930. Although
the Alþingi had been moved to Reykjavík in 1845, it was still considered the center of the land, and all national festivities were celebrated there—and are, to this day.

21   **Hrafnkell himself, should forfeit nothing but his life:**
Hrafnkell Freyr's-goði is the anonymous hero of *Hrafnkell's Saga*. He
revered his horse so much that he swore that he would kill anyone
who rode him without permission. The saga talks of the dire conse-
quences that ensued when his shepherd rode him, and Hrafnkell
killed him without compunction.

21   **nor am I accustomed to forget Sleipnir:** Sleipnir was the
eight-legged horse belonging to Óðinn, the chief god of the Norse
pantheon.

38   **the thousandth anniversary of the settlement of Iceland:**
The traditional date for the first settlement of Iceland is 874.

39   **Norse warriors who served in the Varangian Guard
under the emperor in Constantinople:** The Varangians (Væring-
jar) were an elite unit of highly paid Scandinavian mercenaries serving as part of the Byzantine emperor's imperial guard, founded in
the late tenth century.

39   **No farmer was considered worth his salt if he could not trace his genealogy back to Harald hárfagvi (Fine-Hair):** Harald hárfagvi (Fine-Hair) was the first Norwegian ruler to unify all Norway under a simple crown, late in the ninth century.

39   **or his namesake Harald hilditönn (War-Tooth):** Harald hilditönn (War-Tooth), a semilegendary Danish king, is said to have been defeated at the Battle of Brávellir, in Sweden, after being betrayed by Óðinn.

39   **All Icelandic genealogies can be traced back to the Ynglings and the Scyldings:** The Ynglings were a semilegendary dynasty of kings who ruled Sweden from the end of the third to the middle of the ninth century and were descended from Yngvi_Freyr, the god of fertility. The Scyldings (Skjöldungar) were an equally legendary dynasty of Danish kings descended from Skjöldur, the son of Óðinn.

39   **King Gautrekur of Gotaland:** King Gautrekur Örvi (the Generous) is the eponymous hero of one of the many Legendary Sagas within Iceland. He appears in genealogies Landnámabók (Book of Settlements), and is said to have been a king in Sweden.

39   **Ganger-Hrolf:** Ganger-Hrolf (Göngu-Hrólfur) is better known as Rollo, the viking leader who founded the duchy of Normandy in France.

40   **Gormur gamlí (the Old):** Gormur gamlí (the Old) was a tenth-century king of Denmark; he died in 958 and was interred in one of the great burial mounts at Jelling, in Jutland.

42   **who fought the battle of Brávellir:** Brávellir was a celebrated battle, said to have been fought between the Danish King Harald War-Tooth and his nephew Hríngur, after Óðinn had sowed dissension between them.

58   **one from an old ballad involving the hero Þórður hreða (Menace):** Þórður hreða (Menace) was a Norwegian warrior who fled to Iceland in the tenth century. He is the hero of a fourteenth-

century saga called *Þórður saga hreða.* Like Steinar, he was noted for his craftsmanship.

204   **"Or at least the old ogress Grýla.":** Grýla was the quintessential bugbear of early Icelandic folklore; she was an elemental troll, with fifteen tails (with a hundred bags on each tail for holding captured children). Her name was much used to frighten recalcitrant children.

289   **a berserk fit no less frenzied than when Einarr Skálaglamm fastened the shield:** Einarr Skálaglamm Helgason was Egill Skallagrímsson's poetic protégé in *Egill's Saga.* His nickname means "scale-tinkler." He presents Egill with an ornate shield he had been given by the ruler of Norway. When Egill saw it hanging in his bed-closet he was curious—he thought that Einarr expected him to write about it!

293   **started to hunt for minnows in the Tjörn:** Tjörn is the name of the small lake in the city-center of Reykjavík. The name is related to the word "tarn."

298   **when they accepted an unknown faith in the year 1000:** In the year 1000 (or 999, as scholars now suggest), Iceland was converted from paganism to Christianity by parliamentary decree.

Printed in the United States
by Baker & Taylor Publisher Services

A Note on Sources

In researching this book I have relied on three kinds of sources: unpublished archival materials; interviews; and published materials, including books, newspapers, magazines, and scholarly articles. While I have tried throughout to make the source of my information clear, I have not footnoted every citation because I have not written this book primarily for scholarly readers. Anyone interested in examining these sources or pursuing research on Oberammergau may find the following helpful.

Unless otherwise specified, cited unpublished materials that are originally in German can be found in the Gemeindearchiv Oberammergau. Most cited unpublished materials in English can be located in the archives of the American Jewish Committee in New York City. A small number of unpublished documents cited here can be found in the archives of the Anti-Defamation League of

B'nai B'rith, the YIVO Institute for Jewish Research, and the American Jewish Congress.

A good deal of information was derived from conversations with the following individuals: Phil Baum, Michael Brenner, Annelies Buchwieser, Simon Dahlmeier, Klement Fend, Eugene J. Fischer, Abraham Foxman, Stefan Hageneier, Carsten Häublein, Otto Huber, Leon Klenicki, Gottfried Lang, Philip Levine, Gordon Mork, Michael Raab, Christine Rädlinger, James Rudin, Ingrid Shafer, Leonard Swidler, Christian Stückl, Stanley M. Wagner, and Rudolf Zwink.

An enormous amount has been written about Oberammergau and its Passion play. For a useful bibliography that is especially strong on nineteenth- and early twentieth-century Anglo-American scholarship, see Maximillian J. Rudwin, *A Historical and Bibliographic Survey of the German Religious Drama* (Pittsburgh, 1924). I have turned repeatedly in the course of writing this book to three important, if at times quirky, studies: Hermine Diemer, *Oberammergau and Its Passion Play*, trans. Walter S. Manning, 3rd ed. (Munich, 1922); Roman Fink and Horst Schwarzer, *Everlasting Passion: The Phenomenon of Oberammergau*, trans. Andreas Neumer (Düsseldorf, 1970); and Saul S. Friedman, *The Oberammergau Passion Play: A Lance Against Civilization* (Carbondale, 1984).

Quotations from modern versions of the Oberammergau Passion play are taken from the official texts, in English and in German, for each production. I have also made extensive use of the official guides to the play, also published by Oberammergau.

The following is a list of the published sources used in each chapter. The final chapter (as well as most of the first) is based largely on interviews and my own experiences in Oberammergau.

1. Next Year in Jerusalem

Phil Baum, "Unpurged Passion Play of Oberammergau," *American Jewish Congress Bi-Monthly* (February 19, 1968), 5–6

A Note on Sources

James Bentley, *Oberammergau and the Passion Play: A Guide and a History to Mark the 350th Anniversary* (Harmondsworth, Middlesex, 1984)

Robert Gorham Davis, "Passion at Oberammergau," *Commentary* 29 (March 1960), 198–204

T. F. Driver, "The Play that Carries a Plague," *The Christian Century* 77 (1960), 1016–18

Willard A. Heaps, "Oberammergau Today," *Christianity Today* 63 (December 1946), 1468–69

Adolf Hitler, *Hitler's Secret Conversations, 1941–1944* (New York, 1953)

Anton Lang, *Reminiscences* (Munich, 1930)

2. Staging the Passion

Giuseppe Alberigo, ed., *History of Vatican II*, vol. 1, English version edited by Joseph A. Komonchak (Maryknoll, New York, 1995)

Judith Banki, "Oberammergau 1960 and 1970. A Study in Religious Anti-Semitism" (New York, American Jewish Committee, 1970)

Phil Baum, "Background of Oberammergau Passion Play" (New York, American Jewish Congress, November, 1966)

Thomas H. Bestul, *Texts of the Passion: Latin Devotional Literature and Medieval Society* (Philadelphia, 1996)

Georg Brenninger, "Passionsspiele in Altbayern," in Michael Henker, Eberhard Dünninger, and Evamaria Brockhoff, eds., *Hört, sehet, weint und liebt: Passionsspiele im alpenländischen Raum* (Munich, 1990)

Raymond E. Brown, *The Death of the Messiah* (New York, 1994)

Osbert Burdett, "The Passion Play," in *Critical Essays* (London, 1925)

Elizabethe Corathiel, *The Oberammergau Story* (London, 1959)

Michael Counsell, *Every Pilgrim's Guide to Oberammergau and Its Passion Play* (Norwich, 1998)

A Note on Sources

Criteria for Evaluation of Dramatizations of the Passion, Bishops' Committee for Ecumenical and Interreligious Affairs, National Conference of Catholic Bishops (Washington, D.C., 1988)

John Dominic Crossan, *The Historical Jesus* (New York, 1991)

———, *Who Killed Jesus? Exposing the Roots of Anti-Semitism in the Gospel Story of the Death of Jesus* (New York, 1995)

Philip L. Culbertson, "What Is Left to Believe in Jesus after the Scholars Have Done with Him?" *Journal of Ecumenical Studies* 27 (1991), 1–17

Robert Gorham Davis, "Observer at Oberammergau," *Commentary* 29 (1960), 198–204

John R. Elliott, Jr., *Playing God: Medieval Mysteries on the Modern Stage* (Toronto, 1989)

Ferdinand Feldigl, *Oberammergau and the Passion Play: An Illustrated Guide-book*, trans. Laurence Gibson (Oberammergau, 1910)

Eugene J. Fischer and Leon Klenicki, eds., *In Our Time: The Flowering of Jewish-Catholic Dialogue* (New York, 1990)

Charles Y. Glock and Rodney Stark, *Christian Beliefs and Anti-Semitism* (New York, 1966)

Donald P. Gray, "Jesus was a Jew," in Marvin Perry and Frederick M. Schweitzer, eds., *Jewish-Christian Encounters over the Centuries: Symbiosis, Prejudice, Holocaust, Dialogue* (New York, 1994), 1–26

August Hartmann, ed., *Das Oberammergauer Passionsspiel in seiner Ältesten gestalt* (Leipzig, 1880)

Stephen R. Haynes, "Changing Paradigms: Reformist, Radical, and Rejectionist Approaches to the Relationship between Christianity and Antisemitism," *Journal of Ecumenical Studies* 32 (1995), 63–88

Vernon Heaton, *The Oberammergau Passion Play*, 3rd ed. (London, 1983)

Michael Henker, Eberhard Dünninger, and Evamaria Brockhoff, eds., *Hört, sehet, weint und liebt: Passionsspiele im alpenländischen Raum* (Munich, 1990)

Susannah Heschel, *Abraham Geiger and the Jewish Jesus* (Chicago, 1998)

A Note on Sources

David Houseley and Raymond Goodburn, *A Pilgrim's Guide to Oberammergau and Its Passion Play* (Woodbridge, Suffolk, 1999)

Otto Huber, "Zwischen Passionsandacht und Gesellschaftskritik. Die Passionsspiele des P. Othmar Weis," in Michael Henker, Eberhard Dünninger, and Evamaria Brockhoff, eds., *Hört, sehet, weint und liebt: Passionsspiele im alpenländischen Raum* (Munich, 1990), 187–95

Sylvia P. Jenkins, "The Oberammergau Passion Play: A Literary Study," *German Life and Letters* 5 (1951), 1–10

Roland Kaltenegger, *Oberammergau und die Passionsspiele 1634–1984* (Munich, 1984)

John J. Kelley, "Niederschrift: A Translation of the Minutes of the Secretary of the Village Done after the Dialog with the Hierarchy in Munich, May 26, 1989" (privately circulated, 1989)

————, "The Dilemma of Oberammergau," *Christian Jewish Relations* 23 (1990), 28–32

Leon Klenicki, ed., *Passion Plays and Judaism* (New York, Anti-Defamation League in cooperation with the National Conference of Catholic Bishops, 1996)

Helmut W. Klinner and Michael Henker, eds., *Playing Salvation: Guide to the Permanent Exhibition in the Passion Play Theatre* (Oberammergau, 1993)

Joseph Krauskopf, *A Rabbi's Impressions of the Oberammergau Passion Play* (Philadelphia, 1901)

Eric Lane and Ian Brenson, eds., *Oberammergau: A Passion Play* (London, 1984)

Gottfried Lang and Martha Lang, "The Missed Reform: Conflict and Continuity in a Bavarian Alpine Village," *Anthropology Quarterly* 57 (1984), 100–110

James H. Marrow, *Passion Iconography in Northern European Art of the Late Middle Ages and Early Renaissance: A Study of the Transformation of Sacred Metaphor into Descriptive Narrative* (Kortrijk, Belgium, 1979)

Malcolm McColl, *The Ammergau Passion Play*, 6th ed. (London, 1880)

A Note on Sources

John P. Meier, *A Marginal Jew: Rethinking the Historical Jesus* (New York, 1991)

Mitchell B. Merback, *The Thief, the Cross, and the Wheel: Pain and the Spectacle of Punishment in Medieval and Renaissance Europe* (Chicago, 1999)

Gordon R. Mork, "The 1984 Oberammergau Passion Play in Historical Perspective," *Face to Face* 12 (1985), 15–20

Montrose J. Moses, *The Passion Play of Oberammergau* (New York, 1930)

Lynette R. Muir, *The Biblical Drama of Medieval Europe* (Cambridge, 1995)

J. M. Oesterreicher, "Declaration on the Relationship of the Church to Non-Christian Religions: Introduction and Commentary," in *Commentary on the Documents of Vatican II* (New York, 1969)

"Passion at Oberammergau," *Institute of Jewish Affairs*, Background Paper No. 15 (London, 1969)

F. P. Pickering, *Literature and Art in the Middle Ages* (Coral Gables, 1970)

———, "The Gothic Image of Christ," in *Essays on Medieval German Literature and Iconography* (Cambridge, 1980), 3–30

Leon Poliakov, *The History of Anti-Semitism from the Time of Christ to the Court Jews*, trans. Richard Howard (New York, 1974)

Bernard P. Prusak, "Jews and the Death of Jesus in Post-Vatican II Christologies," *Journal of Ecumenical Studies* 28 (1991), 581–625

Report Oberammergau '70/80 (Oberammergau, 1970)

Ferdinand Rosner, *Passio Nova: Das Oberammergauer Passionsspiel von 1750*, ed. Stephan Schaller (Bern und Frankfurt, 1974)

E. P. Sanders, *Jesus and Judaism* (Philadelphia, 1985)

Stephan Schaller, "Nie Wieder: Verfluchte Synagoge!: Die Rolle des Judentums in der Geschichte des Oberammergauer Passionsspieles," *Schönere Heimat* 69 (1980), 288–92

———, "Survey of 350 Years," *Passionsspiele Oberammergau 1634–1984* (Oberammergau, 1984)

A Note on Sources

Alexander Craig Sellar, "The Passion-Play in the Highlands of
Bavaria," *Blackwood's Magazine* 107 (1870), 381–96

Gerard S. Sloyan, *The Crucifixion of Jesus: History, Myth, Faith*
(Minneapolis, 1995)

Arthur Penryhn Stanley, "The Ammergau Mystery: Or Sacred
Drama of 1860," *Macmillan's Magazine* (October 1860), 463–77

Leonard Swidler, "The Jewishness of Jesus: Some Implications for
Christians," *Journal of Ecumenical Studies* 18 (1981), 104–5

Leonard Swidler and Gerard Sloyan, *A Commentary on the Oberammergau Passionsspiel in Regard to Its Image of Jews and Judaism*
(New York, Anti-Defamation League, 1981)

———, "The Passion of the Jew Jesus: Recommended Changes in
the Oberammergau Passion Play after 1984," *Face to Face* 12
(1985), 24–35

———, eds., *The Oberammergau Passionspiel 1984* (New York, Anti-
Defamation League, 1984)

Marc Tanenbaum, "Time for a New Vow at Oberammergau: Anti-
Semitism of the Play," *The Christian Century* 83 (1966), 1328–29

Geza Vermes, *Jesus the Jew* (London, 1973)

Otmar Weis, "Oberammergauer Passionstext von 1811," in Ferdinand Feldigl, ed., *Denkmäler der Oberammergauer Passionsliter-
atur* (Oberammergau, 1922)

Karl Young, *The Drama of the Medieval Church*, 2 vols. (Oxford:
Clarendon, 1933)

3. The Myths of Oberammergau

Matthew Arnold, "A Persian Passion Play," rpt. in R. H. Super, ed.,
Matthew Arnold: God and the Bible (Ann Arbor, 1970)

Uwe Böker, "English Visitors to Oberammergau: Amelia Matilda
Hull, Jerome K. Jerome, Graham Greene," in Otto Hietsch, ed.,
Bavaria Anglica 1 (1979), 205–24

———, "Oberammergau: A Minor American Myth," *Yearbook of
German-American Studies* 19 (1984), 33–42

A Note on Sources

Isabel Burton, *The Passion-Play at Ober-Ammergau*, ed. W. H. Wilkins (London, 1900)

Richard F. Burton, *A Glance at the 'Passion-Play'* (London, 1881)

Anna S. Bushby, "The Passion Play at Oberammergau in Bavaria," *New Monthly Magazine* 147 (1870), 288–98

Klaus Bussman and Heinz Schilling, eds., *1648: War and Peace in Europe*, 2 vols. (Munich, 1999)

M. D. Conway, "A Passion-Play Pilgrimage," *Harper's Magazine* 43 (1871), 919–29

Elisabethe Corathiel, *The Oberammergau Story* (London, 1959)

Robert F. Coyle, *Passion Play of Oberammergau* (Denver, 1910)

Joseph Alois Daisenberger, *Geschichte des Dorfes Oberammergau* (Munich, 1858)

Wilfrid Dallow, "Oberammergau and Its Passion Play in 1900," *Irish Ecclesiastical Review* 4 (1901), 63–82

Ernest Hermitage Day, *Ober-Ammergau and Its Passion Play* (London, 1910)

Eduard Devrient, *Das Passionschauspiel in Oberammergau und seine Bedeutung für die neue Zeit* (Leipzig, 1851), excerpted in Norbert Jaron and Bärbel Rudin, eds., *Das Oberammergauer Passionsspiel: Eine Chronik in Bildern* (Dortmund, 1984), 34–35

George Hobart Doane, *To and From the Passion Play in the Summer of 1871* (Boston, 1872)

Madeleine Z. Doty, "The Passion Players in War-Time," *Atlantic Monthly* 119 (1917), 832–38

F. W. Farrar, *The Passion Play at Oberammergau* (London, 1891)

Ferdinand Feldigl, *Oberammergau and the Passion Play: An Illustrated Guide-book*, transl. Laurence Gibson (Oberammergau, 1910)

Henry M. Field, *From the Lakes of Killarney to the Golden Horn*, 4th ed. (New York, 1877)

Richard Foulkes, *Church and Stage in Victorian England* (Cambridge, 1997)

A Note on Sources

Raymond Tifft Fuller, *The World's Stage: Oberammergau, 1934* (New York, 1934)

Guido Görres, "Das Theater im Mittelalter und das Passionsspiel in Oberammergau," *Historisch-politische Blätter für das katholische Deutschland* (1840), excerpted in Norbert Jaron and Bärbel Rudin, eds., *Das Oberammergauer Passionsspiel: Eine Chronik in Bildern* (Dortmund, 1984), 30–31

David Houseley and Raymond Goodburn, *A Pilgrim's Guide to Oberammergau and Its Passion Play* (Woodbridge, 1999)

Anna Maria Howitt, "The Miracle-Play in the Ammergau," *Ladies' Home Companion* (1850), rpt. in *Living Age* 27 (1850), 87–92

Impressions of the Oberammergau Passion Play by an Oxonian (London, 1870)

Norbert Jaron and Bärbel Rudin, eds., *Das Oberammergauer Passionsspiel: Eine Chronik in Bildern* (Dortmund, 1984)

Jerome K. Jerome, *Diary of a Pilgrimage* (London, 1891)

David L. Kissel, *The Passions of Oberammergau: A Diachronic Study of a Case of Institutionalized Factionalism in a Bavarian Village* (dissertation, Department of Anthropology, Indiana University, 1981)

Malcolm MacColl, *The Ammergau Passion Play* (London, 1870)

Edith Milner, *Oberammergau and Its Passion Play* (London, 1910)

Charles Musser, *Before the Nickelodeon: Edwin S. Porter and the Edison Manufacturing Company* (Berkeley, 1991)

———, "Passion and the Passion Play: Theatre, Film and Religion in America, 1880–1900," *Film History* 5 (1993), 41–56

Johann Baptist Prechtl, "Das Passionsspiel zu Oberammergau," in *Oberbayerisches Archiv* (1859–61)

J. B. Priestley, "Oberammergau," in *Self-Selected Essays* (London, 1932)

F. J. Rappmannsberger, *Oberammergau: Legende und Wirklichkeit* (Munich, 1960)

Winold Reiss, "Oberammergau Players," *The Century Magazine* 104 (September 1922), 727–42

A Note on Sources

Ferdinand Reyher, "Christ in Oberammergau," *Atlantic Monthly* 130 (1922), 599–607

Eugen Roth, "The Vow," *Oberammergau and Its Passion Play 1960: Official Guide* (Oberammergau, 1960)

Joseph Schröder, *Oberammergau and Its Passion Play*, trans. A.L.O.M. (Oberammergau, 1900)

Bernard Shaw, *Shaw's Music: The Complete Musical Criticism in Three Volumes*, ed. Dan H. Laurence (New York, 1981)

Arthur Penrhyn Stanley, "The Ammergau Mystery; or Sacred Drama of 1860," *Macmillan's Magazine* 2 (October 1860), 463–77

William T. Stead, *The Passion Play As It Is Played To-Day at Ober Ammergau in 1890* (London, 1890)

————, *The Story that Transformed the World* (London, 1891)

Ethel B. H. Tweedie, *The Oberammergau Passion Play* (London, 1890)

Leo Weismantel, *Die Pestnot Anno 1633* ([1933]; Oberammergau, n.d.)

4. In Hitler's Shadow

James Bentley, *Oberammergau and the Passion Play: A Guide and a History to Mark the 350th Anniversary* (Harmondsworth, Middlesex, 1984)

Philip S. Bernstein, "Unchristian Christianity and the Jew: A Rabbi Speaks Out," *Harper's Magazine* (May 1931), 660–71

T. F. Driver, "The Play That Carries a Plague," *The Christian Century* 77 (1960), 1016–18

Robert L. Erenstein, "The Passion Plays in Tegelen: An Investigation into the Function of a Passion Play," *Theatre Research International* 16 (1991), 29–39

Robert P. Erickson and Susannah Heschel, eds., *Betrayal: German Churches and the Holocaust* (Minneapolis, 1999)

Michael von Faulhaber, *Judaism, Christianity and Germany*, trans. George D. Smith (New York, 1934)

A Note on Sources

Saul S. Friedman, "A Response to the Papers Presented," *Face to Face* 12 (1985), 21–24

G. E. R. Gedye, "Nazis Penetrate Oberammergau," *New York Times Magazine* (July 2, 1933), 11–12

Daniel Jonah Goldhagen, *Hitler's Willing Executioners: Ordinary Germans and the Holocaust* (New York, 1996)

Constantin Goschler, "The Attitude towards Jews in Bavaria after the Second World War," *Leo Baeck Institute Year Book* 31 (1991), 443–58

Otto Günzler and Alfred Zwink, *Oberammergau: Famous Village— Famous Visitors* (Munich, 1950)

Adolf Hitler, *Hitler's Secret Conversations, 1941–1944* (New York, 1953)

E. Burton Holmes, *The Burton Holmes Lectures*, vol. 7 (New York, 1901), 115–24

"Is the Passion Play Anti-Semitic?" *Literary Digest* (September 13, 1930), p. 21

Ian Kershaw, *Hitler 1889–1936: Hubris* (London, 1998)

Guenter Levy, "Pius XII, the Jews, and the German Catholic Church," in Robert P. Erickson and Susannah Heschel, eds., *Betrayal: German Churches and the Holocaust* (Minneapolis, 1999), 129–48

Gordon R. Mork, " 'Wicked Jews' and 'Suffering Christians' in the Oberammergau Passion Play," in Leonard Jay Greenspoon and Bryan F. Le Beau, eds., *Representations of Jews through the Ages* (Omaha, Nebraska, 1996), 153–69

Dennis Piszkiewicz, *The Nazi Rocketeers: Dreams of Space and Crimes of War* (Westport, Conn., 1995)

Guy Stern, "The Burning of Books in Nazi Germany, 1933: The American Response," *Simon Wiesenthal Center Annual* 2 (1985), 95–113

We Remember: A Reflection on the Shoah, Vatican Commission for Religious Relations with the Jews (16 March 1998)

Humbert Wolfe, *X at Oberammergau: A Poem* (London, 1935)

———, *Don J. Ewan* (London, 1937)

5. Tradition and the Individual Talent

Arthur Hertzberg, "The Catholic-Jewish Dispute that Won't Go
Away," *Reform Judaism* 28 (1999), 30–33, 90

Arthur Holmberg, *The Theatre of Robert Wilson* (Cambridge, 1996)

Leo Weismantel, *Die Pestnot Anno 1633* ([1933]; Oberammergau,
n.d.)

Acknowledgments

I am deeply grateful to my long-time friends, Robert Griffin (of Tel Aviv University) and Alvin Snider (of the University of Iowa), who are the best of readers. I am also indebted to Christine Rädlinger, an authority on Oberammergau's history, who helped me at many points along the way. My brother Michael Shapiro offered some invaluable suggestions. Several others commented on the work-in-progress, including my in-laws, Barry and Mary DeCourcey Cregan, and my parents, Herbert and Lorraine Shapiro. My neighbors Richard and Peggy Kuhns and their friends Peter and Ruth Gay read an early draft of chapter 4. Their collective criticism and experience have helped make this a better book.

Most of what I have learned about Oberammergau and the controversies over its Passion play has come from those directly involved. While I have listed all those interviewed for this book in the "Note on Sources," I would like to single out for special thanks the generosity of Otto Huber, Leon Klenicki, James Rudin, Ingrid Shafer, and Christian Stückl.

Given my limited knowledge of German, I am deeply grateful for the assistance of Nina Hein, a doctoral student in theater at Columbia University, who assisted me with interviews in Oberammergau, translated documents, and saved me from many errors. I would also like to acknowledge the help of my German instructor, Christopher Gwin.

I could not have written this book without access to a number of important archives: the Gemeindearchiv Oberammergau (and its exceptionally knowledgeable archivist Helmut Klinner), the American Jewish Committee (and its no less helpful archivist, Miriam K. Tierney), as well as the Anti-Defamation League of B'nai B'rith, the YIVO Institute for Jewish Research, and the American Jewish Congress. I have also relied heavily on the collections of the Union Theological Seminary, the Jewish Theological Seminary, Columbia University Libraries, the New York Public Library, and the Dartmouth College Library.

I would also like to thank my friend and literary agent, Anne Edelstein, for sharing my enthusiasm for this project from the outset, as well as Dan Frank, who is all that a writer can wish for in an editor.

My greatest debt is to my wife, Mary Cregan, for her unwavering support and her intellectual honesty.

Printed in the United States
by Baker & Taylor Publisher Services